I0718559

Once Upon a Dream

DEMELZA CARLTON

Three tales in the Romance a Medieval Fairy Tale series

Float: Enchanted Horse Retold

DEMELZA CARLTON

A tale in the Romance a Medieval Fairy Tale series

One

"Don't mess this up," Godfrey muttered, as if being stern with himself could stop the inevitable. Easier to stop the waves carrying his boat to Lord Sebastiano's door, or to command the gondolier to plant his pole so as to resist the tide. A stealthy glance at the gondolier confirmed Godfrey's fears – the man thought him mad, talking to himself.

The boat turned into one of Rialto's numerous identical canals, weaving through the maze as if by magic, until they stopped at a dock that looked no different to the others they'd passed.

"Palazzo Ziano," the gondolier said, offering his hand to Godfrey like his passenger was some fine lady.

Godfrey choked out a laugh and stepped from the boat to the dock without the boatman's assistance. A few coins changed hands and the gondolier poled away, disappearing around a corner before Godfrey could reconsider and call him back.

Godfrey eyed the double doors before him. Paint peeled at the bottom, where the wood had swelled in response to the endless stroking of the waves that even now threatened to lick tantalisingly at his feet. He rapped on the timber with more confidence than he felt, fuelled by desperation to keep his feet dry until he'd at least met with Lord Sebastiano.

The door opened inward, and a servant bowed him inside the cavernous space that evidently served as a warehouse for whatever Sebastiano traded in, when he wasn't transporting things for people.

"I think I've come to the wrong place," Godfrey said. "You see, I'm in Rialto to see

Lord Sebastiano about a cargo his ships were to carry here from the Holy Land. He invited me to visit him at home, but…" This evidently wasn't it. Perhaps the boatman had decided a mere baron's youngest son was not worthy to enter the home of one of the city's patricians.

"Up the stairs. What name shall I tell the master?" the servant asked.

Godfrey's eyes adjusted to the gloom. The wide staircase before him led to a more lordly entrance on the level above. Perhaps he was in the right place after all.

"Godfrey. My father, the Baron of Maraschal, sent me."

"If you will follow me, Master Godfrey?"

Up the stairs and into the house proper, Godfrey's fears fluttered about inside his chest. He didn't want to open his mouth for fear they'd fly out.

"Master Godfrey, the Baron of Maraschal's son," the servant boomed, then stood aside to let Godfrey pass into the room.

Lord Sebastiano rose and moved around his desk to clasp Godfrey's hands in his. "Master Godfrey, it is a pleasure to meet you. Your uncle, Eustace, speaks well of you. He says you work magic with horses."

Godfrey hadn't seen Uncle Eustace in more than ten years, so how he could know such a thing…perhaps his father had sent him a letter. Yes, of course. A letter saying Godfrey would be collecting this shipment of horses.

"A pity you do not have the same power over ships. The convoy you are here for is a week overdue. It is likely nothing, but many cities along the coast have fallen to the Seljuks in the last few years. It would be ill luck indeed if they have attacked my ships…" Sebastiano patted Godfrey's hand before releasing him. "But it is a fool indeed who would attack such a well-armed convoy. Your horses will arrive safely, you'll see, and you'll have them home in time for Easter. Which reminds me…it is Carnevale this week, the final week of feasting before we fast. You must dine with us tonight."

Godfrey looked up to meet Sebastiano's expectant eyes. The invitation was no mere courtesy – the patrician wanted an answer. "I'd be honoured, and delighted," he managed to say.

Sebastiano smiled. "Good. You have caught

me at a good time. I'd planned on visiting the harbour this afternoon. Will you accompany me?"

Godfrey could hardly refuse, and soon found himself back in a boat, moving with surprising swiftness across the lagoon.

Upon hearing that this was Godfrey's first visit to Rialto, Sebastiano maintained a running commentary about everything he saw, from the islands on either side of them to the people in the boats they passed to the fish in the lagoon waters below.

When Sebastiano paused for breath, Godfrey asked, "How long have your family ruled Rialto?"

Sebastiano laughed. "Ah, you must come from the barbarian kingdoms to the north. No one family rules Rialto. We are a republic, and our rulers are elected from among the noblest families in the city, her patricians. But it is no secret that my family can be traced back to Ziano, one of the first twelve tribunes who ruled when our Most Serene Republic was formed, more than four hundred years ago. We have given the city three Dukes to date, and no doubt more will be elected in the future."

A republic? Like the ancient cities, burned and conquered by the Northmen who Sebastiano called barbarians. Yet this city still stood. A city without walls, as it spread across the islands of the lagoon, from the mainland to the harbour. A city so open should surely be an easy target.

"How does this city defend itself, without walls?"

Sebastiano reached over the side of the boat and cupped seawater in his hands. "The sea protects us, for she is as much a part of our city as the people in it. And there is no fiercer protector than a wife and mother defending her own family." He let the water cascade down his hands, trickling back into the lagoon. "And just like a man knows the body of his wife, the men of the lagoon know every channel and shoal, navigating skilfully across all the curves of the seabed. He knows her moods, her passions, and how to skim smoothly through her waves to the deep channels she opens only to him."

Godfrey felt his face grow hot. Likening the cold water to a lover...he'd sooner love a corpse. Maybe madness was part of being a man of Rialto. And yet, he could almost hear a woman's whisper in the waves, inviting him into her depths.

Godfrey shook his head. A foolish notion.

"If you have need of female company while you are in Rialto, I'm sure my sons can help you find a suitable courtesan," Sebastiano said.

Oh, by all that was holy…

Sebastiano laughed. "When I was your age, my father had already found me a bride. Are you betrothed yet, Master Godfrey?"

Wordlessly, Godfrey shook his head. He managed to find his voice. "My older brothers are already married, with babes on the way, so there is no need for me to marry, or produce more heirs. My father has had me managing the horse stud, so when Uncle Eustace was due to send some new breeding stock, he sent me to fetch them."

"Then after dinner tonight, my sons will find you a courtesan," Sebastiano said. When Godfrey opened his mouth to protest, Sebastiano held up his hand to silence him. "You are in Rialto, a city famed for the beauty of its women. I cannot in conscience allow you to leave this jewel of a city without tasting its delights."

Not wanting to anger his host – that would certainly mess things up – Godfrey decided to ask about the numerous posts and flags sticking out of the water. He opened his mouth.

"I think you are in luck, Master Godfrey. My ships have come to greet you." Sebastiano pointed.

A forest of masts grew on the horizon, separating out into more than a dozen ships. Godfrey wouldn't know one vessel from another, but Sebastiano nodded with satisfaction as he surveyed the convoy coming into the harbour.

By the time Godfrey and Sebastiano reached the ship they wanted, the docks were swarming with men, unloading the ships and taking cargo to smaller boats which then set off for the city. Where it would be stored in the warehouses beneath the merchants' homes, Godfrey realised, for there were no storehouses here in the harbour.

"And here are your horses!" Sebastiano said proudly, as he led the way across the gangplank to the deck which had been turned into a makeshift stable.

Six horses occupied the deck, each as magnificent as any other animal in his father's stable. Mounts befitting a king or an emperor, who would breed countless more when they reached home.

"My men will take them ashore to stretch their legs, then they shall board a barge to take them to the mainland. They will be waiting for you at the Sailor's Rest, the inn nearest the docks. The innkeeper there will take good care of them while you enjoy the legendary hospitality of Rialto," Sebastiano said.

And no doubt charge him a hefty sum for every day, Godfrey thought but did not say. In the merchant city of Rialto, everything cost more. His father had given him plenty of coin for the journey, but Godfrey was sure his purse did not run to weeks of revelry. Or the company of one of the city's courtesans.

If he needed a whore so badly, there were plenty in every tavern on the way home, at a fraction of the price. He could keep it in his hose until then.

A roar came from the stable, followed by an

explosion of straw. "What do you think you're doing with my horses, boy?" An old man, clad in stained rags, emerged from the stable. "Watch her footing on the gangplank! She's worth more than your life, and if the mare should be injured…" For an old beggar, he had the commanding voice of a much younger man.

The unfortunate sailor leading the priceless mare ducked his head, as though avoiding a blow from the man.

"Tielo?"

Godfrey started at the sound of his father's nickname – something he'd only heard his mother use – and found the old man staring at him. "No, I'm Godfrey," he said.

The old man straightened, then grimaced. "Tielo's youngest boy?" He hobbled across the deck and down the gangplank until he stood before Godfrey, then peered up at him.

This man looked old enough to be his grandfather, instead of his father's younger brother, but Godfrey asked anyway: "Uncle Eustace? What are you doing here? Shouldn't you be in the Holy City?"

"The city has fallen to the Seljuks. I was

returning from the harbour, where I'd just seen the horses loaded aboard, and they had the city surrounded. Besieged. They'd demolished one wall and you could hear the screams from a mile away. When I saw there was no hope, I turned around and headed back to the harbour, as fast as my horse would carry me. I had to get word out. The Pope must hear of this, and call for a new crusade to free the Holy City from the infidels!" He thrust his fist up into the air to emphasise his point, but this seemed to be more than his body could bear. Eustace fell to his knees and toppled over, out cold.

Sebastiano helped Godfrey haul the unconscious man into a boat, suggesting he take his uncle to his lodgings and summon a healer to see to him. "He is also welcome to join us for dinner, if he recovers," Sebastiano said.

Godfrey mumbled something he hoped sounded obliging as he directed the boatman to the inn where he was staying. The breeze had picked up, whipping the lagoon into small, savage waves that soon woke Eustace. Godfrey could get no sense out of him, aside from a lengthy account of the state of the Holy City.

Men, women and children, chained up and sold into slavery, or slaughtered if they put up the slightest resistance. Oh, but not the women. Any woman who resisted was taken to entertain the soldiers, until they tired of her and left her lying in a pool of her own blood on the ground.

"Is this true?" the gondolier demanded.

Godfrey shook his head, but Eustace reared up. "Of course it's true! I saw it with my own eyes. Raping virgins in the Holy City. Savages, the lot of them. The Pope must hear of it, and call for all good men to put a stop to it! For the Holy Land to be so befouled..."

The gondolier's eyes widened, and he poled faster.

The sun was sinking by the time the healer left Godfrey's lodgings, having dressed the wounds hidden beneath Eustace's rags. He'd given Eustace a draught to make him sleep before extracting an arrowhead from one of the wounds and binding that, too.

"Will he be all right?" Godfrey asked.

The healer shrugged. "If I have stopped the

infection in time, then yes. If one of the wounds festers...I shall return on the morrow."

Godfrey paid the man, then turned to watch his uncle snoring. Amid Eustace's babblings, he'd also told the tale of his escape from the city amid a storm of arrows, some of which had found their mark in his flesh. No wonder he looked twenty years older than Father, instead of ten years younger.

Sebastiano would understand if Godfrey did not turn up for dinner, he was sure. The patrician would accept his apologies. But that meant staying here, watching his uncle sleep, and worrying that he might not wake. Better that Godfrey go out for a while, and return when his uncle woke.

Godfrey dressed in clean garb, then summoned a boatman to take him to Palazzo Ziano for the second time that day.

He barely noticed the journey this time. He could not have answered whether the sun still shone or whether the waves wet him on the way, for all too soon he found himself at Sebastiano's doors. This time, he didn't hesitate to knock.

Sebastiano's dining chamber could have been the twin of the office he'd visited earlier in the day, with the low ceiling and cosy fire making it look like a private room in an inn instead of a nobleman's dining hall. Even the table where Sebastiano sat had benches on both sides, despite sitting on a dais.

"Please, sit," Sebastiano said, rising. He gestured toward the seat across from him. Only then did Godfrey realise what was wrong with the room – Sebastiano sat at what would be the place of honour on his father's table, but with benches on each side of the table, he was offering a seat of equal honour to his guest, and leaving the seat at the head of the table vacant. "How is your uncle?"

Godfrey blinked, bringing his thoughts back to his host and not the man's furniture. "He is resting. He was wounded. It looked like some of the enemy archers used him for target practice. The healer did what he could for him, but…" Godfrey didn't dare finish, for what could he say? That his uncle might die? Sebastiano was Eustace's friend. He would not like to hear such things any more than Godfrey wanted to say them.

Sebastiano nodded gravely. "Sometimes rest and time are better healers than all the potions in the world. Followed closely by the company of one's family, for which I must apologise. I know I promised you would meet my sons, but they – "

Sons. Courtesans. Godfrey had completely forgotten, yet it seemed Sebastiano had not. Did Sebastiano seriously think Godfrey would want to take some painted whore to the bed where his uncle lay dying?

Copper caught the candlelight, dazzling Godfrey into blindness. When he managed to blink away the lights in his eyes, what he saw stole his breath instead.

Soft copper waves floated above a sea the same shade of aqua blue as the lagoon outside, when the sun caressed the water. Her silk gown shimmered in the candlelight, cut as modestly as that belonging to some highborn matron, but the wicked fire in her eyes would have tempted the devil himself – she was no man's faithful wife.

If this woman was the courtesan Sebastiano's sons had chosen, they had plucked an angel from heaven, and he would fall to his knees and beg for a smile from such a paragon. Nay, he'd offer her every coin he possessed and pledge his life in servitude…

Her lips quirked, parting just the slightest bit, and Godfrey was consumed with the desire to kiss her. Kiss her until he ran out of breath, and then he might die happily.

He would sell his father's horses, and the clothes on his back, and then maybe, just maybe…

"May I present my daughter, Lady Penelope?" Sebastiano said.

Godfrey's mouth had dropped open at some point, and as his mind processed the patrician's words, horror locked his jaw so that he could not seem to close it. By all that was holy…he'd mistaken the patrician's daughter for a whore?

If Sebastiano or Lady Penelope knew his thoughts, they'd toss him out the door and straight into the canal to drown. It was the least he'd deserve for such an unforgivable insult.

"Some wine for our guest," Lady Penelope called, with a glance at Sebastiano. "Father, have you not offered him any refreshment yet?

What will he think of such poor hospitality?" She accepted a jug of wine from a servant, and poured a goblet for herself, before offering her own cup to Godfrey. A wicked smile lifted her lips. "Please, drink. My father is lucky you did not threaten to toss him into the canal for such an insult."

Godfrey lifted the wine to his lips, then choked on the first mouthful as her words registered. Either she'd read his mind, or his thoughts were written so plainly across his face, she hadn't needed to. Any moment now, her father would draw his sword and…

"Ah, Vitale, my friend, so good you could join us. Master Godfrey, this is Duke Vitale, the ruler of Rialto. I had hoped he might hear from your uncle the state of affairs in the Holy Land, but as he is not feeling well…"

Godfrey jumped to his feet, bowing at the newcomer. He would not have picked the Duke as any higher rank than Sebastiano, for the only difference between the men's garb was an embroidered cloth hat the Duke wore.

"Have you come from the Holy Land?" the Duke demanded.

Godfrey shook his head. "No, I have come

from the north, but my uncle has told me much of what happened to the city. Perhaps you will allow me to tell you what I can remember."

The Duke sat. "Please do."

Keeping his eyes firmly fixed on the Duke, Godfrey began to repeat his uncle's tales.

For if he looked at her again, he would lose his very soul to her spell.

Two

Penelope stared at the boy Father had invited to dinner. The boy who thought she was the most beautiful woman he'd ever seen, an angel, and a courtesan. As though anyone could be all three.

She'd considered accidentally knocking his cup over, covering his clothes in wine, but there was no wine on the table yet. Mother would not have forgotten such a thing, but she had left this world two summers ago, and supped at a more heavenly feast than this one would be.

The boy's thoughts turned to how much

he'd like to kiss her. Kiss her, and that was all. She'd never met a boy with thoughts so chaste, though she'd read the minds of most of the men in the city, whether she liked it or not. Truth be told, she did not like it, for she'd probably seen more debauchery in their thoughts than any brothel in the city. Her father would be horrified if he knew his virgin daughter could describe over a dozen ways to pleasure a man with her hands and mouth alone…and what prices the whores in town charged for such things.

Luckily, her father had no idea she could read minds, and she intended to keep it that way. So she sat silently, listening to the boy's tales of war and the world outside of Rialto, and wished that one day, she might travel beyond the lagoon. Though not to the Holy Land, by the sound of things, where women were raped, chained, separated from their children, raped again, then sold into slavery where they were likely to never know a night alone in their own bed again. Unlike the whores of Rialto, who could suck enough money out of newly arrived sailors to take the occasional night off…often to meet lovers of their own choosing. Noblemen who might marry them, or at least keep them as courtesans or mistresses, free of the street and sailors.

Everyone dreamed of something, and she was no stranger to those thoughts, either.

This boy – Godfrey, his name was – feared his dreams would be nightmares about the fall of the Holy City. Things of blood and darkness. When he departed that night, he barely glanced at her, so dark were his thoughts that he'd entirely forgotten her existence.

Father invited him to dine with them again, every night he was in the city, and Penelope made sure to sit where she might hear him speak, though he never said a word to her. His uncle was ill, she learned, and as soon as he was well enough to travel, they would both leave. Until then, her father intended to keep the boy in his household as much as possible. She thought little of it, until she caught her brothers discussing Godfrey with their father one day.

"She is too young!"

"We cannot afford it!"

"If we hadn't sent that expedition to the northern seas, perhaps we could afford it, or if it had returned, but it's been a year and there is no word…"

Seeing herself in her brothers' thoughts, Penelope concentrated harder.

Her father had always been one for hiding his thoughts, but his words were clear enough. "Your mother had already given me a son when she was her age. In this house, with your wives and children, do you not think she wants to have the same for herself?"

"But she brings nothing to the household! We take care of your business, Father, bringing wealth in. What will she do but take it away to some other rival family?" That was Pietro, the youngest of her brothers. He'd married a thirty-year-old widow he could not stand the sight of for the size of her dowry alone. She suspected he'd rather stick his manhood into a bag of gold and get his pleasure that way than go anywhere near his wife.

Domenico was the oldest and most reasonable, so it was no surprise to hear him say, "Perhaps a widower without an heir…someone who has more need of a young, fertile wife, than any kind of dowry."

"No. I will not send Penelope into a miserable marriage, where she will be widowed young."

"Perhaps you should ask Penelope who she wants to marry," Orso suggested, trying hard not to laugh. "If she has a particular old man in mind, maybe she won't be miserable. She spends all her time weaving and sewing. Maybe a wool merchant, or one who sells silk…Ha, or a lace merchant, where she can learn to make Rialto's finest lace for pure profit, just like in the stories." He liked to stir up trouble, tossing out the idea more to see Father's reaction than anything else, but there was a tiny grain of hope that Father might accept his idea. Sending a convoy north had been his idea, and the loss gnawed at him.

"Enough!" Father said. "I will choose who Penelope marries, not any of you. Whether she marries another patrician, or some patrician's son, or even some foreign nobleman, the decision is mine to make."

Penelope had long ago come to terms with this, though she'd raged against it as a child. Now, she was more interested in her father's thoughts, in which she could see a clear picture of Godfrey. He was the foreign nobleman he had in mind.

That night at dinner, she watched Godfrey, and was surprised to see how many times he gazed at her before looking away again. But he was less successful at turning his thoughts away from her. In fact, he thought about her with such ardour it was enough to warm her cheeks, though his thoughts never strayed to anything more passionate than a kiss. And the more he thought about kissing her, the more she warmed to the idea.

She retired early that night, but she could not sleep. Was Father seriously considering marrying her to that boy? She had to admit, she liked him better than most of the other men she'd met, but not to the point of passion, or love. Her brothers and even her father might scoff at such a notion, but she'd read the thoughts of enough people to know there were love matches, and marriages where passion played a big part. They were rare, true, but not unknown. She'd tasted Godfrey's eager desire for her, so why could she not arouse the same passion in herself at the thought of him?

When the next day dawned, she resolved to find her father, and ask him whether he meant to marry her to Godfrey.

But she slept late, and by the time she made her way to the dining chamber, her father and brothers had gone, leaving her to break her fast alone. Servants brought her bread, oil and fruit. She ripped off a piece of bread, dipped it on the oil and munched on it slowly, eyeing the bowl of fruit with distaste. It looked like last year's peaches swimming in honey, much too sweet for her taste. No, she longed for the first spring peaches, fresh picked from the tree, and summer berries, so bursting with juice they stained her fingers, but this winter didn't seem to want to end.

"Do we have any oranges?" she asked.

Silence greeted her – the servants had all gone, to do whatever duties they normally did this late in the morning. She sighed. Her brothers' wives would have just repeated the question, louder, until a servant produced what the woman wanted, but Penelope had grown up in this house with these servants, and most of them still saw her as a child. A child who had been in trouble many more times for climbing the trees in the orchard than for raising her voice.

She stopped to wrap a cloak around her shoulders from the hook by the door before heading outside into the garden. Frost rimed the trees, making her wish she'd grabbed gloves as well, but that would only take longer. She wanted oranges now, not later.

Penelope surveyed the trees, but there was no low hanging fruit today. No, all the ripe oranges were higher up, where the sun kissed them. Ah, she could do with a little sun, too. And it wasn't like anyone was watching…

She found a ladder frozen to one of the tree trunks, but didn't have the strength to pry it free, so she climbed it instead, stepping into the canopy as easily as she would if it was the landing at the top of the stairs. It had been years since she'd climbed trees, but she hadn't forgotten. She tested each branch before putting her weight on it, reaching higher and higher until she found a clump of oranges as red as the sun. She twisted them free and stuffed the cold globes into the pockets of her cloak until she could not carry any more. Then she made her way down to the ground again.

"Is no one home? He demands to see the master!"

"Lord Sebastiano and his sons are at the Ducal Palace, and the wives are all visiting their families today."

"What about Lady Penelope?"

"I brought her breakfast in the dining room myself, but now she's nowhere to be found."

"If it's someone important, perhaps you should send a boy down to the Palace to fetch the master. Who is it?"

"That boy who has dined here all week, making moon eyes at Lady Penelope. Godefroi, or some barbarous northern name like it."

Godfrey. If Penelope couldn't ask her father, perhaps she could ask the boy himself if they had a betrothal cooked up between them.

She crept down the ladder, jumping down the last few rungs to land with an audible thump on the frozen ground. She strode toward the two servants, lifting her head high as she hoped they would not question her. "Send him into the dining chamber. I will greet him, hear whatever message he has for my father, and see him on his way," Penelope ordered, not breaking stride as she swept into the house.

She barely had time to drop her orange-burdened cloak beneath the table before she had to turn and greet Godfrey.

He looked like he'd had less sleep than her, but there was nothing in his thoughts to tell her why.

"My lady," he breathed, bowing low. The only image in his head was of her – her hair haloing her like some sort of angel, with a crown of…

She swore under her breath and desperately tried to comb the leaves out of her hair before he looked at her again.

"Would you like some refreshment? Bread, fruit…wine?" she asked.

He stared fixedly at the floor, shaking his head. "I cannot. My uncle died of his wounds last night, and I must return home. His final wish was to be buried in our family crypt, and I gave my word."

Her hands flew to her mouth. "Heavens, Master Godfrey, I'm so sorry. May God rest his soul. I'm sure he was a good man, as are you for granting his wish."

He looked up in surprise. "Thank you, my lady. You are kind to say so. I wish I could have stayed longer." For her, his thoughts added. "But I must bid you farewell, and I'd hoped to give your father my apologies, too, for leaving with so little warning."

She took her hands in his. "I will tell him all you have told me. On my father's behalf, as well as my own, I wish you a safe journey home."

"Thank you. I pray I will be able to return soon, for your father and the Duke both assured me that the men of Rialto will take up the crusade to free the Holy Land, and I have no doubt that once the rest of Christendom hears, thousands more will take up their swords to defend the faith. When the trade routes open again, I shall return." He lifted her hands to his lips and kissed them.

Her skin tingled as though his lips burned her…and yet, she did not want to pull away.

Nor did he. He wanted to take her with him – had intended to ask her father for her hand. But now he was in mourning for his uncle, he could not.

Could she marry this man she barely knew?

If he'd asked for her today, could she have borne sharing a bed with him?

There was one way to find out. She wet her lips, marching forward to close the distance between them. Godfrey dropped her hands and backed away, but she followed, backing him up against the wall. Now or never.

She seized his shoulders and kissed him. Though she'd experienced a thousand kisses in the thoughts of others, this was the first one that had touched her lips. Clumsy at first, for he was as inexperienced as she, but not for long. Passion took over, and she wasn't sure if it was his or hers, rushing through her like flames, as her body pressed against his and they kissed again.

He was all lean and hard, in all the right places, but his touch was gentle as he pulled her close, and deepened the kiss.

Images of ships and armies crowded her mind, thoughts that had nothing to do with her or Godfrey, as someone else approached the dining chamber.

Her father and brothers!

Reluctantly, she pulled away, straightening her clothes as she put a decorous distance between them. Godfrey might want to marry her, and he kissed like the very devil himself, but her father had not agreed to a betrothal yet.

But she would. He had only to ask.

Godfrey heard the approaching voices and his confused expression vanished, to be replaced by calm composure.

When her father entered the room, Godfrey bowed and took his leave. He shot one meaningful glance at Penelope, who heard his vow to return for her as surely as if he'd spoken the words aloud, before he departed.

Penelope forced out a smile. "So what did the Duke have to say? Are we to save the Holy Land?"

Father sighed heavily. "He will raise an army, and a fleet to carry them. They will depart in the spring."

She ignored the doubts shadowing his thoughts. "Then Duke Vitale will free them all by the summer, and Master Godfrey will return." She tried to believe the words with all her might, but they rang hollow.

"With no family left here or in the Holy Land, Godfrey has no need to return. Even if the Holy City is ours again by summer, I doubt we will ever see him again."

She stopped dead. "But…I thought you planned for me to marry him. I heard you say…"

Domenico choked on his ale and Orso laughed aloud. Pietro's brow just scrunched together like he wanted to shout at her, but didn't dare.

Father shook his head. "Our fortunes would have to be in a sorry state indeed before I allowed you to marry some foreign horse trader. No, you will marry a man worth of you, my little duck. But not for some time."

Penelope longed for her father to be wrong, but she knew in her heart that he was not.

It would be three years before she saw Godfrey again. Three years that saw Duke Vitale and his grand army to their graves, and a new crusade had begun.

And the world would never be the same.

Three

"Crusaders must be the most saintly knights in Christendom," Melisende said dreamily. "I'm surprised you aren't going to join them, now you're a knight, Godfrey. Isn't knighthood all about honour? Travelling so far from home to lay down your very life to save the Holy City…so honourable you cannot help but be named a saint."

"More like the least saintly," Father interrupted, setting down his wine cup. "Though I have no doubt Godfrey earned his knighthood with honour, the truth of knighthood is little more than being able to sit upon a horse without falling off, and knowing one end of a sword from the other. Most of them have only taken up the cross for the glory of it, or the promised pardon of all their sins. They are men who are not heroes at home, or who have no hope of heaven without a good deed so great, it erases everything else they have done. Younger sons and troublemakers – those their fathers would not miss, if they do not return. Unlike my sons, who are very much needed here at home." He signalled for a servant to refill his wine cup. "I am delighted that none of your brothers have decided to join this fool scheme."

Too busy dealing with the damage and thievery those supposed saints had wreaked as they rode across Father's lands, Godfrey mused silently. His brothers still had not returned, so he was the only one of Father's sons in the dining hall that day. Probably because he was the youngest, his knighthood so newly minted that he didn't yet answer when someone addressed him as Sir Knight. He could handle a horse and a sword, but little else, so it was no wonder he was not yet trusted enough to act on his own, like his older brothers.

Especially after his first solo task for his father had resulted in the death of Uncle Eustace and the end of all trade with the Holy Land. No one wanted that sort of ill luck again, so Godfrey was kept on a short rein, close to home.

He did not mind. His brothers would manage the estate, while he could focus on what he did best – working with the horses. His great grandfather had brought home some particularly fine horses when he went crusading, before Uncle Eustace had lost his life bringing more, and they'd bred a herd that was the envy of kings and emperors alike. Kings and emperors who were only too happy to buy the beasts when they came up for sale. The new colt that was born last week came from two particularly good bloodlines. If he could train it as well as he had the beast's sisters, he would be a mount fit for a king. Perhaps tomorrow…

"Godfrey!"

Godfrey blinked, focussing on his father. "Yes?"

"Tell your sister what the crusading army has done."

Fathered a bunch of bastards on as many girls as they could find, Godfrey thought but daren't say. No, Melisende should not hear about the plague of brutal rapes that had beset their lands. He wondered what would happen when their pack of rapists met the army of Seljuk ones. All one side had to do was don dresses and hide their weapons beneath them and victory would be assured, for the other army would be caught with their hose about their ankles. That would be a sight to see.

Ah…what had Father asked again? Oh, that's right.

"They slaughtered and ate a herd of dairy cows in the next village – nothing left – and then burned one of the wheat fields with one of their roasting fires, days before harvest. Other villages have lost all their poultry. One tavern brought out all their barrels of beer – which the crusaders took off with, not paying the tavernkeeper a single copper." And when he'd protested, the knights had laughed, seized the man's wife and daughters and…Godfrey swallowed. "We've kept the horses in the walled yard, instead of letting them out into the fields, so they don't see them. This army is like ants, taking and devouring everything in their path. It will be good when they are gone."

"They're camped outside town for now, but they'll ride on tomorrow," Father said. "Then they will be someone else's problem."

Godfrey glanced at Melisende, whose attention was fixed on her food. She probably hadn't heard a word. Her mind flew from one idea to another like a butterfly in a field full of flowers. He wished he could think as quickly as she could, but he suspected that if anyone else's mind worked as lightning-fast as hers, it would surely explode.

When he was done eating, he excused himself to go check on the horses.

He found them restless, annoyed at having to take their turns running about the walled yard, stuck in the stables for longer than they were accustomed. Good thing he'd brought a sack of early apples to share. He took his time, giving treats and stroking flanks, whispering promises of time in the fields tomorrow, until he was satisfied that he'd calmed them enough for the night.

And night it was, for darkness had fallen by the time he left the stables. Even the grooms had gone to bed. If he had any sense, he should do the same.

He bypassed the Great Hall, taking the servants' stairs up to the family chambers. He made it halfway up before he encountered a ghost.

The ghost squeaked, then lowered her white wool hood and whispered, "Godfrey! What are you doing here? Looming out of the darkness like that, you nearly made me scream and wake the whole house!"

"I'm going to bed. Where are you going?" he asked.

Melisende tossed her head, pressing her lips together with all the obstinacy Godfrey knew well.

"If you don't tell me, I'll be forced to tell Father, and he'll send men out to bring you back," Godfrey warned.

Her eyes widened in horror. "Oh, don't tell Father!" She grasped his arm with both hands. "Swear you will not tell Father, and I will tell you."

"Are you meeting a lover?" he demanded, feeling foolish the moment the words left his mouth.

Her expression turned thunderous. "Swear to me, Godfrey, or I shall tell you nothing."

She might be his younger sister, and much

smaller than himself, but she made up for it in the breadth of her stubbornness. This was a battle Godfrey could not win.

He sighed, exhaling from the very depths of his soul. "Very well. I swear I shall not tell Father."

She nodded. "I am going up to St Michael's Spire, to watch the army march out on the morrow."

It was Godfrey's turn to nod. The Spire was a tower on the highest point around. A monastery had once stood there, since fallen into ruin, but the belltower remained, manned by guards from Father's own men. Melisende would sleep as safely there as here at home. Perhaps even more so, for there was little to tempt the crusaders up the winding path to the mountain eyrie.

"Would you like me to come with you to protect you on the road?" Godfrey asked.

She snorted. "Of course not. With your big boots clomping along beside me, everyone from the castle to the town will know there's someone on the road alone, ripe for robbing. If I go alone, no one will even know I was there."

He hung his head. She had always been the

stealthiest of Father's children — a better hunter than any of her brothers. He suspected she had inherited their mother's gift for magic, though he'd never seen her cast a spell. "As you wish." He headed up the stairs, turning sideways to squeeze past her.

Her hand against his shoulder halted him. "Godfrey." Her eyes held hurt. "You're a good and honourable knight, but you cannot protect everyone. We both know my fate will take me far from here."

Yes, but Father had not said who she would marry yet. Though he would soon, for she was of an age for a husband. She'd be a castle chatelaine, managing an estate as large as this one for her husband. While Godfrey stayed home, breeding horses instead of heirs, and his brothers managed Father's estate.

"Safe journey," he managed to say, before resuming his ascent. He swore as he stumbled and nearly fell.

"You, too, brother," he heard Melisende say from far below.

Four

Sun shone on the lagoon today, turning the usually grey waters into aquamarine so clear Penelope fancied she could see the fish swimming in it. The slight warmth made her think spring might finally come to the lagoon after this cold winter. Her foolish thought was whirled away in a gust of wintry wind that had her pulling her wool cloak more closely about her. No, spring would be a long time coming, for Carnevale had just begun and it would run for weeks yet.

Already, the nuns greeted the day's visitors with gasps and shrieks, for most of them were masked. She stood on the island shore, away from the dock, knowing she would not receive any visitors today. Her father was a busy man, now he was the newly crowned Duke of Rialto, working hard to give the people the peace he had promised.

He'd granted her peace, too – the day after his coronation, he'd sent her here to the convent at Saint Angelo of Concordia, where she had naught but nuns and weaving to keep her occupied until she married.

Or so he thought.

"The green cloak suits you. I'm glad you like it."

So lost had Penelope been in her own thoughts, she hadn't heard his approaching footsteps, nor noticed the man in his familiar mask. At least he wasn't wearing the hat. The hat no one could clean the previous duke's blood from completely. Poor Duke Vitale, to survive war and plague, only to die on an assassin's blade as he stepped out of his own front door to go to mass.

Penelope dropped a graceful curtsey. "Monsignor was most kind to send me such a gift for Yule. The convent here is much colder than the Ducal Palace." She lifted her face to the breeze. "Perhaps it is the wind coming off the water."

The eyes behind the mask tightened in concern. "If you need warmer clothes, furs, more wine, only say, and it will be yours. But I cannot let you come home. It is not safe."

Father feared he would be the next to fall to an assassin's knife, and he wished to spare her the sight of his mangled body. On the slim chance that his fears were realised, she didn't want to see him bathed in blood, either, so she allowed him the lie.

"Whereas here, I am so safe, the worst I shall do is catch a chill. Unless I catch a husband soon," she said.

She did not need to read her father's mind to know it would not be soon. His heavy sigh told its own tale.

"Would you prefer to be a princess, or remain a lady here in Rialto?" Father asked.

No mention of Godfrey. Not any more.

She should forget him, and mostly, she had, except when talk turned to marriage, or the need for Father to make her a princess.

There were no kings in Rialto – the Duke

reigned with his Council of the Wise until he died, or resigned. She was the nearest thing to a princess in the whole Republic. To truly make her a princess, Father would have to marry her off to some foreign prince, sending her far from home to form an alliance that would help Rialto.

"I would prefer to be the wife of a good husband, like you were to Mother," Penelope said.

Off came the mask. The Duke was done hiding his face. "If Vitale were still alive, I might be able to give you that. But now…we are beset by enemies on all sides. If your marriage could bring us peace in but one quarter…I must try." He did not say how much he feared for his life, for he was not the sort of warrior Duke Vitale had been, to lead an army to victory. Only to lose that army to a plague, and his life to an assassin's blade. He'd been Father's friend, too.

"Any word on which quarter it will be, Father?" she asked. She plucked the names from his head as they appeared. "Otto or Frederick of Aachen, Alexios of Byzas…" She wanted to add Godfrey's name to the list, but after Duke Vitale had failed to free any of the captured cities, let alone the Holy Land, there had been no word from Godfrey or his family for three years. He'd probably forgotten all about her, marrying some northern girl who popped out fat babies like a hen laying eggs.

"Not Frederick! His father is trying to marry him to some southern spinster princess, sole heir to the throne, so he can have the southern Northmen's crown."

Not Frederick, then. And not someone in the south, either, if they had no men for her to marry.

"Who, then?"

Another heart-weary sigh. "If I had an answer, I would give it to you. The negotiations are slow, taking many months for letters to pass between my court and theirs. And some of our envoys have been detained…" Father closed his mouth before he could say more.

Penelope lifted the words from his head instead: "…detained and imprisoned by the Emperor or his vassals. And those who are released are almost unrecognisable…" At the image Father began to conjure in his mind, she shut his thoughts out as best she could. What she could not ignore was his shudder of horror at the torture his men had been subjected to.

She had to marry someone. She hoped it would not be the same man responsible for torturing her countrymen. What such a man might do to her…

But princes had servants to do such things for them, surely. Men they employed to do the things no man could possibly take pleasure in.

She swallowed her unsavoury thoughts, focussing instead on her father. "Then I thank you for the visit, for I know how little time you have to spare now. I hope you will have an answer soon. In the meantime, I shall…weave a wedding dress fit for a princess." Penelope forced out a smile, finishing up with a curtsey.

Duke Sebastiano kissed her cheek before covering his face with his falcon mask once more. "You are a good girl. If only I had a dozen other daughters just like you. Maybe then I might make peace with everyone."

"If anyone can find a way, you can," she said, more out of love than a belief that she was telling the truth. Her father was a good man. If there was a path out of the political chaos the world had become, she knew he would work day and night to find it, or at least the man who could.

Despite her green cloak, she did not envy him a bit.

Five

Godfrey tried to sleep, but he couldn't stop worrying about Melisende. The crusader army was camped on the other side of town from both the Spire and the castle, but he'd seen plenty of evidence that not all the men stayed in the camp. He should have gone with her, or broken his oath and told his father anyway.

If anything happened to her, he would never forgive himself.

Finally, he rose, not caring who heard him on his way to the stable in the predawn darkness. He woke Pegasus, the swiftest of the horses in the stable, and was soon headed up the hill toward the Spire. The moon had not yet set, lighting his path so that he did not need a torch, even though dawn was little more than a smudge of grey on the eastern horizon.

By the time he reached the base of the Spire, it was light enough to discern the difference between the tower and the rock behind it. Leaving Pegasus in the pen that held the Spire ponies, he opened the door to the tower.

"Ho, the tower! It's Godfrey, coming up to see the view!"

Male voices urged him to come up. Melisende was likely saving her comments about how unwelcome he was for when he reached the top of the winding stairs, Godfrey thought wryly as he hastened toward the belfry.

Beatus and Clemens offered him a drink from the jug of cider on the table between them, but Melisende was nowhere to be seen.

"Where is she?" Godfrey asked, pouring himself a cup of cider.

"Who?" asked Beatus, tearing his gaze away from the window.

"My sister, Lady Melisende."

The two men stared at one another, confusion clear on their faces.

"She is not here, Sir Godfrey," Clemens said kindly.

Both men had served his father since before he was born, watching him play with a wooden sword before being allowed to trade blows with them in the practice yard. They knew he was slower than his brothers, and their kindness was not condescension.

But he couldn't help clenching his fists in frustration. He felt as stupid as they thought him to be. "But she said she'd be here. Have you seen her tonight?" After a moment, he added, "Or anyone else?"

For if she'd come here to meet a lover, it was not Clemens or Beatus.

Two heads shook. "Not since Firmin and Justus left at sunset, and our watch began."

Godfrey's heart sank. Either he'd been right to worry, or she'd remembered Father's disgust for the crusaders, changed her mind and crept up to bed. No one would have heard her returning home, just as no one would have heard her go if he had not met her on the way.

He prayed she was home, asleep, and much wiser than her brother.

He missed his footing more than once on his way down the spiral stair, so he wisely let Pegasus choose her own pace on the steep mountain track. He breathed a sigh of relief when they reached the road, only to be greeted by the daytime guards.

"You need to see this, Sir Godfrey," said Justus, parting the bushes beside the road.

Godfrey swallowed. He prayed he was wrong, before raising his head to look.

A bundle of white wool lay in the bushes, folded in half as though ready to be placed in a chest to be stored for the winter.

Justus nudged the bundle with his foot, rolling it over.

Bile rose up in Godfrey's throat at the ruin of what had once been a human face, but was little more than bloody pulp now. Her gown, and the shift beneath it, were ripped from neck to hem, and so stained in blood one might have thought the cloth was meant to be red.

Justus touched a hand to her throat. "There's no heartbeat. She's dead."

Godfrey nodded, taking in the girl's injuries,

for she had no modesty left to preserve. Bleeding out from the vicious cuts to her thighs and belly, she'd crawled into the woods to die after her rape and beating. Another in a long list of victims who could be laid at the crusaders' doors. Sins they would never answer for, if they freed the Holy City.

"Do you recognise her?" Godfrey asked.

Justus coughed. "I'd know that cloak anywhere. 'Tis Lady Melisende, whose stillroom potions kept my mother alive through the winter, when everyone else said she'd never make it."

No. She was asleep in her bed. Home. Safe. Had to be.

"Are you sure?" Godfrey croaked.

The guards exchanged a glance, as if questioning his intelligence. Godfrey had never felt as stupid as he did right now.

"It's the stars embroidered on the hem. When the weather grew warmer, Lady Melisende forgot her cloak one afternoon, and my mother did the stars as thanks for your sister's care." Justus would not meet Godfrey's eyes. "Would you like help lifting her onto your horse to take home?"

If Godfrey's thoughts had been slow before, they moved at the pace of pitch now. It couldn't be her. Yet it had to be. What he'd dreaded had come to pass, and it was his fault. Now, with her death on his conscience, he would be forced to break the final oath he'd made to her, and tell his father.

It took Godfrey three tries to mount his horse, so Justus and Firmin did not wait for an answer. The two men wrapped the body in the cloak, before passing it up to him. Godfrey couldn't think of the limp bundle as his sister as he rode home with it.

Father sat on the dais in the Great Hall, breaking his fast as he gave orders for the day.

Godfrey's feet kept carrying him forward, though the body in his arms weighed him down so much he feared his next step would send him crashing into the cellar below.

He laid the bundle at the foot of the dais.

"They got Melisende, Father." His throat closed as he choked back a sob. "Those damned crusaders killed her." And I didn't stop them, he thought but did not say. This was his fault. His, and no one else's. "I vow to you, on her soul, that I will seek out the men who did this, and see that they face justice. If I have to follow the army to the gates of the Holy City itself, I will find them, and see that they pay."

Godfrey bowed his head to where the cloak's hood hid his sister's ravaged face, unable to look his father in the eye. "I will pack my things and set off immediately."

He rose and hurried out of the hall. He was a killer and an oathbreaker, no better than any of the crusaders. If he wanted forgiveness for his sins, he would have to not only seek justice for Melisende, but he'd have to see that the crusade succeeded.

He vowed to do everything in his power to ensure no more crusades were needed, so this would never happen again.

<h1 style="text-align:center">Six</h1>

"There you are!"

Penelope had barely a moment to register Marzia's presence before the girl grasped Penelope's hand in both of hers and began to pull her toward the convent.

"I've been looking for you everywhere. What possessed you to stand out here in the cold? Why, the breeze blows right through you here – it's a wonder you haven't turned into an icicle. Your hands are colder than the lagoon! I insist you come inside by the fire, before you catch a chill."

Penelope didn't need to glance at the waves

to know her father had already vanished from sight, headed home to the much larger islands that made up the main part of the Republic of Rialto. Maybe Marzia's sunny thoughts were exactly the panacea she needed to cure her own dark misgivings.

Penelope allowed herself to be led into the womb-like warmth of the convent parlour, where the more sensible members of the community entertained their guests. Not everyone wore masks for Carnevale – most of the nuns went bare-faced, like Marzia, Penelope and the other…well, Penelope supposed they were officially novices, the girls who were not yet nuns and those who lived within the walls of Saint Angelo of Concordia while they waited to be married.

People parted to allow her passage through the room to the fireplace, where the roaring blaze kept all but the convent dogs at a safe distance.

Marzia produced a sheet of paper and held it out to Penelope. "My brother sent me a letter. Now the mourning period for Father is over, he thinks it is time for me to marry. He says that if his negotiations continue, I will be married by the summer!"

Penelope skimmed the letter, finding nothing new. After Vitale's death, it made sense for his heir to take over his father's role in making a marriage agreement for her. Such was the way of the world. If women were allowed to choose their own husbands, businesses would fail as dowry money went into less suitable hands than those belonging to their fellow merchants, or their sons. Or so many of the men of the city thought.

But she knew Marzia's secret worries about never marrying, now her father was dead. This news was welcome relief for her.

So, "Congratulations. That is good news," Penelope said.

Marzia's eyes shone. "Isn't it? But I must know if I will be happy in marriage. That's why I need you!"

Oh no. Penelope opened her mouth to protest.

"You see, there's a fortune teller," Marzia continued. "She says she can tell my future by merely looking at my hand. But I haven't the courage see her alone. I'm frightened that my future will be dark. If you come with me, to share your fortitude with me, then perhaps I can stand to hear what she has to say."

Penelope followed Marzia's gaze to the old woman seated in a corner of the parlour. At least, that's what she appeared to be. But as Marzia grasped Penelope's hand and led her closer, she began to see the inconsistencies in the woman's costume. Her rags were the remains of several gowns stitched together haphazardly, with little regard for the fine fabric they were made from. The woman's face was a cleverly made Carnivale mask, complete with wrinkles, so that what little she could see of it that wasn't hidden by the hood of her fine wool cloak appeared to be her real face and not artifice. The woman's hand was unusually large, dwarfing the cup in her hand, though most of it was hidden in her voluminous sleeve. Her boots were larger than even the abbess's, and the abbess had big feet for a woman.

Penelope let her mind brush the fortune teller's thoughts.

"Marzia, what you think is a fortune teller is in fact a fraud. In fact, I think she's a – "

"Some people deny the existence of magic

in the world. So caught up in their own business, they think little of the happiness of others. That's why they will always be alone," the old woman croaked sourly, her eyes fixed on Penelope.

Penelope pressed her lips together. A few more words and she might have given away the secret of her gift. Not even her father knew she could read minds, and she had no intention of handing her secret over to this charlatan. A charlatan who knew too much already, to be issuing predictions about her future that seemed likely to come true.

"Not me," Marzia declared, depositing a small pile of silver on the table before the fortune teller. She perched on one end of the bench, pulling Penelope down beside her. "If you can truly tell me my future, I would pay you ten times that."

The greedy glitter Penelope expected in the fortune teller's eyes failed to appear.

"Give me your hand, my little strawberry," the fortune teller said.

Marzia blushed almost as red as her gown, and extended her fingers.

The fortune teller captured her hand like a

coveted treasure, cupping it carefully as she turned it palm up. Penelope glimpsed well-manicured nails on distinctly unwrinkled fingers before the fortune teller began to speak.

"This is a happy hand. A very happy hand..."

Had Penelope imagined it, or had the fortune teller's voice grown deeper?

"You will be happily married to a man who will adore you. You will live in a fine house overlooking the campo where his family has lived for generations, and your children – "

"How many children will I have?" Marzia interrupted eagerly.

"As many as you desire, and your husband Marco..."

An overwhelming wave of desire engulfed Penelope, accompanied by the image of a young man entwined with Marzia, naked in a bed of silk. A young man with big hands, big feet, and a huge...

Closing her eyes to shut out the image, Penelope rose and backed away from the fake fortune teller.

Marco of the mighty manhood, she

presumed, was now so enamoured of Marzia that he didn't even notice Penelope leaving.

No, not just enamoured – madly in love with her. And who wouldn't be? Penelope's friend was as lovely inside as she was out, and she deserved happiness.

Penelope sighed. If Marzia would have a devoted husband, then perhaps the man was right, and Penelope would spend the rest of her life alone, whether she married or not. For love in marriage was as rare as a flying horse in the merchant city.

Seven

The horde of humanity and horses stretched as far as Godfrey could see. Some had tents or pavilions, while others looked like they'd slept under a hedge and wished they were still there. So much for riding out at dawn. Yesterday's army had become this morning's rabble. Time enough for him to find Melisende's murderers, and bring them before his father to face justice.

"What are you looking for? Did you lose your squire, Sir Knight?"

Godfrey blinked. He hadn't seen the grey-clad man, leaning against a tree beside the road.

"Have you seen anyone else come along this road?" Godfrey demanded.

The grey man pulled a bottle from his belt, yanked out the stopper and drank deeply. He waited until he'd corked the bottle and wiped his mouth on his sleeve before he spoke. "I've seen an entire crusade, Sir Knight. Or did you think magic put all these men here?" He spread his arms wide to encompass the chaos that was the crusader camp.

Godfrey felt his face redden in embarrassment. The grey man must think him a fool, and perhaps he was right. "I mean…since they made camp. Anyone who came this way, leaving the camp, before returning. Likely before dawn."

The grey man nodded, looking thoughtful. "I'll ask you again, Sir Knight. Who are you looking for?"

Godfrey blew out a frustrated breath. "I don't know. I found a girl's body by the road, and I'm looking for the man who killed her."

For a moment, Godfrey thought the grey man looked relieved, but his expression shifted as quickly as breath in the breeze. Perhaps he had only imagined it.

"You're looking for men with blood on their hands. Take your pick, then, Sir Knight. In this army, there are none without sin. You need but cast the first stone, and you shall surely hit a man who has killed."

Godfrey didn't have time for this. He slid down from his horse and seized the man's shoulder. "Cease your mockery, man. A girl is dead, and she deserves justice. Will you help me, or no?"

The grey man brushed him off, meeting his eyes like a man who knew he was Godfrey's equal. The thickly woven wool beneath Godfrey's hand had told him this was no common labourer.

"If you have any honour, sir, I beg you. Tell me what you know. The girl did not deserve her fate, and honour demands I find the men who deserve death more surely than she did."

The grey man gave a sharp nod. "It's Zoticus, without the sir. I'm no knight, nor do I wish to be. Too much throwing your weight about and riding whatever can carry you, willing or not. The men you want to speak to are the leaders of this rabble, knights all. Sirs

Enguerrand, Guiscard, Onfroi and Roland."

Godfrey stepped back. "Thank you, Master Zoticus. Where might I find these knights you have named?"

"Probably asleep in their pavilions, resting after their successful hunt. For if they were awake, the men would be already on the march, obeying the barked orders from their betters." Zoticus cupped a hand to his ear. "Hark, but I do not hear them. Best you leave before you do. Go and see the girl gets a decent burial. You may be sure she died in battle – think of it as an honourable end."

Godfrey shook his head. "She must have justice. I must find the men who did this to her and bring them before my father, so he can judge and punish them for their crimes."

"And what do you think their army will do? At a word from one of these knights, every man among them will fight. Do you have an army that can defeat them?" Zoticus raised his eyebrows. "Are you such a formidable warrior that you could strike all four of them down before they can utter a word?"

Godfrey was under no illusions about his prowess with a sword. He was too slow to be much of a match for anyone. Even Melisende could beat him in the practice ring on occasion, so swift and nimble was she. But if she had not managed to fight her way free from four armed men, Godfrey had no hope.

"I do not fear death, but I cannot die until justice is served." Godfrey moistened his lips. "There must be a way."

Zoticus winked. "Oh, there is, Sir Knight. But you might not think it honourable for such a noble knight like yourself."

He closed his eyes. "I seek justice, for I have no honour to speak of until she is avenged." Godfrey swallowed. "How can I make them pay for what they have done?"

Zoticus lowered his voice. "Even the most combat hardened knight cannot defend against everything in the heat of battle. Especially the blow that comes from an ally. No one need ever know the enemy blow was struck from within their own ranks. And in battle, each knight leads his own men – they will not know the fate of the others until the battle is over."

Godfrey stared at him, trying to puzzle out all possible meanings of the grey man's words. "You mean…I should befriend them, ride with them, until we ride into battle against the unbelievers…and then assassinate them?" Hardly honourable, but then whoever had killed Melisende had no honour, either. They were all damned together, but it would all be for Melisende. Unless this man was lying and he or someone else had killed his sister… "What if it wasn't them?" he blurted out.

Zoticus smiled, but the expression seemed as grim and grey as his tunic. "It will be many months before we reach the Holy Land, and maybe even longer before the first battle begins. If you ride with us, you will soon see what sort of men they are."

Godfrey nodded. From what little he knew of him, Zoticus gave sound advice. Though the grey man could not be more than a few years older than Godfrey himself.

"Good," Zoticus said. "When battle begins, I shall find you. Enguerrand and Roland are mean fighters, and you might have need of another blade to help you in your quest." He held out his arm, one warrior offering assistance to another.

Godfrey clasped it. "Thank you, Master Zoticus." He rode on, through the camp.

It wasn't until he was deep among the crusaders that he realised Zoticus' plan was far too detailed for something he'd thought up in the moments since they'd met. In fact, it sounded like something he'd been planning for some time.

Zoticus had some stake here, too, which he had not chosen to share.

It mattered not. The men who had killed Melisende would pay for it, and that was enough for Godfrey. If they paid for their other crimes, too, for surely they had committed many, then he was the last man to protest against such justice.

The crusade would be long enough for Godfrey to take the measure of more than one man along the way.

Eight

Cloudy skies turned the lagoon waters iron grey, as if to armour the waves against the pelting rain. The weather's war kept most visitors away from the convent, but the clouds and the waves reached a stalemate eventually, as they always did, and some brave boats ventured out again.

Penelope heard their thoughts as first the fishermen, then the merchants with supplies for the outer islands rowed past. Their prayers for profit and a safe voyage were little more than a hum in the back of her mind, as she worked with her loom. She had finished

Marzia's wedding dress before the year ended, but now she fancied making a veil to match. It would use the last of the blue wool, too, from that peculiar dye batch that was precisely the colour of Vitale's family coat of arms. It brought out the colour of Marzia's eyes, too.

Not for the first time, she blessed her father's gift of horn shutters for the workroom windows here at Saint Angelo's. They let in enough light to allow her to work despite the dark day, yet kept the swift wind from stealing away the heat of her fire. If the light held, she might finish weaving the cloth today, so that she could start sewing the veil before night fell.

Something metal clattered to the table behind her and Penelope jumped to her feet.

"You missed dinner again," Marzia greeted her, folding her arms across her chest. "So I brought you some."

Penelope glanced at the plate. Dinnertime already? She had not eaten since breakfast, and it took a moment to register that she was hungry.

"But the cloth for your wedding veil has come out so perfectly. I wanted to do it all in one piece..." Penelope waved at the sea of blue on her loom.

Marzia looked longingly at the cloth. "For me? Oh, it is so pretty. But how could you know?"

Marzia was practically bursting to tell Penelope her news. She must have truly been caught up in her work not to have noticed the thoughts screaming to be heard from Marzia's mind.

Penelope shook her head, hoping to clear it. "What news?" she asked, feigning ignorance.

Marzia clapped her hands. "Oh, you will never believe it. My brother came to visit me today, and with him he brought…my betrothed! A handsome young nobleman called Marco, just like the fortune teller predicted! He had been intended for the church, but after his father and brothers died in battle under Father's command, he was forced to take over the family business and to find a wife. He did not wish to marry Father's daughter, after what happened, but my brother persuaded him to come here to meet me, and…oh, you won't believe it. The moment he saw me he fell in love!"

At least Marco the fake fortune teller hadn't

lied about that. Perhaps there'd been a little more lust than love, but there was nothing wrong with a man lusting after his wife.

And when that wife was Marzia…

"Of course he did," Penelope said, moving from her loom to the chest by the window. "So it's probably past time I gave you this…" She opened the chest and lifted out the blue gown she'd spent most of the winter working on. "It's a bit plain, but as you're so much better at embroidery than me, I thought you'd prefer to do the fine work yourself, or at least tell me what you want so I can attempt it."

Marzia's eyes shone with tears as her shaking hands reached for the gown. "It's beautiful. I've never seen any cloth so blue. Except for the silk scarf you gave me at Christmas…"

Cut from the same cloth as the gown. "Let's see how well it fits," Penelope suggested. Not bothering to summon a maid, Penelope helped her friend out of her overdress and into the blue gown. She laced it up with eager efficiency, wanting to see if she'd judged the cut correctly. With Marzia's small breasts, cutting it too low in the front would expose far too much flesh. As it was…perhaps a ribbon across the neckline in white or silver would help.

"Can I see?" Marzia asked.

Penelope blinked, annoyed at herself for not thinking. She lifted her hand mirror out of the chest and angled it so that Marzia might see what she looked like.

"It's perfect!" Marzia breathed.

"I thought it would make a lovely wedding dress," Penelope said carefully, tweaking the skirt so it caught the light just right. "Along with the veil."

Marzia's face fell. "Oh, it would, but Marco's family are prolific lace makers, and his family's wedding gift to me is an entire chest of lace. If I don't wear it to the wedding, it would be a terrible insult to his mother and sisters, and they would hate me. I could not bear it if —"

"What colour is the lace?" Penelope interrupted.

"Like fresh cream. I confess that when he first opened the chest, I thought I was looking at a cake," Marzia said with a laugh.

A little at the neckline, perhaps at the

sleeves and at the hem, and if there was enough, edging the veil, too…Marzia would not need embroidery, with lace edging her gown. If there was enough lace, perhaps she could lay it over the veil, letting the blue peep through the design…

"Can you show me?" Penelope asked.

"Yes, it's in my sleeping chamber. But you'll have to come with me, for the chest is so large I cannot hope to lift it." Marzia extended a hand.

Penelope took it, letting her friend pull her out of the workroom to where she kept a king's ransom in lace.

Yard after yard of the stuff, enough to edge this gown and make another one entirely. Or…

Penelope lifted an armload of the linen cut-work lace and offered a prayer of thanks for the talent of Marco's mother as she draped it over Marzia's head. "How about a veil of trailing lace, cut like a cloak, so that it fans out behind you when you walk, but pinned open here and here…"

Between Marzia's shining eyes and her own rising satisfaction, Penelope was soon so wrapped up in her work she had no need to worry about suitors or marriage or anything in her own future. Her thoughts and her hands were filled with the most beautiful wedding gown Rialto nobility had ever seen, on the sweetest bride any man could ever marry.

Nine

Godfrey woke with a groan, his head throbbing like someone had cleaved it in two. If they hadn't, he wished they would, so it would stop hurting so. But there'd been a girl, her clothes so full of holes you could see her skin beneath, blue from cold in the night air, her eyes enormous with fear as Sir Enguerrand and his Unholy Trinity of bastards as cruel as he was encircled her. Her clothes had likely been perfectly serviceable before one of them (Sir Roland, most likely) had tried to grab her and the cloth had torn as she'd tried to get away.

By the time he'd arrived, the knights had starting tearing her clothing away in tiny pieces, not caring when their blades nicked flesh.

Godfrey had downed Guiscard with one punch, but then Enguerrand and Onfroi had been upon him, and Roland had vanished. Godfrey had seen Roland again for barely a moment before blackness had engulfed him.

Now, there was no sign of the four men, or the girl. If scraps of cloth had not still littered the ground, he might have wished it was nothing but a bad dream. If the girl's body wasn't sharing the alley with him, perhaps she'd gotten away.

He tried to sit up and groaned again as a spike of pain blurred his vision and threatened to send him back into oblivion.

It took him an embarrassingly long time to get to his feet – after he'd voided the contents of his stomach – so that he might stagger out of the shadows into the light. He made it three steps before he slipped in a puddle of something foul-smelling and went down again amid a pile of refuse.

If he'd thought the girl's eyes were wide and

terrified before...they bulged almost out of her head now.

And the stench...

Godfrey vomited again, turning his head so that he wouldn't desecrate her corpse any more than he had already. The poor girl had not deserved this fate, any more than Melisende had.

He'd failed them both.

Digging his fingers into the mortar of the wall beside him, Godfrey heaved himself to his feet. Now, he had to find his way back to the inn where he'd left his belongings.

The bustle of Byzas went on around him as Godfrey trudged along the streets, shading his eyes against the painfully bright light that reflected off everything. What had possessed these people to build a city of red and white bricks, or sheathe any of the walls in marble? Oh, what he would give for the familiar dark timbers and stones of home!

But home was an inn, at least until he'd succeeded in his personal crusade to satisfy poor Melisende's honour.

At least it was darker inside the inn, where he asked for a headache draught and a jug of water to be sent up to his room as he made his laborious way up the stairs.

When the potion arrived, he drank it, then washed it down with a cup of weak ale, before washing off the filth from the alley.

"Would you like more water, sir?" the serving girl asked.

Godfrey looked up, surprised to see the servant had stayed. She'd been quick bringing the potion, too. Unlike when he'd arrived, when it had taken half a day before any water had been sent up. The inn had been full of crusaders, and so busy that on his first night here, he'd woken a dozen times to the incessant sound of pounding feet on the stairs from servants and guests alike.

The stairs were silent now, and it appeared the servants had time to stand and wait.

Godfrey swallowed. "Have the army left?"

Her head bobbed. "Yes, sir. They left three days ago."

Three days? He'd been unconscious that long? No wonder the girl's corpse had smelled so awful. She'd been dead for three days or more.

He had no time to waste. "No, I won't be

needing anything else, except for someone to saddle my horse."

"Yes, sir." The servant curtseyed and left.

Godfrey stripped off his filthy clothes and donned a fresh set, then buckled on his leather armour. If he had to ride fast through lands the army had already raped, there would likely be plenty of unhappy inhabitants only too happy to attack a lone knight who'd fallen behind.

Ten

Godfrey reached the inn yard before his horse. Perhaps the maid had forgotten to relay his request to the grooms, or been waylaid, he told himself. Or the stablehands were lazy.

At home, neither he or his father would stand for such sloth from stablehands. After paying more than a stablehand's monthly wages to the inn to keep his horse for the few days he was in the city, Godfrey had no intention of tolerating slothfulness here. Especially when every moment counted, if he wanted to catch up to the army again.

"Ho, the stables!" he shouted, then winced

as the sound seemed to ring in his still tender head. The potion wasn't working properly yet. He repeated his greeting, a little more quietly, as he crossed the threshold.

He'd never entered a stable so silent, except when the horses were all out in the fields. But even then, the stablehands would be mucking out the stalls, filling the stable with the sounds of scraping shovels and swishing brooms. A quick peek into the first stall told him why – there was nothing but fresh straw and water. Every stall was the same, from one end of the cavernous stable to the other.

No wonder his horse wasn't saddled and ready for him, if they'd had to retrieve Pegasus from some field outside the city. Perhaps it would be faster for him to go to Pegasus.

A brief search revealed the grooms sharing a jug of ale outside the kitchen door.

"Where is my horse? A silver coin to the man who can take me to him," Godfrey said, holding up the coin.

The men looked at one another, before a boy blurted out, "But sir, there are no horses here. No horses for nigh on three days. 'Tis like a holiday, blessing us for taking such good care of the holy crusader knights!"

"More like the devil has tempted you into laziness, for I am a knight, and without my horse, I shall not be able to reach the Holy Land," Godfrey said grimly. "I left her here, in your care. I would have returned sooner, but some rogue set upon me in an alley, attacking me from behind, and left me for dead. Now I have returned, I need my horse to rejoin the army." Or Melisende's honour was dead, along with his. It was worse than Rialto – would his bad luck never end?

"What did your horse look like, Sir Knight?" one of the older grooms ventured. "We do not have your horse, but maybe we can tell you who stole him."

"Her," Godfrey corrected. "Pegasus would have been the finest horse in your stable. Perhaps the finest horse you have ever seen, for not even the Emperor has one of our horses yet. She is grey, so pale you might think she was white, and as fast as the wind when she begins to run. Why, a man lucky enough to ride a mare like her might think he was flying."

The groom paled, and muttered swearing came from the others. "A pale grey mare, you say? Such a rare beast was in the stables until three days ago, when Sir Roland insisted she be saddled for the journey. There was a loud argument in the square between Sir Roland and Sir Enguerrand over who owned the horse as right of conquest, or some such knightly thing. Swords were drawn, and there was quite the battle between the two men before Sir Enguerrand won the victory, and left upon the grey horse. Sir Roland was wounded, but he rode out an hour later, on another, lesser beast."

Did none of them have a shred of honour between them? To leave a fellow knight unconscious in an alley, then steal his horse…even if Melisende were still at home safe, Enguerrand and his pack of rogues would deserve to die. Now…he swore that Enguerrand and Roland would be the first to taste his blade.

But in order to do that…he would need to catch them first. And in order to catch them, he would need a horse as swift as Pegasus.

"I need a horse. Not any old nag, but one that can run all day without tiring, and wake the next day to do it again. One that will take me to the army, and the men who stole from me."

Another groom shook his head. "You will find no such horse in the city. The crusader knights bought every horse they could find, and even a few lame donkeys. The only mounts left in the city are children's toys."

"Or the ones in the Emperor's stable," the boy piped up. "I heard he posted extra guards to keep the army out. My brother's a guard at the palace, and he said –"

One of the older men hushed him, but not before Godfrey had time to think it sounded much like the guards they'd set on his own stables at home. And if the Emperor did not yet have one of his family's horses…perhaps he would like to. In exchange for the loan of one of his own…

Any other time, it was the sort of bargain Godfrey could never consider, but with Melisende's honour at stake…a horse was a small price to pay. Even Pegasus.

Godfrey flipped the coin to the boy. "To buy you all another drink, in thanks for your help, if you will all swear to it that the fight between Roland and Enguerrand was over my stolen horse."

The men swiftly swore that they had witnessed the events themselves, just as the first man had told it.

Godfrey nodded, then headed for the palace, and his only chance to make good on his vow. He might not be the best fighter, but he knew the horse trade. All he had to do was convince the Emperor to part with the best horse in his stable…in trade for a far superior animal when Godfrey returned.

Simple, surely.

Eleven

Even without the dress, Marzia would have been the most beautiful bride the people of Rialto had ever seen. Glowing with love for her groom, her face rivalled the sun itself, surrounded by a firmament of lace clouds upon a dreamy blue sky.

If Penelope was even half as happy on her own wedding day, she would consider herself blessed indeed.

Marzia grasped Penelope's hands and refused to board her gondola unless her friend came with her. "I'm so nervous!" the girl said. "What if he changes his mind and doesn't want to marry me? What if..."

Penelope spent most of the trip across the lagoon soothing Marzia's fears, which didn't fade until she spotted Marco outside the church. Marco's thoughts were so loud, Penelope could hear him clear across the campo, before they'd even docked.

The man vowed he would kill anyone who came between him and Marzia, and that death would be slow and torturous should anyone try to take his bride away from him. She was his, and tonight he was going to…

Penelope bit down hard on her lip, willing the magic in her veins to silence her gift, if only for a little while, so she did not see Marco's plans for his bride in their bedchamber tonight. By the time her lip stopped bleeding, they were inside the church and listening to the priest perform the marriage ceremony. Luckily, most of the people present were thinking about their own weddings, whether in the past or the future, if they weren't listening to the priest.

Sometimes her gift was a blessing, but at other times, it seemed more of a curse. Most other witches paid a blood price to cast their spells or use their talents, while her gift let her listen to others' thoughts until she paid a blood price to stop it, a sweet silence that never lasted long enough.

But now…her father's thoughts wandered from the wedding to her, and what her future might hold. Aachen, Byzas, or some merchant prince here at home? He kept returning to Prince Alexios of Byzas, because an alliance between the Emperor of Byzas and the Duke of Rialto might free the Rialtine prisoners the Emperor held in his dungeons, even now. But with Prince Otto's father so rich, he would take her without a dowry, which he might have to, given what foolishness her brothers had invested it in.

Penelope blinked. She'd known her father had set aside a substantial dowry for her, and she'd also known about her brothers' northern expedition. Orso's idea, she knew, but only now did she realise that Pietro had persuaded her father to take her dowry money to finance it, and now they'd lost it all. Instead of bringing home expensive furs from the icy northern wastes, the ships had been taken by pirates, never to be seen again.

So she might not marry at all, or be forced to go north to Aachen, and never see the waters of home again.

Because the merchant prince her father had in mind for her had been Marco, if the man had rejected Marzia the way everyone had expected. Except…Marco was very much a man in love, kissing his bride so tenderly more than one girl thought she might swoon.

Otto or Alexios, then, Penelope told herself. Or no one at all.

Bleakness opened up a terrible, aching hole in her heart. Penelope would be alone all her life, and the sort of love radiating out of Marco and Marzia was something she would never know.

Oh, what a miserable thought. She should be ashamed of herself, thinking such maudlin things on this joyous day.

Perhaps that was why her gift was so arse-about, compared to everyone else. Instead of silencing the joy and fond memories around her, she opened herself to them, pouring that shared joy into the void she had no need to feel.

Today, her friend married the man she

loved, a man who loved her more than anyone else in the world. Tonight, in the privacy of her bed, Penelope might mourn, if she wished, that she would never find such happiness. Few people would, so to see it before her now…it warmed her heart.

And whether she went to Byzas or Aachen or anywhere, she would keep the memory of this day close. Because if her father married her off for a foreign alliance, he did so to keep Marzia and all the other girls like her safe.

Men went away to fight – how would her fate be any different? Penelope had no right to be a coward, when the price of her sacrifice might be lasting peace.

As long as she had all she needed to turn simple thread into clothing that earned its wearer the kind of envy Marzia garnered today, she could make a life anywhere.

Twelve

Godfrey eyed the long line of petitioners before him and swallowed. They stretched the length of the enormous throne room and down the steps to the square outside. He'd be lucky to enter the throne room today, let alone speak to Emperor Manuel.

But what other choice did he have?

He settled in for a long wait.

Climbing the stairs took an hour, and when he reached the throne room, he realised why. Petitioners were heard by a row of men who stood at the base of the dais where the Emperor's throne sat. The Emperor himself looked half asleep, stirring only to wave an indolent hand when one of the men addressed him. No matter what the verdict was, a number of guards would surround the petitioner, who either strode off with them in a sort of stunned disbelief, or screamed and fought while the guards carried him away.

"The previous emperor ordered his own brother's eyes to be plucked out when he offended him. Hell might be preferable to the things that go on in these dungeons," the man in front of Godfrey whispered to his companion.

Godfrey uttered a silent prayer that his petition would not see him sent to the Emperor's dungeons.

"The last petitioner that His Imperial Majesty will hear today, Lord Valerio of Rialto," the herald announced.

Godfrey's heart sank. If he didn't get a horse from the Emperor today, he'd never catch up to the army. Shoulders slumped, he turned to leave the throne room.

A voice boomed out, louder than even the herald: "Your Imperial Majesty, lords and ladies of the court, I am Lord Valerio of Rialto, a magician of great power, and I call on all of you to bear witness to my pledge to use my powers in service of His Imperial Majesty, Emperor Manuel!"

Silence fell across the room as everyone turned to see the magician.

Even Godfrey paused on the threshold to listen, the crowd was too thick for him to see the Rialto magician.

But he did see the Emperor wake from his torpor. "What manner of magic?" the Emperor rumbled.

"The power of flight!"

Murmurings and whisperings swept through the room, as every man asked his neighbour whether they had heard true.

"Show me," the Emperor demanded, rising to his feet.

"The enchanted beast is in the square outside, and I will be only too happy to give Your Imperial Majesty a demonstration," Lord Valerio said.

The crowd parted and Godfrey glimpsed a man in Rialto style robes hurrying toward him, the Emperor striding behind.

Godfrey slipped out the door, setting his

back to the wall at the top of the steps, staying out of the way whilst making sure he could see what happened next.

The magician trotted down the steps, stopping when he reached a crude wooden statue of a horse. He spread his arms wide. "Behold, the legendary enchanted horse, destroyer of cities, since an ancient wizard, my ancestor, first constructed it to bring about the fall of ancient Ilium!"

Several people in the square tittered at this impossible claim. The thing barely looked like a horse, and even Godfrey knew it could not be the horse that brought about Ilium's doom. The horse of legend had carried troops secretly into the city, so that they might open the gates to let the invading army in. This wooden thing, though it might be the size of a real horse, didn't look like it could fit a single man inside it.

The fake magician was destined for the dungeons, Godfrey was sure of it.

As if reading his thoughts, a squad of guards approached the man and his crude horse.

"Allow me to show you its power!" the magician said, leaping upon the horse's back.

All right, it could carry one man, maybe two, like that, but still there was the matter of it moving…

The magician leaned over the horse's neck to touch the place where a bridle might go on a real horse.

Screams erupted from the crowd. It took Godfrey a moment to see why – the horse's hooves had risen from the ground to stand on nothing but air, and still the thing lifted higher.

"Behold, the enchanted horse!" the magician roared as he rose level with the steps, then the roof, and up into the air itself.

Godfrey couldn't seem to close his mouth. It was magic – it had to be. However crude its appearance, a flying horse could indeed sneak men into a city. Free as a bird, they could simply fly over the mighty walls, for Ilium's walls had been legend, surpassed only by the ramparts encircling Byzas today. Anyone who possessed the such a horse could come and go as they pleased, armies and walls notwithstanding. The man who owned it would be unstoppable.

When the magician and his horse landed on the ground, the Emperor himself stepped through the doors to stand on the top step, only a few yards from Godfrey. Godfrey held his breath, not daring to move. Guards held the crowd back both inside and out, yet in his spot, half-hidden by the throne room doors, he'd gone unnoticed. If he could keep it that way just a little longer…

"Give me that horse," the Emperor demanded.

For a moment, Godfrey was reminded of his toddler nephew, from the Emperor's tone right down to his reaching hand. A comical thing to see, from a man old enough to be his father, yet no one laughed.

The magician smiled as he dismounted, then bowed fussily at the Emperor's feet. "I would gladly make it my gift to you, Your Imperial Majesty, but to part with such a precious family heirloom…I would be a fool indeed. But I might be willing to trade for it…"

"What do you want?"

There was no trace of the toddler now — something in the Emperor's tone sent a shiver down Godfrey's spine. This was a man who liked torture.

A man who would never trade for

something he might simply take.

Somehow, the magician missed the danger. "I would not part with a family heirloom to anyone who is not family. But if you were to give me your daughter to be my wife, this grateful groom might be willing to give this priceless horse as a gift to his father-in-law."

The Emperor spluttered, then recovered so quickly Godfrey thought he'd imagined it. "Take the impudent wretch to the dungeons," the Emperor said.

No less than six guards closed in on the magician, seizing him before he could return to his horse. They started to carry him away.

"Any man who touches that horse who is not part of my family will suffer the most terrible curse. Him, and every descendant fate allows the misfortune of being born in his bloodline!" the magician howled.

The crowd edged away from the horse.

"Put the horse in my stable," the Emperor ordered.

The remaining guards didn't move.

"Is no man brave enough to touch that hunk of wood? It's not even a real horse – it's not like it can bite!" the Emperor said. "Surely someone can ride it."

Against all odds, the Emperor himself was offering the only horse who might be able to catch the crusaders.

Madness made the decision for him.

"I can," Godfrey said. "I am Sir Godfrey of Maraschal. My father's barony is home to the greatest horses in the world. I have never met a horse I could not handle, and this will not be the first." He reached the bottom of the steps, then turned and bowed deeply to the Emperor. "At your service, Your Imperial Majesty."

"Very well, Sir Knight. Show us your prowess."

Praying that his momentary madness would not get him killed or cursed, Godfrey forced himself to head toward the horse. There were no stirrups or saddle, but a faint indentation where a stirrup might have hung was enough to help him onto the horse's back. The wood had been rubbed smooth by age or countless riders, but he could still faintly see that the horse had originally been more life-like. Now, the ears were worn down to mere nubs, and the carved mane was all but invisible to all but his probing fingers as he sought whatever the magician had touched on the horse's neck to make it fly.

Nothing…nothing but worn wood, and the increasingly impatient Emperor, about to order his guards to take Godfrey to the dungeons, too.

Godfrey wished he'd had time to win back Melisende's honour. To bring justice to the men who had killed her and stolen his horse, and to complete the crusade that would save his soul and the Holy Land, too. If he could have done all that, then maybe he could have returned to Rialto, to resume trade with Lord Sebastiano, and see his enchanting daughter one more time…

Lady Penelope. He breathed her name like a prayer as the image of her angelic face filled his mind. Then his probing fingers touched something sharp and metallic hidden at the horse's throat, drawing blood as he yelped in pain.

Shouts rose up around him, but the sound faded as he focussed on his last memory of Lady Penelope. If he was to die today, he would die dreaming of her.

Thirteen

Fat Tuesday, the final day of Carnevale, and for the first time, Penelope fully felt the weight of the day. Oh, not its religious significance – nothing so spiritual. No, she felt full to bursting from Marzia and Marco's wedding feast. Glutted on good spirits, she didn't dare drink another cup of wine, lest she lose her wits entirely.

She should return to the convent. A short voyage on the lagoon with the ocean breeze should clear her head. No one would notice her absence. Not even…

Marzia beamed at her. "Are you ready for

the trial? My Marco insists we must all go to the Campo San Marco to see the pigs and bulls on trial, before they are executed, and stay for the feast."

The trial was a strange ritual that had begun during Duke Vitale's rule, where a bishop who had raided and looted some Rialto churches was required to make annual reparation – a bull and a dozen pigs, representing himself and his priests, which were subjected to a criminal trial, convicted and then executed by a mob of the people of Rialto. The slaughtered beasts were then roasted and eaten on the spot.

Penelope had witnessed one such trial, and never wanted to see another. Normal people's thoughts turned savage, intent on capturing and killing the pigs as they ran about in a panic all around the campo. If she attended the trial today, she would likely vomit up every bite she'd eaten since breakfast.

"Come, we must get to the boats!" Marzia said.

Marco seized her around the waist and carried her to a gondola, ordering the boatman to make haste. Even as the boat headed away, Marzia beckoned Penelope to follow.

Shaking her head, Penelope found a boat willing to take her home to Saint Angelo.

For the duration of the trip, she breathed in the clean, salt air, and wished her friend a happy and fruitful marriage.

Sooner than she expected, she stepped ashore at Saint Angelo, paid the boatman, and headed inside.

Blessed quiet enveloped her as the empty convent closed around her. On this last day of indulgence, even the nuns were spending time with their families, preparing for the fast to come on the morrow.

Penelope, however, had indulged enough. She unfastened her cloak as she headed for her chamber, where she might lie down, just for a moment.

The moment her head touched the pillow, sleep claimed her for its own.

Fourteen

The sounds of the crowd had grown so faint, it was as though they'd vanished entirely. Or maybe it was the rushing in his ears, blocking out all other sound. The pain potion had worn off, and Godfrey's head had begun throbbing again. This pain was nothing compared to that which would be inflicted by the Emperor's torturers when he reached the dungeon.

Any moment now, the guards would reach him, pull him off the stupid wooden horse and drag him down to the dungeons. Any moment now…

But the moment did not come.

Godfrey dared to open his eyes. Then squeezed them shut again, praying his eyes were lying to him.

Slowly, he opened them once more.

Mist enveloped him, strange strands that hid both the earth and sky from him, not to mention the crowd and the guards. Then the mist ended, and his breath left him in a panicked shout. Godfrey clung to the horse's neck as if his life depended on it.

For surely it did, floating so high up he could scarcely see the ground. If he lost his grip on the horse, the fall would surely kill him. Below him, the city had gone, to be replaced with ploughed fields ready to bear this year's crops. He was flying.

Godfrey sucked a breath into his starved lungs, then another. A cloudbank loomed ahead of him, and he watched in wonder as it enveloped him like wet fleece, soaking him to the skin. He'd always imagined clouds as fine, fluffy things that would feel like lambswool, but the reality was far more chilling, like bathing in the rain.

When moisture started dripping down his back, he pulled on his helm in the hope that some of the water would roll off it instead of under his tunic. Hunching against the horse's neck, he peered below. The cloud thinned occasionally, giving him a glimpse of fields and a small town, but not the city of Byzas or any sign of the crusading army.

He was a fool, far more foolish than the magician who had brought his enchanted horse to court. Godfrey should never have risen to the Emperor's mad challenge. Instead, he should have headed home, to beg his father's forgiveness for yet another failure. Then settled into his life at home, taking care of the horses.

Never to leave his father's estate. Never to see Lady Penelope again…

Did he imagine it, or did the horse speed up?

No, he must be imagining it. The beast's wooden legs didn't move. It had but one speed, at which it floated through clouds and open sky, taking him to destinations unknown.

Where a worse fate likely awaited him than spending his final days in the Emperor's dungeons.

Godfrey sighed and hung on.

Fifteen

Alone, now and forever, just like Marco had said.

The horrible thought jolted Penelope awake, and no matter how much she tried to, she could not shake it. She was alone at Saint Angelo, and she would be until the nuns returned in the morning. She reached out for the comforting thoughts of someone, anyone, even a fisherman late out on the lagoon.

A screech of outrage and an angry image of something in the sky was the first thing she found.

Penelope almost laughed. No, she was not

alone. The abbess had left her monkey here in its cage, where the beast raged at its sworn enemy, a sea eagle who nested on the sandbank off the end of the island. If she strained her ears, she thought she heard the eagle's answering shriek.

As long as she lived on Saint Angelo, she would never be alone.

While she'd slept, darkness had fallen, so she lit a candle and carried it down to the kitchen. With a day of fasting tomorrow, there was no need for the cook to set bread to rising, but the smell of old yeast haunted the room, reminding her that she'd missed dinner.

Penelope headed to the buttery, where the morning's milk stood in pails, the cream floating on top, waiting to be made into cheese on the morrow. She drank a cup, then ladled another to take back to the kitchen with her.

She sliced up a spiced sausage – likely the last she would taste until Easter – and found some of the morning's bread and a dish of oil to dip it in. It would do.

She finished her supper, then washed it all down with a third cup of milk. Anything but wine.

Full and yawning, she headed back to bed.

Sixteen

A chill had settled into Godfrey's bones, yet still the horse flew, showing no signs of stopping. The sinking sun sent a shiver of alarm through him – without the sun to warm him, he might freeze to death. But he could neither stop the sun nor land the horse, so on he flew, growing colder and colder, as his mind grew more and more sluggish.

He thought he smelled the salt of the sea, but he could not be certain. Perhaps he had only dreamed it. Like he'd dreamed a fire, and a hot meal, and a soft bed instead of the hard horse beneath him.

A seabird's shriek penetrated his doze. No, not a seabird – it sounded more like an eagle than a gull. An eagle deprived of its kill, like when a shepherd saved a lamb.

But there was that sibilant sound behind it, like the river rushing past, or waves breaking on a beach. The bird shrieked again, answered by the almost human screech of what could only be a monkey. For no human could make such a sound, unless they were rendered so insensible from pain that they forgot whatever words they might once have known.

The horse bumped against something, a jolt Godfrey felt through his bones. He lost his grip on the horse's neck and felt himself sliding, sliding…toward his death far below.

He scrabbled for a handhold, but the smooth wood slipped beneath his fingers, slick from all the clouds he'd passed through, and he was falling, falling…

The impact knocked the breath from him. For a moment, Godfrey thought he was dead, but air ripped into his lungs and he felt grass between his fingers. The wind down here had not lessened. If anything, it had grown stronger, making him wish more than ever that he'd brought a heavy cloak with him.

He crawled blindly in the dark until he found a spot where the wind could not reach him. There, he curled up and drifted off into an uneasy sleep.

Seventeen

The sky had barely begun to lighten in warning of the coming dawn when the abbess's monkey started screeching again. Swearing softly, Penelope rose. She eyed the hearth, where a fire was laid, ready to light, but that would take too much time. Instead, she donned her thickest hose inside her fleece-lined boots, wrapped a cloak over her woollen dress, and headed out into the orchard.

At least she'd remembered her gloves this morning, she thought, as frost crunched beneath her boots. The orange trees glowed in the first rays of dawn, placed as they were on the south east corner of the island. A good thing, too, for she hadn't brought a lantern. She filled a basket with ripe oranges, and brought it to the monkey cage. The creature was a Barbary ape, the abbess had told her, brought by ship from the lands far to the west, and it only slept in the cage when the abbess was away. The abbess called it Paz, for the golden colour of its fur, and it was fond of fruit.

This was the first time Penelope had ventured close enough to call it anything, or to feed it, but she cut an orange in half and held it out to the creature. Paz snatched up the orange in one hand, but it kept pointing with the other as it screeched even louder.

Penelope followed the direction of its pointing finger, weaving between the trees and shrubs until she reached the edge of the orchard.

Sure enough, she spotted the sea eagle, perched at the ape's eye level, when he sat in his cage overlooking the trees. But only as she rounded the last berry bush did she fully appreciate the bird's new perch. It looked like a giant flotsam horse, thrown up by the tide to stand upright on the grass. Its time in the water had worn it smooth, so the oak it must have originally been made of had turned shiny black. How long had it drifted, riding the waves, until it made landfall here at Saint Angelo?

She stepped forward to lay her hand on the horse's nose, and the eagle took flight with an affronted shriek, which the monkey drowned out with a rant of its own.

Magic moved beneath her hand, coursing through the horse like blood. Someone particularly powerful had crafted the creature, which must have been almost lifelike before the sea had claimed it. Yet the magic remained, thrumming with more power than she possessed. She bit her lip, concentrating on the magic. The spells upon it had been cast by an enchanter, a man who had fought in many battles, with both wits and sword, who wanted…an end to war. A home, a family. A much-loved wife. The longing was so strong she could almost taste it, though the man was not here.

She took her hands off the horse, yet the ghost of longing remained. Almost as if the man was a ghost himself now.

She sighed, and became aware of the monkey, now punctuating its screeching by banging on the bars of its cage. Hungry for another orange, most likely. She picked up the basket and headed back to the cage.

An armoured man stood beside the bars, staring at the monkey.

Penelope hefted the orange, assessing its weight. She'd thrown stones at gulls as a child, to scare them away from the fishermen's catch, and her aim had been true. An orange might not do more than bruise the man, but it was all she had.

"Step away from the monkey. The abbess does not take kindly to thieves, or men who come to Saint Angelo uninvited," Penelope warned.

The knight whirled, his eyes dark pools within his helm. Pools that she could not read. Nor his thoughts, which were a whirl of confusion still fogged by sleep.

He held up his hands as if in surrender.

Some knight, if he feared a woman.

But no, there was no fear in his mind. Some pain from a long ride, dread of disappointing some ruler, all wrapped in that confusing fog.

"Who are you, and what is your business here?" Penelope demanded. A girl might never rule Rialto, but she knew the effect of an imperious manner, and she had learned from the best.

"I am…I am…I don't know where I am. There was a horse…"

She jerked her head toward the beach. "You mean the wooden one? With magic?"

"An enchanted horse…" he muttered, pulling off his helm as he shambled toward her. No, toward the horse, she realised as he headed past her without pausing.

"You didn't answer my question!" she shouted after him. When he ignored her, she threw the orange at his back.

It hit with a satisfying smack between his shoulder blades. He turned, or tried to, getting his legs so tangled that they tripped him. He landed on his face and didn't rise.

Swearing again, Penelope approached him, confident that she would hear any threats in his thoughts before he had time to act. He was well muscled from his knightly training, or whatever it was that such men did. He had the strength to overpower her, if he wished. But right now, his thoughts were not of violence at all. If anything, he wanted to curl up and sleep.

"You can sleep later. Perhaps the nuns will treat whatever wounds you have. But first, you must answer my questions. Now, get up!"

He merely groaned. Not good.

She knelt beside him and shoved until she rolled him onto his side, then his back. The hood of her cloak came off, letting the wind play with her hair, but she ignored it, focussing instead on the injured man before her.

His eyes met hers and the recognition was mutual.

"Lady Penelope?"

"Godfrey?"

Eighteen

Godfrey managed a sickly smile. Even that hurt. "It's Sir Godfrey now," he said. As if it mattered. Knight or not, he would never be good enough for her.

She grimaced. "So I see. Where are your wounds?" She surveyed his body, then looked thoughtful. "Turn over, so I can see your…back." She blushed.

She knew his arse hurt from riding that horrible horse. A magical horse she'd recognised as such. Godfrey felt his own face grow red. "You truly do read minds."

She reared back, moving away from him.

"Don't be silly. No one can do that."

"Not without magic, they can't," he persisted. "That's how you do it, isn't it? It's magic."

She stopped dead and turned to face him. There wasn't a shadow of fear in her expression as she hissed, "If you so much as think to breathe a word of this to anyone, I will cast a curse on you so cruel you will wish you were dead."

He almost laughed. "That's what the other guy said he'd do if I touched his horse. Yet here I am."

She thrust a finger at the horse. "You stole that horse from the sorcerer who made it?" All colour drained from her face. "You have to go, before you bring trouble here. Go!" She made shooing motions with her hands.

"The horse's previous owner is in a dungeon in Byzas. He will not be following anyone anywhere. The Emperor of Byzas gave the horse to me." Realising she would sense the lie, he amended it to, "Well, he asked for someone to ride it. I mounted and it flew me here. Now, I need to get it back to him. Somehow."

She softened, somehow. "You slept out here

last night? You must be freezing. Come into the kitchen, where you can thaw out in front of the fire while you tell me everything." She held out her hand.

He longed to kiss it, but he doubted she wanted his lips on her gloves.

She laughed. "You and kissing."

Mind reader. Of course. She had read his thoughts that day. And seen fit to grant his wish. Kisses from an angel…

"Come to the kitchen."

Whatever Lady Penelope asked, he could not help but obey. So he did.

Nineteen

It wasn't until she had Godfrey seated beside the kitchen fire, wrapped in her cloak, that she remembered her cooking skills were non-existent, and there were no servants in the kitchen to help her.

But there was bread, and she knew where the cheeses were kept in the buttery. Oh, and she still had most of the oranges she'd picked. They would do nicely in some mulled wine — and even she could manage to make that.

That would do to break her fast, and his. It was the first day of Lent, after all.

She peeled and sliced the oranges, dropping

them into the small pot she'd used for this purpose more times than she could count. "So, you're Sir Godfrey, now? How did you become a knight?"

Godfrey shrugged. "My father thought it was a suitable occupation for a younger son who was good with horses. It took a couple of years to get good enough with a sword to be made a knight, that's all." The moment he closed his mouth, he began berating himself for telling her how useless he was. He was a fool…

She handed him a slice of orange. "I wouldn't call you that. You're the only man clever enough to work out what my gift is. When I first met you, you were more boy than man, and so thin a good ocean breeze might blow you away. Two years of sword practice has put meat on your bones, and given you more confidence than you possessed back then. I didn't recognise you at first." She smiled and sank her teeth into her own slice.

He sighed. "You will think me a fool, when I tell you what I have done."

"We all do foolish things at times. It does not follow that we are all fools." She set the pot over the fire and turned to meet his gaze. "You have my deepest condolences for the loss of your sister, may God rest her soul."

Something broke in him then, releasing a torrent of images that told a far more tragic tale than the words spilling out of him.

The marauding crusader army, finding his sister, joining the crusade…and waking in Byzas. The loss of his favourite horse.

Tears coursed down her cheeks as she tasted his despair, as he suffered blow after blow. A lesser man would have given up, but not Godfrey.

She finished straining the wine and poured two cups. "So you lost one legendary flying horse, and became the unexpected owner of another."

Godfrey shook his head. "No, that thing out there belongs to the Emperor of Byzas. I have no doubt he'll want it back, though I have no idea how to manage that. Short of loading it onto a ship headed there. As for heading to the Holy Land to catch the crusaders who killed my sister…I fear I have lost any chance of that. Why the horse would take me here, of all places…"

Penelope passed him a cup of mulled wine. "Perhaps I can help you. Tell me again about the magician, and what you did to make it fly."

She sipped from her cup as she let his words wash over her, focussing instead on the images running through his mind. A magician who had touched something on the horse's neck to fly. Godfrey had pricked his finger, too, as if paying a blood price…

"Is there magic in your family? Your mother, or grandmother, perhaps?" she interrupted. It was rare for magic to manifest in men, but not unheard of. Men might carry magic in their bloodline, passing it on to their children and grandchildren, but it was girls who tended to show signs of extraordinary gifts from it.

"My mother, and maybe my sister," Godfrey admitted.

If she and Godfrey had a daughter, she would definitely be a witch. Penelope almost choked at the thought. Thank heaven she was the mind reader, and not Godfrey.

"I could take a look at your horse, and see if I can help you get it to fly again," she said.

His eyes lit up. "Would you?" Hope kindled

within him. Hope that he might be able to catch the crusaders, save his sister's honour and avenge her…

He would die, Penelope knew with a certainty she could not explain. If he fought four knights again, or even one of them, he would die. There were enough fools and wicked men in the world. To lose one good man on a fool's errand…no. The world needed good men.

"But I would have to come with you," she added. The moment the words left her lips, she wanted to take them back. She could not leave Rialto. Her father, her friends, the nuns here at Saint Angelo…

His eyes widened. "War is no place for a woman! If you knew the things the infidels have done…or the crusaders…" He fell silent as he realised she'd seen it all in his thoughts. "How can you bear to see such things and not be frightened?" he whispered.

She wet her lips. "Slave ships. When northern armies take prisoners, they bring them here in chains, to be shipped to wherever slaves fetch the best price. I hear…all their thoughts. What they have already suffered.

What life is like on the slave ships. What fate awaits them…" She shuddered.

"By all that's holy…" Godfrey reached out, as though he wanted to take her in his arms and comfort her, but he did not dare.

"The Emperor of Byzas took thousands of Rialto citizens prisoner, and they languish in his dungeons still. Ordinary citizens, merchants and their families, who lived in Byzas until the emperor's troops dragged them from their homes and seized everything they owned." She swallowed. "The previous Duke, Vitale, was supposed to go to war against Byzas to rescue them, but he went crusading first, and lost most of his men. Too many to take Byzas. My father is Duke now, and he promised to bring our people peace. So that our captured citizens are not sent to the slave ships next. And he hopes…hopes that if I marry one of the Emperor's sons, he will let our people go." She let out a breath she hadn't known she'd been holding. Before Godfrey could say anything more, she continued, "I will help you with your horse, if you will take me to Byzas, so I can see the truth for myself. Whether our people are still alive, and whether I can save them."

Because if she knew she could truly save them, she would no longer be a coward. She would tell her father to make the match, and marry her off to some faraway prince. Even if she couldn't save them, she would save Godfrey from dying in a crusade.

Madness had stolen her wits, she was sure of it. She'd never left Rialto. To travel to Byzas, the imperial capital, with a man she barely knew…

A man currently staring at her, with awe in his eyes. He'd thought her an angel before, but now he was certain. "I will take you anywhere you wish. I will defend you and your honour with my life. And I swear upon my sister's memory, I will see you safely home when your work in Byzas is done."

He meant every word.

Only a coward would refuse him. A coward who wanted to go back to her weaving, and not worry about the rest of the world.

She held out her hand. "Then we have an accord, Sir Godfrey. Give me a moment to pack some provisions for the journey and then we shall depart, without anyone the wiser. We'll be back before anyone has a chance to notice my absence."

Twenty

Godfrey followed Lady Penelope out to the garden, where he'd left the enchanted horse. She didn't stop until she stood beside it.

"How do I get on it?" she asked.

He showed her the step cut in the horse's side, offering his knee to help her climb high enough to reach it.

"You look like a natural," he said when she settled onto the horse's back.

She laughed. "Don't lie, Sir Godfrey. I look like what I am – a nervous rider, her first time ever sitting upon a horse."

He didn't dare argue. Instead, he swung up

behind her. Thank all that was holy for his armour, for without it, her body would be pressed against his and he could not help his thoughts from wandering to where they shouldn't…

"This is hardly the time to think about kissing, Sir Godfrey!" she said. "How two people could do such a thing while riding on horseback…it is impossible, I am sure."

He busied himself with tying her sack of provisions to the horse's otherwise useless tail.

"Ready?" she asked. "Now, if memory serves correctly, you pricked your finger on a nail on the horse's neck, pictured your heart's desire, and the horse flew you here."

Godfrey felt his face redden. He knew he did not deserve her, was not worthy to be her husband, but any man who knew her could hardly help but love Lady Penelope. Surely she knew that.

She laughed again, then stopped abruptly. "I'm not laughing at you. But if you knew…most men do not like me. They fear me, finding my eyes too knowing for their liking. If they knew I could read their every thought…they would kill me for sure. It is a rare man indeed who truly values a woman above his own desires. You underestimate your worth, Sir Godfrey."

More likely she overestimated it, out of the goodness of her heart, but he did not say it. She would be a Byzas princess, possibly one day the Empress, and he was a mere baron's son. She did him more honour than he deserved, allowing him to be her knight protector on her visit to Byzas.

She leaned over, feeling for the protruding nail. A sharp intake of breath told him she'd found it, and he watched in wonder as the horse rose smoothly from the ground. Higher and higher they went, until the whole lagoon spread out beneath them.

"I've never seen it like this before. So beautiful," she breathed. The horse stayed where it was, floating just beneath the clouds, as if she had no greater desire than to feast her eyes on the splendour of her home.

On his first flight, he'd been too afraid of falling to admire the view. Lady Penelope was indeed a wonder.

"My valiant knight protector won't let me fall," she said softly, before directing her gaze across the water. "Now, on to Byzas." At her command, the horse began to move.

Twenty-One

Sir Godfrey proved a particularly delightful travelling companion. Not only was he a solid weight at her back, sheltering her from the wind, but he was particularly knowledgeable about the places below them, for he'd travelled through many of them since leaving his home.

In one town, Pegasus had thrown a shoe, and it had taken both Godfrey and Zoticus to rouse the inebriated blacksmith, and several tries before the smith had managed to fasten the shoe on the right hoof. In a tiny hamlet, every man of fighting age had chosen to take up the cross and march with the crusaders.

When he'd left another village, he'd discovered a cat had given birth to a litter of kittens in his saddlebag, and Zoticus had nearly expired with laughter as Godfrey had needed to don his gloves over his bleeding hands to evict the mother and her offspring – wrapped in his warmest woollen tunic, for the cat could not be detached from the wool without ripping it to pieces.

Waterwheels that turned mills, men who lived most of their lives on horseback, their homes little more than tents that travelled in their saddlebags, ruins of cities older than living memory…it was like listening to him telling tales of the infidels conquering the Holy City, only better, because this time his words came with rich images from Godfrey's memory.

"I talk too much, my lady. Surely you have plenty of tales to tell."

She shook her head. "I spend most of my day weaving and sewing. I could tell you a tale about the trials and tribulations of weaving my friend's bridal veil, but I fear it would put you to sleep. I'm much more interested in tales of your adventures. Please…will you tell me what happened to the cat? Did you find her a nice, warm barn somewhere, or…did they even have barns in the place where you found her? Or were you among those tent people?"

He laughed, and continued where he'd left off.

Penelope did not want the ride to end, but she knew it must. At least she had the return journey with him to look forward to – for he was determined to see her safely home.

"Where in Byzas do you wish to go first?" Godfrey asked.

Penelope shrugged. "Just set down somewhere that there will be space." If Byzas was anything like Rialto, there would be open space near the prison and the palace, and both would not be far from one another.

Godfrey chuckled. "At least I am not the only one to underestimate Byzas. Wait until you see the city." He pointed over her shoulder.

Penelope squinted. She thought she could see the ocean, white foam as waves broke on hidden rocks and shoals, and behind it….

She gasped. Walls rose up from the sea itself, impossibly high and white, stretching for miles until they curved back around the largest city she had ever seen. Why, Rialto would fit inside those walls ten times over. Maybe more.

Penelope took a deep breath. "The prison, then. There is no point going to the palace unless I'm sure my people are still alive."

The enchanted horse responded to her wishes, landing in the yard outside the prison. People crowded around the edges of the yard, and on the walls of the prison, pointing.

Penelope had never seen so many people in one place. Not even at the trial of the pigs, when all of Rialto turned out to see justice done.

"I should stay to protect you while you do…whatever you need to," Godfrey said, reaching for his sword.

Fear rippled through the crowd…and Godfrey, too. One sword was little use against a mob of thousands.

He knew it, but his vow would not allow him to leave.

Penelope scanned their thoughts. Their fear was tempered by curiosity – the people were not a mob, and were more likely to run away from the flying horse than toward it.

To tell the Emperor that his horse had returned, she realised the same time as Godfrey did.

"Perhaps we should fly to the palace first, so I can show the Emperor I have returned unharmed with his horse," Godfrey said.

She took a deep breath. "You go to the palace, and do what you must. I will stay here with the horse and…find out what I can." When he hesitated, she added, "Should anyone approach me, I will fly away."

Godfrey eyed the prison walls. "There are archers up there."

She managed a smile. "I shall fly higher than their arrows, and return after dark, when it is safe."

Finally, he nodded. "Promise me you will stay on the horse's back. If there's anything I learned in my knight training, it's that you have the high ground on horseback — and the advantage over anyone who isn't."

She patted the worn wood. "I will be here when you return."

He dismounted, then strode across the yard until he vanished into the crowd.

Alone. Alone, amongst thousands.

Penelope drew in a deep breath, then expelled it slowly. She cast her gift wide, a net encompassing the prison. Pain and despair hit her first — from the dungeons where the guards tortured criminals for information and their own enjoyment — but she moved deeper into the building.

Despair swirled through her mind, thicker here, but the pain had dulled somewhat, to a niggling ache that would not go away.

A child's voice rose above the rest — outraged that he was required to do his schooling without his abacus.

Penelope couldn't help but smile. Definitely the child of some Rialto merchant. She had found them.

Thousands of her people, crowded into cells, filling cellars that had once held provisions. Grim, resolute, worried, fearing no help would come, and yet...still there was hope. They might be prisoners, but they had not been tortured. Families huddled together, hunger gnawing at the edge of their thoughts as they waited for their dinner. A dinner that would be paltry compared to what they'd enjoyed in their own homes, but enough to survive.

Hostages. That's what they were. Not ordinary prisoners, but ones the Emperor planned to release. At least, that's what their leaders believed.

The only way to find out would be to ask the Emperor himself.

Or read his thoughts.

One man among thousands…millions, maybe.

But she knew Godfrey's mind, and he was headed for the Emperor. He approached the palace even now, climbing the steps to the throne room. Telling his business to the herald, who nodded and sent a messenger to the Emperor himself.

The present petitioners were from one of Rialto's rival port cities. Without their hats, she couldn't be certain which one, but the smudged ash on their foreheads marked them as members of the same faith as her own, instead of the eastern one more common in Byzas.

Hatred for the petitioners burned from one of the men at the base of the dais. An old warrior, accustomed to commanding troops, but willing to wade into the fray with his sword until the blade ran red. He wanted to do that now. To slaughter the petitioners and everyone like them who did not share his eastern religion. When the Emperor succumbed to his illness and his young son took the throne, this general intended to seize power, be named regent, and order the massacre. He was practically salivating at the idea.

Shuddering, Penelope sought some thoughts that were less…horrifying. She turned to the child on the dais, who could not have been more than six years old. This was Alexios, the Emperor's eldest son, and his mind was a stormy tantrum the like of which Penelope would have expected in a toddler. He wanted to play and eat sweet things and not stand on the dais with his father. Only the fear of another blow from his father stopped him from giving voice to the screaming tantrum.

Her father planned to marry her to that spoiled child? The marriage could not be consummated for a decade, at least. Would she be able to bear children then? Not for long. And the young Emperor would need heirs…

She shook her head and plunged into the

Emperor's thoughts. He, at least, was listening to the petitioners, but nothing they said would change his mind. They wanted him to give them the imprisoned Rialto merchants' property. Something he could not do, for he'd seized it to fill his empty treasury.

As he would surely seize her, and her dowry...

No wonder Father had not finished negotiating her betrothal to this prince. The Emperor would seize her dowry, leaving her barren and penniless. Probably imprison her with her people, where she would wait until the Emperor died and the bloodbath began...

Her breath caught in her throat, and she could not seem to draw any air in. Choking, she bit down hard on her lip to block all other thoughts from her head except her own.

Spots obscured her vision, as she became aware that the constriction in her throat was real, not imagined, as a man's hands tightened around her neck.

Fly...fly! She threw herself forward on the horse's neck, desperately reaching for the nail.

But blackness found her first.

Twenty-Two

"This audience is at an end. All those who desire an audience with His Imperial Majesty, assemble outside the doors at dawn on the morrow!" the herald announced.

Godfrey jerked out of his reverie, and moved to follow the crowd. The herald seized his arm. "Not you. You are commanded to stay, and show the Emperor this horse immediately."

Immediately meant something different in Byzas, Godfrey soon learned. The Emperor required refreshments and a change of clothing while his coach and a squad of guards were assembled at the palace gates. This included a horse for Godfrey to ride as he led the procession. He had to duck his head to hide his amusement at this unasked-for gift of a palace horse, too late for it to be of any use to him.

But it would get him back to Penelope sooner. He wished he hadn't left her alone, but what danger could she come to in broad daylight in a very public square? As she'd said, she had the enchanted horse – she could easily fly away from trouble. Yet he could not help worrying.

The crowd outside the prison had dispersed, probably headed home for dinner. Or perhaps they didn't trust their monarch not to send them to the dungeons for getting in his way. Neither would have surprised Godfrey, not after what Penelope had told him. To imprison thousands of your own people simply because they came from a particular city. One of your loyal subject cities, no less. It beggared belief.

A shout came from ahead, and Godfrey urged his horse to move faster.

He reached the yard outside the prison...the empty yard. No horse, no Penelope. "Oh

God." Godfrey slid from his horse and dropped to his knees to pray she was safe.

"Up there! Shoot him, shoot him!"

The cry came from behind him, and it took Godfrey a moment to realise what the guards were pointing at. The enchanted horse floated high above, with a cloaked figure atop it, and a bundle draped across the horse's neck. Something dropped from the bundle, plummeting to the ground.

Godfrey scrambled to his feet and ran to reach it first. It was Lady Penelope's boot, still warm.

Someone had stolen her and the horse.

"Don't shoot!" Godfrey bellowed, waving his arms. "He's got Lady Penelope of Rialto!"

"Who?" the Emperor demanded, sticking his head out of the carriage window like some peculiar kind of sideways turtle.

"That's the magician! He used some sort of magic to escape from his cell!" one of the guards at the prison gate shouted.

The Emperor's eyes narrowed. "And his countrywoman helped him escape. I knew Rialtines weren't to be trusted, and this proves it."

"She did…she wouldn't…" Godfrey began. But he didn't know, not truly. Perhaps she had planned this all along, duping him into helping her…

No. If she'd gone willingly, she would have sat astride the horse, as she had on the way here. Not thrown across the horse like baggage. Somehow, the magician had overpowered her so he could steal the horse from her. That's what had happened.

"The man who brings me that magician's head may have my daughter's hand in marriage. And if you bring me the woman as well, I will give you anything you ask." The Emperor met Godfrey's gaze for a moment, before disappearing back inside his carriage. The carriage and escorts circled around the yard, then headed back the way they'd come.

Leaving Godfrey alone in the yard with the Emperor's horse beside him and the enchanted horse shrinking in the distance as it headed north. Back toward Rialto.

Godfrey tucked the boot into his belt and mounted up. Where Penelope led, he would follow. The magician would lose his head, and all would be right in the world again.

Twenty-Three

Pain woke Penelope. Her midsection ached like her courses had come early, and her head pounded worse than any hangover she'd ever endured. One of her feet was blissfully numb, but she did not know why.

She forced her eyes open, but the darkness remained. It took her a moment to realise it was night time – how long had she been unconscious? And where was she?

She felt around carefully with her hands, and found nothing but smooth, hard wood. Somehow, she'd fallen asleep on the horse. No, not fallen asleep. Someone had choked the air from her lungs, rendering her unconscious, and left her…outside the prison, in an unfamiliar city?

No, she could feel a breeze upon her face. A breeze not unlike the cold caress of the clouds as she'd flown with Godfrey…

Penelope swallowed. She was flying on the enchanted horse, thrown across it like some chattel. And the man riding it had done this. A man who was definitely not Godfrey. Why take her at all? Why not leave her behind?

She concentrated on his thoughts, holding tight to the horse as she tried to divine his intentions. His attention was fixed on the land below. No, the lagoon below, for in the pre-dawn light she could discern the islands of Rialto. Home.

His thoughts clashed with hers, a wave of anger and betrayal at a city he wished would vanish beneath the waves. Because he could never go back there, after being exiled. A rich city, a religious city, where he'd been ready to settle down happily until they threw him out. But even then, his luck had held. He'd found the ancient, enchanted horse, in the ruins of a forgotten city, and flown back, offering it to the Duke for a pardon and a marriage alliance. But the damned Duke had dismissed him and his horse…

Penelope was startled to see her own father's face in the man's thoughts. This man had wanted her to be his wife? Who was he? Not some foreign prince, if he'd made his home in Rialto.

Home. So close…

She fumbled about on the horse's neck, searching for the nail that would draw her blood and give her control of the beast. Her greatest desire right now was to go home, and take this man to her father. He'd nearly strangled her, then kidnapped her – more than enough reason to deserve death, the punishment that would be meted out to a returned exile.

An exile she had no doubt he deserved, whatever he'd done.

The man's voice interrupted her thoughts. "Oh, you're awake, are you? No, don't do that…"

Without warning, he slammed her head against the horse, hard, and darkness took her again.

Twenty-Four

Rialto never changed, Godfrey thought, as a gondolier – perhaps the same one as before – poled him to the Ducal Palace. Where Penelope's father now lived.

Godfrey gave his name to a manservant, and settled down to wait. The ruler of Rialto was a busy man. Much like the Emperor of Byzas, he would have far more important matters to deal with than an uninvited visit from a foreign knight.

"Sir Godfrey! What a pleasure!"

Godfrey's head jerked up. Rialto might not have changed, but Sebastiano had aged considerably in the years since he'd last seen him. But the Duke's smile was as genuine as ever.

"My l – I mean, Monsignor…I've come about Lady Penelope." Godfrey swallowed. How did you tell a man you'd run away with his daughter, only to have her stolen from you, and spirited away? Duke Sebastiano might be older than his father, but Godfrey had no doubt the man could best him with a sword. Penelope's honour would demand no less than his death.

Sebastiano smiled indulgently. "The sweetest daughter any man could be blessed with. She has joined the convent at Saint Angelo of Concordia, and I cannot imagine a more fitting place for such an angel. I visit her there as often as time permits."

Godfrey had to pause to process the Duke's words. He had found her at a convent, but she hadn't mentioned being a nun. No, she'd definitely talked about marriage. Unless she'd lied…

And rescued the magician, his traitorous mind added.

Godfrey shook his head. He wouldn't

believe that of her. Couldn't.

"When did you last visit her?" Godfrey managed to say.

Sebastiano looked thoughtful. "Why, it must be a week ago, perhaps longer. She left the convent to attend a friend's wedding, on the last day before Lent. My duties as Duke keep me busy here."

He didn't know. Didn't know that he'd taken her.

Or maybe he did, and the Duke was lying, to keep Godfrey from seeing her again.

"Could you…send word to her that I am here? I wish to know that she is well," Godfrey said, hating the awkwardness in his voice, but what else was he to say? He could hardly tell him the truth. He wouldn't leave here alive.

"I had planned on sending her a gift this very day. A chest of fine silk skeins, for her weaving. The finest weavers and dressmakers in the city have begged to be allowed to clothe her, but she will have none of them. She weaves and makes her own clothes. She even made her friend's wedding dress for the wedding last week, though neither the bride or groom was a pauper. Why, my daughter is the envy of every dressmaker in the city, for none can make gowns like she does." Sebastiano beckoned to a servant. "I shall send a note with it now, to tell her of your visit, and your kind enquiry after her health."

The note was written and despatched, before the Duke invited Godfrey to join him for dinner, later in the day.

Godfrey could not refuse, so with a promise to return later in the day, he departed.

He considered hiring a boat to take him to the convent, so he could see for himself if she was there, but he had no guarantees that she would see him. Even if she did, could he bear to look her in the eye, knowing she'd betrayed him? If she had…

Even her father likened her to an angel. Surely they couldn't both be mistaken.

He wasn't sure what he wanted to hear — that she'd betrayed him, but was now safe at home, or that the magician had kidnapped her, and she was now in the devil only knew what kind of danger.

A branch scraped his shoulder, and for a moment, he thought it was a grasping hand. No, just bare sticks, the first signs of spring blossom starting to show on the branches above. He didn't know what sort of tree it was, or what fruit it might bear in the heat of summer. Penelope would – that day they'd kissed, she'd had leaves in her hair, and he'd plucked one to keep. He still had it at home somewhere, a reminder of that perfect moment.

He prowled through the trees, until he found a small church dedicated to Saint Mark. Patron saint of this city. The city Penelope said her marriage would help to save. No, not just the city, but its people – the prisoners the Emperor kept in his dungeons. Was even that a lie?

God, he did not know any more. What was true and what was right and what he should do. First Melisende, then the unknown girl in Byzas, and now Penelope…what kind of knight was he, if he could not protect those who could not protect themselves? Never mind Melisende's killers – he was the one who didn't deserve absolution from joining the crusade. That's why he'd lost the army, and the enchanted horse, and now Penelope, too.

Maybe the magician was right, and he was

cursed.

Godfrey fell to his knees and prayed. Not for himself – he didn't deserve the saint's attention – but for Penelope, who had seemed so earnestly to want to save her city. To keep her safe. Because if he could save only one woman in his life, it would be her.

Hours later, or so it seemed, a hand touched his shoulder.

"Sir Godfrey, the Duke is about to sit down to dinner."

Godfrey climbed laboriously to his feet – he must have been kneeling for longer than he'd realised – and followed the servant to the Ducal Palace.

The dining room seemed empty without Penelope, though the Duke and plenty of servants were present. Godfrey wasn't sure why he'd hoped…

"Sir Godfrey, please, sit." The Duke gestured to the seat across from him. "I must beg you to forgive my servants for interrupting you while you were at prayer, but I had an inkling you might need to hear this news sooner rather than later."

Godfrey sat, and a cup of wine was thrust

into his hand. He wanted to deny his desire to hear whatever news the Duke might have, but he couldn't. Not if it pertained to Penelope.

Let her be safe at the convent. Safe and well, no matter what else she had done. Safe and well, and he would forgive her anything, Godfrey prayed silently.

"The servant I sent to the convent has returned," the Duke began. "It seems my daughter is not at home. No one has seen her since the start of Lent."

Godfrey's heart sank down into his boots. He could not bear to meet her father's eyes, knowing it was his fault this had happened.

Wordlessly, he pulled out her boot and set it on the table. He wished it still retained her warmth, but it had gone cold before he'd even left Byzas.

"What has happened to her?" the Duke demanded.

Did the Duke have dungeons, where he tortured people? Godfrey wasn't sure he cared. Not knowing what had happened to Penelope, while knowing it was his fault, was agonising enough.

Godfrey wet his lips, hoping the Duke was

not a mind reader like his daughter. "She was taken from the convent by a man on an enchanted, flying horse. He took her to Byzas, where she was seen briefly. She dropped her boot as he flew off with her, headed north. I had hoped he came here, as the magician claimed to have come from Rialto."

The colour drained from Sebastiano's face. "A man with a magical flying horse? Oh, no. Poor Penelope."

"What? Who is Lord Valerio?" Godfrey demanded.

"I know of no man of that name. But I do know a man who claimed to have an enchanted, flying horse. Leonardo Gabrieli, a pretend priest who seduced nuns and other virtuous women, then accused them of being possessed by the devil so that he might end the affair, before returning to hear their confession and accept money for many masses to be said for their souls. Money he kept for himself, for he was not a priest at all. He was exiled when it all came out, for the courts deemed death too good for him.

"One of my trading ships marooned him on an uninhabited island to the south, and that was all I heard of him, until a few months ago. He sent me a letter, thanking me for choosing that island, for there, he'd unearthed a trove of riches, including a priceless magical artefact – an enchanted, flying horse. He offered it to me in exchange for recalling him from exile, and giving him my daughter to be his wife. Naturally, I refused. No father who loved his daughter would willingly give her to the very devil himself."

Godfrey squeezed his eyes shut. What had he done?

He rose. "I swear to you, I will find her, and bring her home to you. The Emperor himself has already called for the magician's head. I pray I will be the first to find him, so I can deliver that to you, as well."

The Duke rose, too. "Bring her home safely, and I will give you anything you ask."

Rescuing Penelope from the devil's clutches would be miracle enough for Godfrey, but he did not say that to the Duke. "I would walk through the gates of hell itself, if that's what it takes to find her," Godfrey said instead. Seeing as he was probably headed to hell anyway now…

Sebastiano slumped into his seat. "Pray it does not come to that, Sir Godfrey."

Twenty-Five

"At this rate, we might have to ride to the Holy Land itself before we find a suitable quarry," Prince Magnus complained. "The crusaders have wiped out anything larger than a mouse."

The other courtiers laughed, though it sounded forced, but Count Vesone did not. Prince Magnus might be a spoiled child who knew between little and nothing about hunting, but he was not wrong about this. Count Vesone's lands would take decades to recover from the ravenous host that had devoured everything in their path on their way to save the Holy Land. He only hoped the price he and others paid would be worth it. That Emperor Frederick and his army would return victorious. Anything else was…unconscionable. Just the thought of Prince Magnus on the throne…

"I'm hungry!"

Count Vesone gestured for his servants to start laying out the midday meal. The teenage prince was annoying most of the time, but when he was hungry, he was unbearable. Better men had met with hunting accidents in the past…

Besides, there was little point to hunting in an empty forest.

A forest that had fallen silent.

For all Magnus's complaints, there had been birds, and rustlings from small creatures. But now there were none.

A woman's scream rent the air, a shrill blast from her lungs followed by an equally piercing plea for, "Help!"

Vesone leaped easily into the saddle, while the other courtiers stood frozen, as though they'd never heard a woman scream before. If Magnus were truly to become Emperor one day, he should have been the one to issue the command, but he was as slack-jawed as the rest.

"Come, we must help her!" Vesone called as he rode in the direction he thought the voice had come from.

As if to spur him on, she screamed again.

Not waiting for the others to catch up, he urged his horse to speed up.

He found them in a clearing – the very spot he'd hoped to reach for their midday meal. The man had the girl backed up against a tree, one hand around her neck, a knife in the other.

"Step away from the girl," Vesone commanded, laying his hand on his sword.

The man glanced behind him, but his grip only tightened on the girl. "This is no business of yours, sir. I'm merely teaching my wife a lesson in obedience, something she has been slow to learn, and we are here so that we will not disturb the neighbours with the noise." The knife came to the neckline of her gown, poised between her breasts. "Isn't that right, wife?"

"I am no man's wife, least of all this piece of exiled scum!" the girl said, baring her teeth. "I am Lady Penelope of Rialto, and he kidnapped me, knocked me unconscious and dragged me here –" His grip on her throat tightened, choking off her words and her air.

Vesone expected her to claw at her throat, to get him to release her, as the bloodied scratches on his hand said she already had, but the girl surprised him. She grabbed for the knife, and succeeded in making him lower the blade, but not before it had sliced down the front of her gown.

"I said step away from the girl." Vesone dismounted and drew his sword. He didn't know who to believe. If the man was right, it would take him very little time to discover the truth from whatever nearby village they'd come from, and he could do what he wished with his unwilling wife.

If he was lying and the girl was telling the truth, justice must be served.

The girl kicked him in the shins, forcing him to loosen his grip on her as he stumbled back.

"I demand justice!" she said. "This man is Leonardo Gabrieli, exiled from Rialto by my father, the Duke of Rialto, for crimes so numerous and vile, death was deemed too good for him. For daring to enter the Rialto lagoon, his punishment is instant death, and I demand immediate justice from the lord of these lands!"

A whistle sounded from behind Vesone. Magnus and the others had finally joined him, and the young prince's eyes were fixed on Lady Penelope.

And no wonder, for Gabrieli's blade had slashed her gown open to the waist, baring her breasts and the red line of trickling blood between them. Perfect breasts heaving, as her eyes fixed firmly on Vesone. Demanding his assistance, as any lady of her breeding would.

"Lying whore!" Gabrieli hissed, raising his fist to strike her.

Vesone didn't hesitate. He thrust his sword between the two, so Gabrieli's blow landed on the blade, cleaving his arm open to the bone.

Gabrieli howled, turning his knife on Vesone instead.

An arrow sprouted from Gabrieli's throat. Gurgling, the man clawed at it, before falling to his knees. His eyes burned at Vesone, blaming him for his impending death, before the light in them died and he toppled over at Lady Penelope's feet.

She looked down with distaste, and only then did she notice her own nakedness. She tried to pull her torn gown up to cover her breasts, no longer the lady in charge. Now she looked like a frightened girl as her eyes met Vesone's again.

"I call it a successful hunt after all!" Magnus cried, holding his bow high over his head in triumph. "I claim the kill, and the prize."

Lady Penelope gave a delicate shudder, shaking her head almost imperceptibly. Magnus meant to claim her as his prize, Vesone realised in disgust.

Vesone unfastened his cloak and wrapped it around Lady Penelope. "Come, my lady. I am Count Vesone, and these are my lands. Now that justice is done, please accept my hospitality, and the services of my healer."

She hesitated a moment, then gave him her hand, and allowed him to help her onto his horse. She sat at the back of the saddle, not touching the stirrups or the reins. As though she had no idea how to ride a horse.

Or had Gabrieli injured her worse than he'd thought? By all that was holy…how did he ask a lady to speak of unspeakable things?

She managed a timid smile. "Thank you for such timely action, Count Vesone. If you had not intervened, I fear that brute would have had his way with me. He was a magician, possessed of diabolical powers that could bring things to life. He rode on that wooden horse, using his magic to make it move." She pointed at a life-sized carving of a horse. Though it stood in the middle of the clearing, he hadn't noticed it until now.

"Then it shouldn't be left here, for anyone to find. Not if it is tainted by dark magic," Vesone said, beckoning for a servant to come forward. He left orders for the carving to be brought into his castle, where it was to be locked in a dungeon. Just in case.

He eyed Lady Penelope, averting his gaze from the pouting prince who couldn't keep his eyes off the injured girl. She would need an escort, for if she lost too much blood, she might fall from the saddle.

As if reading his thoughts, the girl swayed, appearing pained.

"Continue the hunt. I will take Lady Penelope home to find a healer," Vesone said. He mounted the horse before her. "Hold on to me, my lady."

Twenty-Six

Count Vesone's castle was like something out of a story. A square, stone building, several storeys high, with a tower keep stuck to one side, soaring above it.

The tower occupied his thoughts, too – for that's where he planned to put her. For her safety, he told himself repeatedly, as he planned to place guards on the level below hers, and perhaps the stairs as well.

The Count was true to his word, shouting for a healer as he helped her down from his horse. "Can you walk?" he asked anxiously, already stretching his arms out to carry her.

Her wounds stung, especially where her clothes clung to them, but the cuts were shallow enough. She could climb the spiral stair to the top of the tower. Better than being carried up them, for all the Count's gallantry.

"I can," she said softly, pressing a hand to her chest as if it pained her. He fancied himself her honourable protector, and it cost her nothing to feign weakness. She was aching, tired, in need of a bath and a good night's sleep, and she had no idea how to get home without his help. He would help, too – he was no twisty Byzas courtier, to simper and smile while debating how best to kill her. Nor was he a gold-driven Rialto merchant lord, trying to work out the best way to profit from the situation.

He led the way up the tower stairs, pausing occasionally to make sure she followed. "This was the original keep, built by my ancestors in the time of Charles the Great. My great-grandfather had the second castle built, and he pledged to build a cloister on his land, too. Construction took longer than he expected, and for a time, the nuns stayed here, in the tower, until the cloister was finished."

From one convent to another, Penelope thought. She was destined to die an old maid, just like Marco the fake fortune teller said.

Vesone caught her frown. "It fell into disuse until my father died, and my widowed mother decided to take the tower room for her own. She has been gone these ten years, but the servants keep it as she left it, a chamber befitting their dowager countess, for she was well loved. There will be clothes and all the things a lady needs there. You may take whatever you wish. If anything is not to your liking, I will make arrangements to improve it for you, for you cannot travel until your wounds have healed." And it would take time to assemble a suitably large guard to protect her on her journey home to Rialto, if indeed she was who she said, he added in his head.

Penelope nodded. Every step higher became more and more of an effort. If she'd known there would be so many steps, maybe she would have allowed the Count to carry her. Now, she just hoped the climb would soon end so that she might rest.

When she reached the top, the brightness in the room dazzled her, forcing her to stop. She blinked, bringing into focus the windows letting in so much light. They were made of horn, much like the ones she'd had at home, but cut into a delicate diamond pattern. "It's beautiful," she breathed.

Vesone bowed. "I'm sure you wish to rest. When the healer arrives, I'll see that she is sent to you immediately."

He departed before she could respond, but Penelope was too busy examining her new quarters to notice.

The dowager countess had been a weaver, too, judging by the loom placed in the brightest part of the room. Chests around the walls held linens, silks, and wool in myriad colours – all waiting to be woven into something new.

A small chest at the end of the narrow bed held what remained of the woman's clothes, all in mourning black and grey. Penelope grimaced. She had no intention of mourning the magician, but she'd prefer even grey garments to ones stained with blood.

There was water in the jug, so she decided to wash while she waited for the healer.

Off came the Count's cloak, but her own

clothes were another matter. Her torn gown and chemise had stuck to her wounds as the blood clotted, and she hissed with pain as she pulled them free. Her cuts started bleeding anew as her shredded bodice settled over her skirt like some horrible parody of Marzia's wedding lace. The bloodstained wash water trickling down to turn it red did not help matters.

"Oh, don't do that, dear. Let me clean those cuts properly," a new voice said.

Only now aware that she was bare to the waist, Penelope lifted her arms to cover her breasts from the newcomer's sight.

The middle-aged woman made a clucking sound in her throat. "Healers see plenty of skin, dear. Let's get you out of that ruined gown and onto the bed so I can tend you."

Penelope took a moment to skim through the woman's thoughts to determine that she truly was a healer before she stretched out on the bed. A blissful sigh escaped her at the much-needed softness.

The healer set to work, unpacking her satchel on the table.

"You're a lucky one. If this cut had gone any

lower, and just a little deeper, it would have opened your belly, and you would not have lived this long," the healer said as she worked. Some of her ministrations stung, but Penelope gritted her teeth and wished the ordeal to be over.

"But without you, the future won't work, so I suppose even fate has her favourites. Can't kill the loom you're weaving on," the healer continued.

"What?" Penelope blurted out. Her head felt clear, but the healer's words made her brain feel fuzzy all over again.

The healer shot her a sharp glance. "Empires rise and fall, and only a select few will ever know why. You have the power to make peace between emperors and kings, Lady of Rialto. But power calls to power, so you will give the world five powerful queens, though you will never take the throne for your own."

"How…" Penelope began, reaching for the woman's thoughts. A jumble of images waited for her. Her own face, but older, never alone. A dark-haired woman, her skin tinted faintly blue, as if underwater. A girl surrounded by fire, battling a dragon. A blonde teenager holding a thorny rose, heedless of the blood trickling down her hands. A fair girl with red-rimmed eyes, eyes that reflected fire both without and within. A redhead across the water, an army breaking like waves at her feet. And herself as she was now, hair flying in the wind, as she flew the enchanted horse high above three armies, marching on Rialto. "You're a seer!"

The healer inclined her head. "Yes, and I've been seeing visions of you for as long as I can remember. You're younger than I thought you'd be. I'd wager you haven't even bedded that handsome husband of yours yet." She winked.

"I will marry after all?" Hope rose in Penelope's breast. "Are you sure?"

The healer chuckled. "Nothing is certain in a seer's visions — for your gift has shown them to you as surely as mine has given them to me. But when the fate of empires rests on you choosing wisely, I can say with certainty that one of the queens will be the daughter of your union with the man you love." She blinked. "Or will love, if you don't yet."

"Who?"

"I'm only a seer. I see the future, not the secrets of your heart. That's your gift, dear." The healer patted her shoulder. "If you put on a clean shift, I'll take these rags away for you, for I've done all I can for you now. Rest, recover, and when you're ready, the opportunity to leave will come. Your fate lies far from here, over the water." And with that, the healer left.

"Wait…I don't even know your name!" Penelope called after the woman.

"You may call me Mistress Dalia, though I doubt we'll meet again. Have courage, Lady Penelope, and keep busy."

Twenty-Seven

"I don't care what promises you made! You are nothing without my father, and in his absence, I am the highest authority here. I will have her!"

At first, Penelope though the petulant cry belonged to a woman, but a quick peep into the spoiled brat's thoughts revealed it to be the boy she'd seen yesterday. The one who'd been so overwhelmed with desire at the sight of her bare breasts, desire that had reached fever pitch when blood welled, and he'd killed the magician to get to her. Without the Count's quick thinking to cover her and spirit her away, heaven only knew what the boy would do.

"She is Lady Penelope of Rialto. The Duke of Rialto's daughter. If you have her against his will, you will start a war. An attack on her person is an attack on Rialto itself, and not something those merchants will take lightly."

"But I want her!" the boy whined. "She's only a duke's daughter. No one would know…"

"Rialto has no king. No emperor. They are ruled by a duke – a duke who happens to be her father. As far as Rialto and the rest of the world is concerned, that girl is a princess, at the very least. The man who kidnapped her…there will be pursuit. Even now, Rialto's armies will be searching for her. If they find out she was here and came to harm, they will have no mercy. I will send a letter to her father tonight, telling him she has been found, safe and well, asking how we might best return her home. For if we do not and she is found here…all our lives will be forfeit."

"Then fetch a priest – I'll marry her, and bed her right away! What God has joined, no man may sunder."

Ugh. Penelope shuddered at the image in

the boy's head – of her own naked body, bloodied as if from a battle, thrown down on the ground as he had his way with her.

"If her father finds out she has been forced into a marriage not of his making, he'll sunder plenty. Starting with separating your head from your body. Please reconsider, Your Highness. Your father would never forgive me for starting a war or being responsible for the death of his favourite son."

The prince's pride nearly exploded at the Count's glib lie. "Then send the letter to her father. Tell him the Emperor's favourite son wishes to marry her."

Relief flooded through Vesone. "I will, Your Highness."

"Good. Now, take me to her. I want to tell her myself." Another lie. What the prince wanted was to see her naked again, and he hoped to catch her undressed, at the mercy of a healer.

"But she has been through a terrible ordeal, Your Highness. I fear if we disturb her before she is properly recovered, it may cause irreparable harm…"

"Don't be silly, Vesone! She's going to

marry me. That's the best news she could ever hear. I have no doubt it will put her in the best spirits!"

Penelope wanted to laugh at the prospect of sharing a bed with that bloodthirsty toad. Better than the vipers of Byzas, but not by much.

"I'll even honour her with a kiss!"

Could she endure kissing a toad without throwing up? She suspected she was about to find out, as she heard the sound of feet on the spiral stair. She glanced around, wishing she had something she might use as a weapon to defend herself. But she was no warrior – she was a weaver. Which, in this room, might be enough…

Penelope placed herself behind the loom. A distaff sat propped against the wall, within easy reach, and the unusually large shuttle would work in a pinch. Why, this one might do double duty as a rolling pin in the kitchens. A formidable weapon indeed, if she had the strength to wield it.

And if she didn't?

She sank onto the stool, her knees no longer willing to hold her. So much for the healer wishing her courage, for hers had fled through some tiny gap in the horn windows.

The boy appeared in the doorway, closely followed by Count Vesone.

"Lady Penelope of Rialto, may I present Prince Magnus, son of His Imperial Majesty?" Vesone said.

Bloodlust burned in the prince's eyes, until his gaze fell upon her modest grey gown. Then fury replaced it. "What is she doing here?" He waved his hand up and down. "And why is she wearing that?"

Vesone bowed as low as he could. "My deepest apologies for the interruption, Lady Penelope. His Highness commanded me to take him to you, and as I have always been His Imperial Majesty's loyal servant..." If he'd refused, the prince would have demanded his head. The prince did not understand that, as the Duke of Rialto's daughter, she was the prince's equal, if not his better, for Emperor Frederick was not fool enough to make an enemy of Rialto.

Only a queen could cow the prince. So a queen she must be.

Penelope inclined her head, not bothering

to rise. "Thank you, Count Vesone. He looks like a fine boy. I'm sure Emperor Frederick is very proud." She forced herself to lower her gaze to the empty loom. She picked up the shuttle and pretended to go back to her weaving.

This only angered the prince even more.

"Stop that!" the prince insisted, striding forward. He reached for the spindle.

Without thinking, she rapped the spindle across his fingers. "Don't touch my work! You'll ruin it."

His eyes widened in fear as he stuck his stinging fingers in his mouth. Then he looked at the loom. "There's nothing there!"

Of course, he was right. She hadn't even strung the warp threads on the loom, let alone begun weaving properly. A ridiculous tale of her mother's came to mind, and she said, "Just because you cannot see it, does not mean it's not there. Rialto weavers are among the finest in the world, and Rialto lace so fine that it is almost invisible to the common eye."

If he'd heard the same tale, he'd challenge the lie at once, but it seemed the prince had not. He was too busy pouting at being struck, and plotting how he would have his revenge when they were married. "Keep weaving, then. When you are well, I want to see you wearing a gown made of this on our wedding day." The prince turned and trotted down the steps. All the way down, wondering whether the fabric on the loom was real or if she'd gone mad. Only a madwoman would dare strike a prince…who knew what else she might do? The wedding would have to wait until the Count's healer had cured her madness, for he would not tolerate being struck again.

Vesone stared mournfully at her, as if he wanted to say something, but could not form the words. He thought her mad, too.

If madness might buy her time, then mad she would be.

"How do you like my Rialto lace, Count Vesone?" Penelope asked, gesturing at her empty loom. "Is the colour too bright, or should I add more of that gold silk to it? I'm sure I saw some…" She moved to the nearest chest and began rifling through it, looking for the imaginary gold thread.

With her back turned, she should not have seen him poke a finger, then his whole hand, through where the cloth should be. But of course, she saw all that in the Count's mind, and more.

"Get well, Lady Penelope," he muttered, as he hurried down after the prince.

To write a letter telling her father she'd lost her wits, and to send someone to collect her soon.

Ooh, there was gold thread here – skeins of the stuff. While she waited, she might weave something real, as well. Heaven forbid that she should wear a widow's mourning clothes when her father's men showed up. No, she wanted to wear the brightest colours imaginable on that joyful day.

Twenty-Eight

Godfrey had lost count of the days he'd been riding north, not to mention the tiny inns where he'd spent the night. They all seemed the same, with watery ale, thin stew with more vegetables than meat, and beds with mattresses worn so thin it was a wonder he slept at all.

"I have a tale that can top them all," a newcomer boasted, slapping both hands on the bar. "Keep my cup filled with ale all night, and I will tell you everything!"

Judging by the excitement this caused in the small country inn, Godfrey suspected news had been hard to come by of late. A pile of coins formed on the bar – enough to buy the man a meal as well as enough ale to see him sleep for days, no matter what mattress he lay upon.

The innkeeper dipped a mug into the ale barrel and set it before the storyteller.

The newcomer took a deep breath. "Now, every man here has heard of the Holy Crusade our Imperial Majesty, Emperor Frederick is on, right? Him and two of his sons, while the oldest stayed at home to rule in his father's place. The younger boys all got fostered out across the kingdom. One of the princes, he got sent to a castle not far from here. It belongs to the Count of Vesone."

The storyteller paused, to drink the health of the Count he served, before continuing: "One day, the Count takes the young prince hunting. They go deep into the woods, far from any road or town, where no one goes. And they hear a woman scream. A woman where there should be no one.

"So they ride deeper into the forest to find her. When they do, they are just in time to save her from a terrible rogue who has stolen her away, and means to steal her virtue, too."

He drained his ale, then waited for a refill.

"The girl is fair fainting from fear, but the Count manages to revive her, and asks for her tale. How she came to that place, and who she and her attacker were."

The storyteller slapped his hands on the bar. "Who do you think she was?"

Various men shouted names, from their favourite whore right up to queens from legend. He shook his head, laughing at them all.

"She said the man was a magician, who flew her from her home on a magic horse. Then she said she was the Duke of Rialto's daughter, the highest lady in that land. The Count, being the wise man that he is, believed her at once, for such was obvious from her noble bearing, and offered her the hospitality of his home."

Again, the assembled men toasted the Count's health. Godfrey's grip tightened on his cup as he willed the storyteller to continue.

"Ah, but the prince…do not forget the young prince! Not yet a man, but near enough to know a beautiful woman when he sees one. And she was – the most beautiful girl there ever was seen, dazzling the poor prince, who fell instantly in love with the girl."

There was some laughter at this. They had never seen her, Godfrey had to remind himself. She would enchant most men, if it truly was Penelope.

"Sadly, she fainted again before she could fall in love with him, and they carried her to the Count's castle. A healer came to see to the girl, and said she would live. The prince was delighted, and sat by her bedside, day and night, waiting for his beloved to wake up."

Anger burned in Godfrey's gut. The boy might be a prince, but how dare he remain in Penelope's bedchamber while she slept? She would be horrified if she knew.

"It was some time before she awoke, this beautiful lady, and she beheld her prince, her rescuer. The prince fell to his knees, overcome with her beauty once more, as he beseeched her to marry him."

Another pause as the storyteller drained his ale. One man congratulated him on a good story, hoping the prince would be happy. The storyteller nearly choked at this, and the taproom fell silent.

"Happy? The prince? Oh, the story is not

over yet. For the damsel in distress, the sweet maiden who had swooned in his arms, was a completely new creature upon waking. As though possessed of the devil himself, she attacked the prince so violently that he feared for his life, and fled her chamber. The Count was forced to lock the girl in the top room of the tower, so that she could not hurt anyone in her madness."

No. Penelope would not threaten a man's life. She might throw an orange at him, but want to kill him? Godfrey could not believe it of her. This girl must be someone else, pretending to be Penelope.

The storyteller brandished a scroll case. "The Count has sent me with a letter to the Duke of Rialto, asking him to send someone to fetch his mad daughter. But the prince, oh the poor prince! The prince wants the Duke's permission to marry the girl, mad or no, and offers a reward to the man who can cure the girl's madness. To the man who can lift the curse from her – for it is the magician's curse, I have no doubt, likely whispered with his last breath as he lay dying – the prince will give a bag of gold and his sister's hand in marriage."

Cheers erupted, as the patrons drank to the health of the prince, the storyteller and the promised princess.

Godfrey had to wait until the crowd around the storyteller had dispersed before he dared approach the man.

When the storyteller turned to head up the stairs to the room he'd undoubtedly secured for the night, Godfrey made his move.

"Is that sailor's tale you told true, man?" he asked.

The storyteller turned around, narrowing his eyes. He'd had several mugs of ale, but not enough to be drunk, Godfrey judged. "I swear it on my life," the storyteller said.

Imprisoning Penelope… "Did the Count truly lock her in a prison?"

"In a tower," the storyteller corrected. "The dowager countess's bower, in fact. Not a prison at all, but where the Count's late mother did her weaving and sewing. Far superior to any other sleeping chamber in the castle proper. The prince still means to marry her, when someone lifts the madness. In the meantime, she can be heard, working on the dowager countess's loom. It is the only thing that calms her."

Penelope had mentioned her affinity for weaving and sewing. Perhaps…

Godfrey held up a silver coin – more money than the inn patrons had laid on the bar, much of which had ended in the storyteller's pockets. "Tell me her name."

The storyteller eyed the coin. "I cannot quite recall. It was a long name, a name from legend. Panacea. No, that's not right. Persephone? No…ah, I remember now. It was Penelope."

His throat suddenly too dry to speak, Godfrey handed over the coin and dismissed the man.

He'd found her.

When the sun's first rays touched the earth the next day, Godfrey was already well on his way north to Vesone. To save Penelope from princes, counts and whatever curse the magician had cast.

Twenty-Nine

Word had spread of her supposed madness. Servants tiptoed in and out of her chamber, fearful of her notice. Penelope longed to say something that would dispel the miasma of fear that surrounded her, but she didn't dare. Fear was the only thing that kept the prince away, though more than once she'd heard him climb the stairs to peep through the keyhole to her chamber. Hoping to catch her in a state of undress, she knew.

The next time a servant came, she'd complained about the door's eyes staring at her and demanded a screen to hide her from view.

The poor maid had nearly flown down the steps, but the screen had arrived soon after, to the prince's endless muttered frustration.

The loom was a good one, and she wove until she ran out of gold silk. It was not enough to make a whole gown, so she searched through the chests for more.

The dowager countess had left enough supplies to make a lifetime of clothing, but she hadn't liked gold thread much. Or maybe she had, and she'd used it all. She'd also liked weaving green wool, with swathes of cloth filling three chests.

Perhaps Penelope should make a gown from the already woven wool, to wear while she wove something brighter than the dark green the countess had favoured. She started to spread the cloth out, measuring it with her eyes. There might be enough for one gown, and half enough again for a cloak to match, but it would be best to do the cloak entirely in dark green. Then she might melt into the forest, and no one would see her.

Which she would not do until she had no other option.

Penelope dug through the chest, lifting aside

a bundle of black wool to find more green. Yet this cloth was not the same as the rest. Soft, like felt, yet gleaming like silk. If she'd been asked, she would have described it as short fur, if any creature alive had moss green fur. Yet the stuff had clearly been woven on a loom of some sort.

She laid it out atop the wool. Enough for a gown, and she could trim it with the gold silk. She would keep the scraps of the green stuff, though, in the hope that she might manage to replicate such strange cloth. The green wool would become a cloak, then, for this stuff shimmered too much when it caught the light.

She would cut and sew the gown and the cloak in secret, hiding them when she heard the thoughts of anyone climbing the stairs. When they reached her room, they would find her seated at the loom, weaving the invisible Rialto lace that made them all think she was mad.

What she would give to see real Rialto lace again. To feel the stuff under her fingers as she'd fashioned it into a wedding dress for Marzia…Penelope wiped away a tear that had appeared, inexplicably, on her cheek. She would go home. It might take all her courage, and fortitude, and endurance, and many other virtues she wasn't sure she possessed, but Count Vesone had written to her father, and her father would send someone to escort her home, if he could not come himself.

When she saw him again, she would wear a green cloak, over a green and gold gown made of the mysterious cloth. Ready to give the world…was it five queens? And bring two emperors to heel. Her. One woman, a weaver, who would be happy to spend the rest of her life simply creating clothing.

Perhaps that was it – she would clothe five queens in such magnificence that men swooned and lost their hearts to them. Even emperors were men, too, with all the urges of the flesh.

But these mysterious queens must wait, for her own gown came first. Yes, the gown, then the cloak.

Decision made, she set to work.

Thirty

Vesone's castle was much like his father's, Godfrey mused. Sitting on a hill at a distance from the town…but Vesone's tower was part of the castle, not on a neighbouring, higher hill, like his father's. A tower where the Count kept Penelope, if his messenger was to be believed. He squinted at the tower windows, hoping for a glimpse of her, but they were all shuttered. Never mind. If his plan worked, he would see her soon enough.

He'd sold his horse at the last town, covering his armour with a coarse robe like those worn by the Benedictine monks.

Nobody at this town paid him any attention as he headed past the inn, toward the monastery on the edge of town.

"I'm Brother Iudas, a mendicant friar from Saint Angelo of Concordia," he told the first monk he met. "My abbott told me to travel here, for he was told in a dream that my healing skills were sorely needed."

The monk frowned. "We have a good healer here already, who can cure many an illness. You may stay for a night, if the Abbott agrees, but your own superior must be mistaken."

Godfrey lowered his voice. "My abbott is never mistaken, and I know he is not now. On the road, I heard tell of a terrible affliction that has befallen someone at the castle. I am no ordinary healer. God has blessed me with the miracle of being able to cure madness."

He prayed he would be forgiven for the lie. Though it would not be entirely a lie if he could restore Penelope to her sane self. If such a thing was even necessary...

The monk nodded. "I will take you to the Abbott. Father Danilo will know what to do."

Father Danilo and the Abbott were one and the same, so Godfrey only had to repeat his tale once, adding details about Saint Angelo until the man seemed satisfied.

The priest was only too willing to take him up to the castle, for he confided, "Count Vesone is very worried for the young woman. He feels responsible for not protecting her properly, and is willing to do anything within his power to be able to return her to her father, healed."

No more than Godfrey himself. He hoped the priest's assessment of the Count was indeed accurate.

The priest took him to the Great Hall, where a servant promised to tell the Count of his arrival, before begging the priest to pay a visit to the servant's mother, who lay dying in her bed.

Godfrey waved the priest away. "Go, see to the poor woman's soul. I can meet with the Count alone."

The servant thanked them both profusely, beckoning Godfrey to follow him up to his master's solar, because, "I can see you are a holy man of God, and I will vouch for your goodness myself."

Feeling more uncomfortable by the minute,

Godfrey followed the man upstairs.

"My lord, this is Friar Iudas, who Father Danilo assures me is an expert in matters of madness and possession."

"Send him in."

The servant waved Godfrey into the room, then shut the door behind him.

The silver-haired man dressed in plain wool might have been the castle steward, not its master, but the vair collar on his cloak gave away his high station. "Do you believe I gave the devil leave to take lodging in my home, Friar?"

Godfrey considered for a moment, then replied, "I believe the devil is a tricky beast, one which may hide its true nature in order to steal souls it does not deserve. I have seen madness from other sources, too – sometimes a curse can make men behave contrary to their natures. I would need to see the patient for myself before I could give you an honest answer to your question, my lord."

The Count nodded. "Very well. I'll take you to her."

Part of Godfrey wanted to tell the Count to wait, but the rest of him was simply too eager to see Penelope again. If it was Penelope…

He fairly flew up the stairs to reach her, stopping only when they reached the closed door at the top.

Count Vesone rapped on it three times. "Lady Penelope, may I enter?"

That voice. "Yes, of course, Count Vesone."

Godfrey nearly fell to his knees to thank heaven and all their saints for their help in finding her. Not least of all Saint Iudas, patron saint of hopeless causes. But he remembered himself, and hoped the Count didn't notice.

"Are you coming, Friar?" Vesone asked in a low voice.

Godfrey swallowed. "I will stay here, and observe unseen. If the devil sees me, he will surely recognise me, and perhaps set the poor girl upon me, where she might be hurt."

The Count nodded. "Very well." He strode into the room, and asked Penelope about her weaving.

Godfrey edged into the room, placing himself behind a large screen that presumably blocked draughts from the door, and looked his fill.

She was dressed in dove grey, which made

her brilliant hair stand out all the more. She kept her eyes down on her loom as she told Vesone about her work. A soft smile played about her lips, just as it had when she'd listened to Godfrey's stories.

Perfect Penelope, showing no signs of madness or ill health. His prayers were answered.

After a while, the Count finished his conversation, and made to leave. Godfrey hustled out of the way before she saw him, for if she recognised him and called him by name, the Count would know he had been tricked.

When the door closed behind him, the Count shook his head. "Madness has taken hold of her wits completely, I am afraid. She speaks of cloth that does not exist, yet to listen to her, one would believe she could see it! Is it the devil, or a curse, Friar? And, more importantly, can you cure it?"

Cloth that did not exist? There was a tale his uncle had once told him about such cloth. Cloth sold by a greedy Rialto merchant to a particularly prideful emperor. A pretence, so that those who knew the merchant might see the emperor as he truly was.

Penelope could be feigning madness, but why would she do so? He needed to speak to her alone.

Godfrey deepened his frown. "I am not certain. I must know more. Tell me, how often does she attend church?"

"Never. Why, she has not even been to confession, though it is Lent."

Godfrey nodded thoughtfully. "See that she attends confession tomorrow. With Father Danilo's help, I will prepare a trap for the devil, if indeed there is a devil, and force the beast out of her."

It was the Count's turn to frown. "And if you cannot?"

"Pray that I can, my lord."

Thirty-One

"The Count says you must dress for church, milady, and prepare for confession," the maid told her when she brought Penelope's breakfast.

Oh, how many sins she would have to confess. Or was that conceal?

Feigning madness, striking a prince, wishing the prince would choke on his dinner and die, her satisfaction at the magician's death…the list was long, and not one she cared to confess to a priest who might tell all of it to Vesone.

She chose to wear the green gown, trimmed with gold, as she'd finished sewing it only yesterday. No one but she and the maid would see it, though, for she left the tower shrouded in one of the dowager's dark mourning cloaks.

Half a dozen of Vesone's men surrounded her to shepherd her into town. Not to the church, but the monastery. None of the men seemed to know why, for their minds were filled with more questions than her own. They left her at the door, where she was escorted by a single monk to the refectory.

She almost told him she had no need for an escort, for this building was the twin of Saint Angelo. She'd heard a tale that Saint Angelo had originally been built for monks, who had given it to their sisters when a more suitable site, closer to the city, had been gifted to the community. Now she saw the truth of it.

Yet this refectory had one item that the one at Saint Angelo did not – an ornately carved confessional, where laypeople might confess their sins to the priests in the community, and receive absolution at the hands of these holy men.

The monk opened the door for her, and then closed it when she was inside. Trapped inside a tiny box, barely big enough for one person…oh, there was a good reason why she only endured this once a year.

The priest was no less fearful as he entered his own wooden cell.

"Forgive me, Father, for I have sinned. It has been close to a year since my last confession," she began, wondering what to say next.

"Tell me your sins, child," the priest prompted.

The priest's fear increased, and Penelope took a moment to work out why.

She almost laughed when she realised he was frightened of her. Well, not her exactly, but the demon he believed possessed her, driving her to madness. And he had some sort of plan to rid her of the creature, a plan that involved both the Count and a newcomer to the community, a holy man whose business was disposing of demons.

"Child?" the priest repeated.

Penelope shook her head. If the priest meant to hand her over for the ministrations of some quack, she fully intended to make him question his own conscience, too. "My greatest sin is overwhelming fear, Father. Fear that the plan in place for me will be more than I can bear. Fear that that I may never go home again. Fear that I will be held prisoner here…I fear every day, Father, that those who profess to help me do not have my best interests at heart, and that I am wrong to have faith in them and their plans for me." Even Dalia the seer expected too much of her. She was one woman – how could she be the one to make kingdoms rise and fall? Elevate not one, but five queens?

"You must have faith, child, in God's plan, and no other…" He thought she referred to the demon and its plans, not his own. Or hers.

"I fear I have lost my faith, Father. And I know not where to find it."

He seemed satisfied with this response. "Then that will be your penance. You will pray until your faith once again finds you."

No, that didn't make sense. "But, Father – "

The door to her cell opened, and a strong hand grasped hers.

"My brother will take you to my private chapel, where you will remain in prayer until your faith is renewed," the priest said.

"No – "

Do not resist, my lady, and your prayers will be answered, along with my own.

The words hung in the air, unspoken, yet clear in her mind.

She stared at the monk who held her hand. With his face hidden beneath his cowl, she could see nothing but the strong fingers that enveloped hers.

Come with me, my lady.

She wished she had the power to push her own thoughts into the minds of others, instead of the other way around. She would tell his man to stay out of her head and shove his prayers up his own arse. She bit down hard to stop the words from leaving her lips.

The monk bowed his head in obedience – almost as if he'd heard her! – and moved away, tugging her after him.

Try as she might, she could not break free from his grip. She would be forced to follow him.

He pulled her into a short passage, then kicked the door shut behind them. Only then did he tug off his cloak and drop it on the floor.

Godfrey stood before her, grinning.

Her mouth dropped open, and no words came out.

Please do not say you have lost faith in me, my lady. I have searched so long to find you.

She threw her arms around his neck and kissed him. Not the tentative sort of kiss they'd shared in her father's house, all those years ago, but something crafted out of all-consuming passion and fire that burned all her doubts away.

"Get me out of here, Godfrey," she begged, breathless.

He pressed a finger to his lips, and pulled her though the passage and down into the chapel proper. Candles sat on every surface, with filled candelabras forming a rough circle around the centre of the floor. Someone had scrawled strange symbols on the flagstones, in what looked like a mix of chalk and blood.

"Godfrey, what – "

He shook his head, his finger not leaving his lips.

The priest is listening. He has never performed an exorcism before, and hopes to learn how by spying upon us. And the Count sent his own spy, a young squire who hid behind the confessional, so that he might hear what you said. I know he has not gone far…

The clear images in his mind illustrated the tale. Godfrey had mistaken Prince Magnus for a squire – what a blow to the boy's pride, if he but knew.

I have a plan, but in order for it to work, we will need the enchanted horse. Do you know where it is?

Penelope shook her head. She hadn't seen it since the day the magician died. When blood had bubbled up from his mouth, as he'd gasped for his last breath…

Even closing her eyes could not shut the image out. Her lips sought Godfrey's, so that she might lose herself in the warmth of his embrace. The warmth of his thoughts, as he wrapped his arms around her, before he pushed her up against a low wall of some sort, his body pressed against hers, the heat of them together more than she could bear, and yet…and yet, she wanted to lean back, to open herself to him, in every way possible…and he…he wanted…

To make love to her on the altar.

By all that was holy, they could not do something so wicked!

I did not know you could do that.

She looked up at him, a question in her eyes.

I heard you, as clearly as if you'd spoken the words aloud. Just like when you said I should shove my prayers…

Her cheeks flamed.

Please forgive me. You may not have guessed, but I have attempted few quests, and I have not yet succeeded in completing any of them. I promised your father and you that I would bring you safely home, and I mean to do so. But if you do not know where the horse is…

Penelope took a deep breath, then lifted her lips to his ear. "The Count has it. He had his servants bring it to the castle, but he locked it away, for he fears it."

She felt the sigh gust out of him, as relief relaxed his shoulders. Then all she could feel was his lips on hers as he whirled her around, incoherent with joy.

Her heart swelled within her chest, sharing his joy…or expressing her own? Who could say? Reading the secrets of her heart was her gift… Dalia's words washed over her, revealing the truth she had not known until now.

It wasn't joy, or not just joy. Her heart swelled with love for Godfrey, the knight who would save her, whatever the cost.

She bit her lip, tasting blood, then fixed her gaze on Godfrey's face. *Do whatever you must to free me of this place. I trust you.*

He bowed deeply. *I am honoured by your trust, my lady.*

Thirty-Two

His lips burned from her kisses. Though he knew he was not worthy of a single one, he had not been able to resist her. Nor had he wanted to.

But when she'd said she trusted him, he knew her honour depended on him finding the fortitude to play the part he'd created for himself.

So he did not allow his lips to linger on hers for another moment, no matter how he longed for her touch. He donned his hooded monk robe once more, willing her to trust him still, as he scooped her up in his arms.

She stared at him, shocked.

I am going to tell them I attempted an exorcism, but the demon fought so hard, I feared it might kill you. You swooned, and I will wait until you wake before I try again. Tomorrow.

She nodded in understanding, then lay back in his arms in a most artful swoon.

He would have given everything he owned to see her lying in his arms like this. Now, he didn't want to let go.

If you let go, I shall fall, so I implore you, do NOT let go. He could even hear her tart tone, as though she'd spoken the words aloud.

Never, my lady.

If only she could be his lady…

He half expected the guards waiting outside the monastery gates to take Penelope from him, but they kept a healthy distance from her as they surrounded him, and escorted them back to the castle. He carried her up the tower stairs and laid her on her bed, cloak, boots and all, wishing he dared to steal one more kiss, but he could feel the maid hovering behind him, waiting to tend to her mistress. He had to force himself to leave her chamber and close the door.

The Count pounced on him. "Is she healed?"

Lady Penelope was as perfect as the day he first met her, he wanted to say but did not dare, or all this would be for naught.

Godfrey sighed deeply and hung his head. "The devil within her is uncommonly strong. We fought long and hard, until her delicate body could take no more, and she fell into a deep swoon. But before she did, the devil said he had been driven from his true vessel by a magician, and had been forced to possess the girl against his will. His true vessel was much larger, a sort of sinister, dark horse, or so he said." He tried to appear puzzled. "Have you ever seen such a thing? Or has the girl?"

Vesone slumped. "Yes, there was a large, wooden horse where we found her. I feared it was something dangerous, so I locked it in the dungeons."

Godfrey forced himself to look surprised. "So there is such a thing? Demons are so skilled at lying, I suspected there would not be, but if there is…we must take the chance. Both the girl and the demon will be weak for some days yet, so we should act quickly. Let her sleep now, but when she wakes, have her and the horse brought to the town square, along with all the incense you can find. Then, I shall force the demon from her and into the horse, before I burn it to ash."

Vesone bowed deeply. "If you succeed in curing her, you will have my gratitude, and that of His Highness as well. As men of your order do not marry, perhaps a different reward will be offered…"

Godfrey shook his head. "Freeing the maiden of this diabolical taint will be reward enough." Lies, every word. He hoped the Count did not know it.

"You are truly a saint," the Count said.

Oh, if only he knew.

Thirty-Three

"My lady, you must wake. If you cannot walk, the master's men will carry you. Maybe even the prince himself."

Little toad. The distasteful thought of the prince made Penelope open her eyes. She'd rather throw herself from the top window of the tower than let the prince get his hands on her.

Especially after Godfrey's kisses yesterday, before he'd carried her in his arms…

She wished she truly was the swooning type, so that she might sleep and dream of it all over again. But it was tomorrow, the morrow

Godfrey had promised her, when he would take her home.

She wore the green gown again, and the cloak she'd made, with a pair of boots the dowager no longer needed. Just like yesterday, guards surrounded her for the short walk to town, but instead of the monastery, they took her to the town square, where a number of bonfires had been prepared. They circled around the familiar figure of the enchanted horse.

A number of townspeople stood in the square, asking whispered questions of one another. None seemed to know why there were bonfires or a horse, until someone spotted her.

"They're going to burn the devil out of that girl."

She wasn't sure whether the man had spoken aloud or merely thought the words, but the statement spread like wildfire until everyone seemed to be staring at her in a mix of fear, excitement and dread. None of them had seen an exorcism before, or a devil, but they were determined to witness this.

As long as they didn't truly mean to burn

her.

Godfrey wouldn't do that.

But if this wasn't his doing…

Two guards pushed her into the circle and backed away from the wood piles.

She whirled, just in time to see the first bonfire kindle into flame. All around her, torches were thrust into the oil soaked branches, until they belched out smoke, rising up into the sky.

She wanted to back away, but the fire blazed on all sides. There was nowhere to run.

Her back hit something hard. The enchanted horse. She climbed onto its back, reaching for the nail that would draw her blood.

Please, do not leave without me, my lady. Godfrey slid onto the horse's back behind her, wrapping both arms about her waist.

The smoke was so thick, she could not see the crowd, though she could hear their shouts. She and Godfrey rose up, level with the rooftops, then higher still, following the smoke that hid them until they reached the clouds.

Safe. Free.

Thank all that was holy, for her courage was

spent.

Penelope burst into tears, letting her fear drain out of her with the endless salt water. Somehow, she'd turned to bury her face in Godfrey's tunic, and his arms around her were exactly the kind of comfort she needed.

"Lady Penelope, with your permission, I would like to take you somewhere you will be safe, where you can rest, a stop along the way to taking you home to Rialto."

It took her a moment to realise he'd spoken aloud. She swallowed, her throat dry and scratchy from the smoke. "Yes," she managed to say.

She felt Godfrey reach forward over the horse's neck, heard his gasp as the nail drew blood. Then the horse turned beneath them, heading to the destination of his desire.

As long as it had a bed and water to wash with, she would be happy, was her last coherent thought as she drowsed in his arms.

Thirty-Four

Lady Penelope was still asleep when the wooden horse landed in the courtyard outside Godfrey's father's castle. The place had not changed a bit – not that he'd expected it to.

No servant came to see to his horse, but it wasn't as though this one needed feeding, grooming or even rest. Penelope probably did, though, so he took her up the servants' stair to Melisende's chamber. He did not dare undress her, but he took the liberty of removing her boots, and unfastening her cloak, before laying it atop her for a coverlet.

He left her there, where no one would

disturb her, and went to wash and change into fresh clothes. Questioning the first servant he found, Godfrey discovered his father was at dinner in the Great Hall, and he hastened to join him.

His father's booming laughter rang out. Godfrey tensed. His brothers must be home, then. They would not be happy to see him, for surely Father would have told them about his part in Melisende's death. Poor Melisende – he had failed her in life, and now in death, too, for he would never redeem her honour now. It was a miracle Penelope trusted him, given what a failure he'd been.

Now he had to admit his failure to his father.

Godfrey threw open the doors of the Great Hall, and marched in.

"Godfrey! Is that truly you? We thought you were dead!"

Godfrey bowed to his father. "No, by some miracle, I still live and breathe, Father."

"It must be a miracle, for I just finished telling the Baron of Mareschal how you died of your wounds, after you slew Sir Enguerrand and his companions."

Godfrey blinked. At his father's right hand sat Zoticus. Who…had just said Enguerrand and the Unholy Trinity were dead? Along with he himself…

The slightest nod from Zoticus confirmed his suspicions. All four were slain by Zoticus's hand. Which meant…Melisende's honour was restored.

"So, by what miracle are you here? When I saw you fall that final time, I could have sworn you were dead, or I would not have told your father so," Zoticus said.

It took him a moment to put Zoticus's words together in his head and make sure his story matched.

Godfrey managed a pained smile. "I thought so, too, my friend, but it seems the world is not done with me yet. I woke up on a healer's cot on a ship, wishing I was dead, but most assuredly alive. When the ship landed in Rialto, I was well enough to pay my respects to the Duke, who sent me on a quest to recover his daughter." Godfrey accepted a cup of wine. "The lady is tired from her ordeal, so she is resting upstairs right now. We will continue our journey in the morning. And what of you, my friend? I thought you were intent on freeing the Holy Land."

Zoticus shrugged. "It seems the Holy Land will be harder to free than we hoped it would be. A Seljuk army, numbering in the millions, swept down on us from out of nowhere, and slaughtered many of us where we stood. If it were not for your horse with her winged feet, I might not have made it through the battle, let alone back here to bring the news to your father of your successful quest to redeem your sister's honour."

It took Godfrey a long moment to understand what the man had said. Luckily, he did not have to swallow his surprise, for there was more than enough news to astound anyone. "The crusade is over? And you brought Pegasus home?"

Zoticus nodded.

"Thank you." The words came out flat as Godfrey sat down, overwhelmed. "I am in your debt."

Zoticus waved the debt away. "Nonsense. We are friends. Your horse saved my life. I brought her home. Debt repaid."

Godfrey made polite conversation for a few

more minutes before he found his eyelids sagging, threatening to put him to sleep. He excused himself, and headed up to his own bedchamber.

They would have a long way to go in the morning, but for now, both he and Penelope could sleep safely.

And Melisende's soul might know repose, too.

Thirty-Five

Penelope woke in a room with corners. Definitely not her tower room.

"Are you awake, Your Highness?"

She didn't recognise the curtseying maid, either.

"Where am I?" Penelope asked.

"Mistress Melisende's room, at the Baron of Maraschal's castle. Sir Godfrey ordered me to attend you. I wasn't sure if you wanted to dress or break your fast first. I was only in training to be Mistress Melisende's maid. I never thought I might have the honour of serving a princess." She curtseyed so low, she could have sat cross-legged on the floor.

"I'm not a princess. I'm Lady Penelope of Rialto."

The maid did not rise. "Sir Godfrey said the titles were different where you come from. That they do not call you a princess, yet princes beg for the honour of your hand. Forgive me if I offend you, Your Highness."

It wasn't the maid's fault Godfrey had told her such things. "Where is Sir Godfrey now?"

"With the horses, as always. I can send for him, if that is your wish?"

Penelope shook her head. "No. Help me dress, then take me to him."

The maid agonised over the gowns that had once belonged to Mistress Melisende, none of which she thought was good enough for a princess, until Penelope pointed at one in pale blue wool and insisted upon it. She almost regretted her choice when the maid laced it up over her chemise, for it was obvious that Melisende had been much narrower in the chest than Penelope. As it was, the lacing pushed her breasts up and out, like the bawdiest tavern whore. Only by fastening her chemise close about her throat could Penelope manage any kind of modesty.

The maid slid silk hose up her legs while Penelope braided her own hair. She felt the maid's disappointment at not being able to try out what she imagined were court fashions, which was quickly eclipsed with horror as Penelope donned the dowager's boots she'd arrived in, but the girl did not say anything aloud.

Penelope hoped the girl might one day meet a real princess, who would undoubtedly fulfil all her dreams of grandeur. Penelope herself would never be royalty – had the seer not said so? The thought was more freeing than she'd thought it would be.

The maid led the way outside the castle walls, where fields held…what was the name of a group of horses? Was it a herd? She wasn't sure, but there sure were a lot of them. Prancing, dancing, and galloping about, their hooves making the most thunderous sounds as they hit the turf. So…wild.

She backed away from the energetic beasts, only to feel something warm and solid stop her retreat.

Something blew a gust of wind down her

shift from high above, and she shrieked.

"Easy, Pegasus. This is Lady Penelope, and I'm sure she doesn't appreciate you blowing your breakfast down the front of her gown."

There was straw caught in her lacings. Now she not only felt like a tavern whore, but one who'd taken a tumble in the hay. And here was Godfrey, holding the bridle of the most enormous white horse, beaming at her as though he had no idea what she was thinking.

"My sister would be green with envy if she ever saw how well that gown fits you. You look breathtaking, as always, my lady." Godfrey bowed.

From another man, it might have been empty flattery. From him, it was the honest truth.

"Would you like to join me for a ride?" He gestured at the field of frolicking horses. "Pegasus here is the fastest, and my favourite, but you may choose any of them you wish. That bay over there will be sent to Emperor Frederick, once the beast is gelded and trained, and the king in Kasmirus has laid claim to the next colt Pegasus produces. We don't sell breeding stock, only geldings, but the offers we've had for even a single Maraschal mare…it's more money than I've ever seen, that's for sure. But Father will not budge. With the exception of Pegasus, none of the mares leave Maraschal. And no one rides them but our family and those who work for us."

Hysterical laughter bubbled out of her. "Are you offering me a job, riding these capricious beasts I cannot even imagine how to control? I'd sooner go back to my tower than climb on the back of a beast with a mind of its own, and hooves that could crush my head!" She turned and hurried back to the safety of the castle.

"Penelope. Penelope, wait!"

If she turned around, she'd see those huge horses again. And the incredulous look on Godfrey's face. She did not want to hear his thoughts at that moment, his contempt at her fear of horses.

"Lady Penelope, have you never ridden a horse before? Not once?"

She stopped, not sure how to admit her shame.

"Of course, there are no roads in Rialto, and horses cannot walk on water. But I never imagined…" Godfrey paused. "Lady Penelope, would you do me the honour of allowing me to take you for your first horse ride? I promise to keep you safe. If any horse here should even think of harming you, I will see the beast butchered for the table before day's end."

She'd left whatever courage she possessed in that smoky town square yesterday. No. She shied away from his outstretched hand.

"Not even if we ride double, as we did on the enchanted horse? I would never let you fall, Penelope."

She swallowed. She knew every word was the truth, but…

"Emperors and kings would envy you, for this is an offer I have never made to anyone else. One ride, on the finest horse in the world. First around the field, and then, if you like, a bit longer. I would not offer if I didn't think you would enjoy it."

Oh, how could she refuse? He had done so much for her, and all he wanted was to share a simple pleasure that was the greatest gift he thought he could offer.

He grinned, as if she'd spoken into his mind. Perhaps she had. Godfrey swung up into the horse's saddle, and held out his arms to help her up.

By all that was holy…

She landed in his lap. He wasn't wearing armour today, but he didn't feel any less hard behind her or beneath her.

"Shouldn't I be sitting behind you? I thought that's what ladies do in stories about knights."

Godfrey burst out laughing. "If we're ever riding into a battle and I'm wearing armour, then you can sit behind me while I shield you. But if you're going to learn to ride today, you'll need to be the one in front, holding the reins. You're the knight in training, which I guess makes me…the lady."

She had to laugh at that. Just the thought of Godfrey in a gown…

Godfrey reached around her, his arms warm at her waist. "Now, hold the reins like this, and nudge the horse with your knees, like this."

The horse set off at a slow walk. Godfrey showed her how to persuade the horse to turn when they reached a corner of the field, but she suspected this one would have turned anyway. They made it back to their starting point without any mishaps, and she dared to relax.

"More?" Godfrey asked.

She swallowed and nodded.

"I'll take you on Pegasus's favourite trail," Godfrey said, steering the horse away from the castle. "No need to tell her what to do here, she knows the way. All you'll have to do is hang on."

He leaned forward, pushing her down against the horse's neck. For a moment, she resisted.

"Be easy, and lean into it," he murmured into her ear. "Read the horse's mind, if you will not read mine, and do what I do."

She relented, letting her body move with his, and the horse. It was almost soothing, the slow lumbering gait…

"Go," Godfrey breathed.

The horse burst into flight, in a flurry of thundering hooves and rushing wind and…and…Godfrey's laughter in her ear as he urged the horse on. Not that the beast needed the encouragement. For Penelope could feel the horse's mind, too, a rush of exhilaration at running so fast. It was almost as though man and mare shared the same thought…

A low stone wall approached at alarming speed. She felt muscles bunch, tighten, and all three of them went soaring over the top of it, with barely a pause in the mare's stride. She heard a whooping sound, and it took a moment to realise it came from her own mouth.

She could feel Godfrey laughing behind her, and she laughed right along with him. The wooden horse had never felt anywhere near as fast or as exciting as this.

When the horse felt she'd galloped enough, she started to slow down. By the time they reached the river, Penelope thought she could have matched pace with her, walking beside her. But she had no desire to move from her current position, wedged firmly between the man she loved and his horse.

Until the horse stopped beside the river, and dropped her head for a drink.

Only Godfrey's grip around her middle kept her from sliding into the river, face first. He swung her off the horse, then dismounted behind her.

There was a question in his eyes, but his thoughts were so tangled, she wasn't sure which one he wanted answered.

So, she said, "Thank you. For the ride, for your patience, and for not giving up on me."

"I could not let a woman of your courage, and your determination, remain in fear of one of the gentlest, noblest creatures that ever lived," Godfrey said. "You've ridden a flying horse, and it didn't daunt you at all. I clung to its back for a good half hour before I dared to open my eyes, and then I was so afraid of falling off I didn't dare move until it landed in your orchard. I've ridden real horses for as long as I can remember, and I was terrified of a wooden one." He ducked his head, not meeting her eyes.

"I know. While you were telling me about it in the kitchen, I was watching the memories that flashed through your mind."

"Then you know I'm not much of a knight. Horses I can handle, but quests and swords and all the other things are not my strength."

She smiled. "You saved me just fine. That makes you the finest knight I've ever known."

Godfrey didn't agree, but he had the good manners not to say it aloud. "But a poor host, taking you riding before breakfast. I should take you and Pegasus home, so you can enjoy proper Maraschal hospitality and Pegasus can get a rub down."

"Will Pegasus fly again?" she asked.

Godfrey eyed the horse. "Not willingly. She prefers open fields to the road, and the road is the fastest way back."

"Then will you be the knight this time, so I can experience being a lady?"

Godfrey laughed. "Even if you donned my armour, brandished a sword, and rode Pegasus into battle, you would still be very much a lady."

A lady who had to go home to Rialto, and do what was right. Make peace, marry, and make her father happy. Never mind whatever the future held for empires and queens. Oh, how she wished she could stay here with him. And his horse.

Perhaps if she thought hard enough, she might find a way to do all of those things.

Thirty-Six

Penelope settled deeper into Godfrey's arms as they flew, letting out a sigh of contentment. She couldn't explain why she felt so comfortable with a man she barely knew, yet she did. His embrace felt like the most natural place to be, and her thoughts strayed back to their kiss in the chapel. The sheer thrill, bubbling through her blood, as their lips touched, before the heat between them had burned deeper. Into a desire to do the unforgivable, and use the altar for a communion of body and soul that had nothing to do with the church or anyone else but the two of them. The reverence in his every touch had only made desire burn hotter, and now they were so close again, the fire had begun to smoulder within.

Of all the men in the world, Godfrey was the only one she wanted. And she had begun to believe she might be able to have him.

Penelope laughed softly. "I had begun to believe that all men below a certain age thought only with what lies between their legs, but – "

"Forgive me, Lady Penelope," Godfrey interrupted, and the delicious memory evaporated as though it had never been.

Suddenly bereft, it took her a moment to realise that the memory she'd seen was as much his as hers – they'd both been thinking about the same thing. So was the urge to lie down on the altar his idea or hers?

He continued, "I'd forgotten how you can read my thoughts, and being so close to you, I allowed my thoughts to wander into a place where they did not belong."

His thoughts fixed on an icy stream, and the memory of jumping into the water. So cold even she gasped, pressing back against him and the reassuring warmth that the immersion was no more than a memory.

"Your thoughts mirrored my own, and you're wrong. You're not like the other men I've known. Most of them think of mastering me, possessing me, with a violence like that suffered by your sister. They do not see a face, merely a body. They mean to leave me broken, beaten, conquered, my defences battered by what they believe is a mighty battering ram but is in fact little more than a piece of gristle." She shook her head to clear the images of Magnus, Marco, and even the magician's lustful thoughts. "But your thoughts are of me, of us, of the joy in coming together, touching, wanting…" The icy clouds they flew through were not enough to cool her flaming cheeks. "I think we should find a town with an inn."

Even as she voiced her wish, she felt the horse tilt beneath them, descending. Their descent pushed Godfrey even closer to her, and she could feel him hardening at the close contact. She wasn't sure which of them blushed more.

"Please forgive me," he breathed in her ear.

The steep walls of a hilltop town loomed

out of the dark, and they skimmed over the top of them, landing in a churchyard. She helped Godfrey push the horse between some bushes before taking his hand. "Now to find that inn," she said.

He pulled his hand out of her grasp. "Lady Penelope, we cannot. You are the daughter of a duke, a duchess of Rialto. Emperors and princes are willing to go to war for you, offering a world of wealth for the right to marry you. You are destined to be an empress, a queen. I am merely a knight, and a younger son at that. All your other suitors can offer you crowns, whereas all I can give you is a chamber to share with me in my father's castle, and perhaps a horse to ride. I may dream of becoming your lover, but your place is far loftier than my lowly bed. I lost my honour a long time ago, but I am honourable enough not to steal yours."

If she'd offered herself to Magnus, he would have stripped her naked by now. The magician would have done unspeakable things to her already. Yet Godfrey, sweet, honourable knight that he was, begged her to think of her own honour.

"I'm no duchess. Rank in Rialto is not like other places. My father's position is his alone, which he occupies only after the other nobles in Rialto voted to place him there. I'm as noble as you — Lady Penelope, the same rank as any knight. And so I shall remain. I will not marry the child prince of Byzas, to live in a pit of vipers, waiting for one to strike me down. I will not share a bed with that rabid cur Prince Magnus, a violent man-child who believes it is his right to have his way with women when they are unwilling." She took a deep breath. "If you truly wish to save me from a loveless marriage that will kill me as surely as any sword, then you must claim me for yourself. All honour demands is that you do so before a witness, a man of God, and that I am willing to do the same."

She felt hope rise in his breast, stealing his breath as, for a moment, he considered being granted his wish. A wish he did not believe he deserved.

Before Godfrey could protest, she marched up to the church's side door and rapped smartly on the timber. She could sense the sleepy priest inside, surprised by her knock, but coming to answer it anyway.

She threw back the hood of her cloak, smoothing her hair and straightening her clothes. The priest would not see much in the darkness, so she would need to convey everything with her voice alone.

The door swung open, and the priest lifted a lantern so that he could squint at them. "Yes?"

Penelope lifted her chin. "Good evening, Father. We wish to be married. Immediately."

The priest opened his mouth to protest.

She reached for the pouch of coins at Godfrey's belt and pulled out a handful. "We will pay you well for your trouble."

The door opened wider. "Come in."

The priest led them to the altar, and Godfrey grasped her shoulder. "Are you sure about this?" he hissed.

She merely gave voice to the thoughts running through his head, for they were no different to her own. "Marriage is for life. What God has united, no man can break apart. Be he emperor or prince or duke. You can refuse to take the oath, but I know my heart, and this is the future I choose. Marry me, Godfrey, and I will be your wife. Yours to protect…and to love."

"Are you ready to say your vows?" the priest asked.

Penelope nodded. After a moment, so did Godfrey.

"Then kneel," the priest commanded.

The priest asked for her vow. She knew her eyes were supposed to be fixed on the cross behind the altar, but she could not help looking at Godfrey.

"I vow to love and honour you, all the days of my life," she said, squeezing their joined hands. Oh, how she wished he could read her thoughts. Then he'd know she longed for this as much as he did. It might be madness, but it was the kind of madness she wanted her life long.

He wet his lips, lifting his eyes to meet her gaze. "I vow to love, honour and protect you, all the days of my life," he said.

The priest said a few more words, before pronouncing them married. United.

She wasn't sure which was more powerful – Godfrey's exultation, or her own. Did it matter?

She reached out with her mind for the inn,

and found it beside the closed city gates. They were as surprised as the priest to see them, but the innkeeper was happy to accept gold in exchange for a meal and his best room.

He sent servants up with warm water to wash with, and a meal neither of them were hungry for yet. They only wanted each other.

Godfrey shooed the servants out and bolted the door.

Their eyes met and Penelope couldn't suppress her grin. "Kiss me. Please."

It was but a moment and she was in his arms again, her lips meeting his as naturally as they had in the chapel. Only this time, they would not be parted again.

Thirty-Seven

Penelope could have kissed Godfrey forever, but even newlyweds had to pause for breath. And Godfrey had more in mind than kissing, which set her cheeks aflame all over again.

"My lady, let me wash away all the memories of your ordeal." He gestured for her to sit down.

Obediently, she did.

Godfrey stood behind her, then set his hands on her shoulders and leaned forward. "I will spend the rest of my life trying to earn the precious gift you have given me," he whispered, sliding his fingers down so they rested over her collarbone.

He meant herself, Penelope realised, finding it hard to read his thoughts amid the cloud of her own desire. She wanted him to move his hands lower, to cup her breasts, to…

He unfastened her cloak, then moved away from her to hang it up. She barely had a moment to register his absence before he knelt at her feet. Off came her boots, until he cupped her stockinged foot in his hands. The silk had felt substantial enough while they were flying, but now it might as well be as ephemeral as mist, melting away in the heat of his touch as his fingers slid up her leg. Her garter halted him, but only for a moment before he ventured higher still, laying a hand on her bare thigh.

A question burned in his eyes and she had to concentrate to see the thought forming in his mind. If her stockings only went up to her knees, and he had his hands beneath all her skirts, he had only to lift them higher and she would be bare to the waist and ready for him…

She trembled at the thought, but she swallowed and nodded. Never had she been so nervous, and at the same time so eager. If he were to lift her skirts and move between her thighs, she would willingly rise to meet him. Maybe even leap into his lap.

Godfrey smiled as though he could read her thoughts now, then lowered his hand to untie her garter. He slid her stocking off slowly, stroking the silk down her skin until she shivered again, before he did the same with her other stocking. Now she knew why women covered their ankles in public. To feel the breeze caress her skin like her husband was now would drive her to distraction. Was driving her to distraction.

He lifted the hem of her skirts, bundling them into her lap to bare her legs.

Yes. Oh, yes. Please.

Godfrey laughed softly, then reached for the jug of water and a cloth. "Time to wash away the travel dust and the memories," he said, a moment before the warm, damp cloth touched her thigh. With deft strokes, he washed her leg from hip to heel, drawing ever closer to her most secret places, without actually touching her there. One leg, then the other, leaving her skin tingling and the rest of her aching for its turn.

He set the water on the table and clambered to his feet, then held out his hands. "Rise, my lady."

Her skirts tumbled down about her ankles, covering her again, yet she'd never felt so naked. The ghostly echo of his caresses even as his hands held hers, combined with the hunger in his eyes as he looked at her, saw her…it stole her breath away.

She threw her arms around his neck and kissed him. His hand cupped the back of her neck as he deepened the kiss. A thousand butterflies burst into flight in her breast, as he unfastened her shift and bared her neck and shoulders. But for the lacing of her gown, he would have exposed her breasts as well. Her fingers moved almost of their own accord to rectify the situation, but he caught her hands in his and looped them around his neck once more.

"Patience, my lady," he said, reaching for the wash cloth.

She closed her eyes as he stroked the cloth over her shoulders, down her throat, tracing her collarbone before caressing the tops of her breasts. Then the cloth was gone, replaced by his lips, kissing a trail of fire across her skin. Penelope threw her head back and moaned aloud.

He could just pick her up, push up her skirts and pin her against the wall. She would open to him like a flower to the sun, like a…

Like a prostitute in an alley, down by the docks.

The thought was his, not hers, but it was tinted with amusement. He was teasing her, deliberately imagining things that might make her change her mind. Almost as if he wished she would come to her senses and see him for what he was.

A brave, honourable knight who had come to save her when no one else would. Her knight, and now her husband.

She would meet his challenge, for she had read the thoughts of sailors and whores alike. And she intended to enjoy her first night with him far more than any prostitute who had to fake her pleasure for her customers' coin. "I believe 'tis cheaper to have stand-up sex in an alley than in a bed in a brothel. But if my husband insists, the alley behind the inn is empty at the moment…"

Godfrey's mouth dropped open with shock. He hadn't expected such salty language from his convent-raised lady. He recovered quickly. "When I make love to you for the first time, it shall be in a bed. For if you truly are determined to consummate this marriage, madness though it may be, I will give you no cause to regret your choice."

From levity to seriousness in a moment, yet even with her blood fair boiling with desire, she knew this was the wisest course. "I have no regrets," she said simply, undoing the lacings of her gown before he could stop her. Her clothes wilted to the floor, along with any whispering doubts she might have had. She stood naked before him, arms spread. "Behold, your willing bride."

He looked her up and down for a long moment, his thoughts revealing nothing but the curves of her body, pale skin that had never seen the sun now revealed in the lantern light for him alone.

"Just an ordinary woman. Not worth waging a war over." She managed a small smile, hoping her equally small jest might provoke some reaction from him.

He reached for the jug of wine, then poured himself a cup. He lifted it to his lips as he regarded her again. Godfrey drank deeply, his thoughts darting about her body like a swarm of bees. The silkiness of her skin, the pink pearls of her nipples, the tight curls at the juncture of her thighs, the weight of her breasts in his hands, the softness of her behind as he pulled her to him, the flush of her cheeks as her eyes kindled with desire, piercing his very soul with longing.

His soul, or hers? She wasn't sure any more where his thoughts ended and hers began.

"Restraint be damned. I cannot resist you any longer," he growled. He seized her and kissed her. She expected him to be rough, but his every movement was firm and deliberate. He would never hurt her.

She pressed against him, gasping as her tender nipples rasped against his tunic, a new one he'd brought from home. Better than being dressed like a friar, a man vowed to celibacy. That would never do.

It was her turn to lift his hem, to tug the tunic over his head and throw it onto the floor.

Then her turn to gasp again as she traced the muscles he'd hidden beneath the shapeless garment. Why, he was built like the ancient statues, all hard ridges, but warm like no statue she'd ever seen. She hadn't believed it was possible to want him more, and yet...

He scooped her up effortlessly and tossed her onto the bed, where she found she could regard him properly, so she just lay back on her elbows and looked.

A wry smile twisted his lips, as he spread his arms wide, just as she had. "Behold, your knight without his armour."

Fine muscles indeed, with a trail of hair that led into his hose and further...hardness. Her cheeks heated again, searing her mouth to desert dryness. She wanted to tell him to take off his hose, to come to bed, to kiss her, to claim her, to do all the things he'd dreamed about and more, but her voice seemed to have died. "Please," she whispered, the only word she could say.

The hose vanished as if by magic, and he lay his body beside hers on the bed. He slid a finger under her chin, lifting her eyes to meet his, and all individual thoughts were lost. She was his, and he was hers, two waves crashing together in an ocean of desire that consumed them both. Utterly. Completely.

When the swirling, tempestuous waves within her reached their peak, she found her voice again, screaming Godfrey's name until she had no breath left. But he was there, kissing the breath back into her body, coaxing her to new, undreamed-of heights until he, too, shouted her name to the heavens, and it seemed that two souls were truly one.

Thirty-Eight

The sun was well and truly risen by the time Godfrey and Penelope managed to get the enchanted horse into the sky again. No matter how much he told himself they should hurry, he could not seem to bring himself to care. She was his willing wife, madness though it seemed, and no one could take away the pleasure they'd shared last night. Truly, he did not deserve her.

"What is THAT? It looks like…a wave coming in and swallowing the road, or…I don't know. And there's another one over there, too…"

Godfrey followed her pointing finger. "That's an army on the move. Two armies on the move. Both headed for Rialto." Dread curdled in his stomach. "But Rialto has warships and defences, right?" He peered across the water. "I can see the ships now!"

Penelope leaned forward, squinting. "Rialto has no warships at the moment, not since Duke Vitale died. Father hasn't commissioned a new war fleet yet. Those are Northmen vessels, built for rougher and deeper seas than ours. Which would mean…three armies headed for Rialto."

Her calm tone was maddening. Perhaps she didn't know what an army could do to a city. What the infidels had done to the Holy City. What the crusaders had done to…everywhere they went.

"We have to do something. Warn them. Or we won't be safe here." You won't be safe here.

Penelope shook her head. "Rialto is not like other cities. No army has ever taken it, and they will not do so now. We will fly to my father's palace, and tell him what is coming. And then…we wait. For them to send their envoys. Then the negotiations will begin."

"But they have armies…"

"Armies cannot walk on water, and those deep water ships cannot negotiate the shoals and shallows of the Rialto lagoon. There are not enough gondolas in the lagoon to transport one army, let alone three, and even then, they might not be willing to pay the boatmen's price." She patted Godfrey's arm. "I may not know much about swords or horses or battle, but I was born in Rialto, raised listening to merchants making bargains every minute of every day. When the envoys come, and they will, I will work out what they want, and are willing to sacrifice for it. I will tell you, and you will advise my father and his council accordingly. When there are three armies camped around Rialto, the safest place to be is Rialto itself. You shall see."

Either she was incredibly naïve, or she knew more about politics than Godfrey could even imagine. Neither was a particularly comforting thought, but, because he had no better plan, he headed for the Ducal Palace. For whatever the armies meant to do, he had a quest to fulfil.

Thirty-Nine

By the time they reached the Ducal Palace, Father was already busy with his council, and the reception hall was full of important people, also waiting their turn to see him.

Penelope settled in for a long wait, made more pleasant when the servants recognised her and brought refreshments.

"How long will this take?" Godfrey asked, peering at the other groups, unaware that he'd said the same thing as three other men at almost the exact same time.

Penelope shrugged. "As long as it takes. It looks like the armies sent envoys ahead of them, and most of them are already here. The Northmen…they are upset because they heard Emperor Frederick's son was to marry me instead of their king's sister, as there is a longstanding betrothal. All Emperor Frederick has to do is agree to celebrate the marriage immediately, and they will be satisfied.

"Now, Frederick's people are less easy to please. Your father received Count Vesone's letter, and sent his answer to Prince Magnus, who considers his refusal a great insult to himself and his father. He has persuaded his brothers and their army to support him, but all he really wants is to marry some woman other than the Northmen's king's sister. I think the betrothal is with his older brother, anyway, but I can't be sure.

"Oh, and there's the matter of Frederick's claim to the title of Emperor. It appears the present Pope has not approved it, and Frederick is willing to negotiate with him to make things official. But in order to do that, he'll need the support of the Northmen, and Rialto. Perhaps even Emperor Manuel, as well. So even if they've ostensibly come here at Magnus's insistence, they have more important things to discuss.

"The army from Byzas...now they're interesting. The Emperor still holds our people in his prison, but he's willing to negotiate for their release if we hand him...hmm, I believe he wants the magician. And possibly his flying horse. He's come here in search of him because Gabrieli admitted to being from Rialto, and he was headed this way when he left Byzas.

"Ah, but Emperor Manuel has a problem. If he releases our people, they will demand compensation for their stolen goods and businesses, and that will beggar the royal treasury, so he will be willing to do anything for gold to fill those empty coffers, up to and including marrying his young sons to rich women. The Northmen bride comes with a crown, but little dowry, which is why he wanted me. When he finds out I am already married, he will look elsewhere – likely to Emperor Frederick, who might have an eligible daughter or two. Manuel's daughter might do for Magnus – she's old enough for marriage, and has a peculiar hobby involving torture implements in her father's dungeons, so the two of them should get along nicely.

"So…with a few marriage alliances, and a fair bit of gold changing hands, we can probably send most of them away from here, not entirely unhappy."

Godfrey shook his head. He would never understand politics like she did. Never. "And what does Rialto want?"

She smiled. "Oh, the same as always. More autonomy, fewer tariffs and taxes. More opportunities to make money. My father and his council are all from good merchant families – they will act to further Rialto's trade interests. Merely hosting these negotiations will increase Rialto's power immeasurably, for it is in all their interests to see Rialto endure, to prolong the peace."

"And what about the Pope? What will he want?"

Penelope laughed. "A man of God, head of the church…I am sure he wants many holy things, as is proper. But most of all, he will want a new crusade, particularly after the failure of this last one, and he knows Rialto is the best port to launch one from. If Rialto calls, he will come, and at least listen to what these kings and emperors have to say. So that when he or his successor calls for another crusade, Rialto will rebuild its war fleet, and answer his call."

"Lady Penelope, Duke Sebastiano will see you now."

This earned them the animosity of most of the other men in the room, but this didn't seem to bother Penelope. She followed her father's man to his office, where she abandoned all decorum and ran to embrace her father.

The Duke did not want to let her go, holding her at arm's length as he studied her face, her clothes, and even her boots.

"Are you well?" he asked cautiously.

Penelope laughed. "Well enough to try to sell a man the finest Rialto lace, so fine only men who are truly noble may see it. My ill luck that Count Vesone was an honest man, who thought me mad when he could not see the cloth."

The Duke managed a weak smile. "And the rogue who kidnapped you?"

"Gabrieli is dead. Slain by Magnus, one of Emperor Frederick's sons. I believe Emperor

Manuel offered his daughter in marriage to the man who could bring him Gabrieli's head, so you might want to suggest the alliance yourself."

Sebastiano nodded thoughtfully. "I suspect you have quite a tale to tell. I fear I have little time to spare today, but if your tale might help to explain why three armies are circling our fair city, perhaps I must make the time."

The Duke called for refreshments, before Penelope and Godfrey told their tale.

Finally, Godfrey reached the part where they'd arrived at his father's house, and reached over to pour another cup of wine, but the jug was empty.

"I fear there is little more to tell, Father, for I know you are busy. I have never seen your reception hall so full," Penelope said.

Sebastiano nodded, then turned to Godfrey. "Thank you. I cannot express how grateful I am that you brought her back. If there is ever anything I can do for you…"

Godfrey swallowed. It was now or never. "There is only one thing I would ask of you. A small thing, really. I – "

"We," Penelope interrupted, squeezing

Godfrey's hand.

"We would like to ask you to bless our marriage."

Father suddenly grew very still. Then he shook himself and said, "Sir Godfrey, would you be so kind as to take the wine jug and find a servant who will refill it? I can't imagine where they have all gone to."

Godfrey glanced at her and registered her slight nod before taking the wine jug. "Of course, Monsignor."

He slipped out of the room.

Father considered several suitable ways to start the conversation, but Penelope had waited long enough.

She wet her lips. "The Byzas princes are children, their treasury is empty, and it is only a matter of time before a palace coup occurs. Frederick's elder sons might be nice enough, but they have a feudal government that we have no desire to see here. To marry one of them would put Rialto at risk. Gabrieli, Marco, and all the young merchants or merchants' sons here…they would want my dowry, and even I know it was lost somewhere in the northern seas. My brothers would not allow you to beggar the family business to make another family rich. Was there ever anyone you considered good enough to marry me?"

Father sighed. "You're right. No, I never met a man I considered good enough for you. The one thing you asked me for, a husband who will make you happy, that I cannot give you."

"Sir Godfrey makes me happy. He searched everywhere until he found me, and stole me from under the nose of Prince Magnus himself, who planned to force me into marriage."

"But…a horse trader?"

Penelope smiled. "We visited his family home. His father is a feudal baron, it's true, but Godfrey has older brothers who will inherit the title, while he is merely a knight. And the horses – such horses! The finest ever bred. Emperor Frederick knows the value of them already, and Emperor Manuel can be made to know it, in time. There is some value in being the merchant who represents both the buyers' and the breeders' interests, particularly when many of them are kings."

"You should have been born a boy. I swear,

you are more astute than your brothers, when it comes to some things."

"But then I wouldn't be able to be your favourite daughter. Or Sir Godfrey's wife."

Father's forehead crinkled. "Do you truly wish to marry the man? Will he make you happy?"

Penelope rose. "Godfrey and I are already married, and he does make me happy." And if you give us your blessing, we will stay until the peace treaties are signed, but if you do not, we shall leave, she thought as she fixed her gaze on her father.

He sighed. "I will tell the servants to prepare a guest apartment for you both here in the palace. I have plans for the campo, and I would love to ask you what you think."

Penelope beamed. "Thank you, Father."

Forty

The summer sun shone on Penelope's bare feet as she dangled them over the canal. The enchanted horse lurked beneath the surface, ready to be buried and forgotten when the canal was filled in on the morrow.

She reached for another peach. The trees had been moved to another island, and where they had once grown was now covered in cobblestones, set in such a way that they looked like fish scales. Soon, the whole campo, including the canal beneath her feet, would be paved over to become Saint Mark's Square, where two emperors, a Northman king, the

Pope, and her father would sign the peace treaties that divided the world between them. Three princes and three princesses would be married, and the hostilities would be over.

They would all stay to witness the annual ceremony where the Duke walked out to the edge of the sandbank protecting the city and said the city's marriage vows to the sea. This year, the Pope had not only agreed to officiate, but he'd given the Duke a gold ring to throw into the water to signify how he blessed the union.

It seemed almost an anticlimax to have weddings instead of a big battle, but that's how things were done in the Republic of Rialto.

"What do you want to do next?" Godfrey asked Penelope.

She threw her peach stone into the canal. "Hope there is something cool to drink in the kitchen. It used to be lovely here under the trees, but now the sun beats down on you unmercifully."

He chuckled. "I mean after the treaties are signed. Would you like to live here, or come home with me, where we can ride every day, or did you have some other adventure in mind?"

Penelope considered. "I would like to spend the rest of the summer somewhere cooler. And there's my dowry…My brothers used it to finance a shipping expedition to the northern seas, but the ship and cargo were taken by pirates, after reaching Beacon Isle. Once the treaty is signed, we could find a ship headed to northern waters, and see if we can find my dowry…along with the rest of the pirate treasure."

Godfrey laughed, then realised she hadn't joined him. "You mean you are serious?"

Penelope shrugged. "It's a sizeable sum. Well worth tracking down, so that any children we have might have the money to join my family business in Rialto, if that is their wish, or buy more breeding stock for your horse herds." She smiled. "More importantly, it is another adventure, where we will not have to worry about saving one another. Just…enjoy things as they happen. Will you take me on an adventure, Sir Godfrey? Just a knight and his lady, no one else?"

He could not refuse her anything, and she knew it. "If you want an adventure, my lovely lady wife, then you shall have one. I hear the pirates around Beacon Isle are quite lovely this time of year."

Steal:
Forty Thieves Retold

DEMELZA CARLTON

A tale in the Romance a Medieval Fairy Tale series

One

"These figures can't be right. Are you sure, Peter? I'm going to check them over again."

Peter pulled the ledger out of Mithra's hands. "Yes, they're correct. Father is going to be delighted. This month has to be the most profitable one he's ever known. War is good for business, contrary to anything those grumbling old men say in Rialto. Father was a wise man to leave his family behind and set up here. I would never have been born, because younger brothers aren't allowed to marry and have children, and you would be forced to take an apprenticeship under your sour old uncle. I bless whatever prophet, false or otherwise, who persuaded the Seljuk army to attack Edessa and leave us here at Dorylaeum as the largest city left trading with Rialto!" He jumped to his feet and spread his arms wide. "This war will make our fortunes, Mithra! And to celebrate, I'm taking you to dinner."

Mithra could not refuse such a generous offer, for while they might be fellow apprentices at present, Peter stood to inherit all of his father's substantial merchant business one day, and Mithra's father was a woodcutter whose most valuable possessions were the three donkeys and a handcart he used to collect firewood every day.

Not for the first time, Mithra wondered why his father had apprenticed him to a successful merchant like Simon, when he'd never have the money to buy trade goods to sell at a profit, like Simon or Mithra's uncle, Kasim.

Unless Mithra married a girl with a large dowry, as Kasim had. But Mithra's heart would not allow him to do something so mercenary. His parents had married for love and Mithra meant to do the same, if the girl of his heart's desire would have him. Speaking of which…

"There she is!" Peter said, gesturing toward the counter.

Cagri blushed prettily at something her customer had said, then tugged at her veil to cover a curl which had escaped. Mithra had a sudden vision of her curls all escaping at once, reaching for him and then twining about him like serpents, before bringing him to her as an offering. One look from her deep, dark eyes would hypnotise him so he felt no need to struggle out of her snare, and he would happily serve her all his days.

It was as though one of the ancient goddesses had been made mortal and forced to hand out bountiful trays of bread to the descendants of her former worshippers.

"Wipe your mouth – you're drooling again!" Peter hissed.

Mithra swiped his sleeve across his face, only to find it dry. He shot a hurt look that only made Peter grin wider.

"I can't blame you. Lechem's bakery has both the sweetest and the most savoury delights in the whole city." At another look from Mithra, Peter added, "I'm only talking about the food. You're the one who thinks Lechem's daughter is sweeter than any pastry. My father has some Rialto lady lined up to marry me, who will likely look elsewhere if she knows I even looked at another woman before I beheld her. To hear Father tell it, Rialto ladies are so jealous they should all wear green!"

Mithra managed a smile, but he didn't feel it. The famed city of Rialto was half a world away, the necessary gateway to trade in the north, but he would never reach it if he married for love, let alone see its ladies. But winning Cagri as his wife would surely be worth it…

"I will miss the food from here. The north does not have the same spices," the man in front of them lamented.

"So take some with you. Some to trade, some to be added to your food, and use your profits from the voyage to buy more when you return!" his companion said.

The first man shook his head. "I fear it will not be safe to return."

"Why not? Has your mind become so

addled you're now believing stories about sea monsters? Or the ones about girls who sit beside the northern sea and sing up storms? Sailors' tales, all of them, and not a drop of truth to be found."

"'Tis not imaginary monsters I fear, but stories from the south. Did you not hear? The Seljuk army is headed here next. They mean to drive all Crusaders back into the north, and take their land for their own."

A third man chimed in, "Then we close the gates, and prove why the ancients built a fort here in the first place! Dorylaeum has never been taken by an enemy, and it will not be conquered now! This city has stood for more than two thousand years, and may it stand for two thousand more!"

A ragged cheer went up at these words, but it died away quickly.

The last time two armies had met on the plains outside the city, the Crusaders had beaten the Seljuks, and though more than fifty years had passed, the Seljuks had no intention of forgiving the Crusaders' descendants for it. The stories of atrocities the Crusaders committed when they reached what they called the Holy City – thousands of citizens killed or sold into slavery – were mirrored by the tales of what the Seljuks had done to Edessa. Dorylaeum was a prosperous city where people of various different faiths lived in relative peace. It was this delicate balance that allowed the city to thrive as it did.

"The Crusaders will come, and save the city again," Peter said. "They have undoubtedly heard word of what happened in Edessa, and are building an army to take the city back even as we speak. If both armies meet outside Dorylaeum again, we will be able to cheer them from the walls!"

Cagri's eyes grew wide. "They would truly fight to defend us, right outside the city walls?" Her hands flew to her heart as her eyelashes fluttered. "Oh, I could not bear to watch. I would be far too frightened."

"I'm sure one of our brave defenders on the walls would be willing to hold your hand, to bolster your courage with his own. Right, Mithra?" Peter dug his elbow painfully into Mithra's ribs.

Mithra opened his mouth, but no sound came out. By all that was holy, she was so beautiful, she stole his very breath away.

"If you were there, I might be able to bear it," Cagri breathed.

But her eyes were on Peter, not Mithra.

A voice behind Mithra shouted, "It's the Seljuks that would save us from the Crusaders! Last time they came, they slaughtered whole cities and ate the babies! What else can you expect from northern barbarians?"

"Crusaders are not cannibals!" Peter burst out. "They are holy knights…"

The argument raged hotly as Mithra took their meal and carried it outside, following Peter and the other shouting men into the street.

Blows were exchanged, but it was not long before the fight broke up, with little more than bruises and a few bloodied knuckles and noses. This was what passed for peace in Dorylaeum, and Mithra could only hope it lasted.

Peter pinched his still-bleeding nose in his handkerchief. "So what are you going to do to prepare for this war?" he asked thickly.

Pray that war would not venture inside the city walls, probably, Mithra thought but did not say. For either army might kill them all.

"Come on, Mithra, this war will make all our fortunes! Maybe even make you enough so that Lechem will come looking for you to beg you to marry his daughter. What will you do to profit from the coming war?" Peter pressed.

Mithra thought for a moment, as he bit into his meat-filled pastry. He suppressed a moan at how good it tasted. With Cagri as his wife, he would eat like a king. But in order to win her, and her father's permission, he would need a plan.

He closed his eyes. "When the armies come, the city will shut the gates. If there is a siege, we will run short of firewood, for no one will dare cross a battlefield to cut wood. So Father and I need to fill our storerooms with all the wood we can, before they arrive."

Peter nodded. "After the battle is won, there will be funeral pyres, too, don't forget. And both our families should buy good stores of food, before the prices go up, in case there is a siege. If not, we can always sell them as supplies to the soldiers."

"We should take inventory of what food and drink your father has in his warehouses, and whether it can be sold at a higher profit here than shipping it north."

"The Crusaders will want the wine we received last week. I wonder if we'll get another shipment before the army arrives…"

They headed back to Peter's house, discussing plans for the coming war as if it was nothing more than another commercial opportunity. And perhaps it was.

But why did the pastry in Mithra's belly insist on churning like the sea in a storm?

One thing Mithra did know: whoever came to the city, whether Crusaders or Seljuks or both, the coming battle would change his life forever.

<h1 style="text-align:center">Two</h1>

The first riders arrived shortly after dawn, and the rest followed like a biblical flood that refused to be stopped. Melisende watched them from the top of the keep, and even when she was called down to dinner, still the river of knights marched through her head, banners flying, proclaiming to heaven itself that they would avenge her.

She longed to march with them.

"Is the meat particularly good today?" Father asked. "Or are your thoughts not on your food at all?"

She blinked, focussing on her almost empty

trencher. She could not remember tasting her dinner at all. No matter. "Crusaders must be the most saintly knights in Christendom," Melisende said dreamily.

Her brother simply stared at her. As though it wounded him that she didn't think he was as good as them. Poor Godfrey.

She continued, "I'm surprised you aren't going to join them, now you're a knight, Godfrey. Isn't knighthood all about honour? Travelling so far from home to lay down your very life to save the Holy City...so honourable you cannot help but be named a saint." If Godfrey went, then surely her father would agree to let her go. It was said that a king and queen were leading their people in this crusade. Her father could hardly object to his own daughter going if it was suitable for queens.

But Father frowned. "More like the least saintly. Though I have no doubt Godfrey earned his knighthood with honour, the truth of knighthood is little more than being able to sit upon a horse without falling off, and knowing one end of a sword from the other. Most of them have only taken up the cross for the glory of it, or the promised pardon of all their sins. They are men who are not heroes at home, or who have no hope of heaven without a good deed so great, it erases everything else they have done. Younger sons and troublemakers – those their fathers would not miss, if they do not return. Unlike my sons, who are very much needed here at home." He signalled for a servant to refill his wine cup. "I am delighted that none of your brothers have decided to join this fool scheme."

Melisende's heart sank. Godfrey was nothing if not an obedient son. Especially after he'd somehow made a mess of trade negotiations in Rialto. No one would tell her the details about what he'd done, but from the whispers she'd heard, it had something to do with someone's daughter. She knew it couldn't have been that bad – knightly Godfrey wouldn't dishonour a lady – but perhaps he'd managed to offend her somehow. Most likely by refusing to kiss or touch her, if the stories she'd heard about Rialto women were true.

"I'm sure my brothers will find plenty of other foolish things to do instead," Melisende said sweetly.

"Your brothers are not foolish. They might

make mistakes occasionally, but none of them are foolish," Father said.

"Then why hasn't Godfrey returned to Rialto, when we all know how much he longs to?" she asked.

From her father's shocked expression, she decided her arrow had struck its mark. Finally, someone would tell her what he'd done.

"Godfrey's trip to Rialto was ill-timed, is all, and the reason he hasn't returned is nothing to do with anything he did. Godfrey knows all too well why this crusade is foolishness from start to finish, as well as what kind of men will form the bulk of that army."

"Stop talking in riddles, Father. I'm no longer a child, and it won't be long before I am old enough to be mistress of my own destiny. What happened?"

"Godfrey, tell her."

But her brother's eyes were down on his food, his thoughts as base as the horses he loved so much. Sometimes she wondered if his mind was addled, he seemed to think so slowly.

"Godfrey!"

Godfrey blinked, finally looking up to meet

Father's gaze. "Yes?"

"Tell your sister what the crusading army has done."

Her heart sank again. She didn't care about the Crusaders – she wanted to know about Rialto. And if neither of them was going to tell her…then she did not need to listen to them any more.

When Godfrey finished talking, he excused himself to check on the horses, and Melisende took that as her opportunity to leave, as well.

Yet when she reached the top of the keep, the last of the Crusaders were gone, likely into the valley and the town below.

If she wanted to see them again before they left, she'd have to follow them down, or climb up to St Michael's Spire, the watchtower that stood on the hill between Father's keep and the valley.

Whatever direction she chose, she would definitely need a warm cloak tonight. Which meant a detour to her chamber to fetch one, before she had to decide.

Three

When Mithra reached home, he found it empty. His father was evidently using the last few hours of daylight to cut as much wood as possible. His was a good example to follow, and Mithra was nothing if not a dutiful son.

Mithra dug out the old handcart that his father had used before he'd become the proud owner of first one, then two, and now three donkeys, all of which were out working with him right now. Mithra might not have time for a full day's work, but he'd probably manage to fill the handcart before it was too dark to see and the guards shut the city gates.

He headed down to the bend in the river, hoping to find some trees washed down by the recent rains. Luck was with him today. The sodden branches cleaved to his axe like willing lovers. Like he hoped Cagri would, when she became his wife.

He couldn't imagine her being anything but eager. She always had such a ready smile, always willing to get whatever a customer wanted. That kind of willingness in a wife, wanting to be bedded whenever he wished…why, it was the kind of happiness a man could only dream of.

Mithra didn't dare dream for long, for dreaming wasn't doing, and he wouldn't have a wife at all until he had the kind of wealth that made wooing a wife a worthwhile pastime. So he hacked and he stacked, until he'd reduced a goodly bunch of branches into a cartload of firewood to sell, once it had dried out. He estimated there was at least another cartload left, but he could return in the morning for that, before he was expected at Simon's shop.

It wasn't a fortune yet, but it was a start, Mithra told himself as he trudged home with the weight of the handcart trundling along behind him. He'd need a lot more before Father's store rooms were full. He could only hope both armies held off for as long as possible.

Four

Melisende waited until it was dark before stealing down the servants' stairs. The house had been silent for some time, so if she was quick and quiet, no one would be the wiser until morning.

But luck was not with her tonight, for she ran headlong into a solid form headed up the narrow stair.

Between the definitely masculine exclamation and his horsy smell, she knew she'd found no servant.

"Godfrey! What are you doing here? Looming out of the darkness like that, you nearly made me scream and wake the whole house!" she said.

"I'm going to bed." He eyed her. "Where are you going?"

It was on the tip of her tongue to tell him she was merely going down to the kitchen to fetch something to help her sleep. But not even Godfrey was stupid enough to believe she'd wear a cloak to the kitchen. She could lie and say she'd been summoned to town to help someone, for she was the best healer the town had, but if by some miracle he divined her true purpose for going to town, he would try to stop her.

"If you don't tell me, I'll be forced to tell Father, and he'll send men out to bring you back," Godfrey warned.

"Oh, don't tell Father!" she burst out. She grasped his arm with both hands. "Swear you will not tell Father, and I will tell you."

"Are you meeting a lover?" he demanded.

Trust a man to think of something so silly. As if she would allow one of the boys in town to so much as touch her.

"Swear to me, Godfrey, or I shall tell you nothing."

Long he looked at her, until finally he gave in, as she knew he would. "Very well. I swear I shall not tell Father."

She nodded. "I am going up to St Michael's Spire." There would be little to see in the darkness, so before he could ask why, she added, "To watch the army march out on the morrow." Let him think she would walk up the hill to the watchtower slowly, arriving in time see the dawn. While her other brothers might suspect her talents, she was certain Godfrey did not know about them.

He nodded as if he understood, and she breathed an inward sigh of relief.

"Would you like me to come with you to protect you on the road?" Godfrey asked.

She choked back a laugh. "Of course not. With your big boots clomping along beside me, everyone from the castle to the town will know there's someone on the road alone, ripe for robbing. If I go alone, no one will even know I was there."

He hung his head, and she felt bad for bringing up his shortcomings. Heaven knew he had a good heart and plenty of courage, even if his wits worked a little slower than most. "As you wish," he said. He headed up the stairs, turning sideways to squeeze past her.

No, she could not let them part so. Though she might change her mind, she would regret this moment if the plan she had begun to form came to fruition.

"Godfrey."

He stopped and turned.

She took a deep breath. "You're a good and honourable knight, but you cannot protect everyone. We both know my fate will take me far from here." To the Holy Land, she wanted to say, but she could not, for he'd surely stop her.

"Safe journey," he said, resuming his ascent.

She smiled in the dark. He only meant to the Spire, not all the way to the Holy Land, but still he wished her well.

"You, too, brother," she said softly as she headed out to meet her fate.

"They're here, they're here!" a small boy shouted as he ran past Simon's shop.

Both Peter's and Mithra's ears pricked up. There was no need to ask who – the whole city had been humming with rumours about how close or far away the Seljuk army were.

"Go and see what the fuss is about," Simon said, shooing the young men out into the street.

"Last to reach the walls has to sweep out the shop!" Peter called over his shoulder as he set off at a run.

Mithra laughed and followed. They wove

through crowded streets, dodging other, equally curious citizens, until they reached the wall at practically the same moment. While others queued to get through the gates, Peter pointed at the steps leading up, and led the way to the top of the walls, where several guards stood watching.

No need to ask where the army was coming from, for all eyes were fixed on a distant dust cloud. A cloud that grew larger even as they watched.

"There must be hundreds of them," Peter breathed.

"Thousands," one of the guards corrected.

When finally the shapes of men on horseback emerged from the cloud, Mithra began to believe him. Rank upon rank, they rode out, heading for Dorylaeum, only to stop less than a mile from the gate.

"What are they doing?" Peter asked.

They were milling about by the river, much like the wives waiting outside Lechem's bakery each morning before it opened.

"They're waiting," a guard said.

"For what?"

But no one had an answer, until a man the

others appeared to defer to starting waving his arms in a determined fashion and his men moved to where he'd directed them.

"Close the gates!" someone shouted, and the rumble of the gates moving into place thrummed through their feet.

On the plain below, the army didn't move into some sort of attacking formation, as Mithra had expected. Instead, most of the men dismounted and began to make camp.

Peter raced home to tell his father the news, while Mithra stayed to watch. He'd heard tales of the massive fortifications the ancients had constructed when besieging cities, and he had to admit he was curious to see how such things were done.

He stayed standing on the walls until it was too dark to see, but all he saw of the camp were cookfires dotting the plain.

When morning came, it seemed a siege or even some sort of fortification were not part of the army's plan. They'd settled en masse beside the river, with no intention of attacking the city.

Consequently, by the time Mithra reached the city gates with his handcart, they were already open, and he wasn't the only one heading out about his business.

Now he'd cleared the riverbanks, he had to move deeper into the forest to collect firewood, but the wood wasn't as wet, so it was easier to haul the cart home when he was done. The sun was high in the sky by the time he emerged from the woods, and he had to hurry back or risk being late to work.

When he reached Simon's shop, Mithra was surprised to find it wasn't open yet. He'd been apprenticed here for long enough to manage the shop by himself, though, so he opened the doors and pasted what he hoped was a helpful smile on his face, for the streets were full of soldiers and citizens doing brisk business that neither Peter or Simon would want to miss out on.

When the sun set, he closed the shop, and set off for Simon's house to see why no one had come to the bazaar that day. With him, he lugged a clinking bag of the day's takings, which he planned to proudly present to Master Simon as proof that he'd successfully completed his apprenticeship.

Six

Out the side door, following the wall around to the gate until she reached the road, and Melisende was free. Moonlight illuminated her path, setting her cloak aglow. It was a sign, she decided. Definitely a divine one. She was doing the right thing.

Melisende bit her lip, tasting the magic that flowed through her veins, and began to run. Trees and fields flew past, while the road was firm beneath her boots. Her brothers would never know the sheer exhilaration of this kind of speed – not even on Pegasus, Godfrey's favourite horse, at full gallop. Godfrey did not know that she'd raced his horse many a time, and the mare had never won a race. Not that the mare had minded – she'd loved to run almost as much as Melisende.

The road forked ahead, leading down to the town or up to St Michael's Spire. She paused for a moment, looking up. She could ascend the hill and look down on the army from the isolation of the high tower, as she'd said she would, or she could head down into the thick of things, and become part of the wondrous undertaking that was a crusade.

She had stood apart long enough. Melisende turned toward the town, only to find someone running toward her. The girl's panting breaths were louder than the patter of her footsteps on the road.

The girl slowed to a stop, then doubled over to catch her breath. "Lady Melisende? What are you doing here? It is not safe, not with the army encamped just outside town."

It was safe enough when you moved too swiftly to see. Not that Melisende intended to share her secret with one of the village girls. She knew the voice but...Melisende squinted at the girl's face. "Jella?" she asked.

"Yes," Jella wheezed.

"What are you doing out here without your cloak? You'll freeze, or worse, catch a cold again, and be in bed for a week. How will your father keep up with business in the inn with you lying abed?" Melisende unfastened her own cloak and wrapped it around the girl's shoulders. "There. That should help."

Jella's eyes grew wide, shining in the moonlight. "Oh, no, Lady Melisende, this cloak is far too fine for me. I couldn't…"

Melisende's hand clamped over Jella's frozen fingers, stilling them, before she tied the cloak at the girl's throat. "Return it to the castle when you are done with it, then. I have others." She reached into her bag and drew out a plain brown one that had once belonged to her brothers. They'd all outgrown it, with their broad shoulders, but it fit her just fine. "Now, what are you doing out here? Are you coming up to the castle to fetch me? Is someone sick?"

Jella shook her head. "Father sent me up to the watchtower with a message for Uncle Beatus. He said to stay up there until the army leaves. They're bad men, my lady. You should not be out here. It isn't safe."

She darted a glance behind her.

Melisende heard it, too.

"Horses. Must be men from the army. Quick, hide, my lady!" Jella ran into the trees beside the road, blundering about until she half-fell into a bush.

Hoofbeats approached, accompanied by bawdy calls from the riders.

No, these were not the kind of men she wanted to meet. These were Crusaders with souls so deeply steeped in sin, they were desperate for redemption. God help the Holy Land if these were the best they could send.

That's where she came in, wasn't it? To lend the army a small mite of virtue, so that this grand undertaking might win. She had no choice but to go with them, no matter what her father said.

Melisende bit her lip and began to run again.

When Mithra reached the prestigious Crusaders' Quarter where Peter's family lived, the lanterns had been lit and there seemed a lot of people moving about at a time when they were usually enjoying their evening meal. Perhaps it was some sort of Christian holy day that he'd forgotten, Mithra told himself.

But all the people he saw were soldiers, or labourers who lived in the poorer part of town where Mithra and his father lived. A cart stopped outside the house that belonged to Peter's neighbour, a Rialto horse merchant who'd returned to Rialto some time ago, and several labourers started loading chests from the house into the cart.

Maybe the merchant didn't meant to come back, and he'd sent for his things, Mithra thought, until he saw a cart outside Simon's house, too. This cart wasn't empty – it held long, cloth-wrapped bundles like the one being carried out of Simon's door right now. A bundle that looked suspiciously like…

The breeze fluttered the cloth, pulling it away from the horrors it covered. Mithra saw Peter's face, wide eyed and staring, before one of the soldiers pushed the cloth back where it belonged. Peter's body was flung into the cart atop the others, just as another bundle was brought out.

Mithra didn't want to, but he forced himself to step forward to lift the sheet on this body. Simon's face was crusted in blood, barely recognisable, but the man could be no one else.

"Hey! Who are you? Are they your family?" a soldier demanded, drawing his sword to bar Mithra's path.

Mithra shook his head. "I was apprenticed to this man. My father and I live beside the

Meat District, behind the markets."

"And who is your father?"

"Ali Baba, younger brother of Kasim, who lives in the Merchants' Quarter." Though more merchants lived here in the Crusaders' Quarter than the Merchants' Quarter, Mithra thought but did not say.

The soldier lifted his eyebrows and sheathed his sword. "You're not apprenticed here any more. The family is dead. Infidels will not be tolerated in this city, and all their goods are forfeit." He waved at the cart full of the horse merchant's things, which had now moved up to Simon's door. Or what had been Simon's door. "If you know of any other infidels in the city, tell us where they are hiding, and you will be rewarded. Anyone who helps them hide will die a traitor's death alongside the infidels."

The breeze seized Peter's shroud, and whipped it away, showing the corpse in all its gore. Peter's tunic was black with blood, except where someone had sawed a hole in his tunic and the belly beneath, spilling out his entrails for the flies to feast on.

Mithra choked back the horrified sound that tried to escape from his throat.

Had it been only yesterday that he and Peter had planned to profit from the arrival of this army? Yet here Peter and his whole family lay dead – good people, for all their faith was different to his own – while he lived. Worse, he'd spent the whole day politely doing business with the men who'd murdered his master.

He'd barely eaten all day, but Mithra managed to stumble into an alley before retching up everything down to a mouthful of bile. It wasn't until he reached up to wipe his mouth that he realised he still carried a bag of Simon's gold.

One day, when the army left and it was safe to travel again, he would take it to Simon's family in Rialto, and tell them what had happened.

Until then, he would keep it safe, for by the time the army's bloody work was done, it would be all that was left of his friend and the family he'd loved almost as dearly as his own.

He felt laugher bubble up in his throat as a horrible thought struck him, but he forced it back down. He, a faithful Muslim of the same faith as the Seljuks, now waited for the

Christian Crusaders to arrive, so that he might lay his Christian friend's soul to rest in the way Peter would have wanted. The Crusaders would arrive too late to save Peter's body, but they might help save Mithra's soul.

Eight

Mithra didn't have the heart to go home, for he would have to tell his father about Peter's family's fate, so he wandered the city, with little thought to where he was going until he became aware of his belly complaining of hunger.

He stopped and realised he'd walked all the way to Lechem's bakery, which was currently serving a crowd of people their evening meal. He joined the queue.

Whether it took an age or merely a moment, Mithra did not know, but he found himself standing before the counter. "What would you like?" Cagri asked, her eyes as dull as he felt. Evidently she'd already heard the news.

Mithra ordered a meat pastry – Peter's favourite – and exchanged a few coins for his food.

"I can't believe he's gone," Mithra said.

Cagri blinked. "Who?"

"Peter, of course! We'd come in here together almost every day, and order exactly the same thing. And now…I'll never see him come down from the Crusaders' Quarter, eager to open the shop."

Cagri wrinkled her nose. "What do I care for some Crusader? Probably plotting to kill us all in our beds, the moment he gets the chance! Now, out of the way before I report you as a traitor, too." She shooed him away with a disdainful hand, before her angry expression softened and her eyelashes fluttered. Just like the way she used to look at Peter. "What can I do for you, handsome?" she simpered.

Mithra turned to find two soldiers behind him. His eyes caught on one man's sleeve, darkly spotted with dried blood, as though he'd thrust his sword so hard into his victim that the blood had spattered all the way up his arm.

He could have been the man who killed Peter, or Simon, or any one of the innocent citizens whose bodies had been bundled into shrouds on that cart.

Yet Cagri served them with a smile, as she spat on Peter's memory.

Mithra moved aside, letting the men through, and forced himself to eat the pastry as he watched Cagri with new eyes.

He'd loved her, thought her the sweetest, most beautiful girl he'd ever laid eyes upon, a goddess made flesh.

Now, as he watched her flirt with every man she served, most of them soldiers, he wondered what he could have ever seen in the girl. Her sweet words fell with bitterness on his ears, and he beheld no beauty at all. He avoided her dark zebani eyes that wanted to drink his soul and drag it down to the very depths of torment.

At some point, he must have left the shop, for he found himself wandering the streets again in darkness, tasting bile at the back of his throat, wondering if there would ever be light in the world again.

Nine

Just outside of town, Melisende stopped to change into boys' garb. More castoffs from her brothers that she'd stored in a chest in her chamber, for the boys' clothes fitted no one else now, and the plain tunics and hose were better for sparring than the gowns she wore to please her father.

And herself, on occasion. She had no talent for weaving or spinning or even sewing, but she remembered remedies well enough to take over as mistress of the stillroom when her mother died. So when one of the townsfolk came to seek the ministrations of Lady

Melisende, she took care to look like a lady. Herbs and horses had pleased her mother well enough, but Melisende envied her brothers their freedom. They travelled all over Father's lands, and sometimes even further, when a horse was bought or sold.

She'd made Godfrey tell her about everything in Rialto when he'd reached home, until the others tired of his tales, but she never had. She wasn't sure where this crusade would take her, but she hoped she would see some exotic cities on the way.

She fastened her leather breastplate, grateful for its weight against the cold, for the brown cloak was woefully light compared to the thick, white wool one she'd given Jella. But it would be warmer once they reached the Holy Land, or so she'd heard.

Lastly, she took out the leather helm she'd borrowed from the armoury. With the nose and cheek guards, it would hide her hair and her face.

"You won't need it. Most squires are too young to shave, so smooth cheeks aren't much of a giveaway. I would suggest binding your breasts, for the times you're not wearing your aptly named breastplate."

Melisende whirled at the sound of a decidedly masculine drawl.

A man in grey leaned against a tree, a bottle in one hand as though he was about to lift it to his lips for a drink.

"How long have you been there watching me?" Melisende demanded, feeling her cheeks redden. Long enough to see her undress, she was certain.

"Since you arrived and woke me," the man returned, gesturing toward his bedroll and the remains of a fire.

Now she felt even more embarrassed than ever. "My apologies, sir, for I did not see you."

He waved her words away, as if they were nothing. "No knights here, and for that I am grateful. They're a boorish bunch, for the most part. Best stay away from them. For all their talk of honour, they could not watch a maiden undress without wanting to help her, and exact their own high price for the service."

Melisende frowned. "That does not sound honourable at all to me."

The grey man clapped his hands. "Precisely! So if you wish to keep your honour, or at least hold it a little longer, best keep close to the lover you're playing squire to."

Melisende's mouth dropped open in horror. First her brother, now this man. "I do not have a lover! I am a maiden!"

The grey man did not seem ruffled or even surprised by her outburst. "For now, perhaps, but you cannot think you are the first girl to follow a man into battle. A mistake, in most cases, for if the man had a good squire who fastened his armour properly for him, he'd last longer in battle than most. Yet you're not unfamiliar with armour, so maybe your man might survive. Not to mention the magic you might use to save him."

She'd known the man for barely a moment, and he already knew all her secrets. "What makes you say I have magic?"

A smile touched his lips. "The magic in your blood speaks to the magic in mine. The women in my family are all powerful enchantresses, and you don't grow up around that kind of power without learning to recognise it. Of course, when you appeared in my clearing without casting a portal, I knew there was magic at work, but the bite marks on your lip make it clear that you are a witch." His smile widened. "Or that your lover is a brave man."

She stamped her foot. "For the second time, I do not have a lover! I have no desire to follow some stupid man to war!"

"So why are you here?"

She considered not answering. Lying, perhaps. But in the end, it was the truth that spilled from lips. "Everyone seems so certain the men on this crusade have no honour or virtue to speak of. Without that, how can a crusade succeed? But I recall a tale I heard in church, of a town that was razed to the ground for lack of a virtuous man. If there'd been but one pure person present, the city might have been saved. I'd hoped to persuade my brother to come, but he obeys my father in all things, so he stayed home. And I thought…perhaps it does not have to be a virtuous man at all. Perhaps I could be that one…" She trailed off, suddenly feeling silly. One girl would never be enough to save a city.

But the man only nodded. "Perhaps. One man, or one girl, might make a difference. Or it could be that history is written by the victors, and the people who destroyed that city merely said that the city was full of sinners, instead of simply…other people. As good or bad as anyone else. And the truth is whatever those who survive to tell the tale write after they are done killing." Melancholy shadowed his expression, as he cast his eyes down under the weight of what Melisende could only guess was a terrible memory.

She took a deep breath. "I mean to survive. To return home, where I will tell a tale that is true."

"If that is so, then you will need to be careful. Stay away from those who might do you harm, and when battle is eventually joined, do not stand and fight. Killing leaves a terrible taint on your soul, a stain that you can never wash away. Instead, run. As far and as fast as you can, to a place where you may watch the battle but stay out of sight."

"What honour is there in cowardice?"

"There is very little left of honour in the last moments of life on a battlefield. Especially if you're on the losing side." The grey man gave her a dark look. "It's not too late to head back home."

But it was. She'd made up her mind, and would not turn back now. Melisende shook her head firmly. "I believe my fate lies far from here, and I must go. I can't explain how I know, but…" She shrugged.

"Perhaps your magic makes you a seer of sorts. My mother has always seen the future, and I've never seen one of her predictions to be wrong. Stay or go, 'tis all the same to me. Best stay close to me if you want to live long enough to make it home, though."

Naïve she might be, but she was not as stupid as that. "Why should I trust you? You've already said there's no honour in this army. That means you, too!"

He bowed his head, acknowledging her taunt without taking offence, as her brothers certainly would. "Ah, but I am not a soldier in this army. I merely march with them."

His response only begged more questions, instead of answers. "So you're not a knight, and not a soldier," Melisende said slowly, feeling her thoughts flow as sluggishly as Godfrey's. "What are you?"

"I am a man, much like any other." The answer was too smooth, too practised to be anything other than more evasion.

"But why are you travelling with these men? What is your destination? For you must have one in mind," she persisted.

He eyed her. "Curiosity is the failing of young boys, and of women no matter what their age, yet I will satisfy you, just this once. But I will tell you now, that you will not like the answer." He waited a moment, then went on: "My destination matters not, much like most of these men. I am an assassin on a mission, and once the deed is done, I shall depart."

Melisende took a step back, then another. "You kill people for money!"

He shrugged. "Better than raping, tormenting and then killing them for the sheer fun of it, like most of the others here. The only people who die by my hand deserve it, and if I get paid to deliver justice, where is the harm in that?"

"I'd be mad to trust you!"

"No, you'd be surprisingly sensible. Only a sloppy assassin kills more than they must. As you are not my target, you are perfectly safe with me." He lowered his voice. "Or have you heard rumours saying otherwise?"

Melisende shook her head. "How could I have heard anything about you or any other assassin? I don't even know your name!"

"Ah!" He executed a sweeping bow that wouldn't have been out of place in a royal court. "Zoticus the assassin, at your service." He straightened and grinned. "Should you have need of my services, and the gold to afford them."

She blinked. It was growing lighter, for she could see his face now, as well as the fine wool tunic he wore. He might not be a knight, but he had the manners of a courtier and the clothes of a nobleman. If he truly was an assassin as he said, he could move within the highest circles, and likely held kings and prices in his clientele. Or in his list of victims…

Melisende shivered, then remembered herself. She attempted to drop a curtsey, forgetting she wasn't wearing a gown, and spread the hem of her cloak wide instead. "I am – "

"Don't tell me, or I might call you by name. Especially if you curtsey like no squire ever. Boys bow, and most knights don't bother to learn their squires' names, anyhow, so if you plan to join this benighted crusade, expect to be called Boy or Squire."

She nodded. "All right."

The sound of hooves on the road had her racing to hide behind a tree. She peeped out, cursed, then flattened herself against the trunk.

"So you're not following a lover, but running away from one?" Zoticus asked.

"That's not my lover. He's my brother!" she hissed.

Zoticus grinned. "Oh, then I really must meet this man."

Melisende shot him a dirty look, then bit her lip and bolted.

Ten

Dawn found Mithra at his favourite bath house – favourite because it was formed over a natural hot spring that bubbled up from the earth, and so ancient no one could remember who'd constructed the building that housed it, so the caretaker charged men nothing for bathing in the waters, collecting coin only from those who wanted towels or soap or other services. Mithra usually brought things from home, but no amount of scrubbing could make him feel clean today. Perhaps he should use a couple of hard-won coins to buy some of the bath house soap, to see if it could do any better.

"It's a woman, isn't it?"

Mithra looked up to meet the eyes of a man with a broom. The caretaker, he presumed.

It was everything, he wanted to say, and a woman was both the smallest and worst part of all of it. But the words seemed to stick in his throat.

"Women are the greatest joy and the greatest trouble in a man's life. Your woman's causing you trouble, I think."

Mithra swallowed. "She's not mine. She'll never be mine." Saying the words aloud ripped his heart open anew. How could he have been so wrong about her…

"I'll wager it's because you never tried the thousand and one ways of pleasuring a woman on her. If you'd tried those, she might not have left you." The man raised his eyebrows.

Mithra didn't know what to say. The thousand and one…what?

The man smiled knowingly. "Men are simple, but women…trying to understand them is like trying to catch water with your fingers. They even trouble me, and I'm a eunuch. The things I saw when I was a harem guard..." He shook his head.

Curiosity burned through Mithra's lethargy. His mind simply could not fathom how the man's...no, the eunuch's words could be true. "What is a palace eunuch doing in a lowly bath house?"

The man's smile widened. "Teaching men like you about the thousand and one ways so next time you woo a woman, you will surely win her."

"How much will it cost?" Mithra asked.

The eunuch laughed. "Oh, women pay me well for such knowledge. Gold, jewels, more than a simple man like me needs. How do you think I came to own this bath house? I have no sons, but it seems fitting to share my knowledge with those who might use it. After all, I am but one man, and I cannot serve all the women of the city. A young man like you will catch another wife easily enough, I am sure, and if my words help you win her, then you may pay me whatever price you see fit."

Mithra nodded. It was a wager of sorts. It seemed fair. "Go on."

"There's a reason women cover their bodies, and it isn't modesty. It's because the slightest touch, when done right, can provoke pleasure such as you have only dreamed of..."

Mithra let the eunuch's words wash over him, as he began to wake properly from his torpor.

Yes, he'd lost his best friend, his job, his master, and the girl he thought he'd loved all in the same day. But he still had his father, and Simon's shop, along with the vow he'd sworn.

Mithra would keep working in the shop as long as the soldiers allowed it, or until all of Simon's goods were gone. In the mornings and evenings, he'd collect wood, and use the coin to pay for his passage to Rialto when the army left and it was safe to travel north again.

And when he was done, then perhaps he'd look for a girl who might be willing to be his wife, and try out perhaps a few of the eunuch's thousand and one ways with her. He would have to return to this bath house, however, to hear the eunuch tell them all, until he managed to memorise them, for he suspected he'd missed a few and the man was already detailing the tenth...

Mithra lay back in the hot water. Now he had a plan and perhaps a future. He owed it to

Peter's memory to make good use of both.

Eleven

The sun was high in the sky when Melisende dared to return to the clearing. She found Zoticus preparing a midday meal in his stewpot over a small fire, but no sign of Godfrey.

"Did you tell him about me?" she asked.

Zoticus glanced at her, then turned his attention back to stirring the stewpot. "We spoke about a number of things, but you'll be surprised to hear you didn't come up in the conversation at all."

That wasn't possible. Godfrey must have come looking for her.

"You're lying," she concluded. "Either he asked about me, or you didn't talk at all."

Any normal man should have been offended, but Zoticus didn't seem to care about her accusation. "Or your brother had more important things on his mind. A girl had been murdered, and he came looking for the culprit, or culprits, as is likely the case. I hinted that I might be willing to hunt them down for him, for a price, of course, but he insisted upon bringing the men to justice himself. A pity. He appears to be that very rare creature, an honourable knight. Yet one who holds justice above his own honour. I told him the names of those he sought, and he rode on. I imagine he will see his mission is futile, and come back presently to offer me the job." Zoticus grinned. "Perhaps he is even now finding courage in the bottom of a tankard in the tavern. For a man's first time hiring an assassin can be as nerve-wracking as one's first kill, or so it seems to me."

"Godfrey does not lack for courage. He is not as bright as some men, but he is steady and loyal and stubborn. If he means to bring a murderer to justice, he will do everything in his power to bring it about." In her hurry to defend her brother, she'd forgotten the most important piece of news. "Did he tell you the name of the girl?"

Zoticus lifted his spoon from the pot and sipped delicately from it. "He did not. Perhaps he did not know it. After all, you are not the only girl who rides with this army." He glanced up at her. "Oh, and in case you weren't aware, it's usually a squire's job to cook the meals."

It was Melisende's turn to smile. "Oh, but I'm not really a squire, and you're not a knight. Besides, the only cooking I'm good at is what I do in the stillroom, and there's no need to make medicine taste nice. So if you want a savoury stew worth sipping from the spoon, best cook it yourself, sir."

Zoticus's eyes fairly sparkled at this. "Well, now," he drawled. "A healer is worth their weight in gold in an army like this one. Not to mention invaluable to a man in my trade." He filled two bowls and set one before Melisende. "Tell me what you know of poisons."

She picked up her bowl and sniffed at it with apprehension. The stew did not smell anything but savoury and appetising, but she knew there were poisons that her nose could not detect.

"There are many substances in the world which may heal in small quantities, but kill if the dose is too large," she began. "And others which may bring about a swift death where a healer can offer no other help." Heaven help her, but the stew smelled so good, and she had not eaten all day.

"What's wrong? Not fine enough fare for your ladyship?" Zoticus asked, looking from the untouched bowl to her.

Melisende swallowed. "I'm not a courtier. I like plain fare just fine. It's poison I do not care to consume."

He burst out laughing. "You think I poisoned the food? Oh, you are a suspicious one, Squire! No, upon my honour, you are safe with me and my cooking. I've rarely used poison, though I might need to in the future. I prefer a blade, slipped between a man's ribs or better yet, sliced across his throat , so that he may see the face of his killer, and the last thing he hears is what crime he has committed for which his life is forfeit. When you're as good an assassin as I am, you may choose which missions you take. May I never stoop so low as to murder a maiden whose only crime is her own naiveté." He raised his bottle in the air, as if in a toast, and drank deeply from it.

Melisende dipped her finger in the stew and licked it. It didn't taste poisoned. "If you're lying, then I shall haunt you from the moment I die to your very last breath," she threatened. Then she began to eat in earnest.

Zoticus only smiled.

Twelve

When the army were done with the houses in the former Crusaders' Quarter, they raided the warehouses. Mithra had already transferred everything he could to the shop in the bazaar, but he wasn't able to save it all.

At least the stock he had saved, he sold at a tidy profit to soldiers, mostly. The luxury foodstuffs he and Peter had saved for a siege found their way into the camp outside the gates at far higher prices than Simon's customers in Rialto might have paid.

Last to sell were the northern furs, brought from creatures that knew nothing but snow, that soldiers bought as gifts for their wives back home. What their wives wanted with such stuff, he had no idea, but Mithra was not of a mind to quarrel with men who handed over gold by the handful, boasting that the money was their share of the treasure looted from Crusader houses.

Money which he took home every night and locked in the chest that was now all that stood in his father's store rooms, for the wood he'd collected for the siege he'd managed to sell to the soldiers building funeral pyres for Crusader corpses. A thousand times he'd opened his mouth to tell the soldiers that the men they'd killed were no more Crusaders than he was, and that they'd just been ordinary merchants going about their business before they were murdered. Yet he'd closed his mouth again, all those words unsaid, knowing he would only join the bodies on the pyre for supposedly sympathising with Crusaders.

He wished he had the courage to tell the world that he sympathised more with Peter and Simon than he did with the soldiers camped outside his city, but he didn't want to die. Perhaps that made him a coward, someone the soldiers should look down upon, but even as he closed up the empty shop for the last time, he knew the soldiers would soon look down upon him any way.

A merchant and shopkeeper they would at least pay attention to, but a lowly woodcutter was beneath their notice.

As he saw, once again, when he deposited the last of Simon's gold in the chest, and dragged his handcart out of the house to collect more wood.

On the morrow, he would cut wood all day, carting it back to town, before going back out for more, much like his father did. Every day, he would do the same, until the army left and he could journey to Rialto.

And once his quest was complete, he would return to Dorylaeum, never to leave here again.

He was a woodcutter. He'd been born a woodcutter, and, but for a brief time when he'd been an apprentice who dreamed of becoming a successful merchant, he'd live and die a woodcutter. Just like his father.

Thirteen

By the time Melisende reached Byzas, she was sick of walking, sick of sleeping outside and heartily sick of the smell of sweaty, unwashed men. But when she saw that enormous, sprawling city spread out before her for the first time, she found she regretted nothing.

"It's beautiful," she breathed.

"Yes, like the sun making rainbows in the scum atop a cesspool," Zoticus replied. "I could make my fortune here among the royalty and nobility, who are all so worried the others will stab them in the back they don't trust their own families, and rightly so. Everyone else is probably busy quaking in their boots at the sight of an army this big, but the royals are too satisfied with their own superiority to see Crusaders as a threat. If they were ever to close their gates to a Crusader army…that would be an interesting day."

"But aren't they Christians too?" she asked.

"Yes, but of a different sort. They do not show the same reverence to saints. This city is the last crumbling bastion of a dying empire, built by the ancients, but they are too busy squabbling to see it."

"It looks plenty prosperous to me. Look at those palaces!"

Zoticus did not smile. "They are as opulent inside as out, I promise you. Best not to look too closely at them, for the prisons here are barbarous places, where men are locked up for words and looks as much as their deeds."

She'd learned during the journey that while Zoticus might speak in riddles much of the time, he was both observant and knowledgeable about the lands they travelled through. So if he knew about the prison here…

"How did you escape?" she whispered.

"The position of prison guard is not well paid, and men are constantly needed to fill their ranks. So when I took a contract to kill a prisoner before he could be interrogated by one of the resident torturers, it was the easiest job of my career. The man begged for my blade, eagerly snatching it out of my hand to end his own life. When I left the prison's employ a week later, no one was the wiser as to how the man got his hands on a dagger. Most believed he had hidden it upon his person when he was arrested. After that, they searched the prisoners better, I believe."

That wasn't what she'd expected. "They torture people here? How barbaric!"

Zoticus's lips lifted in one of his enigmatic smiles that she knew signified he thought her too naïve to hear any more on the subject, so he would tell her no more.

They passed through the gates in silence. More than once, she had to hurry to catch up to him in the maze of city streets, because she'd been caught staring at yet another building that shimmered in the sun. She had no idea that houses could be so huge.

"I usually stay at the inn near the street of

bakers. Cheap rooms, and if I do not like the breakfast, there is plenty to choose from nearby," Zoticus said, gesturing toward a building that looked much older than the ones alongside it. "You should use the time we have here to buy whatever new clothes and weapons you need, and some food for the journey. As much as you think you can carry."

Which wasn't much. Not for the first time, she wished she'd brought a horse and saddlebags full of everything she'd need for her journey. Perhaps she'd have enough coin to buy a packhorse, or at least a sturdy pony. She knew the kind of prices her father commanded for his horses, but she wasn't after a mount fit for a king.

A quick trip to the nearest stable had her wondering if her father was charging too little. A tired-looking donkey that was definitely lame was apparently worth its meagre weight in gold, or so the stablemaster said. He would not part with it for a penny less than her father charged for a well-trained gelding, though it would likely end up in some soldier's stewpot before the week was out.

No horse for her, then, Melisende resolved,

taking her time at the blacksmith's instead. A serviceable short sword with no embellishment save the maker's mark cost much the same as one from the smithy at home, though she'd had to wait for the smith to finish re-shoeing a couple of horses before she could make her purchase.

Spare tunics and hose made from a particularly thin kind of linen cost her little, but a good pair of boots small enough for her feet proved impossible to find. There were pretty shoes aplenty, suitable for court or sitting in a chamber, sewing, but for walking halfway around the world, she'd have to wear the boots she'd left home in. At least they were sturdy, for her time running at home stood her in good stead now for all the endless walking. It was a pity she could not run all the way to the Holy Land, but if she arrived alone, without an army at her back, there was little she could do to save anyone.

Besides, she'd missed dinner, and the smell wafting down the bakers' street was trying to steal her attention.

She took her purchases up to the room Zoticus had arranged, took advantage of his absence to wash thoroughly before donning some of her new clothes, and headed out in search of sustenance.

Melisende found the source of the smell was a shop which sold parcels made from thin bread, wrapped around a dark filling that smelled strongly of fish. Yet when she bit into hers, she discovered that the filling consisted entirely of beans, mixed with a spiced sauce that a fish had once swum through, leaving little of its presence but the pungent smell.

She slipped into the shade of an alley to eat her meal, for the road was both hot and busy, only to wish she'd brought something to drink, for the sauce was surprisingly salty. Deciding she could afford to buy a jug of the local wine, she stepped out onto the street before she stopped dead.

Melisende backed into her alley once more, hoping the shadows would hide her while she stared.

It couldn't be Godfrey. It couldn't be.

Yet no other man could possibly ride Pegasus. The only time Father let the mare leave their lands was with Godfrey, who had claimed the horse for his own.

What was he doing here?

Hunting for her, she was sure of it.

Well, she would not let him find her.

She stuffed the remainder of her dinner into her mouth, and set off at a run. She didn't slow until she reached her room at the inn, where she stayed until Zoticus returned.

"You look like you've encountered a ghost," Zoticus said. "You should know that shades rarely cause trouble, and even when they do, they are more intent on avenging their own death than menacing maidens. In the meantime, I have a jug of the local wine that I know will lift your spirits." He brandished the jug in triumph.

Melisende shook her head. "It's my brother. He's here."

"Yes, I thought I'd seen him on the march. I've tried to discourage him as much as I could, small setbacks and the like, but nothing seems to daunt the man, so he has made it all the way to Byzas without turning back. A surprisingly tenacious knight, is Sir Godfrey. I don't see why you don't choose to travel with him instead of my humble self. After all, he has the most magnificent horse, which can carry you and all your clothes, all the way to the Holy Land!"

"If he sees me, he'll only drag me home again. Please, Zoticus. It's only a matter of time before he knows I am here. I'm surprised he hasn't seen me already. Is there nothing you can do that will persuade him to head home without me? I can pay you." Melisende reached for her coin purse.

Zoticus held up his hand. "Now you insult me. I accept payment for assassinations, not for small favours performed for friends. If it is so important to you, I shall stick as close to your brother as his own shadow, until I am certain he has abandoned this crusade."

Only then did Melisende dare to breathe again. "I would be eternally in your debt."

He waved her gratitude away. "Not for eternity. Just until you performed a suitable favour for me in return. After all, friends help each other, do we not?"

She nodded readily, and he left.

It wasn't until later that she began to wonder what sort of favour the assassin might ask for. Then she began to worry. But Zoticus did not return that night, or the next, as apprehension curdled in her stomach. She wasn't sure what would be worse – to go home in disgrace with Godfrey, or assisting the assassin in his work.

And she dreaded finding out.

Fourteen

Some days, Mithra worked alongside his father, cutting a day's worth of wood before loading it onto his handcart to carry back to town. Sometimes it took him two or three trips, compared to only one for his father with his patient donkeys, and by the time he returned from town, his father had moved on, deeper into the forest to cut wood. Then, Mithra would work alone, cutting and lifting and carrying, until it was too dark to see, and the day's work was done.

At least once a day, he took care to make sure his path led him close to the army camp, where some of the soldiers were only too happy to buy firewood from him instead of collecting it for themselves. It saved him a trip to town, and firewood fetched a high price here.

Until one morning, when he found the camp in disarray. The Seljuk army were soon to be on the move again. He stopped to ask one of the men he'd become familiar with, "Are you leaving already? Are the Crusaders coming?" He tried to sound concerned, instead of hopeful that opportunity had come at last.

The soldier shrugged. "I have not seen them, if the Crusaders care to come at all," he said. "But the General has slaves to sell, and he wishes to take them to market while the girls still retain their good looks." He jerked his head toward the middle of the camp.

What the camp had previously hidden, now became clear. A fenced-off enclosure, similar to the one that held the soldiers' horses, sat in the centre of camp. Inside its walls were not beasts of burden, but the women and children Mithra thought had died alongside their menfolk in the Crusaders' Quarter. Perhaps even Peter's mother and sisters. Mithra craned his neck for a better look.

As if to oblige him, several of the soldiers opened the gate, and started herding the poor people into a column that would march between two lines of soldiers. Mithra looked and looked, but he could not discern Peter's family from the woeful women wearing little more than rags, which showed the bruises from their ill-treatment all too well.

Mithra wanted to weep. The guards of the city should have protected these people, instead of letting the soldiers steal them and turn them into slaves. He wanted to rage at the army, to fight them all to free the people he knew did not deserve this. But one man was no match for an army – least of all him. He forced himself to harden his heart. Not to their suffering, which smote him to his very soul, but to this soldier and all his fellows, for what they had done.

When the Crusaders came, he would throw open the gates and welcome them, watching with glee as they cut this despicable army to pieces. He hoped they all met the same fate as Peter and his family.

It wasn't until Mithra reached the shelter of

the forest that he allowed his anger to surface. His axe was the instrument of his wrath, and the trees his hapless victims. He worked until darkness fell and his arms were too tired to lift the axe that felt almost as heavy as his heart, but still his anger burned.

Fifteen

"You'd best be up and about if you hope to break your fast before we are on the march again," Zoticus said with a brightness that Melisende definitely did not share. Surely it was too early for cheerfulness of any kind, especially from a man who had been following her brother for days on end without sleep, or so it seemed.

Melisende rose. She was gratified to see Zoticus turned his back so that she might dress with some degree of modesty. "Where is my brother?" she asked.

"Oh, I do not think he feels like marching

today, or for some days yet. You have no need to worry about him any more."

Dread closed a cold hand around her heart. "He's not…dead, is he?" She knew death meant little to the assassin, but Godfrey was her brother. He didn't deserve to die for simply doing his duty in coming after her, to try and fetch her home.

Zoticus laughed. "No, though he might wish he were when he wakes. He met with a misadventure in an alley last night, and will sleep for some hours yet. When he wakes, I am sure he will wish for nothing more than to be at home in his bed, and likely do everything within his power to make his way there. Of course, once I have done his job for him, meting out justice for this girl he is so determined to avenge, perhaps I shall stop by your father's house to collect a fee for my services. We shall see."

"But he has Pegasus, the swiftest horse alive. This army marches so slowly, he could outpace us in less than a day. You do not know him. He will not stop until justice is served. His honour demands that."

Zoticus sounded thoughtful. "Then it seems

I will have to see that someone steals his horse. An easy matter, with a beast so magnificent. I have just the man in mind. Better yet, once we are far enough away from here, I shall simply steal the horse back, and return him to your brother when I come to visit."

Melisende could not help but shake her head. To an assassin like Zoticus, the world seemed so simple. To her, it grew more and more complicated, the further she got from home. Yet today she had no desire to turn back.

Washed, dressed and ready, she headed downstairs with her belongings in a sack over her shoulder, prepared to break her fast and be on her way.

Sixteen

The day the Crusader army arrived was delivery day for Mithra. Both he and his father went house to house, delivering the week's firewood to the clients who his father had supplied for as long as Mithra could remember. His father took the far side of town, while Mithra made trips between the nearer houses and his own with his handcart.

"The Crusaders have come!"

"The Seljuks have returned!"

"They've come to save us!"

"They mean to murder us in our beds!"

"They seek to avenge their countrymen!"

"Close the gates!"

"Open them!"

"Go home and bar your doors!"

"Grab what weapons you can and fight to defend our city!"

Confusion reigned in the city, and Mithra had no idea what to believe when he was hemmed in on all sides by houses and people on the busy street.

If he could but see them with his own eyes, then it would be clear. Mithra dropped his barrow, and began to run. Not since the day he had matched Peter stride for stride had he ascended the walls so fast. Maybe not even then. Because whatever happened today, his fate was tied up in this army's arrival. Whoever they were and whatever they meant to do, his destiny rode beside them.

Yet when he reached the walls, his own confusion was complete. Oh, he could see the approaching dust cloud, coming from the opposite direction to before. He could vaguely discern the outlines of horses and men, headed for the city. But their purpose or religion he could not determine, and the guards were no help.

Just like the people in the city below, they called the approaching army Crusaders or Seljuks, and bellowed for the gate to be both opened and closed.

By the time anyone knew for sure, the army would be upon them.

Mithra stared at the empty plain, where no trace of the former Seljuk camp now stood. He and the other townspeople had picked it clean, hoping that would scour away their memory of war. Now it seemed the initial slaughter of their citizens was only the beginning.

If Peter's death was the beginning, Mithra did not want to imagine the end. Dorylaeum would be destroyed, he was certain of it.

What could one lowly woodcutter do?

Nothing.

So Mithra stayed where he was, took a deep breath, and allowed himself to think for a moment.

If what he saw was the Seljuk army returning, they could only be hurrying to reach the battleground of their choosing before the Crusaders arrived. That meant the Crusaders were close.

If the Crusaders arrived first, then surely

they meant to take the city, or at least make camp outside it. They would avenge Peter, his family, and all the other Christians who had been killed. When the Seljuks heard of their approach, they would return to the city, and battle would ensue.

One way or another, Mithra's wait would be over.

It took an hour or more before Mithra had the answers he sought. The approaching army were definitely Crusaders, and the herald they'd sent ahead shouted to all who could hear him that the Crusaders would defend their faith and avenge their fallen, for they had sworn a terrible oath and so it must be.

Guards bellowed for the gates to be closed, just as a messenger arrived from the other side of the city, conveying orders from the approaching Seljuk army that the city gates should be shut, as they would not permit a single infidel to pass through those hallowed portals to take shelter with any traitor who remained inside. The Seljuks swore they would defend the city against the infidels, even if it meant laying down their lives, for the Crusaders could not be allowed to kill any more innocents.

Once again, Mithra found himself staring at the bare plain, which was about to become home to not one, but two vast armies. In the city below, he heard panicked cries urging people to bar their doors and pray.

Mithra did neither. He intended to stand on the wall and witness the start of a war he feared no one could win. Whatever the outcome, if he survived the day, he knew his life would be forever changed.

So it was with wide eyes and a heavy heart he watched as two armies, two faiths, and two deep desires for vengeance warred for supremacy on the plain below.

Then the two armies collided and the calm plain erupted into chaos.

Seventeen

On top of a hill in the distance, Melisende glimpsed a city surrounded by high walls. "Is that the Holy City?" she asked.

Zoticus laughed. "No, though it's probably just as old. The ancients built it because of the hot springs beneath the ground, and it became a trading centre. They called it Dorylaeum, and it still goes by that name now."

Melisende couldn't help but stare. It wasn't as big as Byzas, but it was still bigger than anything she'd seen before starting this journey. The high stone walls surrounding it made her father's castle look like a child's fort.

She was fortunate to be travelling in the vanguard today, instead of somewhere in the dusty middle of the column. Zoticus had insisted on travelling with one of the small companies led by knights, instead of one of the larger forces commanded by some foreign king. His strategy seemed to have worked, for the knights paid her and Zoticus little to no attention, even when she walked close enough to them to discern the family crest each wore on his breast. They were not brothers, though they appeared as close as family. She knew them by their crests - the raven, the owl, the bear and the horn.

Some days they rode with their men, but others, like today, they kept close together, muttering about their superiors or laughing over some sport they'd engaged in the night before. Today, they were arguing about something, with much emphatic nodding and arm waving to illustrate their points.

Melisende crept closer in the hope of hearing what they were talking about.

"Once we reach the city, there will be sport aplenty. Why else did I offer our services as scouts? So we might serve in the vanguard today, and have first pick of the city's women," the Bear Knight boasted.

The Raven Knight hunched in his saddle. "I'd sooner have slept between a pair of camp followers than scouting. Damned desert. The days are hot, but the nights are far too cold!"

The Horn Knight offered little more than his loud agreement, as he took a long draught from a wineskin.

"If we'd found a small town or even a roadside inn, you'd all be perfectly satisfied with your scouting mission, having dipped your wick in whatever we found. Who'd have known there'd be no villages along the way?" the Owl Knight said. "If we had, we'd have scouted all the way up to the city, and we'd be safe inside, waiting for the others to catch up."

Melisende smothered the sound of disgust wanting to well up within her. These knights were so base, they considered the success of the crusade to be in the number of women they'd bedded. She'd love to see one of them lose a fight to a proper knight, the sort who protected his lady and fought for her honour. If Godfrey were a better swordsman, she might have wished to have him along to teach these men a much-needed lesson, but it was not to be. If only her own sword skills were better, she'd be willing to take them all on, and show them that a woman was not to be messed with. Perhaps…

"Something is wrong," Zoticus said urgently. He pointed. "The city gates are closed. Dorylaeum is a trading city, where Crusaders and pilgrims have stopped for supplies for more than half a century. Many Christians stayed after the first crusade to help defend the city, and their wives and children…with the sun so high in the sky, the gates should be wide open to welcome the business we bring." He stopped and dropped his bundle of belongings. "Put your armour on."

The other Crusaders glared as they marched around them, but Melisende didn't dare disobey. If Zoticus was worried enough to put his own armour on, then she'd be a fool not to follow his example. She stuck her helm on her head, then struggled to pull her breastplate over it. Swearing, she took her helm off and tried again.

Screams came from the men ahead.

"Archers!" Zoticus hissed.

Melisende dropped her breastplate to look.

Riders poured onto the plain between the Crusaders and the city, sending a storm of arrows into their lines. They fell short of the spot where Zoticus and she stood, but it would not be long before the riders rode into range.

"You remember how you owe me a favour, Squire?" Zoticus asked.

Oh God. Melisende nodded mutely. She knew she was not going to like doing what he asked.

"Drop everything, and RUN, GIRL, RUN!"

Clad in little more than her tunic and hose, without any armour to speak of, Melisende obeyed. She fixed her gaze on the distant forest, and willed her legs to move.

The thunder of hooves behind her had a familiar ring. She dared a glance over her shoulder, and her fears were realised.

Pegasus galloped at full speed toward her. But the mare's rider was the Raven Knight, followed by his friends, instead of her brother.

Hunt. Sport. A murdered girl. Realisation dawned on her that she'd become their quarry, while they forgot the battle that raged around them in their frenzy for the hunt.

But none of the knights knew she'd raced Pegasus since the mare had first learned to run. This was a race the mare could not win.

Melisende bit her lip, tasting the magic that coursed through her veins, and flew.

Eighteen

Melisende ran until she could run no more, and she was forced to lean against a tree as she fought to catch her breath. One, two, thr…

A man's scream behind her had her scrambling up the tree, heedless of the scratches from bark or branches until she reached a height where the leaves thinned and she could see through the canopy.

But what she saw…

The plain she'd looked upon only a moment before was now a heaving sea of blood, as two armies fought for supremacy and their lives, amid screams, growls and roars that seemed to belong more to beasts than to men. Yet the crunch of metal through bone and skin told the truth even to her unwilling ears. They were both beasts and men, armed with deadly weapons and battle rage no beast possessed.

Melisende wept for them, and for her vain hope that she might help this army. She wrapped her arms around her head, trying to muffle the sounds of battle or at least the agonised screams, but they echoed in her ears still.

Finally, her face pressed against the bark of a tree that bore witness to a battle she dared not watch, Melisende prayed to go home. She prayed with a fervour she had not known since she was a little girl, repeating the words until they turned into nonsense in her head, and still the battle raged.

Nineteen

Melisende woke unwillingly, her body feeling bruised as though she'd been thoroughly beaten. Even her face felt tender. Yet as she lifted her face from the hard surface she'd been resting against, she realised she was still in a tree, with the rough bark of the trunk still beneath her hands. How she'd slept through the remains of the battle, she did not know, but daylight faded into darkness, though it had not silenced the screams.

She stretched up, peering above the canopy at the battlefield she'd fled. To one side was a well-lit camp, with scattered campfires between the dark shadows she guessed were soldiers' tents. The screams she heard now came from women, likely the camp followers who had marched with the army and been captured upon their defeat. Some had been whores, while others were cooks and laundresses, servants pressed into service who did not deserve such a fate. Or perhaps they were women from the city, stolen before they'd shut the gates? She was under no illusions that the army she had marched with would have done any different. It was not religion that guided the soldiers' behaviour, she had learned along the way. If their superiors did not guard their appetites, neither would the men. Women were but possessions to them all, things to be had, whether they were willing or not. Her hand strayed to her belt, ready to draw her sword, but the scabbard was gone. Yet another thing she'd dropped in her headlong retreat. What she'd give for the last loaf of bread in her bag, or that cheese she'd been saving…

But her bag and all her other belongings remained upon the battlefield, lost in the darkness. She could not look for them until day dawned, and when it did, the army would find her easy prey.

Like some sort of African ape, this tree had become her new home. Laughter threatened to erupt, but she stifled it. Darkness and silence were the only armour she had now. Too much noise would draw attention from the army camp.

She blinked. Was that a light she'd seen upon the battlefield? No, surely not. And yet...

There was another, and another! She counted more than a dozen before she began to look more closely. Each light was a small lantern, held low by men who leaned over the bodies of the newly fallen, patting down their pockets, putting things into a bag, sometimes even stealing the men's shoes, before moving onto the next.

Melisende recoiled in horror. Whoever they were, these men were looting the bodies of their valuables, stealing from those who could no longer protest.

A gurgling cry went up, and Melisende watched in horror as the wounded man who had protested was stabbed to death before her eyes. He'd been Seljuk, not Crusader – so these thieves were not part of either army, so mercenary they would kill anyone for a few coins. Or this man's jewelled dagger, as it turned out. The weapon caught the light for barely a moment, before it was stuffed into a sack.

Melisende started in surprise. She recognised the sack, for the gay stripes had provoked much laughter from Zoticus when he'd seen it. He'd said that only a woman would choose a pretty sack instead of a plain one, but it appeared he'd been wrong. Thieves were partial to pretty things, too.

She hoped Zoticus had survived the battle. He'd saved her life, assassin or not. She didn't think he truly deserved to die so. The only way there would have been survivors was if they had run as she had.

She'd called it cowardice before, but now she was not so sure. There was no honour in what had been done to those men down there. Now they were being dishonoured in death, robbed of what little they possessed by a strange band of bandits.

She could hardly talk. She was trapped in a tree, with no food and nothing but her eating knife, and no idea where her next meal might come from or whether she'd ever make it home. Melisende wanted to weep but she had no tears left. For the first time, she understood the desire for vengeance that had burned in many Crusaders' words along the way. She wished she had the power to make all men regret the violence they brought to the world, but she was one girl, and they were out there in their thousands. So she fixed her ire upon one man – the thief who carried her striped sack. Her gaze followed him, as he crept from body to body, adding theft after theft to the crime she already condemned him for.

When his corpse robbing was complete, he would have to sleep some time. And when he did, she would use her dagger as Zoticus might have, and take back what was hers.

Twenty

When Mithra arrived at the gates the next morning with his handcart, he was surprised to find them still shut. Nor did the guards know when they would be allowed to open – the Seljuk army outside the walls gave the orders now.

So, with little else to do, Mithra ascended to the top of the walls again. He wasn't the only one who wanted to see what changes a night had wrought. Yet nothing had changed, or so it seemed.

All the bodies still lay where they had fallen in battle, beginning to bloat in the blazing sun.

The Seljuk army had camped by the river, as if they had never left. Nothing remained of the Crusader army.

Well, that was not entirely true. When the two armies had engaged yesterday, part of the Crusader column had broken off and retreated back the way they'd come. The Seljuks had been too busy celebrating their victory to bother going after the rest.

But even as the thought entered his mind, Mithra could see a peculiar procession leaving the army camp and heading for the gates. It started with soldiers, but the stumbling, shambling figures who followed them were a pitiful sight.

At first, Mithra thought that these were the same women they'd stolen from the city the last time they were here, but what remained of their clothes told a different story. These women had come with the Crusaders, and were now considered the spoils of war. More slaves for market, after a night of serving at enemy soldiers' pleasure. Dead eyed women who stared in horror at the carnage on the battlefield, cringing away from their captors, with nowhere to run.

"You may now open the gates," the new herald shouted. "But listen well. If there are any traitors still alive in Dorylaeum, we will seek you out. If you think to shelter one of these foul Crusaders who fled from battle, your fate will be the same as theirs." He pointed at the line of beaten women. "Your wives and children will be sold as slaves. These infidels will not befoul our lands again!"

The herald repeated his words several times, for the benefit of those on the walls or within the city. With every word, Mithra's fury grew. He strode down the steps, his lips pressed tight together so that his own words would not slip out. When the gates ground open, he was the first man through them, looking neither at the battlefield or the army he wished had died there. Finally, he reached the forest, where once again, he took his anger out on the trees. The sun shone above, but for him, the world had gone dark. He could not imagine a world worse than the one he lived in today.

Twenty-One

Dawn seemed to be an unspoken signal between the body thieves. As soon as the sun rose, so did they, melting into the trees before the stirring army camp could see them.

Melisende kept her eyes on her striped sack. She slid down her tree and started to follow them through the forest.

The men were weary from the long night's labour, and rarely looked around to see if anyone was following them. They walked and walked before finally they stopped in a clearing full of horses. Palfreys, destriers, plus a few geldings that looked to have come from her father's stock, they were so superior to the rest – these animals had belonged to Crusader knights, Melisende realised, though these magnificent mounts belonged to this pack of thieves now.

Yet the men moved past the horses, to part of the clearing when no grass grew. What Melisende at first took for a round hill was nothing of the sort. When her eyes adjusted to the gloom, she realised she regarded a large rock, but the thieves stood around it with some reverence.

"You! The traitorous battlefield wench!"

Melisende whirled in shock to find a man behind her. She bit her lip and raced up the nearest tree, faster than a cat.

She climbed until she'd reached what she felt was a safe height. Only then did she dare peer out again.

Instead of following her, the man had sunk to his knees. Only now did she see from his bloodstained tunic that this was not one of the thieves, but the Horn Knight. Somehow, he had survived the battle, and now he looked vainly about, searching for her.

Then the circle of thieves closed around

him, and it didn't matter.

"The girl, the girl...!" he cried.

One of the thieves stepped forward, drew his sword, and thrust it through the man's throat. The Horn Knight gurgled for a moment, before his life left him.

Melisende held her breath. If this many men started looking for the girl he'd seen, she wasn't sure she could move fast enough to escape them all. Silence and stillness were her only weapons now.

The leader cleaned his sword on the former knight's tunic, then pointed at two of his men. "You and you. Search the body for anything of value. Then take the body back to the battlefield. We don't dare leave anything here to mark the spot."

The two men nodded and began the grisly task.

A moment later, a fight broke out between the two.

The leader stepped between them, demanding to know what was the matter.

"His signet ring is missing," one man said.

"Because you stole it!" the second man said.

"Not I! I'm the one who saw where the ring

was on his finger, but there's nothing but pale skin now!"

"You're seeing things, you are!"

The leader held up his hands for silence. "What does it matter? All we have, belongs to us all. We add to the treasure left by our predecessors, and leave more for those who come after us. We are the Forty Thieves!"

The two men grumbled their agreement, finished robbing the man, then carried him between them out of clearing.

The rest of the thieves, including the man still carrying Melisende's striped sack, headed back to the rock. They all fell silent as the leader gave a command that sounded like, "Open something."

None of the men moved. Melisende shrugged, dismissing the man's order as gibberish, until she saw the rock begin to move. A house sized boulder rolled aside smoothly, as though some hidden machinery was at work. It left behind a hole several yards across, and Melisende glimpsed steps spiralling downward.

The thieves were not the slightest bit surprised, moving single file down the steps until the leader went last. He uttered another incantation that Melisende could not make out, before the boulder rolled back into its original place.

Dividing Melisende from everything she owned and the thief carrying it once more.

Twenty-Two

"Ho, woodcutter!"

More than anything, Mithra wanted to ignore the soldier and keep pushing his fully loaded handcart back to town. But the corpses staring up at the sky reminded him that doing so would only earn him a place among them.

Schooling his face into blankness, Mithra turned to face the man who'd shouted. "Yes?"

"How much for this cartload of wood?"

Mithra took a deep breath, doing the calculation in his head, before naming a price no sane man in the city would pay.

He had it in his hands before he could blink.

"The same again for every load you can bring before dark. The General wants these bodies burned."

Mithra nodded and thanked the man, even as the words seemed to choke him, then beat a hasty retreat for the forest. He'd bring one more load, after dark, and steer as far away from the army camp as he could when he brought it.

And in between, he'd hide deep in the forest, where no soldier would bother following him.

He found himself following a trail that some beast had made, which was barely wide enough to allow the cart to pass. More than once, it caught in the undergrowth and he had to hack at grasping branches that hoped to steal the cart from him.

Finally, he emerged into a clearing filled with horses.

"What in heaven's name…"

The words came from a woman, he was certain of it, though Mithra could not see her.

Then a body crashed into his, knocking him to the ground. He scrambled to his feet in time to see his cart shoved behind some bushes before the girl returned.

"I thought you were them returning. Quick, hide, they can't be far!" she urged, setting off at a run for a tree on the other side of the clearing.

Mithra couldn't seem to move, for he was too busy staring. She looked like one of the captured Crusader women who'd been paraded past the walls that very morning, yet she had somehow missed out on their fate. Likely she'd run away into the woods, and they'd lost her in the dark.

He understood why she'd want to hide, but the soldiers knew he was here to collect wood. If they'd followed him, then he needed to get his cart out of that bush and set to work with his axe.

"Do you want to die?" the girl demanded. Out of nowhere, she crashed into him again, somehow pushing him up against a tree. Her slight body pressed against his could not possess the necessary strength for such a thing, and yet Mithra could not deny she had done it. Up close, he could not help but stare at her face. Even as she glared at him, he had to admit she was pretty.

He opened his mouth to tell her so.

She muttered an oath he'd never heard a woman utter before, and clamped her hand over his mouth, shaking her head.

Only then did Mithra hear the sound of approaching footsteps. Two men, dressed like ordinary Dorylaeum citizens. Except ordinary citizens did not carry curved swords.

Wide-eyed, he pulled the girl closer, twisting his body so that it shielded hers.

She'd had the courage to escape the army once. That made her a thousand times braver than he'd ever be. Crusader maiden or not, he would not let them capture her again. He might not be able to save Peter's family or any of the other women, but this time would be different.

Twenty-Three

Heaven help her, but Melisende had never been this close to a man before. Well, except maybe her brothers in the practice ring, until they'd learned that greater strength in close combat was no match for her well-placed foot and the power she could put behind it.

But this wasn't the same.

He was dressed like one of the thieves, which is why she'd taken him for one of them at first, but the barrow he'd been pushing looked like something the farmers back home used to take their cabbages to market.

And just like the peasants back home, he

didn't carry any weapons.

Curse her soft heart, but she did not want to see him die as the Horn Knight had. So she'd used her magic to move him. Now he knew more about her than her own father and brothers. And his body was pressed against hers, nothing but two thin tunics between them that the heat of their bodies made feel like nothing at all.

He had a firm, muscled body, this peasant, if that was what he was. He worked hard at whatever he did. He could have used his strength against her, but he did not take advantage of their closeness. Even the look in his eyes lacked the lust she might have expected. His eyes darted back to the clearing when he heard the two thieves approach, and he became as still as the tree they had chosen for their hiding place.

"What's the password again?" one man asked.

"Open…simsi!" he said, or at least that's what Melisende thought she heard.

The man beside her stiffened as he saw the boulder move. He did not relax until they uttered the evidently magical password again and the boulder closed the entrance to their cave.

"Did you see that?" he breathed.

She gave a sharp nod. "That's the second time I've seen it. The first time was earlier today, when the rest of their band of thieves arrived and went in. I think their chief said there were forty of them, though I didn't think to count them. Then one of the knights who'd fled into the woods when the battle started happened upon them, and they killed him. Those two took his body back to the others. If they found you, they would have killed you just as easily, I am certain."

The man stepped back and bowed. "Then I owe you my life, though I don't even know your name."

She hesitated. Godfrey was gone and so was Zoticus. Did she need to invent a false name, or was she far enough from home that her own would sound false?

Finally, she said, "I am Lady Melisende of Mareschal. I rode with the Crusaders until someone killed them."

A faint blush coloured his cheeks. "So I must offer you my condolences for Lord

Mareschal...?"

She laughed. "There is no such lord. My father is Baron of Mareschal. Of all the men who died here yesterday, I only knew one of them well, and I'm not certain even an army could kill him. If he did survive, I'm sure he's far from here already."

The man nodded. "I am Mithra of Dorylaeum, son of Ali Baba from the same city. I am delighted to meet you, Lady Melisende. Did you know you share your name with the Crusader queen, who lives and rules in what you call the Holy City?"

Queen Melisende. No, she had not. "I'm not her," Melisende said.

"No, you are younger and more beautiful," Mithra said.

Now it was her turn to blush. Then a thought struck her. "Do you know her? Perhaps if I could see her, speak to her, she might help me find a way home."

Mithra hung his head. "I fear I have never met a queen, nor been allowed to speak to one. Even if I did know her, I could not take you to her, for there is an army between here and my home. If any soldier saw you..."

"He'd throw me over his shoulder and dump me in the place they're keeping their other prisoners. Their whores," Melisende spat.

"Their slaves," Mithra corrected. "They take the women and children they capture to sell as slaves."

Somehow, Melisende wasn't sure whether that was better or worse.

A rumble shook the ground beneath them. The boulder was moving again.

"Quick, they're coming out. Hide," she said, climbing the nearest tree.

Mithra sprang up beside her, climbing like he was half monkey. Maybe he was.

"I had no idea Crusader ladies could climb trees as well as a woodcutter," Mithra whispered.

"I grew up with a bunch of older brothers, whose every game was to see who could be the fastest, the strongest, the best." She shrugged. "I was the smallest, and the only girl. While never the strongest, I could always climb the highest. It helped no end when I began to learn how to heal, and prepare medicines. Sometimes the best leaves were only to be found at the top of a tree, and there are certain parasitic herbs that twine up a tree so that the only place to collect them is high above the ground. What my brothers didn't realise is that every hour spent in the stillroom or the sickroom is only after many hours spent in the forests and fields – "

She fell silent as the thieves began to emerge.

When they headed for the horses, she searched for the one with her striped sack, but every man was empty handed. Which meant her things were still inside the cave.

Once again, the leader was last, muttering his magic words to close the cave behind him.

"Where to next, Captain?" one thief asked.

The leader thought for a moment, then said, "With armies marching along the trade routes, no merchant will venture out, so all our usual haunts will have slim pickings until the war is done. So, we follow the remnants of the Crusader army. Some of them were surely wounded, and they'll fall behind. We can pick them off as they do. When they next go into battle, we'll be there to take first pick of both what's on the bodies and in the baggage train."

Disgusting scavengers. Preying upon wounded men and fallen soldiers. If bandits like these ever entered her father's lands, her brothers would scour them from the earth. She wished she could do the same here.

If only she were a powerful enchantress, capable of casting spells that incapacitated dozens of men at a time. Or that could turn the tide of battle, transforming defeat into victory.

Instead, even when she did use her magic, she'd managed to lose her last loaf of bread to a common thief.

The thieves mounted up and rode out, walking their horses in single file along a game trail until Melisende could no longer hear the unhurried hoofbeats.

"I counted forty of them. Did you?" Mithra asked.

She'd been so busy raging against them, she'd forgotten to count the thieves. Put to shame by a common woodcutter.

Melisende confessed that she'd been too distracted to do so.

Mithra gave her a sympathetic nod, his eyes dark with concern. "You've been through quite an ordeal. When I think of the other women…why, you are quite remarkable."

Other women now in the hands of the enemy. Women the Crusader knights should have protected, instead of running away like the honourless cowards they were. This crusade was doomed to fail from the beginning. She should not have come.

"Don't cry," Mithra said. "Here, don't you want to see what those thieves keep in their secret cave?"

Actually, she did not much care. Except that her own things were there…

Melisende wiped her eyes. Crying was for children. "We should wait to make sure they don't return. It would not do to be found inside, for surely that boulder is the only way in or out."

Mithra's eyes grew wide. "I had not thought of that. Best we wait, then, as you say, wise Lady Melisende."

That made her laugh. She definitely wasn't wise. Then again, the man might be teasing her. He looked to be about the same age as her brothers, and they liked to tease her all the time.

"If I was so wise, I would have stayed home, instead of coming here on this foolish crusade," she said.

Mithra looked thoughtful. "My master used to say wisdom comes from experience, making mistakes that you must learn from. The wisest men have made many mistakes."

"Master? Are you a slave?"

Mithra stared at her for a long moment, before he said, "Things must be very different in the north, if you cannot tell the difference between a slave and a free man. Though I suppose being an apprentice is a little like being a slave, for my father paid my master to teach me his trade, which meant working very hard without being paid."

"But…you are a man now, too old to be an apprentice, surely. Most of the boys back home became journeymen younger than my brother was when he was made a squire."

Mithra nodded. "In some trades, it is so. The trade guilds say who is good enough to become a master, but not all trades have a guild in Dorylaeum. Without a guild, we are all either apprentices or merchants. Perhaps if my master had lived a little longer, he would have helped me to become a merchant. Or his son, who would happily have partnered with me in a trade venture."

"How did they die?" Melisende asked.

Mithra's expression darkened. "It is a dark tale, one not fit for a woman's ears, but when the woman has been in battle and survived to tell the tale…perhaps you are made of sterner stuff than the norm."

Melisende didn't think he'd be as impressed if he knew she'd run, climbed a tree and slept through most of the battle, so she merely said, "Tell me."

By the time Mithra told her about his master's death, she wished she could hide her face and weep for these men she had not known. But there was worse to come.

The Seljuks sounded no better than the men she'd marched with.

"Peter counted on the Crusaders to come and save him. Perhaps it is for the best that he did not live to see their defeat," Mithra said sadly.

"I'm not sure any more that a crusade can save anyone. Saving a city by sacking it and killing the inhabitants…I fear they are all mad!"

"So you have no desire to rejoin the crusade, if you could?" Mithra asked.

Melisende shook her head. "The only thing I want now is to go home."

Twenty-Four

The silence stretched between them, but Mithra did not know how to break it. If he was trapped in a foreign land, far from home, hiding from an army that wanted to torture and enslave him, he didn't think he would have her calm composure. He'd be anxious to take action, leaving caution behind in the dust, and probably get himself killed.

Yet Melisende had kept them both alive.

"It's been some time. When they left, they talked of catching up to the rest of the Crusader army. They would have had to hurry. It should be safe to see what they keep in their cave now," Melisende said, descending.

He'd been so busy talking to her, he'd completely forgotten about his own curiosity. He mumbled his agreement and climbed down after her.

Lady Melisende moved to stand in the same spot where the thief captain had, took a deep breath, and said, "Open simsi."

Nothing happened.

Melisende cleared her throat with some annoyance. Louder this time, she repeated, "Open simsi."

The boulder did not move.

Most girls he knew would have given way to anger by now, or at least stamped their feet, but Lady Melisende merely took another breath and asked, "Is there something else the man did to make it open?"

Mithra shrugged. "I think he only said something." She'd been here longer, and heard the incantation more times than he had, so surely she knew it better.

"Perhaps…perhaps it's blood magic, which requires a blood price to work," she said. She took her dagger, pressed the point to her finger and waited until a drop of blood welled up. Then she wiped it on the rock. "Open simsi."

Still nothing.

Finally, Mithra said, "I thought he said sesame. You know, like the seed."

She looked puzzled. "What sort of seed?"

"Sesame seed. You know, it's small and straw-coloured. You can press them to make oil that's good to cook with, or you can use the seeds in cooking. Mixed with honey and spices, some of the bakers in town make the most delicious cakes…" He opened his eyes to find her staring at her. "You don't know sesame?"

Melisende shook her head. "We don't have that sort of seed at home. Besides, why would he talk about seeds when he wants a massive rock to move? Simsi is the old word for mountain where I come from. So when he said, 'Open simsi,' he's telling the mountain to open. Isn't there some sort of proverb about mountains moving for a particular prophet? It makes much more sense."

Mithra had to admit what she said was true, but the unmoving stone seemed to say otherwise. "I still think I heard sesame," he said.

"Then you try to command the boulder," Melisende said, folding her arms across her breast.

Mithra did not want to look like a fool, but he wasn't sure he had a choice. The rock hadn't moved for her, so the worst that could happen would be that he might fail, too.

What did it matter? She probably didn't think much of him, anyway. He was nothing but a lowly woodcutter, while she was a lady who lived in some Crusader castle, far to the north, protected by her knightly brothers.

Who would likely run him through with their swords if they saw him speaking to their sister.

Mithra sighed. "Open sesame," he said.

The rock gave an ominous rumble, then rolled aside.

Mithra looked around, worried that someone might have heard it, and know that intruders were about to enter their cave. But no one came.

"I'll go first, shall I? After all, that's best, just in case they've left a guard inside," Mithra said, brandishing his axe as if he was eager to meet his foe, when that was definitely not the case.

But no matter what fear he felt, he could not allow her to come to more danger because of him. He'd opened the cave, after all.

Not waiting for Melisende's assent, he descended into the dark.

Twenty-Five

As she headed down the steps, at first Melisende wished she'd brought a lantern, for if this place was anything like the cellars back home, she would be standing in the pitch dark within a few yards of the bottom of the stairs. But this cave was no cellar, for it seemed that the thieves had left the lantern burning when they'd left.

Did that mean they had left a guard with it?

Fear almost drove her back up the steps to the surface, but she dared not show cowardice in front of the woodcutter. Especially as he walked in front of her, so he would bear the brunt of any attack.

If anything, the cave brightened, the further she walked into it. Yet the lights seemed to come from a dozen different places, all up near the ceiling. When she held her hand up near one, she was surprised to feel a draught creeping down her fingers. She marvelled at the thought that air and light could come from the surface that were invisible to those who walked above. If anyone had known such a wondrous cavern lay beneath, they surely would have tried to find a way inside.

"Can you believe it?" Mithra stood with his arms outspread, his eyes wide with wonder.

Melisende smiled, biting back a comment that the cellars in Dorylaeum were evidently much smaller than those back home.

Instead, she scanned the underground chamber, searching for her things. Finally, she glimpsed the coloured stripes, hiding beneath several other sacks that looked dull in comparison.

She struggled to shove them aside, before getting her hands on the striped sack and pulling it from beneath its drab fellows.

It was heavier than she remembered, likely

full of things looted from the battlefield bodies. Having no desire for stolen treasures, Melisende upended her bag on the stone floor. Coins cascaded out – copper, silver, and more gold than she remembered possessing at the beginning of her journey. Jewelled daggers and brooches made up the rest, with no sign of her spare clothes, or her sword.

Her stomach growled a reminder of what else was missing.

Oh, that vile thief! She pawed through the tinkling hoard, but still she didn't find what she sought. Instead, she swore.

"What is the matter?" Mithra asked.

"That ill begotten whoreson stole my cheese!"

Mithra burst out laughing. "Truly, I have never heard a woman use language so colourful. And what do you care for some old cheese? There is enough gold here to buy you a lifetime's worth of cheese, and all the cheese your children could ever want, too."

Melisende blinked. She rose from her crouch and surveyed the room properly for the first time. As she took in what she had missed while intent on the search for her sack, her eyes grew wide. "It must have taken more than one band of thieves to amass this much wealth," she said. "Not even a dozen such bands in their entire lifetime…"

The plain sacks she'd shifted had started to spill out their contents. Each held a fortune in gold and jewels. Yet they were stacked higher than her head, and wider than her arms could reach. Gold statues gleamed in the far corner, looking at first like men, until she looked more closely and realised they bore the heads of beasts. Chests and jars and barrels, stacked a dozen deep, reached almost to the ceiling of the cavern. On all sides, she saw the wealth of more than a dozen kings' treasuries, with dozens more hiding in the shadows.

Melisende pressed her lips together. "I don't care where they got it. I don't care how many years they've been collecting it. They stole my things, and as I can't take them back, I shall fill the bag they stole from me with their gold, to pay for what they took." She began picking up the coins from the pile on the floor, flicking aside the jewels. She was no grave robber. When she was done with the gold, she started on the silver.

"In payment for the cheese," she said.

Then the coppers.

"For my loaf of bread, and my cloak."

When there were no more coins on the floor, she tied the sack shut and rose, throwing it over her shoulder. "The gold should pay for my passage home, with a little left over for a bath and a meal and a night in a real bed in your city's best inn. If you can recommend one, I would be grateful," she said.

Once again, she found Mithra staring at her. "All this wealth does not belong to anyone. You said it yourself – these thieves stole it. With just a small part of this, you could live comfortably without having to work another day of your life." He shook his head. "And yet you take one bag, and copper coins for bread?"

It was Melisende's turn to stare. No amount of money could stop her from having to work every day of her life. Not for money or reward, but because it was expected of her. A woman in her position had the responsibility of looking after the people on her father's – or her husband's – estate. Hours spent in the stillroom, drying herbs or preparing medicines. Hours more seeing to the sick, and bringing charity to those who needed it. Her father's horse herds and the tithes from their tenants bought them everything they needed, but no amount of money could buy good health. That took time and care and more than a little love. Yet this man from a faraway land knew nothing of her life at home. She did not know where to start to even try to make him understand. "What would you do with it, then?" she challenged.

His eyes gleamed in the darkness. "I would buy a house for my father and mother, so they need not ever pay rent again to a greedy landlord. I would pay the food merchants in the marketplace to deliver provisions to their house every week, so that they would never have to go hungry again. I would tell the inn where my mother works to hire a new cook, so that the only people my mother would cook for, and then only if she wishes it, would be my father and me. If she did not want to cook any more, I would hire a woman to do it for her. Or a girl she might train as her apprentice, perhaps. I would pay for two orphaned boys to be my father's apprentices, to help him cut and fetch firewood until they were old enough to do the job on their own, so that my father need no longer work. I would go to all the merchants my master traded with, and start doing business with them once again. I would take apprentices of my own, bright, poor boys, or those with no parents, and no hope of someone paying for them to have an apprenticeship, so that they might learn the trade as I did. If it were possible, I would pay every soldier in that army up there to desert their General and go home, never to take up arms again. And I would travel to Rialto, to see my master's family, to tell them what happened to Simon and Peter and the others, and give them what gold I managed to salvage before the army stole all their worldly goods." Mithra took a deep breath, then let it out slowly, as if he had so many things in his mind, he had to pause to decide what to say next.

"Then you should take it," she said. "But if those soldiers are anything like the crusading army I marched with, no amount of coin given them will ever be enough. They wish to take, and conquer, and they will not stop, not even if God himself commanded it. So do all the good you can, but I pray, do not give a single copper coin to those soldiers. Or the Crusaders, if they ever return. Hide it until they are gone, and use the money to repair the damage they have done." She closed her eyes. "All I ask is that you help me buy passage home."

Mithra nodded gravely. "You have saved my life. I can refuse you nothing. I will do everything in my power to help you find hospitality in my city, and, after that, a way home."

His words were spoken like an oath, and she believed them.

"I will go now, and return in the morning," he said. "Here, take this." He held out a small pouch that had been fastened to his belt. "It was to be my midday meal. I'm sure it is poor fare for a lady such as yourself, and I will see that you have better when you enter the city, but I hope it may tide you over until I can find a way to sneak you past the army camp without being captured."

He took a bag of coins on his way out, hiding it under a load of fresh cut wood Melisende helped him stack on his handcart before he left.

Wrapped in a cloak she'd borrowed from the cavern, Melisende curled up in a tree with broad enough branches to cradle her body safely, and settled in for what she hoped would be her last night sleeping outside.

Twenty-Six

Grabbing a handful of coins from the bag before stashing it beneath a pile of firewood, Mithra headed first for the market. If Lady Melisende meant to enter the city, she would need to look like a local woman. There was a merchant who sold secondhand clothes which might be suitable.

He picked the first three gowns he saw, all the sort of thing his mother might wear, and added a couple of veils. He debated whether to buy some sort of underdress, too, but just the thought of Lady Melisende wearing nothing more than one of those thin, filmy things made him blush, so he decided against it. Let her buy her own underthings, for she had no shortage of coin. The thing was to get her into the city.

Ah, but she'd wanted a cloak, too, he remembered. He found one that was the same shade of green as her eyes, and added that to his pile.

The merchant who owned the shop never took his eyes off Mithra for a moment. As though he expected him to try to steal his shabby stock. Mithra wanted to tell the man that he could afford to take Lady Melisende to the silk merchant at the other end of the bazaar, but he restrained himself. He'd pay for his purchases, then go and see if the inn up in the Merchants' Quarter had any rooms free.

"How much?" Mithra asked, reaching into his money pouch.

The merchant lifted each item, eyed it for a long moment, before setting it down and going to the next, as though he hadn't watch Mithra select every one. Finally, he rested one hand on the pile of clothes and stretched out the other, palm up. "Fifty coppers," he said loftily.

Mithra thought it sounded a little high, but then he'd never bought women's clothing before. He didn't have time to haggle. He took out a coin and set it on the table.

The merchant's eyes grew wide. He snatched up the coin, then bit it.

Too late, Mithra realised he'd pulled out gold instead of silver. He dug through his pouch and pulled out a handful of copper. "Here…"

"Thief! A lowly labourer like you could not come upon gold like this honestly. I knew you were a thief the moment I saw you. Guard, guard!"

Instead of a guard, the merchant had managed to get the attention of a pair of soldiers, who hurried over.

Mithra swore, threw the coins back into his pouch, and bolted.

At first, he ran through the middle of the market, dodging between people until he found the alley he wanted. He dived for the narrow gap between one shop and another, then headed into the maze of alleys and back passages that only a boy who'd grown up in the bazaar truly knew. The soldiers lost him in seconds, and by the time he emerged from the side door of Simon's old shop, wearing the set of clean clothes he'd kept there when he worked in the shop, they were nowhere in sight.

Holding his head proudly like the merchant he'd once hoped to become, he headed for the inn.

The taproom was almost empty, but for two soldiers who eyed him suspiciously when he entered. "Are you new to the city?" one of them asked.

They both had their hands on their swords, as if waiting for him to deliver a less than favourable answer.

"No, I was born here," Mithra said easily. "I worked in one of the shops a few doors down, until we had to close because we'd run out of goods to sell. I'm expecting a new shipment of silk and spices from the east soon, and I wanted to see if there would be any rooms free for the caravan master when he arrives."

"All the rooms are free," said the innkeeper, with a surly glance at the soldiers. "We've had no new guests since the army arrived, and all the old ones left. Your friend will be assured of the best room in the house. As long as he doesn't mind answering a lot of questions from these men first."

Mithra's heart sank. If Lady Melisende came here, the soldiers would capture her for sure. He managed a smile. "I shall tell him when he arrives."

It was the same at the next inn, and the next, right down to the cheap one by the gates where his mother worked.

Darkness was falling, and he had no clothes for Melisende, and nowhere for her to sleep.

Perhaps his aunt might have some old clothes that Melisende might be able to wear. Praying his luck would change, Mithra headed for his uncle's house.

To his surprise, Aunt Seda answered the door.

"What happened to the maid?" Mithra asked.

Seda frowned. "The girl ran away. I don't know what's the trouble with these modern girls, not wanting to do good, honest work. One night she was here, and the next morning – gone! Now I need a new one and I don't know where to find one. I don't suppose you know of any girls where you live who are good workers?"

Most of the girls where Mithra lived were all good workers, spending every hour of the day working at whatever jobs they already had, if they weren't taking care of their family. Sometimes, like his mother, they did both. None of them were in need of another job.

"If I do, I shall send her straight to you, dear aunt," Mithra promised.

She smiled. "You always were a good boy. If only Kasim and I could have had a son like you…"

"My mother sent me to ask if you have any old clothes you no longer need. There are a couple of poor widows near us who are dependent on the kindness of the city, as they have no family to care for them…"

Seda nodded. "Of course, of course. Perhaps you can help me lift the lids on the chests, for I have no maid to do it for me now."

Mithra dutifully followed his aunt inside and helped her search through her clothes until he had an armful of things that might fit Melisende.

"Oh, and there are these things of Kasim's which no longer fit him. I fear he's grown quite stout, and I've had to order new tunics from the tailor's for him. A new belt, too, for he cannot fasten the old one. It's still quite fine. I'm sure it would fit you."

His aunt would not let him go until he'd at least fastened the new belt around his waist, and then she fussed about him, shifting things from his old belt to the new one. He reached for his coin pouch at the same time as she did, spilling the contents everywhere.

Seda whispered a gentle oath – not the sort that burned his ears, like Melisende's – and knelt to help him collect the coins.

When he had everything back where it belonged, Mithra thanked his aunt, bundled up the clothes into an old sack, and headed home.

Now night had fallen, he saw more soldiers in the streets, but he just bowed his head, like any tired labourer at the end of a long day, and they mostly ignored him.

Lady Melisende had no hope of hiding in Dorylaeum with all these soldiers around. They would know her for a Crusader maiden in a moment.

But if they thought she was a lowly servant, someone beneath their notice, she might have a chance.

An idea began to form in the back of his mind. By morning, he hoped to have the whole scheme thought out, before he presented it to Melisende and prayed she would agree to it.

Twenty-Seven

"I don't believe a simple change of clothes will convince them I'm not a Crusader," Melisende said, looking down at the shapeless dress with distaste.

"Says the Crusader maiden who made an entire army think she was a boy for the march here," Mithra returned.

That made her pause. "Are people really so silly that they only see what is on the surface?" It was a sobering thought, and a saddening one.

"People see what they expect to see. Soldiers expected to see a boy in armour, marching with them, and so that's what they saw. The Dorylaeum guards expect to see a modestly clad woman, escorted by her husband or brother or whoever, as do the Seljuk soldiers. If you wear this, they will take one look and dismiss you as beneath their notice."

"Men always notice women. Sometimes they try to hide it, but, trust me, we know when we are being watched."

Mithra blushed. "I only glanced over my shoulder to see if you were finished dressing. When I realised you were not, I turned my back again."

Melisende's mouth dropped open in surprise. More at his honesty than his admission. She gave herself a mental shake, telling herself he couldn't have seen much more than her bare back, for she'd turned her back on him, too, and…oh, what did it matter, anyway? She'd be headed home soon and she'd never see this woodcutter again.

"Let's go," he said, giving his handcart a push.

Panic rose up in her throat, but she forced it down. If Mithra had wanted to betray her to the soldiers, he'd have done so yesterday, without coming back and bringing her these scratchy clothes. With her hair covered by one veil and another that hid most of her face, there was nothing for the soldiers to see except a walking sack. She felt like a leper.

She glanced nervously at the army camp as they stepped out of the shadow of the forest. If they caught her, they certainly wouldn't treat her like a leper. Lecherous soldiers couldn't keep their hands off the women they had caught. Not to mention wearing what felt like a tent that ballooned around her while she walked would make it harder to run if she had to. Even with her magic, could she reach the cover of the trees?

"Keep your eyes on the ground. Pretend you're so painfully shy that you can't bear to see someone looking at you. Hunch your shoulders a little, and bow your head, like you're afraid of being beaten. Don't look around, don't stare, and definitely don't meet anyone's gaze.."

She aimed a glare at the back of his head before doing as he commanded. If her brothers could see her now, they would laugh so hard they pissed themselves. She bowed her head to no one, and to do it now on the orders of some foreign peasant…if her life did not depend on it, she wasn't sure she could bear it.

It took an eternity to cross the battlefield, even with the bodies gone. She didn't dare wonder where they'd gone.

Finally, they slowed as they reached the gates.

"Good evening," Mithra said.

The guards returned his greeting, and they exchanged pleasantries for a moment until someone said, "Who's the girl?"

A tug on her sleeve made her shuffle closer to the handcart. She relaxed a little when she realised it was Mithra, then tensed again under the guards' sudden scrutiny.

"This is my betrothed, Melis. She came to find me to invite me to dinner with her family, and she was afraid to walk back through the forest on her own, so she waited to walk with me."

One of the guards sniggered, while the other laughed aloud. "Oh, it's called walking, now, is it?"

Mithra lifted his shoulders in a shrug. "Well,

our families won't let us wed yet, what with the war and all, and we've been waiting so long…what else is a man to do but go for a walk in the woods?"

More laughter as the guards waved them through, wishing him a hasty wedding.

Melisende's face burned. If she meet anyone's eyes now, they'd see her mortification. Much safer to keep her gaze firmly on the ground.

When they were far enough away from the gate for no one to hear, she hissed, "Damn your impertinent hide, Mithra. Now everyone thinks I am your whore! I should strike you down for that. Were my brothers here, they would cut out your lying tongue."

Mithra kept his voice low. "No, they do not. Those two guards believe you are my betrothed, soon to be my obedient bride. From the moment I told them you were mine, they averted their eyes and looked only at me."

"They think we fornicated in the forest!" she persisted.

"Would you rather they knew the truth?"

No, for it would mean her death, and likely his as well.

"Take me to the inn. I want to wash," she snapped.

He hesitated for a moment, then said, "Come with me while I take my cart home, and then I shall take you to where you can stay."

She followed him to the door of what she might have called a tiny cottage, were the roof made of thatch and not stone. He tucked the handcart into a corner of the yard, then led the way down a new street.

The hovels on either side did not give the air of a prosperous place to stay.

"Are you sure the best inn is this way?" she demanded.

Mithra sighed. "Indeed it is, but I cannot take you there, nor to any other inn in the city, for there are soldiers waiting at all of them to put any newcomer to the question. A woman travelling alone is unusual enough, but one who arrives now, when there are no travellers left in the city…you would be caught and questioned for certain. So, in the absence of a suitable inn, I have found somewhere you might stay without suspicion until the army departs and you can seek passage home."

They passed several soldiers along the way, some of whom appeared to be patrolling, while others seemed to be looking for some off-duty entertainment.

She had to wait until the soldiers were far enough away before she said tartly, "It had better not be a brothel."

"Though you swear like one of their best customers, no, I would not dream of taking you to such a place."

Somewhat satisfied, she followed him through the poor district and into one that looked more prosperous.

"This is more like it," she said, looking at the larger houses with satisfaction.

Mithra chose one and rapped smartly at the door.

A well-dressed woman wearing a veil much like Melisende's answered it. "Good evening, nephew."

"Aunt Seda, this is Melis, the maid you wanted. She is formerly from a Crusader household, so she might not be as familiar with our ways, but she is capable and a quick learner. If you can give her somewhere suitable to sleep, she will serve you well."

Melisende did not have more than a moment to collect her wits before the woman had grabbed her arm and dragged her inside, closing the door on Mithra's only mildly apologetic countenance.

A maid? Truly? And shortening her name, so it sounded like malice. Perhaps she should have let the thieves kill him after all.

Twenty-Eight

When Mithra reached home, he found both his parents waiting for him, with a familiar sack on the table between them.

"Mother!" he said with surprise. "Does no one at the Gatehouse want supper tonight? I can't remember the last time you came home so early."

"No one at the Gatehouse wants a cook tonight, or any other night," Mother said. "With few visitors to the city and people scared to go out after dark on account of all the soldiers in the streets, the innkeeper's wife will do all their cooking from now on. I thought perhaps I could help you and your father, at least until there are travellers on the roads again, but when I went into the storeroom to fetch the handcart, I found this." She pointed at the sack.

His father took up the tale. "When I arrived home, your mother asked me about it, but I'd never seen it before. I certainly hadn't put it there, or carefully hidden it beneath a pile of fresh cut firewood. And when we opened it…" He tipped it up and gold cascaded across the table. "I know you sold Simon's goods and keep the money you made from them in a chest, but the dust atop it tells me you haven't touched that in weeks, and even if you sold every item in his warehouses, you could not have amassed so much gold. If it were filled with coppers, maybe, or even a few silver coins, but gold…this is a king's ransom here. Tell me – did you steal the Seljuk army's war chest?"

He wished he had, for without money, surely the soldiers would have to go home. But Mithra did not dare lie to his parents.

"I was cutting wood in the forest yesterday," he began.

He told them everything about the thieves, their magic cave, and all it contained. The only detail he left out was any mention of Lady Melisende.

Though she likely wouldn't forgive him for making her work as his aunt's maid, she definitely would not forgive him if she shared her secrets.

When Mithra had finished his tale, his father said, "My son, you have done a terrible thing. While there is little crime in stealing from a thief, the Forty Thieves are known for their ruthless methods and the power of their vengeance. If they find out you have taken what belongs to them, they will hunt you to the very ends of the earth, kill you, and slaughter everyone you have ever known or loved. To protect us from their wrath, we must bury the gold deep in the garden, and no one must ever know we have it."

In vain did Mithra argue that the coin could be spent in such a way without revealing the source of their wealth, but his parents would hear none of it.

On the morrow, both he and his father went out to cut wood again, for all the world as if nothing had changed.

And for a time, it seemed that little had. But not for long.

Twenty-Nine

To her surprise, Melisende found that being Seda's maid was not so onerous a job as it seemed. The thin pallet she was expected to sleep on was as uncomfortable as any of the nights she'd spent sleeping on the ground near Zoticus, but her duties seemed to consist solely of fetching and carrying things for either the cook or Seda herself.

Back at home, as mistress of the stillroom and succourer of the sick, she'd been far busier.

While she stayed inside the house, she wasn't expected to wear the heavy veil she'd donned to get through the gates, and the cook seemed resigned to having to explain even the simplest task to her. Apparently, the woman had trained a great many maids.

Every day, she was expected to sweep the steps, and she took a moment to ascertain whether there were soldiers still patrolling the streets, or whether she might leave. Every day, she found them still there, so when she was finished, she headed back inside again, to fetch some meat for the cook, or to find the slippers Seda had lost since putting them down only a moment ago.

One day melted into the next, and she was surprised to discover she'd been a servant for more than two weeks before she met the master of the house, who'd been travelling to another town to see what had become of a shipment of trade goods which had not yet arrived.

He was a great, lumpy jelly of a man, with greedy eyes that matched his girth. His gaze touched on everything and made her feel like scrubbing.

He had a manservant who served his dinner, but the cook still expected her to carry the platters to the table, and Melisende felt his eyes on her every time she entered the room.

She was glad when the cook let her retire as soon as she'd brought in dessert, for with Master Kasim home, the evening meal would end quite late and it was better to wash the dishes in the morning, when they'd had time to soak.

Only that morning, she'd discovered a plentiful supply of straw in the hayloft above the stables, and after several trips from the loft to her tiny bedchamber, she now had a bed even her brothers would envy.

She fell asleep almost instantly, only to wake in the dark with her heart pounding and no reason for it that she could see.

Then she heard heavy breathing when she knew she was holding her breath.

She was up and out of bed in an instant, trying to escape from her tiny room, but a solid shadow blocked the doorway.

A shadow that shoved her up against the wall.

"Take those clothes off, girl," a male voice said.

A draught chilled her legs as she realised

he'd seized hold of the hem of her gown and was trying to haul it up over her head.

"Go to hell," she snarled, tearing out of his grasp.

Then his full weight hit her, knocking her to the floor. He forced his lips against hers, in a slobbery kiss that made her retch.

She bit him.

He howled and lashed out at her, but she smashed her knee into his groin and fought her way free before any of his blows landed.

Then she bit her own lip, and magic seemed to infuse the air around her. She moved while it did not.

"Come back here, girl. I am the master of this house, and you will obey me!" Kasim roared.

"Touch me again and I'll cut off your wizened little prick, and shove it so far up your arse, all you'll taste for the next month will be your own balls," Melisende hissed, drawing her dagger.

He staggered to his feet, blundering past her in the dark toward his own chamber.

She breathed a sigh of relief and sheathed her dagger.

"I'll be back with my belt, and when I do, you'll learn obedience, bitch!" Kasim shouted.

Not bloody likely.

She paused only to pull on her boots and grab her cloak to cover herself before she raced out into the street. She wasn't sure where she was headed, but anywhere was better than here.

Thirty

Melisende stopped to catch her breath, and discovered she'd run clean across town to Mithra's house. She found him asleep in a loft above the storerooms, so she shook him awake.

Before he had time to speak, she said, "Did you know that your uncle is a lecherous toad who deserves to burn in hell for all eternity for trying to use his servants like whores?"

Mithra managed to sit up. "I had heard that he beat some of his servants, but I never imagined the beatings were anything but deserved. From what my aunt said…"

"Seda is a simpering fool who spends her days making clothes for the children she'll never have because her husband is too busy forcing himself on his servants in their own beds to spend any time in hers!"

"Well, we did suspect there was no love between them and he only married her for her father's money, but Seda is the only person I knew who would take you in without asking questions, even if it meant you had to pretend to be her maid for a few days. I'd hoped the army might leave before now, but they seem determined to stay. I'm as trapped as you, Melisende – I don't know what else to do."

She forced her hands down by her sides, in an effort to resist shaking Mithra again. Perhaps he truly didn't know what a villain his uncle was, or he hadn't until now. Seda's house had been a suitable place to hide, if Kasim hadn't come home.

"Perhaps if I talk to my uncle – "

She cut him off. "I talked to him. I told him I'd cut off his manhood if he ever touched me again. He went off in search of something to beat me with, or at least that's what I think he was shouting about. I don't know. That's when

I left to come here."

"Right. All right." Mithra rubbed his face with his hands.

"It is most certainly NOT all right."

"No, but I don't know what else I can do. If you stay here, my parents would soon find out about you, which means the rest of the street would know within the week, and someone would sell you to the soldiers sooner than that. The only safe place for you is Seda's house. If you can stay away from my uncle…"

"He came to my bed!"

"Is there anywhere else you might sleep? Their house is much bigger than ours. Perhaps in the stables…"

Melisende wanted to slap him – if her father knew she had to sleep in a stable! – but her father wouldn't be pleased with her sleeping anywhere but her chamber at home. Grudgingly, she offered, "There is a hayloft above the stables which you can only reach by a ladder, which I could pull up after me. I doubt he'd find me there."

"Then that is what you must do. I'm sorry, Lady Melisende, that I cannot offer you better accommodations, but I am merely a woodcutter, and what you see here is how I live. If it were safe to enter any of the inns, I would take you to one at once, but the soldiers… the soldiers…I'm trying to keep you safe in the only way I can. If only the angels had sent you a better protector. One of their own, or a knight, maybe, but I am merely…me. Forgive me."

Now she regretted her outburst. What man in her village at home – let alone a woodcutter – would offer her such assistance, if they'd found her in the woods alone? He'd done nothing but help her, in any way he could. His uncle might be a piece of filth, but Mithra was a good man.

"There is nothing to forgive," she said. On a whim, she kissed his cheek. For a moment, she thought a spark had passed between them, but surely she had imagined it. "I will go, and ascend to my new hayloft bedchamber."

He took a deep breath. "If you wish, I could come with you, and stand guard while you sleep."

She'd never wanted a man in her bedchamber, but if she was to trust any man in it, it would be Mithra. "I would like – "

A thunderous hammering came from the front door. "Ali Baba, I know you are home! Open the door this instant!"

"It's him!" Mithra hissed. "I don't know what he's doing here, but if he finds you...Go, Melisende, go! I will keep him here for as long as I can, so that you are safe in your eyrie when he returns."

Once again, Melisende bolted, but more than once, she caught herself glancing behind to see if he was following.

No, not Kasim. Instead, she hoped for Mithra.

Thirty-One

By the time Mithra reached the front door, he found not only had his father opened it but Kasim had already bulled his way inside.

After feeling the full force of Melisende's fury, Mithra was more than ready to fight the man himself. His father knew nothing of Melisende, or what had transpired in Kasim's house tonight, so it seemed safest to be civil. To start with, at least.

"Good evening, Uncle," Mithra said. "Is there some urgent matter that you wish father's help with, that you must visit so late?"

Uncle Kasim's eyes narrowed. "Yes, most

urgent. You did not seem to think so. We are family! I allow you to live in this house at so low a rent it is positively criminal, yet when the tables are turned, I find you are not willing to share your good fortune with me."

Mithra and his father exchanged confused glances. This had nothing to do with Melisende, so even Mithra had no idea what the man meant.

"My most esteemed brother," Ali Baba began. "Have you perhaps drunk a little too much wine? My wife has recently lost her position as Gatehouse cook, but I would hardly consider that good fortune."

Kasim's brows lowered until they almost met over his hawk-like nose. "Pah! What do I care about your wife or the pennies they pay her? Not when you possess gold so plentiful you did not even notice that these were missing!" He pulled something out of the pouch at his waist and tossed it at the table. The coins flew across the surface before tinkling to the floor.

Ali Baba bent to retrieve them. When he raised his head above the table, his expression had turned from confusion to dread. Carefully, he laid the three gold coins on the table.

"Do not lie to me, brother. Your son dropped these at my house weeks ago, and only found them tonight. Where are the rest?" Kasim demanded.

Ali Baba closed his eyes. "I will show you." He rose.

Mithra was faster. "No. I shall. I found them in a cave in the forest when I was out cutting wood."

"Aha!" Kasim turned to his brother. "Did you think you could keep such wealth to yourself? Are we not brothers, who share everything?"

If Kasim's words were true, then he would have invited them to live with him in the Merchants' Quarter, instead of charging them what was actually quite a normal rate of rent for a cottage here.

"I'll take you now if you like," Mithra offered.

Kasim's eyes gleamed with even more greed than usual. "Not without bringing some beasts to carry the treasure home. What is to stop you from stealing it the moment I am gone and hiding it somewhere else? No, I shall take my share now. Wait right here, while I go get some horses."

Mithra started in panic. If Kasim went to his stables and found Melisende…

"No, not horses! What you want is mules. Sturdy beasts, who are used to carrying great weights. If you mean to carry your half of the treasure away with you, you will need as many mules as you can find."

Kasim nodded thoughtfully. "You see, brother? Your son knows the value of family, if you do not. Perhaps I shall make him my heir if my barren wife does not bother to give me a son."

Mithra had no desire for anything his uncle had touched, but he was not a fool, either. With or without the thieves' gold, inheriting his uncle's business at some point in the future could not be a bad thing.

"Thank you, Uncle. I will wait here while you get the mules."

Wearing a grin so wide he truly resembled the toad Melisende had called him, Kasim dashed out into the darkness.

Thirty-Two

It was nearly noon by the time Mithra and his uncle reached the cave. They'd started out shortly after dawn, but Kasim had insisted upon far too many mules, all roped together. Even with Mithra at the front and Kasim bringing up the rear, the animals managed to tangle the ropes in trees more than a dozen times before they had travelled a mile.

Then his uncle started complaining about the heat, and the distance, followed by how ungrateful Mithra and his whole family were. At this point, Mithra was more than ready to leave his uncle in the woods to find his way out on his own.

But he was family, and there was more wealth in the cave than Mithra and his family could ever use, so he did not see a problem sharing it with his uncle.

Before they'd left, his father had warned him to be careful, and Mithra meant to be.

So when he finally reached the clearing and ascertained that it was empty, Mithra finally dared to breathe a sigh of relief.

"I don't see a cave. Where is this magical place?" Kasim complained.

Mithra merely walked over to the boulder and said, "Open sesame."

Just as before, the cavern opened.

"After you, Uncle," Mithra said with a bow.

For a moment, Kasim looked suspicious, before he peered down the steps. He must have caught the glitter of gold or something else that changed his mind, for he trotted down the first few steps, before turning to block Mithra's path.

"You stay up here and mind the mules," he said. "I shall choose what treasure to take as my share, and you may have the rest."

Mithra shrugged. If his father had his way,

their share would be nothing at all, at least until they had run out of the gold he'd already brought home. Seeing as he hadn't spent anything yet, that could take quite some time.

Deciding that his uncle would probably be a while, and that the man would shout if he needed him, Mithra tied the lead mule's rope to a tree and found a suitable bush to shade him while he caught up on some much needed sleep.

Mithra woke some time later to angry shouts. At first he thought they'd come from his uncle, until he realised that he'd heard several voices shouting at once, and his uncle's was not one of them.

Carefully, Mithra rose up onto his knees and peered between the branches. His worst fears were realised – a large number of men occupied the clearing with the mules, and they were most unhappy at having to share.

"Look! Someone has moved the stone!" One thief pointed, but they all turned to look.

Mithra's heart sank. He had to warn his uncle, but he didn't know how. He could not reach the cave without running through the thieves, who would surely kill him on sight.

His only hope was that his uncle had heard them, and that he'd found somewhere inside the cave to hide until the thieves had left.

So Mithra held his breath, and waited. The thieves approach the cave entrance, their steps stealthy, and their swords drawn. Down the steps they went, two at a time, sealing the entrance behind them.

When Mithra was certain that all forty of them had gone in, only then did he dare move. He raced across the clearing, and climbed the tree where he and Melisende had sat when they'd first learned the secrets of the cave.

He waited and he waited, until finally, the boulder moved and the thieves emerged. Mithra counted forty men, with no sign of his uncle among them.

"That will serve as a lesson to anyone who thinks to steal from us," the leader said. "Untie the mules. We shall sell them to recover the cost of what has already been stolen from us."

His men took the mules and departed.

Mithra stayed in his tree, waiting until he was certain they had all gone. Then he waited a little more until the sun seemed ready to sink beneath the horizon. He wished he could go home, get his father and together they could find out what had happened to his uncle. But Mithra was a man, not a frightened child, which is what he knew his father would say. Besides, his uncle might still be alive.

With that heartening thought, Mithra told the stone to shift aside.

He descended into the gloom, allowing his eyes to adjust to the dim twilight as he called softly, "Uncle? Uncle Kasim? It's me, Mithra. They've gone, it's safe to come out." He waited a moment, then repeated the words, several times, but still he got no answer. He stepped off the bottom step and trod in something soft. Mithra glanced down, then recoiled in horror.

Beneath his boot was a hand that ended in a bloody stump where the wrist should be. Another hand lay several yards away, with two arms and a torso in pieces between them. The legs and feet were off to the right, while his uncle's head had rolled almost to the wall on his left.

Mithra fought not to lose what little he'd eaten that morning. He wasn't sure what he'd expected to find, but his uncle's dismembered body was not it.

What would he tell his father?

Or his aunt?

Not wanting to leave his uncle's remains there, Mithra bundled the pieces into a bale of cloth, wrapping the winding sheet around them until he was sure he had them all secure. Then he forced the grisly bundle into the biggest sack he could find, and began the long journey home.

Thirty-Three

When he finally reached home, it was past sunset and the lamps had been lit. Mithra paused at the door, trying to decide where to take his uncle's body. He caught the sound of feminine voices inside, and thanked whatever watchful angel had slowed his steps. If his mother had a visitor, he couldn't bring the body inside.

He laid the sack on his handcart instead, gathering up an armload of firewood to lay over it to conceal it.

"Mithra, is that you?" his father asked. Shuffling footsteps sounded before his father was silhouetted in the doorway. "Where is Kasim? Seda arrived just before sundown, hysterical with worry that she hadn't seen him since he left last night. Your mother is trying to calm her down, for if Kasim were to see her like this…"

He would beat her, Mithra knew with a certainty he would not have possessed if it wasn't for Melisende's story last night. But his father had known.

Though he hated to even think it, Mithra suspected his uncle might have deserved his fate.

"Uncle Kasim is dead. Killed by the thieves, who happened upon us while Uncle was collecting treasure from the cave. I managed to hide, but Uncle…" He gestured toward the sack. "They chopped his body into pieces. I could not leave him there. What should I do now?"

Mithra had spent years learning the trade of both a merchant and a woodcutter, but neither had prepared him for a situation like this. Surely his father would know.

His father stood in thoughtful silence for a moment, then said, "You must take him home.

Put his body in the cellar or somewhere cool, and see that he is laid out for his funeral. I will keep your aunt here for as long as I can, to give you time to do what you must. See that her maid has a sleeping draught ready for her when she arrives, if you need more time."

Melisende. Melisende would help, and hopefully know what to do. She'd been a healer. Did that mean she'd had to lay out bodies for funerals before? Because no healer could save everyone…

Mithra found himself nodding, lifting up the handles of his handcart to deliver Kasim home for the last time.

He trudged through the streets with his cart, forcing his voice to sound cheerful as he told every soldier he met how he was on his last firewood delivery of the night. None of them seemed to care, or feel the need to shift the thin layer of branches camouflaging Kasim's remains.

Mithra reached Kasim's door and knocked softly.

He knew the angels had answered his prayer when Melisende opened it.

Mithra's breath whooshed out of him in a

great gust of relief. He'd never been so glad to see anyone in his life.

"Help me with this," he said, pushing the barrow toward the cellar entrance.

Hesitantly, Melisende followed.

"Close the door," he said, seizing the firewood and stacking it with the rest. That left only the sack on the handcart, which he could not seem to bring himself to open.

Melisende didn't share his qualms. She strode across the cellar and reached for the fastening. "What's in here?"

All his life, he'd been brought up to believe women should be sheltered, not subjected to a man's life of blood and toil. Especially highborn ones like her. His instincts screamed at him to be silent.

But if he didn't tell her, she'd find out for herself, and she deserved a warning before having Kasim's blood on her hands.

"It's Kasim. Hacked up into little pieces and bundled into a sack."

He waited for her to faint or scream or some such ladylike thing that Seda would definitely have done.

Melisende blinked. "That is…very kind of

you, but you didn't need to kill him for me. Uh, thank you, I suppose. I only threatened to cut off his manhood. Not…everything. But if this is how such things are done here, I guess I should be grateful. At home, this would be considered murder and you'd be in trouble for it. Are things so different out here in the desert?"

Mithra's breath caught in his throat. She thought he'd brought his uncle's body as a gift? A laugh burst out of him, the sound startling her as much as him.

It took him a moment to get himself under control enough to speak. "I didn't kill him. The Forty Thieves did. You see…" Mithra spilled out the whole story, not leaving out anything, including his own cowardice.

Melisende's eyes widened. "They'll come here next. If what you said is true, they'll find out who he is and come after his family. We'll have to hide his death long enough to make it look like something else. Some sort of sickness, maybe, so no one suspects…but Seda is still out looking for him. I'll tell her…I found him in the cellar, unconscious and wounded, after he fell down the stairs, and that

I've made up a sickbed for him there, so that I might tend to his wounds. Infection that proceeds to necrosis…I'll go to the apothecary for medicine in the morning, and keep returning to say he is worse until…well, until the blood poisoning could reasonably kill him. Fastest would be a gut wound, which would take less than a week. Hence the need to mention necrosis and a wound, to account for the smell at the funeral." She gave a little nod. "That should work."

Mithra could not help staring. "You thought all that up right then?"

Melisende shrugged. "Mostly. It's only a rough plan. It will surely need more thought if it's to work. Would your family visit if your uncle is sick?" At his nod, she continued, "Then you must definitely visit every day, and see that everyone you meet knows of Kasim's illness. You say your father knows, so only you and he should come down to the cellar to see Kasim. I will try to stitch the body together as best I can, then cover it with a sheet, so that at least to anyone who looks into the cellar, he will appear to be a sick man instead of a dead one. And buy some herbs to burn to cover the smell…"

Mithra nodded, trying to commit all the details to memory, so that he might help her in any way he could. He didn't know what he'd do without her.

Thirty-Four

Melisende was surprised at how smoothly her plan went. She'd dealt with one or two cases like the one she'd described to Mithra, so it was easy to state the right symptoms to the apothecary.

She'd stitched the mostly bloodless body together, then bandaged it tightly and bundled it into some of Kasim's clothes. The bloodied rags and sack Mithra had brought the body in were burned with some of Mithra's firewood, leaving no sign of what had really happened to Kasim.

Dealing with Seda was another matter. At

first, she'd insisted on seeing her husband, saying it was her duty as a good wife, but she'd gagged at the smell from the stairs and scuttled out again. By the end of the day, Melisende had her convinced that sending her maid to nurse the man was more than anyone would expect of a good wife. Perhaps if Kasim had been a better husband, or done something to deserve his wife's love, it might not have been so easy, but as it was…

Mithra and his family came every day, spending long hours with Seda. Mithra escaped to find Melisende as often as he dared, meeting her in the stables so they could get away from the ghastly smell in the cellar. Melisende brought a selection of food from the kitchen, which they shared, while they told each other tales about their lives before the crusade.

For the first time in her life, she told someone what it felt like to use her magic to run with horses or to travel swiftly when someone's life depended on it. For Mithra had seen how fast she could run, when she'd used her momentum against him, and there was no point in pretending it was a secret between them.

He in turn told her about Peter and Simon and the family he'd spent his apprenticeship with. Several times, he'd started to say how much she'd like Peter, but stopped himself. Then, a shadow would pass across his face before he changed the subject.

Melisende had wanted to hug him, each and every time, but if Mithra was anything like her brothers, he'd only push her and her girlish sentimentality away. Then again, none of her brothers had ever lost their best friend in what Mithra said had been a particularly brutal murder.

But their idyll soon came to an end, when Melisende had to go to the apothecary to buy a sleeping draught to help calm Kasim's newly widowed wife.

Seda was not allowed to attend her own husband's funeral, Melisende learned, for that was a men's affair alone. Mithra and Ali Baba had stayed for long enough to leave Mithra's mother, Banu, to comfort the grieving widow, before they departed with Kasim's coffin.

Then the women, Seda's friends, started to arrive.

Melisende was run off her feet, fetching

things from the kitchen to feed the hungry hordes. Banu – a cook herself, if Melisende remembered Mithra's words correctly – worked alongside the cook, issuing a stream of orders that Melisende hurried to obey. She hadn't worked this hard since the last Yule feast at home when her mother was still alive.

But when the day was done and Melisende thought she might be able to creep up to bed, the cook sent her to clean out Kasim's bedchamber, and another across the passage that was reserved for guests, if Kasim had ever had any.

"Why?" Melisende asked crossly.

"Because tomorrow, Kasim's heir moves into his new house, and the family's rooms must be clean, or they will dismiss you as a bad servant," the cook said.

If they did that, they'd deserve whatever retribution the Forty Thieves visited upon them, Melisende thought. But then her sluggish mind turned up another thought that wouldn't go away. "But Seda is his widow. Isn't the house hers?"

She'd heard Seda say something about how she'd grown up in this house, which had belonged to her father.

"Of course not. She couldn't inherit, but her father had no sons, so he willed it to her husband instead. When Kasim died, everything he owned passed to his nearest male heir. Luckily for her, he's a kind man, who will let her stay."

"Who is he?" Melisende asked. If he was anywhere near as bad as Kasim, she wanted to be warned.

"Ali Baba."

Mithra's father. Which meant…

"Mithra's moving in here?" Melisende blurted out.

"That's the young master to you, girl. He'll be taking over his uncle's shop and all the rest of the business, so Master Mithra will be a much more important man. He won't be a woodcutter any more." The cook headed off, with a satisfied air as if she expected her orders to be obeyed.

Melisende smiled. Master Mithra. Merchant Mithra. She knew how much he longed to be able to practice his trade again, and tomorrow he would finally achieve his dream. It was fitting that he slept in a fine bed in his uncle's best room.

And she was in a position to provide it.

Suddenly possessed of a new burst of energy, Melisende set to work.

Tomorrow was going to be a good day.

Thirty-Five

Mithra arrived at Kasim's shop well before dawn, hoping to have time to go over the books and stock before opening the shop at the normal time later on that morning. Yet when he opened the door and raised his lantern to look inside, Mithra had to remind himself that it was not his uncle's shop any more. It was his, his father had told him, and his alone. His father had expressed hope that Simon's teachings during Mithra's long apprenticeship would stand him in good stead to keep the shop as profitable as it had been under his uncle's aegis.

Mithra hoped so too.

Yet as he lit the lamps – far too few, in his opinion – he did not feel the same confidence he had in Simon's shop. This place looked dim and dingy, which meant the goods could not catch a buyer's eye as easily as if they were brightly lit.

Mithra shook his head. Never mind the lights. He could make changes on the morrow, when he had a day's trade under his belt which he could then compare to the next day's takings, to see if there had been any improvement. As Simon had often said, the numbers did not lie.

But first, he had to find the numbers, and Kasim's books could be anywhere.

After an hour of looking, Mithra began to despair of ever finding Kasim's records in the cluttered shop. But when he turned too swiftly and tipped over a pile of brass bells that seem to want to roll everywhere, he found a dusty bookshelf tucked under a table which contained records dating back to before Seda's father's time. Selecting the most recent volume, Mithra sat down and began to read.

It took Mithra several hours to determine

with any certainty how bad a businessman his uncle had been, by which time he knew he'd need to read all the records, to work out just how much mess the shop was in.

Mithra did not open the shop on the first day, nor the second. In fact, it was almost a full week before he dared to open the awning and allow people inside.

He needn't have bothered. No one seemed to want to enter the dark space, and those who looked like they might consider it were chased away by the surly looks of the man who owned the shop next door. The same man who had accused Mithra of being a thief, when he tried to buy clothes from the man. Mithra began to realise why his uncle's business had been doing so badly.

That had to change, he resolved. Kasim's shop had plenty of stock, but it was piled up haphazardly in such a way that no one could find what they wanted. Mithra had looked in vain for any record of Kasim's warehouse, where some of this clutter might be stored, only to find that he had sold it more than a year ago, to some Crusader merchant who likely had no use for it now.

Mithra had lost count of the number of times he'd wished he were back in Simon's well-lit, well-laid-out shop, in its prime place in the market. Mithra had no doubt if he got some of Kasim's goods to Simon's shop, they would sell so much better. In fact…

Mithra took a fresh piece of parchment and began to take stock. If he used this place as his warehouse, and opened up Simon's shop, Mithra might be able to actually sell something.

Simon had owned his shop, and still no one seemed to have tried to take possession of it, so Mithra decided to try his luck.

Before dawn the next day, he began moving a selection of stock that he thought might capture soldiers' eyes into Simon's shop. He was still arranging his wares when the other shops around him began to open, and more than one soldier had taken advantage of the open awning to come and ask Mithra if he would be opening for business again.

And then came the magic words.

"Because I was hoping you might have…"

A customer who told him exactly what he wanted was the easiest sale a merchant could make, Mithra knew.

And that afternoon, he opened.

By the time he closed, he had sold out of several items, including those benighted brass bells, and he lingered a little longer in the market to bring another shipment from Kasim's shop to Simon's.

The next day, he did more business in a day than Kasim had in his last month.

Not that he could celebrate yet. His numbers told him that he'd only achieved an average sales day for Simon's shop, with its superior position and all. He could do better than this.

After several days, setting up the shop differently every morning, and filling it with new stock every night, Mithra made a new record.

For the first time, he sold more goods in a day than Simon's shop had ever sold since the start of his apprenticeship. If there had been a merchants' guild in Dorylaeum, they might have awarded him mastery on the spot. As it was, Mithra found himself trying out a new name in his head, testing out how it felt.

Master Mithra. Master Merchant Mithra.

He laughed to himself. Never in his wildest

dreams had he imagined this would be possible for him.

Something he could thank his uncle for…

No. This was Melisende's doing. If she had not arrived, and shown him the thieves' cave, Kasim would be still alive, slowly running his own shop down into bankruptcy.

He owed her everything. And yet she still served as a maid in his uncle's house, waiting for the army to leave so that she might go home.

He shook his head. Melisende had not said a word of complaint, which surely made her an angel – his guardian angel, if such things existed. He could not give her the object of her desire just yet, but he owed her at least a gift, as a token of thanks for all she had done.

He scanned the marketplace, trying to find something suitable. This was made near impossible by the fact that most of the shops, like his own, had pulled their awnings down and closed for the night.

But some lanterns were still lit, including the one at the bakery where Cagri worked.

She stood at the counter, serving supper to a long line of customers, while the smell of yeast from the back room told him that the bread for tomorrow was already rising.

"So how can I help you?" Cagri asked, fluttering those eyelashes that used to send his heart fluttering, too.

But he saw no light of recognition in her eyes, and her words were hollow, when he knew that she said the same thing and looked the same way at any prosperous young man who entered her shop. How could he have ever thought her beautiful? Or imagined that he loved her?

He'd been such a fool.

And then he'd met Melisende…

The Crusader maiden who had never heard of sesame before, or tasted a cake made of the stuff.

"Do you have any sesame cakes left?" Mithra asked.

They only had one, and a small one at that.

When Cagri read the disappointment in his eyes, she offered all manner of other things instead, including a delivery of a whole box of cakes upon the morrow, if he wished.

No. One was enough. He would give it to Melisende, and watch her expression as she ate it. Most likely, she would hate it, for Peter's sisters had not been fond of them, he recalled. They did not like the seeds that caught in their teeth, or some other such silliness.

It mattered not. He would keep his promise to Melisende, and tell her how grateful he was for all of her assistance. They lived under the same roof, yet he had not seen her since his uncle's funeral, and that had been weeks ago.

He paid for his purchase, and headed out into the night. And if there was a spring in his step in anticipation of seeing her again, Mithra did not mind at all.

<h1 style="text-align:center;font-style:italic">Thirty-Six</h1>

"What of the maid? She's lasted longer than most of them, and she seems a willing enough worker."

Melisende had been about to enter the kitchen, but at the sound of Mithra's mother's voice, she waited a moment. She needed to hear this.

The cook spoke next. "She works, yes, but she's not like any of the others we had before. This one has Crusader blood in her. Some Crusader's bastard, I'd wager, who'd never worked a day in her life before she came here. You wouldn't believe the things I had to show her how to do!"

Only because the cook wanted everything done in such a particular way, no one would have known what she wanted before she told them, Melisende fumed. She'd scolded Melisende for boiling water wrong. When Melisende had bottled more potions than this woman had made meals, despite being half her age. If it weren't for Mithra, she would have left this place a long time ago. Oh, and the army. If they'd left. Yes, that's what she'd meant.

"Seda said she's the best maid she's ever had. She's helped her with her hair and gown more than any of the other girls. Like she was a lady's maid or something before. Maybe to some Crusader lady…"

"If she's lost one position in a fine house, you can be sure she's got her eye out for another one. Lady of this one, perhaps. You should find your son a wife as soon as possible, Banu. Before she seduces him. You know Crusader girls are neither modest or obedient. If I had a coin for every insolent look that girl has given me, I would be rich enough to pay someone to cook for me!"

Incredulous, not insolent. Melisende shook her head. Never mind. It wasn't like she needed a herbal infusion to help her sleep. She was tired enough most nights as it was.

Tonight was no different. She'd barely laid her head upon her pillow and she was asleep.

What felt like less than a moment later, she awoke again, to the sound of footsteps outside her room. Kasim was dead and buried, she told herself, as she rose as silently as she could and crept to the wall, where she'd hung up her clothes and her knife.

"Melisende? Are you in here?"

She let the sheathed knife fall. Mithra was hardly a threat. "Give me a moment to dress," she called, tugging a gown over her shift. At home, she'd have needed to lace up the gown, but the shapeless garments that were the fashion here had no lacings at all. Probably a good thing, for she suspected Mithra would not know how to help her lace a gown.

She stepped out into the passage, which was lit by a lantern at Mithra's feet. He must have just arrived home from his shop, because she'd filled every lamp in the house more times than she could count, and that lantern wasn't one of them.

"What do you need?" she asked briskly. At this late hour, it had to be something urgent.

"I need…to thank you. For everything you've done that's changed my fortunes so much I can scarcely believe it's possible."

"You woke me up…to thank me?"

"I didn't realise you'd be asleep so early. Or maybe I just didn't realise how late it was. I've been working so many hours in the shop…"

Melisende felt a rush of sympathy for him. It wasn't all that long ago that she'd struggled to learn a whole new occupation, and her body still hadn't adjusted to the workload. She summoned a smile as she took his hand. "Come, I'll make you a healing draught that will help you sleep, so you'll be well-rested in the morning."

"In the kitchen?" He didn't sound particularly eager to accept her offer.

"Of course." For all the size of this house and its outbuildings, there was no stillroom, so the kitchen it must be.

"Just that my mother and the cook are talking about finding me a wife, and comparing the various virtues of all the local girls. If I go in there…"

Suddenly, this shadowy hallway seemed the best place to be.

"I don't need anything, anyway. I had my supper at the shop, while I was doing the day's figures. Then, I decided it was time to celebrate, and I realised I had a promise to keep."

To take her home. That had been weeks ago, and the army still showed no sign of leaving. Maybe she'd be a housemaid forever.

Melisende shook her head. "I can't expect you to work miracles, Mithra. Without your help, I wouldn't have been safe for all these weeks. You found me food and lodging…" Even if she did have to work for it, she thought but didn't say. It wasn't his fault he hadn't been born in a castle or grand house, with rooms to spare for as many guests as he liked. Well, now his father's house had that, but the soldiers still marched through the streets, so she could hardly proclaim her true identity yet.

"Yes! Food! I finally remembered to get you a sesame cake!"

He held out something round, roughly the

size of his palm.

Now she needed her knife to cut a cake. Melisende wanted to laugh, but one look at his earnest expression and she didn't dare.

Instead, she gingerly took the cake from him and bit into it. A cloyingly sweet, sticky mass hit her tongue. A mass that proved surprisingly chewy, despite the gritty seeds that gave the cake its name. Finally, she managed to swallow.

"What did you think?" he asked eagerly.

"It's…good?" she managed to say. She ventured another bite. If anything, this time it tasted even sweeter, coating her mouth in stickiness. She'd need a drink after this. Would Mithra be offended if she went to draw a bucket of water from the well?

"Here." As if guessing her thoughts, he held out his water bottle.

Taking the leather flask in her free hand, she drank deeply before trying to hand it back.

He waved it away. "Keep it until you're done. Peter's father used to buy us each one on special feast days. When I tried my first one, I stuck my head in the water barrel. Peter laughed so hard he spat cake everywhere."

She held out what remained of the cake. "Then you should have some. Truly, I cannot eat another bite."

She washed her hands while he finished it off.

"Peter would have loved to meet you," he said.

"I can't imagine what it must be like, to have so many memories of someone, and then to have them plucked from your life, as if they'd never existed," Melisende said. She leaned in to kiss his cheek. "Thank you for sharing this with me."

Maybe it was dark, or maybe she'd misjudged. Or maybe he'd turned his head at just the wrong moment, and that's why she missed.

But the moment her mouth met his, time stopped.

And it was more magical than anything she'd ever done in her life.

Until his lips left hers.

Only then did she realise that time had not stopped, though it had felt like it.

Somehow, she'd twined her arms around his neck, and wound her legs around his waist. His hard body pinned her back to the wall, holding her up, while his hands were busy elsewhere. When he'd tangled his fingers in her hair, somehow her braid had come undone, the way the rest of her body wanted to. His other hand cupped her face as tenderly as if she was his most treasured possession. The look in his eyes said he wanted her to be.

Then he set her down and stepped away, hanging his head. "Forgive me, Lady Melisende. I forgot myself. For a moment, I thought I was better than I am. But it seems I am no better than my uncle, stealing what was never mine to take. Maybe I deserve the same fate."

He turned on his heel and was gone.

Melisende's knees did not have the strength to hold her, so she slid down the wall to sit on the floor instead. Her lips burned from his kiss, a kiss sweeter than any cake, which made her hunger for all manner of forbidden things.

"Oh, Mithra. You can't steal a kiss when it's freely given. And after that, you have only to ask, and I would give you a million more." Much more.

She squeezed her eyes shut. The cook was

right, though Melisende had not known it until now. She did want to seduce Mithra.

If the army did not depart soon, allowing her to leave, she'd do it, too. For she knew she could not resist him.

She laughed softly to herself. All her life, she'd laughed at the girls who flirted, trying to win the attention of whatever man they fancied. All it took was one kiss to turn her into the worst of them all.

Reluctantly, she returned to her bed, expecting sleep to elude her. Instead, she fell instantly into a dream where Mithra returned with more kisses and caresses.

When she woke the next morning, no amount of water could cool her burning blushes.

Thirty-Seven

On the morrow, Mithra threw himself into his work once more. When he went to Rialto, he would offer to purchase Simon's shop from his family, and that would take more gold than he currently had. Unless he used the coins he'd taken from the thieves' cave…

No. To do that would be to draw attention to the fact that someone other than Kasim knew the thieves' secret, and they would come after him and his family.

And Melisende…

Mithra buried his face in his hands at the thought of her. He'd come to her chamber last night to thank her, to give her a gift and tell her he had not forgotten his promise to help her.

Instead, he'd behaved no better than his uncle, pinning her against the wall so that she could not escape while his mouth plundered hers, stealing kisses he did not deserve.

She'd been so frozen with fear she hadn't even tried to fight back. He was as bad as his uncle, no better than the soldiers who'd stolen all those Crusader girls and used them for their own sordid pleasure. Why, he'd forced this highborn lady into servitude. She cooked and scrubbed floors when he was the one who should be fetching things for her, serving her…

He was a fool. While he might be a merchant now, he would not remain one for long if he didn't buy more goods to trade. He'd go back to being a penniless woodcutter, what he would always, always be. No match for a Crusader lady.

He couldn't even meet his mother's eyes, knowing she wanted him to wed, when the only woman he wanted was one he could not have.

So he worked, and he worked, and one day he went back out the army camp and asked to see the General. He offered to buy all the remaining goods in the Crusaders' warehouses, and the General agreed.

He sold Kasim's shop to the clothes merchant, shifted what little stock that remained to Simon's shop, and set off for the Warehouse District. While he found many warehouses – Simon's included, sadly – that had been plundered of everything they contained, others, like the one Kasim had sold, were relatively untouched, and they contained a wealth far beyond what he'd paid to the General.

Now he had an excuse not to return to the house until very late at night, leaving early every morning, consolidating all his trade goods in the warehouses with the stoutest doors, while he decided what to sell here and what to ship off to other markets, when the army left. And they would. They had to, for, faithless wretch that he was, he owed it to Melisende to take her home, like he'd promised. Then, and only then, would she be safe from him.

Thirty-Eight

"Excuse me, but are you Master Mithra?" a little boy asked.

Mithra looked up from his books. The urchin could have been him at that age.

"I am," Mithra said.

"Got a message for you, Master. Your father says to come home quick, because there's someone to see you. Some merchant from far away looking to trade. Says he did business with your uncle."

One of Kasim's business contacts. The first he'd heard of, as Kasim hadn't kept records of who had sold him things. His father was right

– he needed to meet this man.

"Thank you," he told the boy, tossing him a coin.

The boy had bolted out of sight by the time Mithra made it out into the street, but it didn't matter. He knew the way home.

The house was a blaze of lights – even the stables had the lanterns lit, and he could hear horses inside it for the first time in as long as he could remember. He stuck his head inside and exchanged nods with the two men tending the horses. He recognised them both as grooms who worked at one of the city's inns. Well, they had worked there – maybe they'd lost their jobs like his mother had.

It appeared they had a new job now – more horses than Mithra thought would fit in this stable, but then he was no expert when it came to animals. Trees and trade were where his talents lay. And trade was what he wanted.

He headed up to the house, where his father was no doubt entertaining their mysterious merchant guest in the dining chamber.

Outside the door, he paused to listen to their conversation.

"You would not believe it, but we were a

day's ride from anywhere, and out of the desert marched a line of mules, all roped together! I stepped up to take the lead animal's halter, and they all just stopped. I let out a shout to tell everyone they were safe and it was not a company of soldiers come to kill us all, and we soon had the fire lit again, with dinner back on the spit. I knew a horse dealer here in town, so I brought them to him today, hoping they'd fetch a fair price. But you know horse dealers – he tried to offer me far too little. So I said I'd sell them to my friend Kasim, a merchant I know who always needs more mules, and he'll give me a fair price. He always has in the past..."

There was no mention of any mules in Kasim's books, Mithra knew, for he'd been through them twice. Not even the mules he'd purchased on the day he died. Whoever this merchant was, he must be mistaken.

"So he said he'd take another look at them, and when he did, he said these were Kasim's mules, for he'd sold them to him just last week!"

Unless Kasim's ghost had been buying mules, someone was lying. Likely the horse dealer, for Mithra knew Simon had had bad dealings with him in the past.

Approaching footsteps made him turn. It was just the cook, bringing a tray of food.

Best that she didn't catch him lurking out here. Mithra entered the room.

Father introduced his son to the merchant, "Judah of Kerioth, a Christian," or so Ali Baba said.

The man certainly dressed like a Crusader, but his name seemed familiar, while the man himself did not. Perhaps Simon or his uncle had mentioned him.

Mithra accepted a cup of wine, watching as the cook refilled the merchant's cup. He drank far more than Father, and seemed to be sweating excessively in the heat.

"A Christian in Dorylaeum! It has been some months since we've seen one. Please, tell me your secret. How did you manage to evade the Seljuk army?" Mithra asked.

For if this man could, then he could take Melisende home.

"What Seljuk army? I saw no such thing, though we had heard they were about. We had a terrible fright one night when a pack of mules came upon us in the dark. You will not believe me..." The merchant began his tale again.

Mithra considered stopping him, but instead he let his thoughts drift. Let the man get comfortable, and enjoy their house's hospitality. A well-fed man would be well disposed to trade with Mithra, and for a favourable price. For whatever this merchant dealt in, if Mithra could find a way to sell it, he wanted to buy it all. At the best price, of course.

On the morrow, when their deal was concluded, then he could tell Melisende the good news and begin planning their journey.

Thirty-Nine

"Two of the lamps have gone out. Go and refill them all," the cook commanded, coming back to the kitchen with an empty tray.

Melisende bit back a curse. "I can't. I used the last of the lamp oil to fill the lamps in the guest chamber I've just finished preparing for the master's visitor."

The cook's oath was not as quiet as Melisende's. Then her eyes lit up. "The man's an oil merchant. He won't mind if you take some from one of his jars — there were dozens of them!"

Melisende frowned. "Stealing from a guest

goes against the laws of hospitality." Though she knew her culture and the cook's were very different, the laws of hospitality were universal.

The cook waved away her worries. "Not when the guest intends to sell that oil to the master. They'll bargain about the price over dinner, but by morning, those jars will belong to the master. Why else would he have brought them here, instead of to an inn or his own warehouse?"

Melisende had no answer for her, so she grabbed a jug and headed out to the stables. She'd been tempted to offer to take care of the guest's horses herself and tell the cook to hire a maid for the night, instead of grooms, but airing and washing linens was infinitely more preferable than shovelling horse shit, which was what the grooms would be doing come morning. So she'd held her tongue and nodded meekly, which had earned her a suspicious glance from the cook, but she'd managed the spring cleaning in her father's castle often enough to prepare a room on her own.

Then, as now, her thoughts had wandered when doing such menial work, and today they'd flown outside the city gates, where this travelling merchant had come from. A Christian, the cook had said, which meant the army must be gone, or he'd found a way to sneak around them. Either way, it would be a simple matter for her to bundle up her meagre belongings and take the same route away from Dorylaeum. She could go home…

But not before she'd had a chance to bid farewell to Mithra. He usually returned home late, long after she'd retired for the night, so she hadn't seen him since the night they'd kissed, but tonight she'd wait. Besides, she had lamps to fill and who knew what other chores to keep her busy for a while.

She swung open the stable door, marvelling at the bustle of activity in the echoing, empty space where she and Mithra had taken refuge during Kasim's imaginary illness. Horses occupied every stall, plus anywhere they'd found space to tether the extra beasts once the stalls were full. There was no sign of any oil, or a vessel which might contain the stuff.

Maybe in the tackroom, Melisende thought as she pushed open the door.

"Don't do that, miss, for the zebani in there will surely trample you to death!" a groom said, thrusting an arm between her and the open doorway.

Melisende glimpsed a set of flying hooves, which made a thunderous clatter as they hit the floor.

"See, miss? A creature come straight from hell itself!"

Surely not.

Silver destriers were rare, and if they'd been closer to home, Melisende would have wagered every coin she had that this fearsome animal had come from her father's stable. The horse reared again, and she was certain of it.

"Moonlight?" she called softly.

The gelding's ears pricked. Down went the hooves, and he lifted his nose to blow warm air across her outstretched hand. She waited a moment, then patted the horse's flank as her gaze swept the room. No oil jars here, either.

Something was amiss. Melisende just knew it.

"Are all the horses like this one?" she asked.

"No, miss, most are nice and calm. Happy to get something to eat. That one turns his nose up at everything and tries to trample anyone who approaches him. It's a wonder he let you near him."

Not a wonder at all, when you knew Moonlight and his twin brother Moonfire had learned to run alongside Melisende in the fields behind her father's castle. No, the wonder was how an oil merchant could afford a mount like Moonlight.

"Show me the other horses," she commanded.

The groom eyed her askance for a moment, before his shoulders drooped and he headed toward the stalls. "They're all just horses, miss."

It was true, and yet it wasn't. Melisende knew more about northern horse stock than most men alive, and these were no common horses. Palfreys, most of them, with a couple more destriers, along with a handful she thought might be packhorses. In the last stall, she had another surprise — a pale horse that could have been Moonlight's twin, at first glance, but this one was younger. Likely born during that long, cold winter when the snow had stayed on the ground well into spring, and the mares had kept warm by letting the stallions cover them. How many colts had been born that spring? Three, four? All named for the weather that year. "Snow? Sleet?" she tried. "Ice?" Then it came to her. "Frost!"

The palfrey lifted his head over the stall door, ears pricked. Melisende rushed to stroke him, too.

No mere merchant could afford two of her father's horses. Why, even Mithra, with all the gold in the thieves' cave, might not have enough for two of them.

These horses had belonged to knights, or princes, or noblemen with plenty of gold to spare. Men who had likely died on that battlefield. These were Crusaders' horses, all of them. Had this merchant bought them from the Seljuk army?

But no. The army hadn't taken the horses — they'd already been stolen by the Forty Thieves.

Thieves would sell to a Christian merchant, Melisende told herself, but even that felt wrong. Surely thieves would know better than to sell horses of this calibre to be used as pack animals.

She'd think on it later, while she filled the lamps. Meanwhile, she still needed to find the oil.

"Where are the oil jars these horses were carrying?" she asked, half expecting the groom to deny any knowledge of them. After all, these horses didn't look like they'd been carrying heavy loads for many miles. They didn't look like they'd carried anything heavy at all.

"We put those in the cellar," the groom said. He led her to the yard and pointed. "Over there."

The cellar where Kasim's body had lain during his imaginary illness, which still smelled faintly of corruption. Of course.

She thanked the groom, and marched toward the cellar. When she threw the doors open, she saw a curious sight. The promised oil jars were lined up along the walls, much like the golden statues in the thieves' cave. A jug hung from the neck of each, swaying a little in the air flow from the open door.

She examined the first jug critically. It was made of cheap, thin clay, easily broken but able to hold a large quantity of oil. Suitable for lowering into the jar to scoop out a measure of oil, then pour it into her own sturdier vessel.

She unfasted the lid so that she might lower the jug inside.

"Is it time yet?"

She almost jumped out of her skin as the voice seemed to come from nowhere. No, from inside the jar!

"Because we've been talking, Captain. Does this thief have any daughters, or a comely young wife or two? It doesn't seem right to kill them all and burn down the house when we might take the women with us to enjoy later…"

Murmurs of assent came from the other jars.

The Forty Thieves had not sold the horses. They were here!

And if she didn't do something, they meant to leap from their jars and slaughter Mithra and his family before burning this place to the ground. Not to mention what they might do to her.

Her mind whirling with panic, she knew what she needed was time. Time to think, to get help, to decide what to do.

So she lifted up her jug, speaking into it to make her voice deep enough to pass for a man's as she said, "We shall see. The house is heavily guarded, so we must wait until they are all asleep or the guards will stop us. Wait for my signal, and I'll see you get the woman you deserve."

None, if she had any say in it, Melisende said to herself.

"When I tap on your jar, three times, tap back, so I know you understand," she added.

She walked along the row of jars, tapping on them and hearing her signal echoed back from every one except the last. She tapped again, but no sound came from it. Annoyed, she kicked the jar, only to hear the slosh of liquid inside.

So there was some oil, after all.

Melisende lifted off the lid and peered inside. An impossible idea kindled in her mind.

Forty

All the jugs sat on the table, brimful of oil and stoppered with a piece of rag that extended upward like a wisp of smoke. Smoke that would soon become flame.

She took a deep breath. This was her last chance to back out, to change her plan and go summon the guards. To find enough people to keep the thieves from killing Mithra and his family.

But if she left…the thieves might emerge early, and begin their terrible task.

These men had no mercy. She'd seen that when they killed the Horn Knight. They'd slaughter Mithra and take her as their plaything.

No, she had to do this. She had no choice, for she was no man's toy.

She took a torch from the wall and waved it across the tops of the jugs. One, two, then a dozen rags caught alight. She would need to be swift and sure, so fast that she'd finished before the first man had time to react.

Melisende tugged on a pair of heavy leather gloves, hoping they would protect her. Even if they didn't…better burned hands than these men getting their hands on her body.

She bit down hard on her lip, tasting magic as time slowed.

Melisende seized an armload of jugs and raced along the jars. Lift the lid, throw the jug in so that it smashed, spilling flaming oil onto the man inside, then on to the next one.

More jugs. More lids. More breaking clay.

Again, and again.

Until there were no jugs left.

Melisende slumped against the table, reeling while she waited for the world to catch up to what she'd done.

And then the men began to scream.

She fled through the cellar door, barring it behind her before the horrible sounds reached the stables. She hoped no one in the house above heard.

Finally, the cellar fell silent. Melisende counted to a hundred, then did it again, before daring to open the door.

Nothing moved.

She crept down the steps, wrinkling her nose at what smelled like burned bacon.

By all that was holy…did cooked human flesh smell like bacon? No wonder Mithra's family never ate pork.

The smell only strengthened as she ventured deeper into the cellar, ably assisted by the fact that some of the jars were still smouldering.

Glad of the leather gloves she still wore, she set her hands on the rim of the nearest jar and peered inside.

Smoke stung her eyes, but the man inside didn't move. Nor did the next, or the next. She went around the whole room, checking until she was sure each jar held a corpse.

Only then did she dare to breathe again. The Forty Thieves were dead, and Mithra was safe.

Melisende swallowed. She'd killed forty men. Burned them alive. Her, the coward who'd run from the battlefield. She wished she could run now, run home and hide from this horrible thing she'd done.

Instead, she crawled into a corner and cried.

Moments passed, or maybe it was hours. She wasn't sure. What she did know was that she had no tears left. Not for the men she'd burned alive, or for the innocent girl she'd been before she'd slaughtered forty men.

But was it forty? Surely there'd been a sentry of some sort, and the captain they waited for.

Melisende counted the jars. "Thirty-eight, thirty-nine, forty." Yes, she had killed forty men.

She counted the jars again. But this time, when she got to the last one, she peered into inky blackness, for it was still mostly full of oil.

She'd killed thirty-nine of the Forty Thieves. Men who'd sworn vengeance on Mithra's family. If the last one found out what she'd done…

It must be their captain, for that's who they'd expected to come for them. Their captain must be the merchant, sharing a meal with Mithra's father even now, before he'd retire to the guest chamber beside Mithra's room. Mithra, who worked so hard and slept so soundly he wouldn't know there was an assassin in his chamber until the thief struck.

Numbly, Melisende drew a final jug of oil. She ascended the steps, jug held high, as she headed back to the house.

She'd killed thirty-nine men this night. What was one more?

Forty-One

Mithra almost choked on his wine when Melisende walked in with a tray of sweets. Judah's gaze was drawn to her, and she seemed to have eyes only for the merchant, too.

He was one of her people, Mithra told himself. The first she'd seen in weeks. Of course she'd stare, because she knew what the man's presence meant as much as Mithra did: the army was gone, and she could go home.

She served his father first, and then himself, despite Mithra's frantic gestures to serve their guest. Did she not know the most basic parts of the rules of hospitality?

It seemed she did not. Next, she set her tray down and refilled their wine cups, once again neglecting Judah.

"Serve our guest, girl," Ali Baba hissed.

Melisende moved around the table, snatched up a bowl and held it out to Judah.

Except, something seemed to go wrong. She tripped, or the bowl slipped, and instead of being set on the table before the man, it flew out of her hands and smacked into his chest, dribbling its contents down his tunic before clattering to the floor.

Melisende uttered a muffled curse, then dropped to her knees to clean up the mess with a cloth.

Judah glared down at her in fury.

"You must forgive our new maid, Master Judah," Mithra said with a forced smile. "She is still in training, and only just beginning to learn how to serve at table. I'll send her back to the kitchen and…"

Melisende had started to clean the man's tunic, dabbing at it with her cloth while muttering apologies.

Judah clouted her across the head. "Do not touch me, girl!" He lifted his head to meet

Mithra's gaze. "Send the clumsy slut away. Ruining such costly silk. If she were my servant, I'd see her whipped –"

A line of red appeared across the merchant's throat, a line that began to rain, sheeting down his front and his already ruined tunic. His sentence ended in a choking sound as he pitched forward onto his plate.

While his father gaped, Mithra's mind worked faster. "Melisende, how could you do such a thing to a guest? Have you never heard of the laws of hospitality? We shall be cursed forever for this!"

Melisende rose gracefully to her feet and tossed a bloodied knife onto the table. The red jewels set in the gold hilt seemed to remind him of the hellish fires that surely awaited them all.

"That man's no guest. He hasn't eaten or drunk a thing, the whole time he's been here. Instead, he's been throwing it all on the floor beneath the table – see?" She lifted the cloth to reveal the mess Judah had made.

"Perhaps the man is a messy eater. But that's no reason to kill him!" Mithra said.

"He was clutching that dagger down by his

side, under the table. I've seen it before – it was in my bag, and I left it in the thieves' cave. He dropped it when I threw his food at him, and he hit me when I picked it up. He's no merchant, and I'd wager he's no Christian, either. That tunic belonged to a knight I knew, who his men killed before dumping his body on the battlefield. This man is the captain of the Forty Thieves. He came here with his men to kill you all, and burn your house down. If anyone has broken all the laws of hospitality, it's him!" Fire blazed in her eyes. "If you don't believe me, go and look into the oil jars sitting in your cellar, and see what has become of his men."

Then, to his father's shock, Melisende strode over to the sideboard and poured herself a cup of wine. "The Seljuk army is gone, and on the morrow I start my journey home." She raised the cup high. "To your health, and, I hope, a long life, though I will not be here to save you next time." She drank the cup dry, then threw it on the floor and stormed out.

Mithra rose. "Father, we should see what is in the cellar."

"You believe this ill-mannered maid?" Ali Baba sputtered.

It took Mithra a moment to remember that what had sounded quite polite for Melisende, might not seem so to someone who hadn't heard how colourful her vocabulary could be. "Father, she has saved my life several times, and if she says that the Forty Thieves are here to seek vengeance, then I fear that not only is she telling the truth, but I have done her a grave discourtesy." Mithra led the way outside, not caring if his father followed.

The cellar still stank of corruption from Kasim's body, but it was stronger now, thick with the miasma of smoke and burned flesh. Mithra knew the stench of burning bodies, for he'd helped bring wood for more pyres than he cared to count.

"I don't know how, but we both owe her our lives. Forty times over, for the lives she has taken in our defence," Mithra said.

Father looked into one of the jars, then ran back up the cellar steps, retching.

Mithra followed him, his feet heavy with the new debt he now owed Melisende.

Only to find the lady herself, standing in the

yard.

Mithra fell to his knees, then bowed until his forehead touched the dirt before her feet. "There is not enough gold in the world to repay you for the favour you have done for me, and for my family. Please, tell me how you accomplished this miracle."

She stared down at him for a long moment, then held out her hand to help him up. "Inside. Where I don't have to smell…all those cooked pigs."

Mithra could feel his father's eyes on him, but that didn't matter right now. All that mattered was Melisende.

He followed her back to the dining room, poured her a cup of wine, and waited for her to tell her tale.

Forty-Two

Her mouth was dry from talking so much, but she couldn't stop until she'd told it all. "I counted the corpses, realised there was one more man, perhaps the greatest danger of them all, so I came up to the house to find him. When I saw the dagger in his hand, I faltered for a moment, and that's when I spilled the sweets. Fortuitous, perhaps, because it gave me the opportunity to get close to him and do what needed to be done." Why was her cup dry? Surely she could not have drunk all that wine.

Mithra lifted the wine jug, and she shook

her head. "Water," she said.

She drank and drank, but still she could taste the smoke and ash of burned bodies. It had seemed so clear at the time, but now horror washed over her at the thought of how many men she'd killed.

She could feel Ali Baba's eyes on her, watching everything. Whatever he thought of her, it could be no worse than what she thought of herself. Murderer of forty men…

Worse than that, why didn't she feel any guilt for what she'd done?

"It seems to me that we owe you everything. Our lives, our fortune…my son especially," Ali Baba began. "For such a debt, I can refuse you nothing. Anything you ask of me, I shall give you. Your freedom, wealth…anything."

"Father! Melisende is not a slave, and the wealth of the Forty Thieves properly belongs to her! You cannot offer her what is hers already!" Mithra protested.

Ali Baba bowed his head. "If my son, your most passionate defender, is correct, then I have little to offer. Except…my son himself, and my blessing upon your marriage. After all you have done, I would be honoured to accept you as a daughter."

Melisende stared at him. A moment ago, he'd been glowering at her for misbehaving, and now he was offering his son to her like some sort of prize.

Never mind that Mithra was a good man, the sort any girl would be happy to have as a husband. After that kiss the other day, Melisende could not deny she'd been entertaining thoughts of sharing his bed. Surely Ali Baba couldn't know about those thoughts…

Mithra's laughter cut through her reverie. "Father, that would be poor payment indeed! Lady Melisende is no maid, though she has pretended to be one for many weeks now, biding her time until she might go home. She is a Crusader lady, one who managed to escape from both the soldiers and the battle and hide in the forest, where I found her when I went out woodcutting. She saved me from the Forty Thieves, whose treasure trove I'd unwittingly stumbled upon, so I offered to help her hide until she might go home. That is her true heart's desire. She has no wish to be here with us. She wants to go home, and I propose to escort her there safely as soon as possible."

Ali Baba's face fell. "But what of your shop?"

Melisende almost laughed at his abrupt shift in focus. Men and their business — always, business came first.

"The shop is almost empty, with no goods left to sell. If this oil merchant had truly been what he said, then I might have had something, but as it is…I must travel to seek new goods I might trade, or return here to sell. Since Simon's death, I have been planning a trip to Rialto, and now is the time to take it. I shall take Lady Melisende with me, so that I may see her safely home."

Her heart sank. Home. The impossibly distant place she'd barely thought about in some time. She'd been so busy with her life here…

"We shall leave in three days," Mithra continued. "That should be long enough to bury the bodies, seek supplies for the journey, and to source suitable clothes for Lady Melisende."

Ali Baba nodded. "Yes, we must bury the bodies. If anyone knew what had happened here…no, they must not find out. The jars we can bury, too. But what of the horses?"

"We take them with us," Melisende said. "Two of them were born in my father's stables, and the rest will be able to carry goods or fetch a fine price in my homeland. You have a fortune in horseflesh in your stable. More than most men make in a lifetime."

But she'd have to go with him, to see that the horses sold at a proper price. Mithra didn't know horses the way she did.

Once she was home, she'd be happy again, Melisende told herself. She'd see everything she'd missed and wonder why she'd left in the first place. Dorylaeum, the crusade, murdering all those men…it would all seem like a fast-fading dream.

Yes, home was where she belonged. Not here.

She rose. "I shall retire. In the morning, we can begin our preparations for the journey."

Mithra rose too, then bowed deeply. "As my lady wishes."

His lady. A dream, and nothing more, she reminded herself, as she headed off to bed.

<h1 style="text-align:center">Forty-Three</h1>

Rialto was like another world, where the sea crept into the city, in aquamarine streets that Mithra had to remind himself he could not simply walk along.

For what felt like the thousandth time that day, he glanced at Melisende, who appeared to be as entranced as he was. He breathed a sigh of relief. Rialto was new to her, too, then. But his eyes lingered on her, on the layers of linen that looked just like his own clothes, as modest as anything she'd worn in Dorylaeum, and yet…

It was because she didn't wear a veil, he told

himself, but that wasn't true. She hadn't covered her face in the house, or in the stables. Then again, she'd rarely smiled in Dorylaeum, but her lips seemed stuck in a permanent curve since they'd left. Her eyes lit up at the slightest thing, as she pointed to whatever had caught her interest to make sure he didn't miss it.

Melisende was the most delightful travelling companion a man could ever meet. If he hadn't fallen in love with her in Dorylaeum, he'd have done it again a dozen times over on the way to Rialto. It would break his heart when they parted.

But what else could they do? She was a highborn Crusader lady, headed home to her father and likely marriage to some Crusader lord. He was a merchant, newly risen to the position, who had yet to prove himself outside of the Dorylaeum market.

He would focus first on finding Simon's family, and giving them the gold that belonged to them. Perhaps then they would be willing to do business with him, or introduce him to other Rialto merchants who might.

A few enquiries about the Ziano family gave him the address of what he understood was the family patriarch's palace. It wasn't until he stood outside the grand edifice that put every single one of Dorylaeum's finest houses to shame that nerves began to knot in his belly. He was no one. He did not belong here. If he'd known how important Simon's family was, he would not have dared…

"Ooh, Duke Sebastiano Ziano's house! My brother said wonderful things about him when he came home from Rialto. I always hoped I'd get to meet him. What business do you have with him?" Melisende asked.

She'd insisted upon accompanying him, and Mithra hadn't had the heart to refuse her. She knew more than anyone where he'd come from, and how this was no place for a lowly woodcutter like him. But the Duke's servants might allow a Crusader lady inside…

Plenty of people crowded into the Duke's reception hall, yet the servant made the crowd part to allow them through. No, to let Lady Melisende through, Mithra reminded himself. He trailed behind her, carrying the pitifully small chest.

"Lady Melisende of Mareschal, and Master Mithra of Dorylaeum! Two people I never imagined I would get to meet, and yet, you are both here in my house!" The man who greeted them looked like a much older version of Simon, with an open smile that said he meant every word. "You must stay with me while you are here in Rialto. I insist upon it."

A few words to his servants, and he'd not only ordered refreshments for them, but guest rooms and instructions to bring their things from the ship.

Finally, the Duke gestured for them to sit as he took a seat for himself. "Lady Melisende, please forgive me if I seem insensitive to your beauty and the honour you do me in this visit, but your companion carries news of my brother that I have sorely craved for many months." The Duke's eyes turned to Mithra. "His letters are always full of news of you and his son, so I feel as if I know you, Master Mithra. My brother's last letter was full of his plans for returning to Rialto with his family, and leaving you to manage his business in Dorylaeum as his partner. Yet here you are. Please, Master Mithra, what word do you bring of my brother Simon?"

The eagerness in the Duke's eyes smote

Mithra's heart. That Simon had had such plans, plans he'd never shared with him, which might have saved Peter and all his family if he'd only left Dorylaeum sooner.

Haltingly, Mithra began, "Your Grace – "

"Sebastiano, please. Simon looked upon you like a son, which would make you near enough to my nephew."

Mithra nodded. His heart had never felt so heavy. Why, if he fell in the canal outside, his heart alone would drag him to the bottom of the sea. Yet he'd sworn to do this, and he owed it to Simon. "Simon, Peter, and all their family were killed by Seljuk soldiers. The army stormed Dorylaeum, slaughtered all the Christians, and claimed all their goods as their own. I was too late to save them, but I managed to keep the soldiers from looting the shop, and saved what I could from the warehouse. I asked myself what Master Simon would have done in my place, and I hope I was not wrong in opening his shop for business. I sold…everything, mostly to the soldiers themselves, and set the gold aside to return to his family when the Seljuk army had gone." He lifted the chest onto the Duke's desk and opened it so that the man might see the gold inside. It was a small chest, true, but it was full of gold coins. "I have since inherited my uncle's shop, and I had hoped to buy Simon's shop, too, now he has no use for it…" He stopped when he saw the Duke.

Sebastiano buried his face in his hands, openly weeping for the brother he'd lost. "It is as I feared! Simon should have left Dorylaeum long ago, I told him. But he would not listen. And now all that is left of him and his family is a cold box of coins." He closed the lid, and fastened it with a click. Then he pushed the box toward Mithra. "You are a good man, and an honest merchant, to have brought this here to me. But I am the Duke of Rialto, and you have come from a Seljuk city. I cannot accept any gifts from you, nor any gold. Nor can I trade with you, while your city and mine are at war. All I can offer you is what is lost to me — everything my brother owned in Dorylaeum. His house, his shop, any goods that remained — they are yours now, just as Simon intended."

Mithra jumped to his feet. "But I cannot — "

The Duke held up his hand. "You must. For who else is more worthy of my brother's worldly goods than his only surviving son? I know you have a father, who I pray still lives, but one day, like Simon, you will wish to marry, and what if it goes against your father's wishes? Simon always followed his heart, like I did, and he would want you to do the same. With this gift, Simon would have set you free from all familial demands, and granted you the wealth to marry whatever girl you wished. I will gladly do what he could not."

Not whatever girl he wished, Mithra told himself, not daring to look at the woman beside him. The one who would always hold his heart.

Mithra mumbled his acceptance, and was greeted with a grateful smile from the Duke.

A moment later, Mithra was forgotten as the Duke turned to Melisende.

"What news of your brother?" he asked eagerly.

"My brother?"

"Sir Godfrey, of course! You must have good news of his quest. Is that not why he has sent you?"

For the first time since he'd met Melisende, she did not seem to know what to say.

Forty-Four

"My brother was safe at home, the last time I saw him. I have not seen him since the Crusaders left our village. The last I heard, he was in Byzas. But that was months ago. Your Grace knows more about his movements than me, if you have seen him since then," Melisende said.

The Duke's face fell. "So he hasn't found my daughter yet?"

Godfrey had been searching for the killers of some girl he'd found, Melisende remembered. The Duke's daughter could not have been in her village at home. Could she?

"When did your daughter go missing, Your Grace? Was it before the Crusaders left?"

He shook his head. "No, some months after that. They'd already left Byzas, your brother said, when he kidnapped her."

No, Godfrey would never do such a thing! "You believe my brother kidnapped your daughter?" Unless this daughter was the reason he'd come home from Rialto in disgrace. There must be more to it, though…for Godfrey would never do something so dishonourable.

The Duke burst out laughing. "Lady Melisende, you and I both know Sir Godfrey would find it easier to fly than to kidnap a virtuous maiden. No, it was some rogue magician with his terrible arcane arts, he said, who stole my poor Penelope. Godfrey swore he'd go after them, and bring her back. Why would Godfrey steal her when your father and I wanted him to marry her? I won't deny your brother isn't the brightest lad, but he's not as stupid as that!"

Melisende breathed a sigh of relief. The dead girl wasn't the Duke's daughter, and her brother had evidently made amends for whatever crime he'd committed on his first trip to Rialto. While she had her doubts about her brother's ability to bring the girl back, if he found her at all, she didn't dare say so in front of the Duke. Instead, she said, "My brother may not have the sharpest wit, but what he lacks in quickness he makes up for with loyalty and honour and willingness to do whatever is necessary. If anyone can find Lady Penelope, it will be Sir Godfrey." Even if it took him twenty years, Melisende thought but did not say. "I hope she is soon returned to you, Your Grace."

"Yes." He stared at her for a moment, then clapped his hands. "But in her absence, you must join me for dinner. Both of you. I insist."

Before either of them could protest, Melisende and Mithra were herded off by the Duke's servants to a pair of adjacent and very opulent guest chambers, where suitable clothes had already been laid out.

Melisende stared at the gown, made of so much silk she'd rustle like a tree in a high wind at the slightest movement. There would be no running for her tonight.

"Would you like a hot bath, my lady?" a maid asked.

Melisende could not recall the last time she'd known such a luxury. "Oh yes," she said.

Forty-Five

Mithra arrived in the dining room to find only the Duke there. He felt a little less self-conscious in his borrowed finery when he realised the Duke was dressed almost the same.

They talked of small things at first, the weather and the way prices changed when one was at war, before the Duke moved to more serious matters, like when the war might end.

"Because I'm eager to get back to all the longstanding business arrangements in your city and those surrounding it. Wars are bad for business, as everyone knows. Once it's over, we can pick up where we left off, if that is amenable to you. Simon said you knew his business better than he did, and he had contacts everywhere. If I wanted silk, he had six men he could source it from, and another dozen if they did not arrive in time. Once this crusade is complete, you may expect the arrival of one of my sons, for I regret I am too old for such journeys myself." The Duke fell silent as his attention shifted elsewhere.

Mithra followed the man's gaze, and the vision that captivated his own gaze was brilliant enough to leave him gasping for breath.

"She's like an angel, isn't she? The Baron of Mareschal always was one to breed the most beautiful creatures, but he'd never part with one of the mares. I tried to get her for one of my sons – fair begged him, I did, but he'd hear none of it. Not even when I offered to marry her myself. Duchess of Rialto, highest lady in the land, was not good enough for little Lady Melisende. No amount of money would persuade her father to part with her. That's why I agreed to the marriage between his son and my daughter. If only the Seljuks and then the Crusaders hadn't ruined all our plans, eh, Master Mithra?"

But Mithra could not speak. He could only watch as Melisende floated into the room in a cloud of gold silk, which somehow showed every delicious curve of her body even as it covered it in the most modest way possible.

She wore a matching veil so gossamer thin that her hair caught the light through it, gleaming as she turned her head.

"My daughter Penelope made that dress. She wore it to a wedding once, and I think the only man with eyes for the poor bride was the groom! Seeing it on Lady Melisende makes me want to lock her away in the strongest room of the palace, with all the other priceless treasures, so no man could steal her. Do you not agree?"

Lock Melisende away? Mithra recoiled. No man who'd seen her face light up with every breath of wind, or shaft of sunlight, or watched her climb a tree, or run as though she would fly faster than the wind itself, or laugh as a bird alighted on the mast to eat a meal of fresh-caught fish…no man who'd seen her glorious soul shine out through her eyes could even think of committing such a crime against her.

Maybe Melisende's father was right to keep her away from such a man.

Melisende frowned and flicked at her skirt. For all its beauty, the gown restricted her steps, making her mince across the floor instead of the swift strides that came so naturally to her.

"No, Your Grace. All I want to do is set her free from everything that confines her."

The Duke stared at him for a moment, before he began to nod. "Ah, yes. You're a young man in your prime. Of course, bedding a naked angel like that would be bliss indeed."

Horrified that the Duke had taken his words in a way he had not meant them, Mithra opened his mouth to explain.

But Melisende was now close enough to touch, as well as hear every word, so he fell silent as she dropped a graceful curtsey.

Mithra's eyes nearly popped out of his skull as the slight tilt of her body let him see right down the front of her gown to the most perfect pair of breasts…

He closed his eyes. He would treasure that vision until his dying day.

"Your Grace, Master Mithra," she said. "Where is everyone else?"

Sebastiano beamed. "We are everyone, my dear. I have no desire to share you."

An angry sound came out of Mithra's throat before he could stop it.

The Duke added smoothly, "Except maybe with Master Mithra here, of course."

Melisende's smile sparkled like diamonds in the sun. Did he imagine it, or was she looking only at him?

"You must forgive Master Mithra if he is a little surprised to see me," she began. "For in Dorylaeum, you see, the women are not allowed to dine with the men."

"Dinners in Dorylaeum must be dull indeed, for I cannot imagine wishing to deny myself a moment with the beauty that is before me now," the Duke said.

How dare this old man try to seduce her!

"That is precisely the problem," Mithra said. "You see, when a man is so beguiled by a woman's beauty, he may forget to eat or drink or speak to his companions at all. Now that is a dull dinner indeed!"

Melisende laughed merrily, but the Duke did

not join in.

Forty-Six

By the end of the meal, Melisende could scarcely keep her eyes open. She had a vague idea that, as the highest ranking person there, the Duke had to dismiss them before she could retire to bed, but if he didn't do it soon, she was going to fall asleep on the table.

Finally, the Duke rose. "Lady Melisende, forgive me for keeping you up so late. It is rare that I have such fascinating company at dinner. You must allow me to take you for a tour of Rialto on the morrow."

Melisende bobbed a curtsey, not caring how graceful it appeared as long as she didn't fall over. "Your Grace is too kind. Since Godfrey got home from Rialto, for months he talked about the beauty of the churches here, and the exquisite artwork. I confess I have been terribly envious of him for quite some time."

The Duke bowed. "Then on the morrow, your envy will be at an end. And tonight, should you wish to confess and absolve yourself of such a terrible sin, I will see that the priest in my private chapel is available to you."

She opened her mouth to protest, then closed it again as she realised it had been many months since her last confession, and she would be wise to accept the Duke's generous offer. So she muttered something she hoped sounded grateful, and headed up to her room.

She found Mithra a step behind her. Oh, of course – his room was beside hers.

"May I speak to you for a moment?" he asked. "Privately?"

"Of course," she said, following him into his room.

His bed was enormous – just like hers – and seemed to dominate the room. It would definitely dominate her dreams tonight, too, for Mithra was never far from her thoughts.

Melisende chose a chair as far from the bed as possible. "What do you wish to discuss?" she asked.

"What do you intend to confess?" he demanded.

She stared at him. He was not a Christian, but he'd lived with one, so surely he knew about the sanctity of the confessional. Though it was possible that he did not…

"My deepest, darkest secrets, so that I may be forgiven," she said.

Mithra shook his head. "You cannot tell this priest about the Forty Thieves, or their cave, or what happened to them. If anyone were to find out, they would arrest us both and kill us for our crimes!"

"What can I tell him, then?" Melisende demanded.

"Maybe that you ran off on a crusade. Surely you regret running away from your family."

She thought for a moment, longer and harder than she thought she'd need to, but still the answer was the same. "I do not regret it for a moment. The church encouraged this crusade, so the priest would praise me for it, instead of calling it a sin. And I am of age, entitled to run away from my family if and when I desire. Perhaps not wise to do so, but I did it, and I refuse to regret it."

"There must be something!"

There was, and she would probably regret saying it aloud, but it would serve him right for being so obstinate about this. She could confess to whatever she pleased, and no man could stop her.

She rose and met his gaze. "Yes. For some weeks now, I have regretted one thing. Not the crusade, not my time in Dorylaeum, and not any of the things I did there. Except the night the Forty Thieves came."

"You cannot tell him – "

"I don't regret killing them. They were criminals, and I did what was right to protect the man I loved. Maybe if I were a better, kinder person, I would feel guilt for the lives I ended. But the truth is that I did not. I still don't. If you had seen the things they'd done…" Melisende took a deep breath. "I regret that I did not tell your father the truth that night. When he offered me anything I desired, and you said you would take me home…I wish I'd had the courage to say what I wanted. Whether it could be mine or not. I regret not saying what was in my heart."

She looked up to find Mithra staring at her. He'd done that plenty over dinner, but this time it was different.

He stepped forward and grasped her hands. "My father's debt is mine as much as his. Anything you want, if it is within my power, I would give it to you. You have but to name it, Lady Melisende, and it is yours."

She didn't want to look at him, and yet she could not tear her eyes away. Tears blurred her vision. "You. I wanted…for one brilliant moment, I wanted to marry you."

"But I am a lowly woodcutter, a man your father would scarcely notice. You've had marriage offers from dukes that he's refused. He would never agree to let me marry you."

"My father can go play hide the sausage with the Duke…or the devil himself, if he desires, but I'll have none of them. In Dorylaeum, it might be different, but here I am of age, which makes me the mistress of my own destiny. If I wish to marry a penniless young woodcutter, I will. Or if I want to marry a good, kind, wonderful man, whose first thought when he stumbles across a priceless treasure is to help other people, whose kisses burn hotter than the desert sands in the sun...then I would damn anyone to hell who dares to object." Then the fire in her died at the thought of the one man who might object, as he had that night, and silence her on this matter forever.

"Melisende..."

He was going to tell her he didn't love her, wasn't he? It would break her heart, but she would bear it. She must bear it. At least she'd found the courage to confess her feelings to him. To know he did not share them...

"How do weddings among your people work?"

When she looked up, startled, to meet his eyes again, he continued, "You see, it's simple back home. The couple simply sleep together for a night under the same roof, and they're considered married. Seda is now considered my father's second wife, seeing as she lives with him, even though he only shares a bed with my mother. So if it's just a matter of sharing my bed, I'd happily take you as my wife tonight."

Her mouth was dry. Why was her mouth so dry? That burning look in his eyes. It seemed to set some sort of fire inside her. The very thought of his hands, his lips on her skin…

"The bedding…that bit comes after the wedding," she managed to say. "The wedding is where we make promises in front of a priest."

The idea seemed to come to them both at once.

"The Duke said there was a priest at your service in his private chapel. Do you think…?"

Melisende grabbed his hand and strode toward the chapel.

Forty-Seven

Promises said in front of a priest took almost no time at all, and then Mithra had Melisende back in his chamber. By her people's customs, she was his wife. But by his, she would not be truly his wife until she'd cried out his name in joy.

Right. Now was not the time to tell her he'd never bedded a woman before.

There were a thousand and one ways to pleasure a woman, he told himself. If he could remember merely a few of them, it would be enough.

He prayed he would be enough.

Melisende stood staring at the bed with her back to him, her silk gown glimmering in the candlelight. No cave of treasure had ever tempted him half as much as she did right now.

He stepped up behind her, pressing her body against his, as he bent his head to kiss her throat. His fingers worked on the lacings that bound her gown so tightly about her body. On each side, and again at the back.

She shivered in his arms.

"You have no need to fear me, Melisende. I swear, I will never hurt you. Whatever those soldiers did to you, I will not."

She twisted in his arms, so that she faced him. "No soldier has ever touched me. You're the only man who has, and we stopped before you could..." She blushed.

"You're a virgin still?" He scarcely believed it.

Wordlessly, she nodded.

Untouched. How had he not guessed?

"I promise I will never hurt you."

He'd have to be so careful. But with someone so precious, how could he not be?

He would start slow.

Carefully, Mithra leaned in for a kiss.

Oh, but he'd forgotten how one kiss with her could set the world on fire.

"Mithra, oh my God, Mithra!"

He blinked. As if this was their first kiss all over again, somehow he'd backed her up against the wall, with her legs up around his waist, but this time, his fingers were inside her, circling and stroking as her irresistible heat contracted around them.

She threw her head back and screamed his name again.

"You said you'd take me to bed after three times. That's seven, Mithra. Please!" she begged.

Seven. He'd pleasured her seven times already? Only…nine hundred and ninety-four to go.

He undid the final set of lacings, and gold silk slid down her body to puddle on the floor. The next layer was white silk, laced up the front so tightly that her breasts seemed ready to burst out the top. He gave the hem of her shift the slightest tug, and two perfect pink nipples peeked out.

All the ways he could pleasure her by

caressing her breasts popped into his mind. He longed to try them all. But he wanted to take her to bed, too…

"Three more," he said, touching his tongue to one of those exquisite pink pearls.

Forty-Eight

Naked as her name day, her heart still thrumming in her chest from the blindingly perfect pleasure her husband had already given her, more times than she could count, Melisende knew she could not put off that fateful moment any longer. If she did, her courage might fail her.

So she lay down on the bed, propped up by an obscene number of pillows, and said, "Please, Mithra, make me your wife." Then she closed her eyes and prayed he would be swift, like her sisters in law had told her their first times had been.

She heard the swish of fabric – Mithra undressing, she had no doubt – and considered peeking, but the ladies had advised against it. If her husband was large, the sight of him would likely frighten her, and if he was small…well, men were sensitive about their man parts, so she'd been warned not to say anything about them at all.

She felt the pillows beside her shift as her husband's weight settled upon them, instead of on her, as she expected.

Strong hands seized her, lifting her as easily as if she were one of the feather pillows and not a flesh and blood woman. He set her down on his lap, straddling him as though he expected her to ride him like some sort of horse. But the heat of him between her thighs was like no horse. It made her yearn to feel his touch there again, a mixture of hardness and heat that almost made her swoon.

She grabbed his shoulders to steady herself, her hands closing on even more hot, hard flesh.

Melisende's eyes flew open, and for the first time she saw her husband naked. His arms, shoulders and chest were just as muscular as she remembered, when she'd pushed him up against that tree. She wanted to run her hands along every ridge, touch her tongue to every dimple, to kiss…

He wore nothing but a lazy grin as he met her gaze. "I know not what you've heard about Crusader husbands, but marriage among my people is a very different thing. It is up to a wife to take a husband, and if I do not please you, you can divorce me by simply saying so. So, will you take me, Lady Melisende, and wed your body to mine?" His fingers stole between her legs again, stroking slowly.

She opened for him, like a flower who could not resist the sun. "Yes, oh, yes."

And then he glided into her, burning her with the most glorious heat, as his hands closed around her hips once more and ground her against him.

Her sisters in law had talked of pain, but Melisende felt nothing but pleasure and the burning desire for more.

"Oh, God, yes!" she cried. "Oh my God, Mithra, do that again!"

Within moments, they found a rhythm, their bodies rising and falling as one, until waves of pleasure rolled over Melisende and she screamed for joy at the top of her lungs. And again, and again, and again, until they lay together, spent.

"Do I please you, Lady Melisende?" Mithra asked as he stroked her breasts.

She wanted him to take one of her nipples in his mouth, and do that thing with his tongue…

"Oh my God, yes!" Melisende said.

"Well enough to be allowed to share your bed for another night?"

"Every night for the rest of my life. And every day, too," she said dreamily.

Mithra chuckled. "Good. For there are a thousand and one ways to pleasure a woman, and I don't think I've tried more than a dozen so far. If I have my wish, I intend to spend each and every night showing you all the ways I remember. Should I forget any, I know I shall have you to remind me, for it is my hope that every night we share shall be branded into your memory, as every moment we have spent together already is branded into mine. You have saved my life and my family and my fortune. Now you hold my heart, and I will spend the rest of my life showing you how grateful I am for it."

She wanted to reply with equal eloquence, but he touched his tongue to her nipple and all coherent words left her with only a rapturous moan in response.

Some hours later, after they'd made love for the third time and her joyous screams had likely woken half the city, she laid her head on his chest and said sleepily, "When we return home to Dorylaeum, I want you to buy me as big a bed as this one, where we can make love every night."

"And every morning," he replied, wrapping his arms around her.

She lifted her head, eyes widening. "We can do it again in the morning?"

"I understand it is the sweetest way to start the day."

"Wake me at dawn, then, so we can find out together." Her eyes drifted shut.

"I will."

Call:
Pied Piper Retold

DEMELZA CARLTON

A tale in the Romance a Medieval Fairy Tale series

One

"Another one full!" Sara said, carefully tipping the contents of her apron into the sack. The peeled chestnuts cascaded dutifully down onto their fellows, before Sara tied off the top of the sack so she could carry it to the cart. The chestnut harvest had been good this year, and they'd have plenty of flour to see them through 'til spring. Once these had been milled, of course.

"How do you peel them so fast?" Silvana said, staring at her half-full basket. She stabbed her knife into a shell and the nut jumped out, surprising her.

"Practice, and knowing which ones are ready, and which need more time," Sara answered. She seized her empty basket and headed up to the smoke house. She breathed deeply as she ascended the stairs to the upper level, where the racks of sweet-smelling chestnuts dried over the smoke from their smouldering shells on the level below.

It took her right back to her childhood, when her grandfather had first brought her in here. She'd had to stretch up onto her toes to see the rows of round nuts lined up on the racks, and the one that burst open before her eyes. She'd squealed at the glimpse of creamy gold flesh amid all that brown, and her grandfather had helped her peel the nut and take it home.

If she'd known then that she'd inherit the smoke house, along with all the rest of her family's holdings, when sickness had carried away her parents and all her siblings in one horrible summer, and she'd struggled through her first autumn harvest alone, she might have been less excited about that first visit.

But grief no longer stabbed at her heart as it had all those years ago, and she'd spent every harvest since shelling nuts with Tola and Maria, Silvana's mother, until one cold winter's night, when the reaper had called for Maria, too.

If only she had a daughter who would take her place at the table with Silvana, and Tola's daughter Swanhild, when she was gone. Though the way fate had shaped her life so far, Sara herself would probably teach Silvana and Swanhild's daughters to shell the nuts, her fingers as gnarled as the chestnut kernels themselves.

Sara shook herself. Such thoughts were silly. She had no need of a daughter – she had a fine son. Tobias would be a man soon enough, ready to marry and have children of his own. If only his father had lived long enough to see him…

Were those tears on her cheeks? Surely not. It was perspiration from the heat in here. She should fill her basket quickly and head back outside.

By the time she reached the cooler air outside, Silvana had emptied her basket and was headed into the smoke house for a refill.

"Can you teach me to choose the right ones? Both you and Tola work so much faster than me. I'll never be good enough…" Silvana's eyes brimmed with tears.

Sara pried the basket from the girl's hands. "Your mother was always the slowest of the three of us when it came to peeling the nuts, but she was the best at pressing them. Here, take my basket and put them in the pressing barrel. I'll fill yours for you."

"Really?"

Sara gave a nod, and the girl hastened back to the table where Tola still sat.

The morning passed quickly, until the cart could hold no more. Silvana might have spent more time stamping on the nuts in the pressing barrel than picking or peeling them, but Sara didn't mind. She'd done her fair share of dancing in the pressing barrel when she was a girl. Now, her feet would hurt by day's end if she did Silvana's job.

"Will you join us for the midday meal?" Sara asked Silvana.

The girl shook her head, furrowing her brow. "I'll take the cart down to Father at the mill. I must make sure he has his dinner," she said.

Sara nodded. Regulo had not taken his wife's death well, and if he didn't have Silvana still, he might have followed Maria into the grave. Best the girl get home and give him some work to do.

So Sara helped Silvana harness the pony to take the cart to the mill, where Silvana and her father would turn the shelled nuts into flour, to be bagged and distributed as Sara directed. Her family might own the chestnut orchards and the smoke house, along with all the land around, but Sara made sure those who helped with the harvest received their share of the final product, to feed them through the winter. Even Silvana and her father, who took a tithe of what went through the mill. Her family had once owned the mill, too, but some wise ancestor had bequeathed the orchards to one brother and the mill to another, which made Silvana and her father some sort of distant cousin to Sara, several times removed.

"What's in the pot?" Tola asked, bringing Sara's thoughts back to her own home.

Sara grinned. "I hope you're not sick of

chestnuts. I popped some in the pot, along with the peas I shelled this morning and the last of the bacon. It should have thickened nicely by now. Perfect with some bread."

Tola's eyebrows rose. "You're out of bacon already?"

"Tobias eats enough for three men, though he's still a boy. He'll have to do without for a few weeks. As soon as we've cleared the smoke house, Cronus will slaughter some pigs for me and hang them up to smoke. They're fattening up in the forest on fallen chestnuts as we speak."

"Whereas Swanhild eats like a bird. I'd fear for her health, if she didn't spend most days in the forest, harvesting herbs. There's food aplenty for those that know how to find it, and she must." Tola shook her head, then sniffed deeply. "Oh, it is definitely time to eat."

They took their bowls outside to the table where they'd been shelling nuts, sitting in the last of the sun before the mountain shadows stole it from them. But until it did, they enjoyed the view over the lake that lay beside the town. Today, the still surface mirrored the blue sky, illustrating perfectly why the town had earned its name of Mirroten.

"Mercurio is early," Tola remarked.

Sara sopped up the last of her stew with a crust of bread. "He's not due for weeks, and it looks too big to be his boat – are you sure?"

Tola pointed, and Sara could not deny that the ship cutting its way across the lake bore Mercurio's brightly coloured sail.

"Profits must be good, if he has bought a bigger boat."

Both women rose.

"I'd best get home and see what I have to trade. He'll have some rare ingredients from the traders in Rialto, which I've been waiting for," Tola said.

They said their farewells while Sara gathered up the dishes, but Sara lingered outside for a moment. Mercurio the merchant, sailing his boat up and down the river and through the mysterious marshes to the port of Rialto, always brought new and intriguing things from faraway lands. For a price, of course. What treasures would his ship hold this time?

A chill breeze swept down from the mountain as the sun slipped behind a cloud. Sara shivered and hurried inside.

Two

"RUN, GIRL, RUN!"

Zoticus watched the girl's expression change from panic to determined clarity. Her arms flew out like wings, letting go of everything she possessed. Before her things thudded to the ground, Melisende took flight.

He'd seen the sequence a dozen times in his visions of this moment, but somehow the addition of sound made it more real.

The scrunch of sand beneath her boots as she broke into a run, audible even over the distant screams of battle on the other side of the field. Clad in only her tunic and hose,

Melisende moved so swiftly the cloth was plastered against the curves of her blatantly female body.

Eager shouts and the thunder of hooves heralded her pursuit, invisible in the crowd of panicked crusaders.

Zoticus unslung his bow and reached for his first arrow. He sighted along it, then waited.

Four riders emerged from the melee, whipping their horses hard in their frenzy for the hunt. The hunters did not know they would be the prey today.

Sir Enguerrand led the charge, a black raven atop a stolen white horse. Sir Guiscard followed some distance behind, his horse unable to keep up with the fleet-footed mare. Sir Onfroi was hot on his heels, with Sir Roland bringing up the rear on a horse that could scarcely bear his weight.

Zoticus could not abide a man who abused his mount. He lined up his shot, and Roland fell first, rolling on the ground while his relieved horse rode on without him.

Onfroi had chosen to wear armour today, so Zoticus had to choose his target. Ah, there it was – when Onfroi leaned forward over his horse's neck, his breastplate rode up, exposing far more of his side than was safe with archers about. A kidney shot, followed by a second arrow that lodged firmly in the man's left buttock. He, too, went tumbling from the saddle, but unlike Roland, Onfroi's foot caught in the stirrup, and his horse dragged him along the ground, likely doing even more damage.

Guiscard had not bothered to don his armour, so the owl on his tunic was clear to see. Zoticus aimed for above the owl, though, and his aim was true – the first arrow caught him in the back of the neck, sinking in deep.

Enguerrand rode alone, heedless of the loss of his companions, intent only on catching the girl.

A girl whose head whipped back for scarcely a moment. Had she seen the glint of the knight's teeth, bared in a triumphant grin? Or was it her brother's horse that had made her smile before a puff of magic surrounded her, and she vanished.

Magic spirited her across the field and into the trees, faster than any horse could gallop, but Enguerrand could not see it. Instead, he reined in his horse, casting about for the treasure he'd lost.

Only then did he realise he was alone, his men having fallen along the way.

In the space of a moment, Enguerrand seemed to regain his senses, and he fixed his sights on Zoticus. With the girl gone, he set his horse against a different target.

Zoticus stood his ground. He'd seen this in his vision, too, and he knew how it would end. He waited until he could see the horse's eyes, mad at this mistreatment from a man who was not her master.

Now.

"Halt, Pegasus!" Zoticus called, and the obedient mare skidded to a stop.

But Enguerrand did not, flying over the horse's head and over Zoticus, to land awkwardly on the stony ground.

The knight struggled to draw his sword, but he'd broken both arms in his fall. "Help me, and my father will richly reward you!" the man begged.

Zoticus leaned down and pulled Enguerrand's sword from its scabbard. It was a fine weapon – far finer than the man it had been made for. The knight would need neither sword nor scabbard now, so Zoticus unfastened the man's baldrick. More broken bones moved beneath his hand – Enguerrand had shattered several ribs, too, and at least one had punctured his lungs.

"Mercy!" cried the knight. He tried to lift his arm to shield himself, but his strength had already started to fade.

Zoticus considered the shattered man at his feet. Mercy came in many forms. A magical healer might make the knight whole again, but without swift aid he would certainly die, and die in agony.

"Did you offer Babette mercy? Or any of the other girls you hunted and killed like animals?" Zoticus asked, sliding the sword back into its scabbard before tucking both into his bag.

"Who?" the knight asked.

"Did you know any of the girls' names? No? How about Sir Josse, who you cut down with this very blade, so that you might force yourself upon his sister?" Zoticus persisted. He'd heard of men who repented their crimes when faced with death, but he had yet to meet one. Most of the men Zoticus had killed preferred to spit curses with their final breath.

It seemed Enguerrand would not be such a man, either.

"Help!" the knight moaned, trying to crawl away.

Zoticus decided to leave Enguerrand until last, and check on the others.

Guiscard stared sightlessly up at the sky, a broken arrow protruding from his throat. It had gone all the way through, as if shot from a crossbow and not a longbow. A formidable weapon indeed – no wonder the Seljuk archers were so fearsome, armed with these. Zoticus would keep his Seljuk longbow, lest it be useful later.

Onfroi's corpse was not so serene. His horse had grown weary of dragging it, and crushed the offending weight beneath his hooves. The result was that where the knight's head had once been was now a piece of pulped meat.

Roland had not been as lucky. Thrown free from his horse, his roll along the ground had torn the arrows out of his flesh, leaving gaping wounds through which his organs spilled. Much like Enguerrand, Roland's injuries were definitely mortal.

Four men dead, or they would be, by the end of the day. And every man who'd marched with them, thanks to the Seljuk army and the ambush no one but Zoticus had suspected. He could head home and collect payment for a job well done.

Ah, but he owed it to Josse to bring proof to the man's grave that his sister's violators were no more. So Zoticus collected three more swords and three signet rings, before heading back to the moaning, groaning worm that was Enguerrand.

He found Pegasus prancing around the man, shaking her head at him. It wasn't until Zoticus got closer that he realised the wretch had managed to wrap his hand around a rope trailing from the mare's bridle, and she was attempting to break free.

"Easy, Pegasus," he said, holding up his hands. He'd seen Godfrey manage this horse all the way to Byzas, and she'd seemed a biddable enough beast then. Now…

"If you'll just let me get close enough, I'll free you, and we can be on our way. I'll take you home to Godfrey and all your other stable mates," Zoticus continued.

This was apparently not to Pegasus's taste, for she reared up onto her hind legs, then brought her front hooves down hard.

Enguerrand's brains splattered on Zoticus's boots.

Pegasus tossed her head, pulling the reins from Enguerrand's slackened grasp as she stepped back from the corpse she'd created.

Zoticus pulled the ornate raven ring from Enguerrand's hand and stuffed that into his sack with everything else.

"Now, would you like me to take you home, or are you planning on joining the Seljuk army?" he asked the horse.

It was a good thing horses were not susceptible to the plague, or she never would have made it home, Zoticus thought. Nor had she liked the ship, but…

He blinked. A low wooden ceiling floated above, while straw rustled beneath him when he moved. Everything ached like Pegasus had stomped on his whole body. But he'd returned Pegasus to Godfrey long ago, before placing his sword and signet ring collection on Josse's grave.

In fact, the last time he'd felt so weak, he'd been aboard that rat-infested ship, fighting off that benighted plague that had killed off more crusaders than the Seljuks had.

Zoticus groaned. Not again. A pestilence on all plagues, for he was heartily sick of them.

Three

When Tobias left to take the goats up to the high pasture the next morning, Mercurio's stall was already under construction. Not that Mercurio himself was doing the work – oh, no, he had every labourer in town fetching and carrying for him, earning credit they might spend on his goods. Sara's brother-in-law Ahab would be among them, likely setting up the stall and directing everyone else, for it would not do for the head of the town council to be seen doing the work of a common labourer.

She shaded her eyes and peered at the hive

of activity on the lake shore. Ah, good, Mercurio had brought the winter fodder for the town. They'd had a warm, dry summer up in the mountains, but you could never tell if the lowlands had had similarly good haymaking weather until the hay arrived.

In her grandfather's time, the hay they made in the high pastures had seen the village livestock through most winters, but the goat herd had grown since then, even more so with Ahab on the council. He'd helped the town prosper, and it had surely grown, so they could sell their surplus down river, but they'd also had to buy in more things they simply didn't have. Without trade, Mirroten would face a hard winter.

But not this winter. Judging by the parade of bundles coming out of the ship's hold, the hayshed beside the town green would be full to the rafters. A good thing, for the harvest from the high pastures had barely filled her own hayloft this year.

Part of her wanted to go down there and see what Mercurio had to sell, but she still had chestnuts to shell, so she fetched a basket and sat down at the table, where she might watch the impromptu market while she worked.

Mercurio's first customer was Tola, carrying two big baskets of herbs to sell. They took their time, bargaining over each item, until Tola looked satisfied. Only then did Tola deign to look at Mercurio's wares, carefully selecting perhaps half a basket's worth of things before any coins changed hands.

Sara smiled. No wonder Mercurio appeared to be sweating – Tola was the one taking the money, not him. Most people didn't know she'd grown up in Rialto, before coming to Mirroten newly widowed, and she'd learned to bargain from the best.

The next customer was Ahab, and his daughter, Ysabel. Sara was surprised to see the girl, for when she'd asked Ahab if Ysabel could help shell nuts, he'd said she was too ill to leave the house. If she'd recovered, Sara should ask again.

She set down her basket and headed down the hill to the lake.

On her way, she met Father Fazzio, the town priest, carrying a large, cloth-draped bundle.

"Are you selling things to Mercurio, too,

Father?" Sara asked.

Fazzio laughed. "No, Mistress Sara. All I have belongs to Mother Church – what would I have to sell? But Mercurio carries goods and messages from my bishop in Rialto, and he is kind enough to transport our messenger birds back." He lifted the cloth to reveal a cage full of pigeons.

Sara blinked. "I thought the point of messenger birds was that they could fly and carry messages on their own. Wouldn't that be faster than sending them by boat?"

Fazzio's eyes widened, before he laughed again. "Oh, yes, of course, but messenger birds only fly home. You cannot train them to fly back and forth, wherever you please. So these birds are Mirroten pigeons, born and raised here. Mercurio will take them to the bishop, who can then send me messages by releasing these pigeons. Ingenious, no?"

Sara had to agree. Before she could say so, however, little Bernard ran up to the priest to breathlessly ask for him to come and help his grandfather. Fazzio promised to speak to Sara more later, and headed off with the boy.

"Mistress Sara! You grow more beautiful

with each season that passes!"

She arched her eyebrows. "And your flattery, Master Mercurio, rings even more hollow than last time."

He looked hurt. "Mayhap you cannot see it, but I only speak the truth. Come, Ahab, is Sara not the most beautiful woman alive?"

"Beautiful, but heartless, I fear. I have asked her many a time to marry me, but she still mourns my brother, and will until her dying breath," Ahab replied.

At least that's what she'd told Ahab.

"Heartless, indeed," Mercurio said smoothly. "Any other town along the mighty river, I might find a guest bed in the best house, but Mistress Sara would rather I sleep aboard my cold boat than beneath her roof." His eyes glittered, daring her to defend herself.

But to do so, she'd have to admit she'd taken Mercurio as her lover, after her husband had died, and he'd likely be her lover still, if she hadn't seen him with a maiden in one of the other villages downriver. Well, the girl had been a maiden, until she'd succumbed to the trader's flattery. Sara had no intention of lying with a man who had a mistress in every hamlet he docked at.

"I think only of the virtue of the girls in our town. Your reputation as a seducer of women precedes you, as always, Mercurio." Sara smiled sweetly.

Ahab's eyes grew huge. "Come, Ysabel, we should get started on those mattresses. Even with straw this fresh, they will not stuff themselves." He tugged on his daughter's arm to hurry her back up the hill to town.

Sara almost laughed. Ahab had his shortcomings, but he was absolutely devoted to the protection of his only daughter. Speaking of which…

"Ysabel, I still have chestnuts left to shell. If you have time to help, I can promise you a bag of chestnut flour for the trouble," Sara said.

Ysabel turned. "I thank you for the offer, Aunt Sara, but I must do the mattresses. Maybe when they are finished…"

Sara nodded. "The offer is open until all the nuts are done. At least another week."

Ysabel nodded her thanks, then hurried off in her father's wake.

"What do you have to trade, Mistress Sara? I have much that might interest you. Fine silks from across the sea, candles from the Holy Land you might burn in church to pray for your husband's soul…in fact, I have been fortunate enough to acquire an entire cargo of items from the Holy Land and Byzas. If you ever chose to wear anything but mourning clothes, you might like…" Mercurio flung open a chest, then lifted up a swathe of gossamer thin fabric that shimmered in the sunlight. The sunlight seemed to shine right through the bright stripes, too. "The finest silk from the Far East. You would look divine draped in a dress made of this."

"I'd look like a concubine from someone's harem, more like," Sara said. She shook her head. "Maybe next time you come to Mirroten, Mercurio. The miller has barely begun grinding this year's crop of chestnuts, so I cannot say if we will have any surplus to sell this year. It will still be another week before I'm done shelling them, the harvest was so good. After that, I'd hoped to start on the cheeses, though I'm down a dairyhand since Santina died. No one else can work that kind of magic with milk."

Sadly, Santina had not managed to teach her cheesemaking skills to her daughter Ysabel. They'd both fallen ill of the same summer fever, and only young Ysabel had survived, though she'd been delicate ever since.

Mercurio pressed both hands to his chest. "Argh, but you are heartless indeed, Mistress Sara! Not only do you deny me your warm hospitality, but I do not even have one of your glorious cheeses to sweeten my supper!"

Her cheeses were salty, not sweet at all, but Sara chose not to correct him. Instead, she said, "Perhaps you should try to sell some of your holy candles or other things to Father Fazzio, who has some pigeons for you."

"Perhaps next time, you will feel more kindly disposed toward me, Mistress Sara," Mercurio said.

She couldn't suppress her smile. "Perhaps. It will depend on how good a price you give me for my cheeses."

Mercurio bowed deeply. "Mistress Sara, I have always given you my best, and I always will."

No. No matter how good a lover he'd been, she had no intention of allowing him to share her bed again.

"See you next time, Mercurio." She turned on her heel and headed back up the hill.

"Peace, brother. I mean you no harm."

Zoticus blinked, his bleary eyes focussing on the blade he held at the stranger's throat. The religious brother's throat, judging by the man's tonsured head.

Zoticus sheathed his knife. "Forgive me, brother. What with your dark robes and all, I mistook you for Death, come to claim me."

The monk managed a sad smile. "I suspect Death fears you more than you fear him, for he took everyone else in the village, yet you are still here."

"You mean the plague killed them."

The monk bowed his head. "They no longer suffer, yet by some miracle you have been saved. I must take you to see the Abbot."

Zoticus considered arguing, but this Abbot would likely know more than some lowly monk. "May I have a moment to make myself presentable, then?" he asked instead.

The monk smiled. "Of course. Take all the time you need. I must see if there are any other survivors in the inn."

Zoticus chose not to extinguish the hope in the man's eyes with more truth. Now, if he were travelling with Melisende still, the crusader girl with a magical gift for swiftness, he would have made some wry remark that would make the girl's eyes grow round, the better to drink in all the strange sights as they travelled.

But she was a girl no longer, travelling only occasionally with her husband, for they had several children now. And her brother, the brave but foolish Sir Godfrey…ah, it did not do to dwell on the past.

Particularly when in the present, he needed to take a piss.

That taken care of, he found a fresh tunic

and hose, but what he really wanted was a wash. Heaven only knew how many days he'd lain abed, fighting the plague. Something to ask the Abbot.

What little water remaining in the ewer did not look fresh, so he headed out to the inn yard, in search of a well.

He found a horse trough, the water murkier than the bottom of the jug in his room, and shuddered. The well, when he did find it, was tucked behind the stables, beside the inn's kitchen gardens. Even in the warmth of a summer afternoon, the water felt shockingly cold against his skin.

The vision hit him without warning. The bite of cold air on his cheeks, as a woman dashed across a castle bailey, her heavy cloak flying out behind her like a raven's wings. Her ruddy lips parted as if to speak, urgency darkening her eyes.

Zoticus blinked, and the vision was gone. He knew neither the woman nor her castle, but one day he would stand in that very bailey, witness to the lady's flight. That's how his visions worked.

Several minutes later, washed and dressed in

clean garb, he strode out into the town square. Monks carried cloth-wrapped bundles to a cart, before heading back into the cottages where the townspeople had once lived.

A small arm slipped from its wrapping, and Zoticus's blood ran cold. The bundles were all bodies, being taken to the churchyard for burial.

"You should not be here, good sir, if you value your life! Please, I beg you, turn back the way you have come, lest this accursed pestilence take you, too!"

Zoticus spun to face a panicked priest, who seemed to think making shooing motions with his hands would make Zoticus disappear.

"Death didn't want me. One of the monks woke me. I was sleeping in that inn over there." Zoticus pointed.

The priest's eyes widened. He fell to his knees, lifting his face to the sky. "Heavens be praised! A miracle, just as the Abbot predicted!" He fastened his hands on Zoticus's arm. "Sir, you must accompany us back to the Cloister of the Holy Innocents. God himself has saved you, as the Abbot saw in his vision, and you must come!"

Zoticus gently pried his arm free. "You're mistaken, Father. There's nothing holy or miraculous about me. Just a matter of luck, is all." Luck, and magic, but he didn't think this pious priest would want to hear that. "This isn't the first plague I've caught. I went on a crusade once, and our whole ship got sick on the way home. Death doesn't like me, is all."

"Twice saved from the plague…you must be a holy man indeed, sir! I beg you – "

A flash of colour caught Zoticus's eye, and he ignored the priest so he might cross the square to see what it was. One of the bodies had been wrapped in a brightly striped cloak, the sort he'd seen sold in the marketplacc in Byzas. The sort crusaders had bought as gifts to take home for sisters, wives, and daughters who would never receive them. Melisende had bought a sack made of the striped stuff, and he'd teased her mercilessly about it. She'd stubbornly hung onto it, until the day of his vision, when those four dishonoured knights had died by his hand.

But the cloak…crusaders had bought every one in the marketplace, until there was no striped cloth left in the whole city. And those who had survived to head home had fallen at the last in the plague ships, their belongings stored in the holds of those doomed vessels.

Ships Zoticus had told Duke Sebastiano to burn, with everything they contained. Surely the man hadn't been foolish enough to take the infected goods and offer them for sale...

But the Duke was a merchant of Rialto. Commerce ran as readily as blood through the veins of a man of Rialto.

Zoticus should have burned the ships with his own hands. Doused them in oil, then thrown a torch in after.

But surely the plague could not persist for more than a decade. He might not be as skilled a healer as his mother or Melisende, but he knew enough about his family's history to be sure. Later, when he was alone, he would sift through the magical memories of his ancestors, to see what else they knew of plagues that might tell him how this could happen.

Yet the cloak wrapped around yet another plague victim shone bright with accusation. He needed to know how a dead crusader's cloak came to be here, of all places, at the same time as a plague slaughtered the town.

"Will you come to the Cloister?" the priest asked. His eyes shone with a kind of fervent faith Zoticus could only envy, for he had never known such a feeling to dwell within his own breast. "It is a most holy place, with relics from the Holy Innocents preserved beneath the altar. I have no doubt it is God's call that woke you from your deathly sleep, calling you to undertake a pilgrimage, sir, to thank God for the miracle of your deliverance!"

Zoticus blinked. Once again, he found himself unwilling to destroy another man's hope. "Perhaps, Father. But first, I must head for Rialto. I have pressing business there, which cannot wait."

When the pony had finished his breakfast, Sara hitched him up to the cart. She'd loaded the last bag of peeled chestnuts last night, and it was time to see whether Regulo had finished milling the previous load. In better times, the answer would have been yes, and he'd have delivered the freshly milled chestnut flour already, but he wasn't the man he'd once been. Perhaps he never would be.

So she walked alongside the plodding pony and cart, as an excuse to see how Regulo and Silvana fared.

"Good morning, Mistress Sara. You're up

early!"

She blinked. Father Fazzio looked far too cheerful for such an early hour. Then again, she'd rarely seen him anything less than eager to please.

"My son rises with the sun, and if I am not by the door when he departs, he's likely to forget to take his dinner, and it's a long day in the high pastures for a hungry boy," she said.

He nodded and smiled. "I'm sure my mother thought the same of me. Now I am a man grown, it makes little difference. It is not my mother who seeks to feed me, but most of the mothers in the town, convinced a priest living on his own cannot possibly cook for himself!" He laughed. "They do not believe there were no women in the seminary, and that we were all required to learn to cook. Even if I hadn't, still they give me too much. But that is perhaps a good thing, as then I have surplus to give to the families who need more than they have…" He went on to name names.

Sara only nodded. Between herself and the priest, they saw to it that everyone in town had enough to see them through the winter, and none of the names were news to her.

Then she realised he carried another cloth-draped bundle, much smaller than the one he'd had before.

"Are you bringing breakfast to someone in need, Father?" she asked.

He shook his head. "Oh, no, my messenger pigeons would make a poor meal. Especially this one, which only arrived this morning."

"And what news did he bring from…ah, your bishop, I believe?" Sara asked. She could tell from the slump of his shoulders that it couldn't have been good.

"He sent word of a cursed plague, wiping out the port town of Altino. Not a single man, woman or child was spared," Fazzio said, his eyes wide.

Her heart constricted in her chest. She knew what it meant to lose loved ones to sickness. To lose an entire town… "Oh, that is terrible! All those poor people."

"The bishop cautioned us to remain true to our faith, and not be tempted to wickedness, lest the same fate befall us."

Sara made a rude noise. It wasn't anywhere near as impolite as what she'd say to Fazzio's obnoxious bishop, were he here. "While some of the people of Altino might have been less than virtuous, I cannot believe even the children deserved such a fate. Plagues do not come out of nowhere, and they are spread by people."

"Yet there are cases in scripture that tell us such things have happened in the past. Towns where there was not one good man…"

"I know my scripture, too, Father, and while there may not have been one good man in a particular town, I'm certain there were plenty of good women or at least children. Yet the Bible is mysteriously silent about those."

Father Fazzio seemed nervous at the turn their conversation had taken. Perhaps he feared for his soul. "You are mistaken, Mistress Sara. The Holy Gospel of Saint Matthew clearly tells us that Herod slayed the Holy Innocents, at the time of our Saviour's birth. They are surely saints in heaven, along with all the other martyrs who have given their lives to the Holy Church. Perhaps you should come to the church, to pray to those saints, so that they may strengthen your faith in this dark time." Ah, so it wasn't his soul he feared for, but hers. Perhaps he was right to do so.

Perhaps. If only there was less work to do. She might spare a moment to light a candle, once this delivery was done.

"Will you be heading back to the church soon, Father? Perhaps you might say a prayer for me, and a mass for those poor souls who died in Altino."

He shook his head. "I must bring this pigeon to Mercurio, so he can take it back to the bishop. I pray he has not left yet..." The priest hurried off toward the lake.

Sara shrugged, and continued on to the mill. She might not have hours to spare, on her knees in church, but she could and did pray that Mirroten might be safe from the plague that had afflicted Altino. For it was only a short sail down the river, a thought which sent a cold shiver down her spine.

Please, don't let Mirroten suffer the same fate as Altino.

Six

Rialto had grown since Zoticus had seen it last, as the swampy city always seemed to do. And yet, it grew ever more beautiful as the years passed. He knew plenty of women who would wish to know the city's secret, for their beauty only faded as they gained wisdom.

But if the Duke of Rialto had sold plague goods, then Rialto had descended into the depths of stupidity. No one would buy their trade goods if they were known to be tainted. Surely Sebastiano could not be so senseless.

Unless age had stolen his wits…

At the Ducal Palace, he gave his name to a

servant and declined the offer of refreshment, for Duke Sebastiano would not keep him waiting.

Sure enough, Zoticus spotted the servant returning. "His Grace the Duke has no business with you, and he will not see you," the servant said.

"The Duke jests, surely."

The servant shook his head. "The Duke does not jest."

"Duke Sebastiano enjoys a joke as much as I do, I am certain. Take me to him, and you shall see."

The servant stared. "Duke Sebastiano had been dead these last five years. We have a new Duke now."

A cold hand wrapped around Zoticus's heart. Another good man gone. Would he outlive everyone before Death came to claim him?

Zoticus inclined his head. "Then I thank you. I shall visit Palazzo Ziano instead. I imagine Domenico is head of the family now?"

But the servant was already hurrying away.

Zoticus hid his smile. So they did know who he was. Never mind that Zoticus had never killed a man who didn't deserve it – loyal servants were a rare enough breed, without killing them alongside their wayward masters – somehow, his fearsome reputation always preceded him, and made men quake in their boots.

He hoped Sebastiano's sons were as well-informed as the new Duke's servants, or this could be a very tedious trip.

When his boat drew up outside Palazzo Ziano, Zoticus could not help but notice the old water-stained wooden doors had been replaced by shiny new ones clad in bronze. Business had prospered for Sebastiano's family.

Which didn't explain why they'd felt the need to deal in death…

He found two of the sons at home, ensconced in the dining room where he'd shared food and wine with their father. Unlike the new Duke, Domenico and Orso were quick to invite him to join them. Pleased to see that Ziani hospitality had not died with their father, Zoticus was only too happy to take a seat at the table.

"So, did Pietro find you?" Domenico asked,

gesturing for a servant to refill Zoticus's wine cup.

"I don't think so," Zoticus said, taking a bite of his fish pie. No one did seafood quite like the cooks of Rialto. "I was taken ill on the road, and when I recovered, I came straight here from Altino."

"Then you must have seen him! He sent a messenger with a chest full of coin from Altino over a week ago, saying he had some final trade negotiations to tie up before he came home."

It seemed Death liked to fondle Zoticus's heart lately, for he felt that cold touch again. "There is no one left in Altino. A plague struck down everyone in the town, leaving nothing but corpses and ghosts. The only people I saw were some monks burying the dead." And insisting he visit their Abbot at his mountain sanctuary, up to and including giving him detailed directions and a map. Memory niggled, and he paled. "It would not surprise me if the monks succumb to the plague, too. I hope your brother's trade negotiations took him far from there." Or Pietro was likely to be dead, too.

Orso raised his cup. "Knowing Pietro, he's probably counting his coins thrice to make sure he was paid properly. Even I can't believe Father forgot about those ships, but Pietro found them and turned a pretty profit on them!"

Was it his imagination, or did the wine taste sour? It had seemed so sweet only a moment before. Zoticus set his cup down. "What ships? What cargo did they carry?"

Domenico shrugged. "These were old ships. Father loaned them to the previous Duke to carry a military force to Byzas or some such place, I believe, but the Duke lost so many men he could not crew all the ships to sail them home, so they remained at Byzas. Shortly before Father died, he sent for his ships, and he anchored them in the lee of one of the shoals at the far end of the lagoon. There they might have remained, had a storm not heaped so much sand on the shoal that it became an island. An island where the Benedictines wanted to build a monastery, but they couldn't, on account of the ships sitting in the sand. The Benedictines wanted to use the timber, for there was a quantity of good oak in those hulls, but the Council would not let them, for they were Ziani ships."

Orso laughed. "You know Pietro. He smelled gold, and he would hear no argument until he had seen those ships. He headed out into the lagoon that very afternoon, and before the day was done, he had an army of men ready to help him dig the ships out of the sand to refloat them, for they were still sound. And their holds were full of cargo that had been sitting there, safe in the sand. The food was spoiled, of course, mostly eaten by rats, and the rats had turned quite savage, with nothing to eat but one another, but he found chests full of cloth and weapons from Byzas. I claimed a chest of silks to send to my sister. She is companion to the Queen in Aros, now."

Ah, yes. Godfrey's bride, Penelope. "If you love your sister, you will burn that chest and everything it contains. I sailed on those ships when they came to Rialto, and plague carried away all those who sailed with me. I told your father to burn the ships, so the pestilence would not spread." Zoticus rose. "On the morrow, I beg you will take me to these ships, so that I may set a torch to them myself."

Domenico shook his head. "It is too late for that. Pietro and his men packed the cargo onto the three most seaworthy ships, and sold the remaining hulks to the Benedictines. He sold the cargo before he reached Altino, for he sent the coin home. The chests are in the strongroom even now, waiting for Pietro to return and take it to our bankers."

Pietro would not return. Zoticus knew it as surely as he knew more innocent people would die if he did not burn what remained of that cargo and the ships carrying it.

And it would be his fault.

"If Pietro or any of that cargo comes here, you keep it away from everyone else until I return. I'll buy everything from you, I swear, and I'll pay any fair price for it. If you place any value in the friendship I had with your father, with your family, you will let me do this," Zoticus said.

Orso's eyes widened. "I did not know the assassination trade was so profitable."

It wasn't the profit, so much as the number of commissions he'd taken in a long and successful career, coupled with how little he'd spent over the years. Years of bringing death to those who deserved it, for deeds even he did not want to speak of, and he would hand over every copper coin he'd ever earned to deny death an even bigger harvest at his hand.

Zoticus wet his lips. "I assure you I have gold enough to satisfy even you."

"Father's account books say that though the ships are his, the cargo aboard them belonged to you. Pietro said he would search for you, while we kept your portion of the proceeds in our strongroom. The coin is yours to do with as you please, including buy ships, if that is your wish. Rialto-built ships are the best merchant vessels afloat, and rarely sold to men who are not citizens of our fair city, but as Father trusted you with our ships in the past, so will we in the future."

Breath whooshed out of his lungs – relief, though fleeting. There was still much to be done. "Thank you. If you will tell me where Pietro went, and where he planned to go, perhaps that will speed up my search."

"Finding him would place us in your debt," Domenico said.

Zoticus inclined his head. "Consider it a favour, as a friend."

"Only if you sup with us tonight, and remain as a guest in our house until the morrow. In the morning, we will furnish you with a boat and a crew, to help you with your search."

Zoticus sat down. "Gladly. If you do business so smoothly with everyone, I suspect you will soon be the richest merchants in Rialto, if you are not already."

Orso winked. "Perhaps."

Zoticus settled in for a pleasant evening, smiling and laughing with the two men he hoped would never know how many times he'd been asked to dispose of members of their family, though he'd refused every time. The richer they became, the more enemies they created.

Yes, the Ziani brothers had been partially responsible for the plague outbreak in Altino, but these two had not known the risks carried by that fateful cargo. Not like he or their father had. But with Sebastiano dead, the blame fell squarely on his shoulders.

This time, he swore, he would save people instead of killing them.

Seven

By the time Tobias returned home that evening, Sara had spoken to Tola and Gojko the apothecary, and she'd spent the rest of the day attempting to implement all the plague prevention measures she'd learned.

Both his bed and hers were stuffed with fresh hay from the high pastures, mixed liberally with pennyroyal, lady's bedstraw and rosemary. Swanhild had brought her a basket of fresh sage, which they'd both hung in bunches from the rafters to dry.

She'd bought every health-promoting herb, tea and potion they'd had on hand, urging both

Tola and Gojko to make as many as they could, in preparation for a possible plague.

Mercurio had left, so Regulo had his millhands back at work again, and Silvana had promised to bring up a load of flour as soon as the cart was full.

Beorma the brewer had sent over three casks of cider vinegar, and promised a dozen more when he'd finished brewing this season's crop of cider apples. A good thing, too, for she'd used most of the first cask cleaning everything in the house, and now she could smell nothing but vinegar.

"What is that smell?" Tobias asked, wrinkling his nose.

He likely smelled of grass from the high pastures, and the mountain air. Healthy air, free of sickness, if Tola was to be believed.

"It is the smell of cleaning. A plague came to Altino, and many people died. I cleaned the house because Tola said good hygiene helps to stop sickness." Sara wrung her hands. "She also said oranges and lemons would help, but she had not seen any since leaving Rialto. Father Fazzio suggested all we need to do is pray, to stay safe, but surely that is not enough, or someone in Altino might have been saved. You must go only to the high pastures, and come straight home at night, too, for the fewer people you see, the less chance you can catch the plague. Oh, I should ask Ahab to call a special council meeting, so we can discuss how we shall protect the town!"

"There is no plague here, Mother, and perhaps it is not so bad in Altino. They're all the way down the river, by the sea. You've told me yourself that sometimes stories can grow bigger in the telling than they ever were in life…" He reached out and took her hands. By all that was holy, he was beginning to look like his father. "It won't be that bad. You worry too much."

She squeezed his hands, then let go. "Perhaps I worry more than I should. But I'm your mother – it's what mothers do. And, since I lost your father, you're all I have. If I lost you, I'm not sure what I would do."

He grinned. "Well, you're not going to lose me, so that's one thing you won't have to worry about. Soon I'll be a man, and I'll be able to take your place on the council, and you won't have to worry about that, either."

It was his Uncle Ahab's place he would take on the council, not hers, but she didn't say that. Ahab had only joined the council after his brother's death, while she grieved his loss. When she'd surfaced from her grief and Tobias had been old enough for her to attend council meetings, she'd been grateful that Ahab had stayed. Tobias should start attending the meetings soon, so he'd get to know what happened. Soon. When the plague had passed.

"Just…promise me you will keep yourself safe, stay away from anyone in town who appears ill, and spend as much time as possible in the clean, mountain air," Sara said.

Tobias laughed. "You forgot to remind me to watch out for the goats."

She managed a smile. "Well, yes. You've been goatherd long enough, I thought you might have grasped that by now."

"It's been years since I lost one, and I still hold that the kid wasn't moving at all when the eagle carried it off. It might have been already dead."

"Yes, well…"

"What's for supper?"

Poor Tobias, always hungry.

"I've been so busy cleaning today, I almost forgot to cook. Luckily, old Matteo caught more fish than he could eat out on the lake today, so I've made a fish stew and there's fresh bread..."

While she ate supper with her son, at least she didn't have to worry about him not eating enough. Two helpings, and he looked like he was considering a third...

Eight

The raven-winged woman flew through Zoticus's dreams that night. The panic in her eyes set his heart racing, as if he shared her fears.

So, it couldn't be him she feared, though she looked right at him. Something she was fleeing from, maybe…

In the vision, Zoticus focussed on what was behind her. A stone castle, yes, but it was built into the side of a hill. No, more like a mountain, for he could see snow-capped peaks towering into the distance behind the castle.

Not here, then. His vision would not

happen today.

Zoticus blew out a breath. None of his visions had ever affected him so much before. He'd long since learned that they were glimpses of a future he could not change, and they only grew clearer as the event he'd seen approached. So why did this one feel so urgent?

Perhaps she was a possible plague victim he had to save. But pestilence was not something she could run from…and he was not some noble knight, or someone who could work miracles.

Except his own recovery from the plague, which was no miracle, no matter what that monk had believed.

He rose, wishing for just a moment that he could spend every night in a fine feather bed, like the Ziani family did. But the mattress alone would not fit into his travelling bags.

He had two travelling bags – a sack that seemed to carry all his belongings, and a small, rough pouch scarcely large enough to contain his midday meal, had it not been magically enhanced. He spread the pouch flat on his bed, where it looked like little more than a ragged circle two handspans across. An empty circle, which yet contained enough gold to buy Sebastiano's ships, weapons and clothing to let him travel comfortably anywhere in the world, and an assortment of other magical objects that had come in useful on more than one occasion. Moreover, most of them could only be used by someone who had his blood. Well, more accurately, his mother's blood, for she was the powerful enchantress who had enchanted all his things, but because she was his mother, her blood ran through his veins and allowed him to use the items as though he possessed a measure of his sister's or his mother's magic. He was nowhere near as powerful as either of them, of course – Zoraida had singlehandedly fought a dragon! – but it gave him an edge, and kept him alive.

He stretched his hand out over the splayed pouch, thinking about what he would need for his quest.

His quest to find the plague ships and the goods they contained, and perhaps Pietro, too. He'd need a light cloak, yet something tightly woven enough to keep the weather off, and keep him warm at night.

The corner of a striped Byzas cloak appeared in his hand. Zoticus laughed softly. He'd forgotten he had it – a gift given to him by Godfrey, who'd complained that Zoticus wore too much grey. He still wasn't sure if Godfrey had known he was an assassin.

Then again, this quest was about saving lives, not taking them, so perhaps he should wear another colour than grey. When he burned the ships and their cargo, he would wear the silly striped cloak.

But in the meantime, he'd need another cloak, some more clothes, his healing amulet…

When he'd packed all the necessary items into his travelling sack, and made himself look presentable for the day, he tied the pouch to his belt again, and headed down to break his fast.

He found Domenico and Orso already in the dining chamber. Once more, he wondered if he was mistaken. Had they knowingly sold tainted goods, for a bit of extra gold? Or was this all a matter of Pietro's greed, which he had likely already paid the price for?

"I hope you find him, and succeed in finding those ships," said Domenico, almost as if he shared his sister's talent for reading minds.

Zoticus did not need such a talent – he knew truth from lies, and Domenico meant every word. Zoticus relaxed. If the Ziani brothers had been responsible for spreading the plague, he would have been honour bound to return and exact justice from them. As it was, he strongly suspected he would never see these men again.

He ate a few bites, before bidding them both thanks and farewell.

Domenico walked down to the dock with him, pressing a sizeable sack of supplies into his hands for the journey.

Zoticus boarded the small sailing boat, exchanging nods with the two men who crewed her, and with a push of a pole, they were out in the middle of the canal, and Zoticus's quest had truly begun.

He only prayed it would come to a satisfactory end.

Nine

It looked like most of the town had turned up for the council meeting. Even Tobias was there, though he was hiding in the back with Raphael, the apothecary's apprentice, as if he didn't want her to see him.

But she hadn't the heart to send him home, no matter how much she feared for his safety. He deserved to hear all they knew about the plague, and what the council planned to do about it. If he had questions or even suggestions, she'd see that they were heard. She might not sit in the place of honour – that belonged to Ahab – but even from her end of the high table, she would be heard, if she chose to speak up.

Not that she'd need to. The people of Mirroten were a sensible lot, most of the time.

Ahab called for quiet, and the chattering crowd obeyed. He cleared his throat, then said, "I've called you all here to hear some grave news Father Fazzio has received from his bishop. It's best that Father Fazzio tell you himself."

The priest, seated at Ahab's right hand, rose. "The port of Altino has been afflicted with plague."

A low murmur rose from the crowd, though not loud enough to drown out Fazzio's words as he filled in what details he had. None that Sara did not already know, so she let her gaze drift over the crowd.

Tola wasn't there, and nor were some of the frailer members of the town. Most of the children were in bed by now, so there were few young people present, except for Tobias and Raphael, who'd been joined by Swanhild and Silvana.

"What happens if it comes here, too?"

Sara couldn't see who had spoken, but it did

not matter.

Everyone looked worried.

"What shall we do?" was the cry on everyone's lips as they turned to each other in panic.

Sara found herself rising to her feet, her hands out to placate them all. "We are quite a way upriver from Altino, so if we stay here, and avoid contact with anyone who has been to the tainted town, we should be safe. We are well provisioned for the winter, and there is much left to harvest before the first snows fall. If we forgo all trade with towns closer to the coast, we will all see next summer safely. Meanwhile, if you find yourself ill, speak to Tola or Gojko, who know many remedies that will soon see you back in good health. There is nothing to worry about." She tucked her skirts beneath her and sat down.

In the silence that followed, she found the townsfolk nodding, looking relieved. She might not be a leader like Ahab or even her late husband, but the people trusted her to do what was right.

"Of course there is nothing to worry about. Altino was a den of wickedness, full of sailors and infidels and thieves. Mirroten is a beacon of virtue compared to the likes of them! But we cannot forgo trade. What Mistress Sara forgets is that we only have winter fodder because Mercurio brought it on his boat, not even a week ago. And the herbs and medicines Tola and Gojko sell? Also bought from Mercurio! Trade is the lifeblood of our town, and we cannot stop it, any more than we can stop our own hearts from beating without committing a mortal sin.

"What does your bishop advise us to do, so that we do not share the same fate as Altino?" Ahab boomed.

Fazzio didn't even glance at Sara. "The Bishop commands us to stay on the true path. To lead virtuous lives, so we do not invite God's wrath upon us. We should…pray, and never close our doors to those who might seek our assistance or hospitality. Because as His Most Holy Son said in the Gospels, whoever welcomes the least of his flock, welcomes the Lord himself into their home."

Sara bowed her head. She'd offer charity to any member of Mirroten, rich or poor, but to a stranger who might carry the plague and kill them all? Did God really require that of her?

Ahab pounded on the table. "And there you have it. We cannot close off our town to the outside world. God himself forbids it. We will pray, and we shall trade, and we shall stand out as a beacon of virtue in the mountains that will shine out to the very sea itself, so that other towns between us and Altino will know how to save themselves, too."

No. That couldn't be right. Sara opened her mouth to say so.

Someone let out a cheer, and soon the whole hall was filled with happily cheering townsfolk. Any words that might have left Sara's lips were drowned out by their pre-emptive cries of triumph.

A hand landed heavily on her shoulder.

Sara jumped out of her seat, only to find Ahab behind her.

"Next time, stay silent, and you will not look so foolish," he said gently. "You know little about what it takes to run a town, and as a woman, your soft heart will lead you astray. Remember, Adam would be safe in Eden had Eve not tempted him with the apple, after she had surrendered to temptation. You only have a place on this council out of respect to your father. If you lose the respect of the townspeople through further foolishness, you will lose your seat on the council, too. Leave leadership to your betters." Another pat, and he left.

Sara squeezed her eyes shut. She would not let them see her cry. She wouldn't.

Yes, she'd been foolish to speak first. She should have waited, and then spoken her piece. That it had taken Ahab, the son of a goatherder, to point out what she should have seen by herself, rankled the most.

Next time, she would not make the same mistake. She would do everything in her power to save this town, and no amount of condescension would stop her. She would be better.

Next time.

Ten

"There! Do you see those three ships, anchored in that cove? Can you get us closer?" It had been years since he'd boarded one, but Zoticus would recognise those ships anywhere. You didn't forget the floating coffin that had very nearly been your final resting place.

Viator, the owner of the small sailing boat, nodded. Then he turned to his nephew. "Fidelis, take us around the headland."

Zoticus kept out of their way as the two men turned their boat away from Altino to enter the eastern cove instead. When the nearest ship was close enough he hailed it:

"Ho, the ship!"

He tried several times, but nothing moved on deck. The same with the second ship. And the third…

"That isn't a Ziani vessel," Viator said, jerking his head at the third, smaller ship. "That's a river trading boat."

"That's Mercurio's boat," Fidelis agreed.

All three of them shouted for Mercurio, to no avail.

The two sailors looked worried, so Zoticus volunteered, "I'll go aboard, to see if there is anyone there. Or some clue to where they might have gone." He didn't dare give voice to what they were all thinking – that nothing but ghosts sailed these ships now. "I'll meet you on the shore over there." He pointed at a tiny beach.

He stripped down to his tunic, then dived over the side. Though it was still summer, the water was colder than he would have liked. The brisk swim to Mercurio's boat kept him warm, though, and the air did not chill his skin when he climbed aboard.

A swift search soon revealed that the river boat was empty. No goods worth trading, and no dead bodies, either. The other two ships were much the same – no more than a couple of empty water barrels between them. The ships, however, had dead rats floating in the bilge beneath the empty hold.

Zoticus swore. Hard though it was to believe that these ships and cargo had carried the plague for years before spreading it to Altino, the evidence was right here before his eyes.

But where was the third ship, and all the cargo? Not to mention Pietro and the mysterious Mercurio.

The answers, he hoped, lay in Altino, where they would sail next when he rejoined the fishing boat. Too late, he realised he should have asked them to keep their distance, lest the beach be tainted, too. His only hope was to reach it before them, so that he might warn Viator to stay offshore.

He dived into the water once more, stroking for the shore. He didn't stop until the sand crunched beneath his bare feet and it was shallow enough for him to stand. He turned to see that by some trick of the weather, the wind had died down, and he'd beaten the becalmed boat to shore.

"Stay there! The beach might be tainted. I'll swim to you once I'm done taking a closer look," Zoticus shouted.

Viator nodded and said something to Fidelis. A moment later, Fidelis dropped the anchor.

Zoticus let out a breath. They were safe. For it soon became apparent that this beach was far from it.

Above the high tide line sat several torn sacks, their contents spilling out onto the sand, with more rat corpses half-buried in the spoiled grain and flour. From here, Zoticus spied a track that led away from the water. His feet felt leaden as they led him along the track, which soon widened until two wagons could travel along it, side by side, as the wheel tracks showed they had done. Sand dunes and beach scrub gave way to fields of stubble – harvested within the last few weeks, if Zoticus was not mistaken. Likely hay for winter fodder, though it was safe in someone's barn now.

More rat bodies lay between the shorn tussocks, and an eagle eyed him suspiciously, before spreading her wings in an impressive mantle and resuming her meal of decayed rat. There were no dead birds in the field, Zoticus noticed. Perhaps they did not succumb to the plague as readily as rats and humans. He hoped so, for the eagle's sake.

He followed the road to the top of a rise, and drew in a sharp breath. Altino lay spread out before him, beside the rippled river. Fishing boats lined up along the canals, but there was no sign of life. Not even a curl of smoke from someone's cookfire. Even the monks had gone.

Monks who had given him directions to their monastery, and multiple invitations to visit. Zoticus still didn't understand their vehemence. Maybe the Abbot had wanted to engage his services as an assassin, for he could not think of any other reason the man might need him, imagined miracles notwithstanding.

Something to consider after this current quest was complete.

He headed back to the boat, hoping his swim would be enough to wash any pestilence off his clothes and body. Just in case, he warned Viator and Fidelis to keep their distance from him until he'd washed properly and changed into clean garb. His wet tunic went over the side into the water – better to buy another one than risk infecting anyone else. He'd use his healing amulet on himself when darkness fell, to banish any hint of disease in his blood.

But first, he had to burn the ships.

He strung his Seljuk longbow with care, before slipping on the worn finger guard that no one would think to look twice at. Anyone who could not sense the spell on the old leather, anyway. Next, he pulled four arrows from his quiver, each wrapped in a piece of cloth. The slosh of liquid told him none of them had broken yet, though they would soon. These particular hollow shafts were crafted to shatter on impact, showering the target in Greek fire, a substance so flammable, the Church had declared it a mortal sin to use the stuff in battle. He risked excommunication by even possessing it, though he knew no pope would ever dare to do so. There were cardinals aplenty who would pay handsomely for an assassin to bring the Pope's reign to an end.

Even the Seljuk bow should not have been able to fire the heavy arrows across the water to the ships, but that was where the magic finger guard came in – when he wore it, his every shot would find its target, though it helped if he was a decent shot to start with. Magic could only do so much.

He fired two arrows at each ship, far enough apart to spatter the decks in the oily fluid. A final pair of fire arrows finished the job, like orange shooting stars arcing across the water, before they kissed the Greek fire.

Flames raced across the decks of both ships, lighting up the sky more brightly than the sunset in the west. A friendly night breeze blew the smoke away from their boat, so they sat down to watch the ships' final fate as they ate their evening meal.

The burning deck of the first ship collapsed into the hold, taking the mast and reefed sails with it. This was more than the ship's hull could take, for it careened over on its side, revealing a hold that could easily have been mistaken for the gate to hell, before it slipped beneath the water.

Sparks from the fire on the second ship set some of its ropes alight, freeing the sail. The night breeze caught the sail and the second boat heeled over, too, still burning brightly, until it, too, sank.

That left only Mercurio's trading boat and themselves in the cove.

Inevitably, their talk turned to the missing ship.

"It could be anywhere. Any of the port cities along the coast. That's a Rialto merchant galley, the best trading vessel in the world," Fidelis said.

Viator's brow creased as he chewed thoughtfully on a piece of dried fish.

"Pietro said he would remain in Altino, to finalise a deal of some sort. Wherever it went, it left from here, likely before the plague took hold in the town. But before or after the harvest?" Zoticus mused.

"After." Viator took a swig from the jug of wine, then set it down. "Altino and all the coastal towns here send extra hay upriver to the mountain towns, to feed their animals through the winter. Mercurio spends all autumn making his way up and down the river, trading hay and dried fish for the bounty in the mountains. Goat cheeses so sweet you'd swear they were soaked in honey. Chestnut smoked bacon, like nothing else you've ever tasted. And bags of the nuts themselves, to roast upon the fire. Anything worth trading, Mercurio will find the value in it. He will know where your cargo is, and maybe your missing ship, too."

"If he's still alive, and hasn't succumbed to the plague," Zoticus said, debating whether to stuff meat or cheese into his flatbread. He opted for both. His first satisfying bite told him he'd made the right decision. He looked up to find both men staring at him. "What?"

"Is this plague truly so deadly?" Fidelis asked.

Zoticus swallowed. He wished he could make light of things, but they deserved to know the risks they faced. "All of the people in Altino are dead. If Pietro or Mercurio were there, it is likely they died, too. I saw the town from the road that leads to the beach. No movement, no smoke…no life. This plague is like nothing else I have known. There is no cure, and everyone I know who has caught it died of it."

Viator squinted at him. "Except you. Master Orso said you were saved."

Death did not want him. Not yet. But Zoticus dared not tell these men about his visions. "Magic saved me. I have a magical amulet a witch gave me. It protects me. I am still afflicted by disease, like anyone else, but I will not die of it."

Viator nodded. "So it's both a blessing and a curse. A wise witch, whoever gave it to you."

Zoticus laughed. "She is my mother, and I thank you for the compliment. She is wiser than I will ever be. I'm sure she would find this missing ship, and our men, too."

"If Mercurio has it, then he has taken it upriver to trade. We could try following him tomorrow. Not before first light, though, for the river has some treacherous shallows for those that don't know it, much like the shoals around Rialto. It's been years since I've been further inland than Altino, but I'll take you as far as I can," Viator said.

It was as good a guess as any, so Zoticus agreed. It felt right, and he wasn't a man who ignored his intuition.

And it took him into the mountains, where he might meet this woman who haunted his dreams.

Yes, upriver they would go.

Eleven

Towns and villages slipped by as they sailed upriver, each as silent and smokeless as Altino. More than once, he'd caught Fidelis and Viator crossing themselves, murmuring prayers and muttering about ghosts. Even Zoticus had felt the spirits of the newly dead staring at him through the ether, all accusing him of coming too late.

He'd gone ashore at the first three towns, before the stench of death had sickened him too much to do it again.

The dead villagers might not be capable of answering his questions, but they told him enough. The plague had passed through their village, and then swept on up the river, pushed by the sails of the third cursed ship.

It was enough to make him want to weep. So many innocent lives lost, because one greedy merchant had not burned the boats like he'd asked him. Because one careless assassin had left them with that merchant to report that he'd succeeded in killing more men. And he'd saved a horse.

Stupid, foolish…the words he could have heaped on his own head for his folly would never be enough, for they could never restore the lives that had been lost.

"There it is," Fidelis breathed.

"Thank Heaven for small mercies. The ship never reached Mirroten," Viator said.

"What's Mirroten?" Zoticus asked.

Viator pointed. "A short sail further on, there is a great lake. Mirroten is the town on the lakeshore. The people earn their livelihood from the mountains. Many medicinal herbs are only found here, and the chestnut groves grow wonderfully well. And the cheeses…they say it's the mountain pastures, making for finer milk than the lowlands, but my sister says there's old magic here. She should know. She's the town witch." There was pride in his voice at that.

"So once we've dealt with this ship, we can go into town and visit your sister?" Zoticus suggested.

Viator shook his head. "She has not spoken to any of our family for many years. My father forced her to marry a man whose wickedness…ah, if only I'd known. When he drank too much wine, he beat her. One night, he was so drunk he fell in a canal and drowned. She disappeared the same night. At first, we thought her dead, too, but some of her things were gone from the house. Things she would never leave behind.

"I searched for years, until I heard a whisper about a new witch in Mirroten. I sailed up here myself to see, and she threatened to turn me into a fish and cook me for dinner if I ever returned, or breathed a word to our father that she'd survived. She had a child, too, a little girl who looked just like her. So, no, I will not be welcome in Mirroten, though you may have better luck."

Zoticus nodded. He hadn't seen his sister in

years, either, though he knew she'd had children with her husband. She'd probably have set fire to her husband if he'd tried to beat her, though. She'd fought a dragon once and lived, which was more than most men could say.

Fidelis hailed the ship. After the river of death they'd sailed through, Zoticus would have been surprised to hear a response. Of course, there wasn't one.

"Bring me as close as you can, then stand off a ways. I'll swim back," Zoticus said.

Viator did as he asked, and Zoticus soon pulled himself over the gunwales of the missing ship. And swore.

The hold was full, with more casks stacked on deck. A lumpy pallet covered in a striped cloak took most of the leftover space, and the stench coming from it didn't bode well.

Zoticus swallowed, then forced himself to step forward and snatch up the cloak. The corpse beneath it could not have been dead for more than a day, but the summer heat had not been kind. It wasn't Pietro, so he assumed it was Mercurio, the lost river trader.

Pietro must have perished in Altino, like

he'd originally thought.

Fidelis shouted his name, and Zoticus moved to the side of the ship, where the others could see him.

"Have you found them?"

Zoticus wet his lips. "We were too late. They're both dead." Not technically a lie, but he had no intention of letting the two fishermen aboard to see for themselves. "We should return to Rialto, to tell Domenico and Orso that their brother is dead."

"What about my sister?" Viator seemed surprised at his own outburst.

If it was Zoraida, Zoticus wouldn't have hesitated to see for himself. But the plague posed little danger to him, while it could be deadly to Viator and his nephew.

"I'll go up to the town and see if she is well." Zoticus wasn't a praying man, but he was willing to pray for Viator's sister's health. "How long will it take for me to reach the town?"

"Half a mile along the shore, so not long at all. But if Tola is well, she will surely offer you hospitality you cannot refuse. It'll be days before she lets you leave, and only then because you fear you will be sick from eating so much." Viator laughed, but it sounded forced. "If not…"

"If she is ill, then I will do my best to heal her," Zoticus promised. At best, all he could do would be to ease her passing, but that was something, at least. "Go to Rialto. I will meet you there, or send word if I cannot."

Viator clasped his hands together and bowed. "You do me a great service, Master Zoticus. If ever you have need of a fisherman, or a boat, or anything at all, come to me in Rialto. I will leave your things on the riverbank, near the road to town. May God continue to preserve you!"

Preserves. That gave Zoticus an idea. He checked all the casks on deck until he found one that contained lamp oil. Not as effective as Greek fire, but it would still burn, and he could save the stronger stuff for another time.

He splashed the oil across the deck, on the corpse, and as much of the cargo as he could reach. Noises from a cloth-draped bundle made him put the cask down and investigate further. Beneath the cloth was a cage of messenger pigeons, still alive.

He'd seen plenty of dead people on the way here, but not a single dead bird. Perhaps the pigeons, like the eagle in Altino, truly were immune to the plague. He could not stand to burn the birds alive, either, so he opened the cage and let them fly free. They all headed in the same direction – toward the lake.

His next destination, too.

When he ran out of oil, Zoticus leaped over the side of the ship and into the water. The river current was slow here, so it was an easy swim to shore, where Viator had left his sack and his bow. Ah, yes, he would send a fire arrow into this ship, too, and stay until it sank into the river. Only then would this quest be over, so that he might start the new one to see to Viator's sister.

Twelve

Walking into a town with living, breathing people was a surreal experience. He'd seen so much death in the last few days that life seemed too loud. Breathing in the smells of cooking and smoke without the miasma of death made Zoticus almost light-headed.

"Are you well, sir?"

He looked up to meet the eyes of a concerned man. A farm labourer, or Zoticus missed his guess. A commoner who could not tell the difference between a knight and an assassin, but sensed deference would serve him best.

Zoticus wet his lips. "I soon will be, if you could direct me to a witch, or herb-woman, if you have one in this town."

The man's chest puffed out. "Here in Mirroten, we have our own apothecary. You can't miss his house – there is the sign of the mortar and pestle over the door."

Zoticus managed a thin smile. "But I want to see the witch."

"Oh." The man shrugged, before some thought occurred to him that creased his face with suspicion. He squinted at Zoticus. "I hope you don't mean to bring trouble to our town. Mirroten looks after its own, and no mistake. But if it is truly our witch you want, you will find Mistress Tola's house three doors down from the apothecary."

Zoticus thanked the man and continued down the road. Sure enough, he spotted the crudely carved bowl with a stick over the door of the apothecary, but he continued walking.

He smelled the witch's house before he saw it, for she had bunches of herbs strung up to dry beneath the eaves of her cottage. Sage, mostly, but there were rare mountain flowers hiding amid all the leaves. Perhaps he should pretend his business here was herbs, and not mention Viator at all. He'd been meaning to stock up on a few things, anyway, and here was the ideal opportunity.

He raised a hand and knocked on the door. When he received no answer, he pushed the door open and stuck his head inside. "Hello, is the healer home?" He waited a moment, then stepped into the house.

"No, but I am," said a young, feminine voice.

Zoticus blinked. A girl stood on the other side of a counter, her hands on her hips. No longer a child, but not quite a woman, either. Likely Viator's niece, if he was not mistaken.

He bowed. "My pardon, mistress. Perhaps you could tell me where I might find the healer?"

She smiled, an enchanting sight that likely would have half the male population of this town swooning at her feet. "Well now, seeing as you mean me no harm, perhaps I can help you. I know as much as my mother when it comes to healing, maybe more, depending on your ailment." She looked him up and down, as if searching for sickness.

Perhaps she was. He could sense the magic in her blood, though he wasn't sure what shape her gift took.

A vision hit him, of this girl flapping her arms and crying out, before transforming into a swan. He blinked, and he was back in the cottage again.

"If it is the falling sickness you suffer from, sir, then I recommend rue. I have some fresh leaves from which you can make an infusion, or you can buy it powdered for tea, but you might prefer a vial of oil of rue, which is easier to use for a traveller like yourself. I've made a fresh batch just this week, in preparation for autumn coughs and colds, but it is good for the falling sickness, too. Just a drop in the morning after you break your fast…"

She'd seen him freeze as the vision took him, and mistaken it for illness instead of magic. What she did not know was that rue only intensified the visions.

Then another thought struck him.

"How do you know I mean you no harm?" he demanded.

She smiled again. "Because if you did, the enchantment on the door would have turned you into a frog."

So her mother's threat to Viator hadn't been an empty one. "Your mother can transform people into animals?" He'd heard of a family line in the mountains who passed such a gift down the generations. Perhaps Tola was descended from them.

The girl's face twisted. "When she was a girl, yes, but my father tried to beat the magic out of her, so now her magic is not as strong as it was. The door enchantment will only make you believe you are a frog, and you'll behave like one for a day or two, before returning to normal. That's how she escaped my father — she made him think he was a fish."

And he'd drowned in a Rialto canal.

"Then I must speak to your mother. Can you tell me where I can find her, please?"

The girl sighed. "She took some oil of rue up to Elder Ahab's house. His daughter's always been sickly, and she's ailing again. Poor Ysabel."

Zoticus nodded. "So I should look for the biggest, grandest house, and that's where I'll find her?"

She burst out laughing. "Heavens, no! Well,

you might, for Mother and Sara are great friends, but Ahab's house is behind the meeting hall, beside the town green. His family has the rights to use the cottage as long as they repair the fences around the green. You should have heard him swearing when they all blew over in that spring storm a couple of years back!"

The girl would make a good village witch, when the time came. She knew all the town gossip, without revealing anything about herself – he still didn't know what her magical gifts were, or even her name.

"So I will find Mistress Tola at the cottage behind the meeting hall, next to the town green?" he asked.

"Oh, for certain. Unless she has already seen to Ysabel and there is a town council meeting. In fact, I remember her saying there might be a meeting. Maybe then she'll be in the meeting hall."

Zoticus shook his head. So much for certainty. Then again, in a town this small, finding anyone wouldn't be that hard. As long as they were still alive, though that seemed likely.

"Thank you," he said. "You have been most helpful."

"Are you sure you don't want some oil of rue to take with you? You won't get it any fresher, and the price will only go up with winter on the way."

The girl was a witch, but she had the blood of a Rialto merchant in her veins, of that he was certain. Almost against his will, he found himself pulling out his purse. "How much?"

Thirteen

"We need to do more to encourage traders to come here. Now they no longer stop in Altino, traders will come up the river in search of what we can provide. The more people know about our products, the more they will want them! Instead of one trader, we should have a dozen traders, maybe more, sailing up and down the river to take our goods for sale in the markets of Rialto. Better yet, we should send invitations to all the merchants of Rialto, inviting them here for some sort of celebration, so they can see all we can offer, and they can show their wares to us." Ahab's grin beamed around the hall, seeking encouragement to continue. He wanted this so much, and it sounded so promising, even Sara wondered if maybe…

She could see Tola shaking her head.

Someone had to stop him, and now seemed a good moment. "Perhaps after this plague outbreak is over, then we might send someone to Rialto to meet with the merchants," Sara ventured. "Someone who has all of the town's interests in mind. But now, with just Mercurio, we didn't have enough trade goods to fill his new ship. He'll have to return in the autumn, when we have more to sell. With the news of plague in Altino and maybe other places, too, we cannot be too careful. Allowing new people into the town now may bring the pestilence here."

"And who is better equipped to deal with sickness than a healthful place like Mirroten? Why, we have more healing herbs here than anywhere else in the world, I'm certain of it! Why else would Mercurio buy so much from us? We are good, pious people, not steeped in sin like some port full of sailors and unspeakable things. God would never visit a plague on us!"

Oh, by all that was holy…when he started invoking religion, she had no hope of swaying anyone to her side. She'd learned that lesson last meeting. But she had to try. They could not risk…

"Actually, the lady is right. The plague took every soul in Altino, saint and sinner alike. And every town along the river between here and the lagoon. This wasn't God's doing. This was a trader, selling tainted goods to those towns. You're lucky he never reached you, or your people would be dying, too."

Sara stared at owner of the voice. He strode into the hall like he owned it, muscles bulging as he folded his arms across his fine linen tunic. A Rialto merchant, maybe, or some neighbouring lord. A handsome stranger she needed to know more about.

"And who are you?" Ahab asked, bristling like an alarmed hedgehog.

The stranger delivered a courtly bow so practiced, Sara was certain he'd spent time in a royal court. "I am Master Zoticus, and I have come to save your town from the plague."

No title. Not a prince or a lord or a baron

or even a knight. Master Zoticus, indeed.

Sara smelled a rat. "At what cost, Master Zoticus? What price must we pay for your services?"

He bowed deeper still. "I would do it simply for the pleasure of serving you, my lady."

Ahab spluttered incoherently.

Anyone who could render Ahab speechless and support her in keeping Mirroten safe could not be all bad.

For the first time that day, Sara flashed a brilliant smile at the newcomer. She was almost embarrassed to hear her voice come out in a low purr as she said, "Then, Master Zoticus, I accept."

He straightened and his eyes met hers. She could not look away, and nor could he, it seemed. Perhaps she imagined the startled look in his eyes, for it was gone almost as soon as it had appeared.

Then, as swiftly as he had entered the hall, he turned on his heel, and was gone.

Fourteen

The woman in his vision. The sight of her had unnerved him for a moment, but Zoticus was certain no one had noticed. She hadn't appeared the slightest bit perturbed, let alone panicked, and on this warm summer evening, she wore no cloak. Her voice had been delightfully warm, too…

He stopped that thought before it blossomed into something far more troublesome. He'd met many beautiful women, and he'd never let his lust for them get in the way of getting a job done. Currently, she was his client, which made his attraction to her even easier to ignore. Because if he didn't complete this quest, she might die of the plague.

But not before he'd seen the panic in her eyes as her mourning cloak flew behind her.

Which meant someone close to her would die, as she wasn't wearing mourning now.

He had to concentrate on his mission, not some mystery woman.

He found the town's only inn, and the innkeeper allowed him to rent a room if, "You promise not to tell Mistress Sara. She was most particular about not having strangers to stay."

In a town this small, Mistress Sara and anyone else who cared would know he was staying in the inn within a day, but Zoticus merely smiled and gave the woman his word.

The room was larger than the one in Altino, and a lot cleaner, too. This wasn't a town that saw too many visitors, and right now, he was the sole guest at the inn, which suited him fine. He paid extra to have his supper brought up to him, instead of joining the townsfolk in the taproom. Their curiosity about him would not save them from the plague.

Only when the maid had taken away his

empty supper dish did he start his preparations. First, he bolted the door. Next, he extracted a magical candle from his pouch, lit it, and set it on the table. Then, he stretched out on the bed and closed his eyes.

Most magic folk were better at this than him. His mother could do it in a few blinks without anyone being the wiser, though when she really wanted a deep draught of knowledge, she settled in her chair beside the fire. His sister, Zoraida, powerful enchantress though she was, could not touch the vast store of ancestral magic memory that dwelt in her blood. It irritated her no end that a weak enchanter like him could access the knowledge he could barely use.

He'd tried to explain it to her, that it was much the same as dipping into his magic pouch and willing what he wanted to appear in his hand, but Zoraida would have none of it.

Which was probably why she fought dragons and he was here in this tiny mountain town, chasing visions and rumours and hoping he could save them. But tonight, he sought memories – memories of plagues past, how they started and how they were stopped.

He took a deep breath and let the memories flow.

Rats. Fleas. Floods. People dressed in clothing the like of which he'd never seen before. Likely long dead. Boils. Coughing. Something small enough to swim through the blood, like magic itself, but nowhere near as benign. And the dead, still carrying the sickness so even the gravediggers were not safe. Bodies were best burned.

Hours passed, or maybe it was just minutes. Millennia of memories marched past his eyes, the sights seen by thousands of magic users.

Yet when Zoticus surfaced, he knew one thing for certain: there was no cure for the plague. No herb or potion could touch it. A powerful healing spell might help, but healing was a power granted to few, and the touch of a spell so strong would leave its mark on the patient forever.

So, he could not cure it. But he could stop it from spreading, if he could banish every rat and flea from the town.

A Herculean task, if ever there was one.

But for an assassin who'd slain four heavily armed knights before their own armies, it would surely be a simple matter. The vermin stood no chance against him, and nor would the rats and fleas, either.

Fifteen

Silvana brought the wagon, piled high with sacks, a grim look on her face.

"Where is your father?" Sara asked.

"Probably in the inn, asleep on the floor. He's barely been home for days. If I didn't know how to work the mill, none of this would be ground." Silvana sighed. "I keep hoping he'll wake up and see there is still a world without Mother in it, but I'm not sure he even cares about me any more."

"He cares. I'm sure he cares. He just loved your mother so much…" Sara pulled the girl into a hug.

They stood there for what felt like a long time, yet Sara felt no need to break the embrace before Silvana was ready.

Eventually, Silvana pulled away, ducking her head as she sniffled. "I'm sorry. I just miss her so much, and he..."

Sara smiled awkwardly. "I lost my parents within days of one another, when I was not much older than you. My brothers, too. I know it isn't easy, but it's not easy for your father, either. When my husband died...I swear part of me died with him. If I hadn't had Tobias to care for, I might have lost myself in grief, too. Women are stronger than men will ever be, I fear. Not because we want to be, but because we must be. Without us, the world will fall apart. So we shed a few tears when it all becomes too much, but we go back to work when men would rather drink their way to the bottom of a barrel."

"That's not what the stories say. They're full of big, strong heroes who save helpless maidens from monsters," Silvana grumbled.

Sara laughed. "Of course they are. We all have our fantasies, do we not? Women wish men were stronger, and more capable, so they won't need to do everything themselves, and men dream of being in charge, having women begging for their help instead of calling them fools for their latest blunder. Most men would not last a week without a woman to tell him what to do, and see that he has food."

"You're putting me off ever wanting to get married, then."

"Well, there are benefits of having a man around. They tend to chop the wood for you, and carry heavy things, and do some of the work around the farm..." Sara winked. "And in bed at night, a good husband is never too tired to make his wife happy."

Silvana's eyes grew wide with horror. "But that means babies! Noisy, helpless things that need more care than grown men!"

"But babies only happen once every nine months, and usually longer than that. Besides, you may change your mind when you hold your own child in your arms."

"Maybe." Silvana eyed the cart. "Do you want me to unload these?"

Sara considered, then shook her head. "No, let's put the cart away in the barn, and I'll find some labourers to do the heavy lifting. A day or two will not harm the flour – it'll be sitting in the cellar for months."

It took two of them to get the ponies to pull the cart into the barn, before turning them loose in Sara's field to snack on the stubble left over from the summer haymaking.

"Come inside for a cup of cider. I keep it cool in the cellar," Sara said, leading the way into the house while Silvana followed.

"What is that awful noise?" Silvana asked.

Deep in the cellar, Sara could not hear anything. She ascended the steps, listening hard.

Finally, Sara said, "It sounds like the time when Tobias found my grandfather's flute, and tried to play it like the travelling minstrels he'd seen in the town square. Terrible screeching. When he was asleep that night, I made sure to hide the flute where he might never find it again. But he should still be up in the high pasture…"

Now it was her turn to follow Silvana, out the front door and down the road into town. A crowd of townspeople lined the roadside, transfixed by the bizarre parade headed their way.

The screeching music did indeed come from a flute, played by a figure in a brightly striped cloak that flew about him as he twirled and capered down the road. Behind him, a river of brown, black and white, followed.

Those by the roadside recoiled as the piper passed, pressing their backs to walls and fences in an effort to get away from him, though they could not stop staring.

At first, Sara thought it was the music that repelled them, until the river came close enough for Silvana to see what formed the flow.

"It's rats! A whole plague of rats! Thousands of them, following him!" she said. They horrified her even more than babies, judging by her expression.

The piper drew even with Sara, and he stopped to offer her a courtly bow.

"Master Zoticus!" she exclaimed. "What in heaven's name are you doing with all those rats?"

He straightened and grinned at her. "Why, saving your town from pestilence, my lady. Ridding it of all the rats." Another bow, and he resumed playing the flute.

There was a tune to it, of sorts, but it wasn't something one would want to dance to. Master Zoticus was no minstrel, that was for sure. He was a ratcatcher.

"Your pied piper is mad," said a new voice.

Ahab, of course. This time, Sara was inclined to agree with him. She'd never seen a man charm rats before. Why would anyone want to?

Yet Zoticus seemed too sure of himself to be mad.

Little though she liked rats, she wanted to follow him to see where he took them.

No, that would be foolish. She'd have a better view from her worktable behind the house. And she'd avoid the rats.

She watched Zoticus take his river of rats down to the lake, where he boarded a boat — with Matteo at the oars, no less — and headed out over the water.

The rats followed him blindly, jumping off the dock and into the lake. They swam for a bit, until they went under, and did not surface. Hundreds of them at a time.

Sara shuddered. There had to be twoscore rats for every man, woman and child in

Mirroten. Had there really been so many? Or had Zoticus brought them here?

When all the rats had disappeared, Matteo turned the boat around, and Zoticus took an oar to help the old man row back to shore. He'd thrown his striped cloak off, and Sara couldn't help but stare as the muscles in his arms rippled at every stroke.

He was well-fed for a ratcatcher, and likely as strong as any man in Mirroten. He stepped from the boat to the dock with the grace of a practiced sailor, too.

And then he shaded his eyes from the sun, and peered up the hill, to where she stood staring. He directed another deep bow in her direction, and Sara felt her cheeks redden.

"Now there's a man who thinks a lot of himself," Tola said.

Sara started. She'd been so busy watching Zoticus she hadn't even noticed her friend's arrival.

"I bet he's terrible in bed," Tola added.

Sara sighed. Such men usually were. "But it doesn't hurt to dream," she said.

"He'll have half the girls in town dreaming about him tonight, not just you."

Sara shrugged. "As long as I have him to myself in the dream, they may do what they like."

"There's magic about him, Swanhild said. He's still susceptible to her spell, but I think he knew she'd cast it. She said he came looking for me, at first, but it seems he found you and liked you better. He hasn't said a word to me."

There was a strange twisting sensation in Sara's belly, and she wasn't sure if it was good or bad. "Have you come to warn me to be careful?"

Tola snorted. "He didn't set off my door enchantment, and Swanhild said he was well-spoken and polite. I don't believe he means harm to anyone in Mirroten. Maybe I'm wrong, and he'd be delightful in bed. Most men with magic in their blood learn to respect the women in their family, for it must run strong in the female line for it to show up in the boys. Swanhild did say he asked for directions. Most unusual in a man."

"So you think I should seduce him?" Sara asked.

"Oh no. I think you should consider allowing him to seduce you. And if you do allow him to share your bed, promise to tell me about it."

They both laughed, but they also watched Zoticus stride up the road back into town.

Sara wet her lips. Perhaps she would.

Sixteen

Zoticus might not be able to read minds, but he'd known what the woman from his vision was thinking while she watched him today. And while his vision of her wasn't about to happen today, he was pretty sure he knew he'd see her again soon – that very evening, if he wasn't mistaken.

He told himself the rats and fleas were the reason he'd bathed and changed into clean clothes, while leaving today's things to be laundered by the inn's maid. He debated whether to go down to the taproom for dinner, where she might easily find him, but she seemed the sort of lady who would wish to see him privately, and the inn staff would honour her wishes.

So he ate dinner alone in his room, then stretched out on the bed. Whether she arrived early or late, she'd probably appreciate it if he was well-rested for whatever she had in mind. And he'd enjoy it more if he wasn't tired.

He slipped easily into dreams of her, and was woken by a tap at the door.

"Yes?" he said.

"There's someone to see you, Master Zoticus," the maid said. There was a quaver in her voice that hadn't been there before.

It would not do to greet her from his bed. Too presumptuous. He hadn't bothered to undress, so it took him a moment to pull on some boots before he answered, "You can come in." He placed himself by the table, where he'd left a jug of wine and two cups. The inn's best wine, he'd been told, and he'd tasted enough to know it was at least drinkable.

Then the door creaked open, and two men crowded inside. Rough labourers, by the look of them, used to hard work and heavy lifting. Men who could not afford an assassin and who would never be targeted by one, because commoners like them were not above the law, especially when noblemen were the ones who enforced it.

But they were smart enough to fear him.

"Master Zoticus, you are summoned to a meeting at the town hall," one of them said.

"By whom?"

By all that was holy, he wanted to know the name of the woman in his vision. Then again, if she was the sort to summon him to her bed, he wasn't sure if she was worth the trouble.

The two men eyed each other nervously, as if daring the other man to say her name first.

Finally, the one who'd already spoken said, "By Elder Ahab, head of the town council."

Zoticus did his best to hide his surprise. The head of the council had seemed more like a useless puffer fish than any real kind of authority, but this man wasn't lying. So either this Ahab had summoned him, or the woman had told these two the summons was at Ahab's order, and they'd believed her.

He relaxed. Yes, that seemed more likely.

Zoticus swept a light cloak about his shoulders. "What are we waiting for, then? To the town hall we must go!"

The men breathed twin sighs of relief as they accompanied him out of the inn.

Zoticus glimpsed the maid's wide eyes watching from a darkened doorway before she hid her face. Why did they all fear him, when this morning they hadn't cared about how much they stared at him? It couldn't have been the rats, or his skill with the high-pitched enchanted flute his mother had given him. The instrument's shrill whistle was enough to melt earwax, even before she'd enchanted it to summon any creature he cared to name.

Idly, he wondered if it would work on dragons.

Zoticus shook his head. Something to consider later, when he had someone more experienced in fighting dragons by his side.

To his surprise, the sun was already peeping over the horizon. He'd slept longer than he'd thought. Why the lady would want to see him so early in the day…ah, but this was a farming town, not a trading city like Rialto. Days went from dawn until dusk in places like this, and perhaps she'd fallen into the same pattern.

Zoticus stepped into the town hall, where a

lone candle cast more shadows than light.

"Bring him here."

The voice did not belong to a woman.

Zoticus peered into the darkness, waiting for his eyes to adjust. Ah, there was the man who'd spoken.

Ahab sat just outside the candle's pool of light, with a cup in one hand and a jug by his elbow. Judging by his sloppy movements, he'd been drinking a while. Most of the night, if Zoticus was any judge.

"You. Assassin. You brought this evil to my town," he slurred.

For a moment, it felt like someone's cold hand squeezed his heart inside his chest.

But Zoticus's head was quicker than his heart.

He couldn't have brought the plague here. Every rat and flea in the town now lay dead and drowned at the bottom of the lake. He'd arrived in town with only the contents of his magical pouch, and nothing he placed in that pouch survived the enchantment. He'd left a piece of ham in the pocket of his summer cloak when he'd stashed it away, and pulled the same piece out, more than a year later, as fresh as the day it had been sliced.

But this wasn't about ham. It wasn't about him, either.

"What evil might that be?" Zoticus asked.

"Your evil. We're good people. We work hard, go to church, pray and live virtuous lives, but you! You kill for money. Is it not written in God's commandments that we must not kill?"

"And it also says in the Bible that men shouldn't wear both linen and wool, and women shouldn't cook meat with milk," Zoticus replied. He'd read the entire tome, had an illuminated copy in his pouch somewhere, actually, and it made his ancestral memories seem positively orderly in comparison. Not that he'd say that to the pope who'd given him the enormous book. "And the whole book is full of people killing each other, for all manner of crimes, not just mixing linen and wool, or meat and milk."

"Do not lie to me! Are you not Master Zoticus the assassin, who has slayed countless men the world over, enough to fill a river with their blood?" Ahab demanded.

"I am Master Zoticus, and I keep count," Zoticus snapped. "Of the men I have killed, and of their victims. A river? If they had lived, they could have filled an ocean with the blood and tears of their victims, and the families who mourn them, but those victims and their families have justice now because of me!"

"And what of my daughter? Why did you kill her? What crime can sweet Ysabel have committed, that you saw fit to kill her? How much did they pay you?" Ahab's eyes were wild now, with a madness Zoticus recognised, though too late. A grieving father would do anything to revenge a favourite child.

Zoticus shook his head, lifting his hands up in surrender. "I never met your daughter. I cannot have killed her. You are mistaken. Someone else must have done this terrible deed. Perhaps I can help you…"

Ahab pointed a shaking finger at him. "You have done enough. It was you, and no one else, with your evil, that has brought this plague upon us! Upon her, the sweetest girl who ever lived…"

Horror seized Zoticus's tongue, rendering him speechless. Even if he could have spoken, he had no words. He was wrong. The plague had touched this town, and he was too late to save them. He had to warn the woman in his vision…

He turned to leave, but a glancing blow struck his head, and everything went white for a moment. A second blow turned it all black.

Seventeen

Sara found her mind drifting in church that morning. Perhaps it was because Zoticus had been in her dreams so much the night before, she'd woken several times, convinced he was in her bedchamber. Of course he hadn't been, but getting back to sleep hadn't been easy.

Or perhaps it was because Father Fazzio kept droning on and on about how they had to reject evil and protect their virtue, as he'd been doing every day since they'd heard about the plague in Altino. It made her wonder if Fazzio thought the town was a flock of white-clad virgins, the sort who'd never done anything in their lives, let alone commit a single sin.

She suppressed a snort. No one in the town over the age of three could possibly be without sin. And there was the whole concept of original sin, that they'd all inherited from Adam and Eve, or so Father Fazzio had told them back in May, when some of the teenagers in town had tried to celebrate some pagan fertility rite. Actually, she remembered trying something similar with Tobias's father when they'd been that age. Of course, they'd gone up to the high pasture instead of into the forest, so no one had interrupted their private celebration. One they'd repeated every year until Tobias was born. Come to think of it, Tobias might have been conceived up there in the high pasture…perhaps the old fertility rites still had power.

"And we will be conducting a prayer vigil for Ysabel this evening. All are invited to attend," Fazzio finished.

Wait…Ysabel?

When the mass ended, she kept her eyes on Ahab, hoping to catch him before he left. He hurried out of the church, and she could barely keep him in sight as he strode off toward the town green. He reached the door of his cottage, and for a moment, he hesitated with his hand on the door handle.

"Ahab, is Ysabel…is she all right?" Sara called as she approached.

Ahab slowly turned to face her, and he didn't need to open his mouth to answer her.

She pressed her hand to her mouth. "Oh, no. How bad is she? Is there anything I can do?"

A harsh laugh came out of his throat, unlike any noise she'd ever heard him make before. "Oh, you've already done enough. Instead of driving the evil out of town, like any sensible person should have, you let him stay. And he killed her. That vile wretch killed my Ysabel!"

His words made no sense. "Someone killed Ysabel? You mean…she wasn't ill?"

"Before he came, she was fine. She filled all the mattresses on her own – she insisted upon it. But the night he came, she fell ill. Deathly ill. So suddenly it seemed like a curse, something only the most evil wretch could have possibly cast upon her. He had all of the town fawning over him, watching that spectacle yesterday, while his curse stole her life away. That assassin killed my daughter, and I will have justice!"

"Ahab..." she began. The death of his daughter had evidently driven the man mad. "What assassin?"

"Your pied piper, the capering fool I saw you making sheep's eyes at yesterday," Ahab spat. "The man you allowed into our town, who you welcomed into your service...is none other than Master Assassin Zoticus, a demon who has slain more men than the very devil himself. The bishop himself sent warning to Father Fazzio only yesterday that the assassin might be headed our way, and should he arrive here, we should send him straight to the bishop to face justice for his crimes. Alas, the warning arrived too late for Ysabel."

It beggared belief. "But why would anyone want Ysabel dead?" She was perhaps the only person in town who might have fitted Father Fazzio's image of an innocent virgin, for heaven knew the girl had rarely been well enough to spend time with boys her own age.

"You'd have to ask that demon...that wolf in sheep's clothing...but I beg you, do not. Stay away from him, lest he kill you, too. He's already charmed you, like the devil he is, and with his every breath, he expels more pestilence. Save yourself, and stay away. I've had him locked away, where he cannot harm anyone else in the town, and I will send someone to fetch some of the bishop's men, for it will take a heavy guard to escort a demon to Rialto."

Amid all the madness, one thing became clear.

"Ysabel died of the plague? The plague has come to Mirroten?" Sara asked. She didn't want to believe it.

"Carried by that demon of an assassin, Master Zoticus himself!" Ahab yanked open his door, strode into his cottage, then slammed the door in her face.

If the plague had indeed come to Mirroten…

"Heaven help us all," Sara whispered.

Eighteen

Zoticus woke to the sound of something grinding above him. That placed him…in the cellar beneath the mill, most likely. He reached for the back of his head, and found his hair sticky with dried blood, but his healing amulet had taken care of the wound and the headache he probably would have woken with, without magical assistance. He'd worn the amulet around his neck since leaving Rialto – one couldn't be too careful with plague about.

Enough daylight reached the cellar that he knew it was likely the middle of the day outside, and not a good time to escape, if he didn't want to be seen. The town would see enough death with the plague – they didn't need anyone dying at his hands when he escaped. It was best for everybody if he waited until night.

In the meantime, he was at leisure to explore his cell. They'd laid him on a well-stuffed straw pallet, with a blanket that could have been the twin of the one he'd slept under in the inn. A jug of water sat on the floor beside him, along with a basket of food that would feed a family for an entire day. Bread, cheese, apples, and a chunk of meat he suspected had come from a goat.

Drink first, then something to eat. He uncorked the jug and breathed deeply. That definitely wasn't water. Strong cider, if he wasn't mistaken. He wasn't sure if his jailers wanted him drunk and easier to deal with, or whether this was normal prisoner fare for Mirroten. If they treated prisoners so well, it was a surprise they didn't have more of them.

Perhaps he should stay for a few days, until the plague ended their hospitality. He could do with a rest, and the cider would certainly help him with that.

But he still had to warn the woman in his vision.

Zoticus sighed. Tonight, then. After he'd demolished the dinner they'd provided.

Nineteen

It felt surreal returning to the church that evening for Ysabel's vigil. The whole town was there, heads bowed in grief for a girl none of them would have said was deserving of death.

"Did you hear about the assassin?"

Sara lifted her head to find Silvana at her elbow. "I heard something, yes." A little from Ahab, more from Fazzio, and a great deal from Tola, for the man had quite the reputation in Rialto.

"Elder Ahab had him locked in Father's cellar. He means to keep him there for some days. Elder Ahab said he killed Ysabel. Is it true?"

Sara lowered her voice. "Elder Ahab is mad with grief. He is likely to say many things, both true and untrue. I myself have heard him say Master Zoticus killed Ysabel, yet in the next breath he swore she died of the plague. I'm not sure what I fear most – whether Ahab has accused an innocent man of murder, or whether he has imprisoned an assassin so deadly, he will surely exact vengeance on the whole town. Even if he is an assassin…why Ysabel? If someone wanted these lands so badly, surely their assassin would choose a more suitable target…" Her voice died.

Tobias. If anyone wanted her family's lands, they'd have to kill Tobias.

She had to know.

"Go…go in without me. I'll catch up," Sara said, gesturing for Silvana to enter the candle-lit church. The summer night seemed colder than it should, but she let the darkness cloak her as she hurried away.

If she wanted to speak to Zoticus alone, now would be the best time, with everyone at the church. To ask him if he really was an assassin, and whether Tobias was in danger.

And, if so…to do whatever it took to save Tobias.

Because Ahab had loved Ysabel, but it was nothing compared to the fierce love Sara harboured for her only son. As long as she drew breath, she would do everything within her power to save him. From assassins, from the plague…and anything else that threatened him.

Heaven help the man who stood in her way.

She marched down to the silent mill. The cellar had a set of double doors, wide enough to allow a wagon inside, barred with an enormous beam that usually took two men to lift.

Yet when she raised her lantern high to look for something that might allow her to lever it open, she found the beam on the floor, and the doors open wide.

Inside the cellar itself was an empty pallet, and no sign of the man except for the faint outline where he'd lay before he'd left.

Sara snorted softly. It seemed heaven had already helped Master Zoticus. Heaven, or the devil.

Whoever had helped him, it mattered not.

He had to be headed out of town, and there was only one road. If she followed it, she'd soon catch up to him.

He wouldn't escape her so easily.

Twenty

Finally, the sun called it a day. Zoticus stretched, pocketed the last of the bread and cheese, and dug out his lock-picking charm. All right, it was actually a key, but he had yet to find the lock it had been made for. The enchantment allowed it to work without being inserted into a lock, though he did still have to pay a blood price, like with any magic.

Tonight, the door seemed to be particularly stubborn. A drop or two of blood was usually enough, but this time, it wasn't until the key was coated in his blood and threatening to slip out of his fingers that the doors finally opened.

The people of Mirroten really wanted him to stay, didn't they?

He stepped over the beam that had once barred the doors and headed up to the road. No one was about, though there were lights further up the hill, around the church.

Some local saint's day, perhaps, or some other holy day he'd forgotten. He wasn't even sure what day it was any more, let alone the date. The church would have to forgive his absence. The people of Mirroten certainly wouldn't welcome him.

So he followed the road the other way — away from the town. Lake water lapped softly at the dock, reminding him he could borrow a boat and follow the river all the way to the Rialto lagoon. The boat's owner would likely be dead of plague within weeks, so he wouldn't even miss it.

Tempting, but his instincts told him no. Instead, he stayed on the road, just long enough to be well away from Mirroten, before he set up camp.

As the town fell behind him so only moonlight lit his way, Zoticus became aware of a second set of footsteps following him.

He paused. When the footsteps continued, he ghosted into the trees. Godfrey had never understood this was why Zoticus always wore grey. A man didn't need magic to become invisible.

Soon enough, a figure approached. A lantern hanging from their hand illuminated the road around the figure's boots, and little more.

Now it was Zoticus's turn to do the following, but his footfalls were silent and swift. The first the figure knew of his presence was the knife he pressed to her throat.

For with his free arm around her body, he was left in no doubt that she was a woman.

One who was too scared to scream or struggle.

"Why are you following me?" he hissed in her ear.

"First, to find out if you really are an assassin, but I suppose I already have my answer to that," she said.

The woman from his vision.

Her heart beat fast beneath his hand, but there was no fear in her tone.

He relaxed, but didn't yet lower the blade.

"The second was to return your things, which you left in the inn."

Zoticus cursed inwardly. He wasn't normally this careless, but he could afford to replace all of the commonplace items he'd left in the inn.

"And third, I have a commission I wish you to undertake."

Every word was the truth.

He released her and tucked his knife back into his belt. "I choose which commissions I take."

"So I have heard. You don't kill anyone except those you are commissioned to kill, and even then, no one is entirely sure you are responsible. Even Holy Crusaders, at the head of an army."

She had a source of information who was unusually well informed. Better than Ahab or the other townsfolk. If he had to guess, he'd pick, "Mistress Tola, the witch from Rialto?"

"Yes. How did Ysabel die?"

His throat grew tight. "I wasn't there, so I don't know. Her father said it was the plague. If the man was correct…" He didn't have the heart to tell her that everyone she knew would die.

Ah, but she already knew. "If the plague has come to Mirroten, then my people will suffer the same fate as everyone in Altino." Her shoulders slumped.

"Not everyone. I survived." The moment the words left his lips, he regretted them. No matter what the monks said, he could not work miracles, and that's what it would take to save Mirroten if ridding it of rats and fleas was not enough.

"How?"

"Magic, and luck. Luck that I survived the plague once before, coming home from a crusade. And magic…magic which won't work on anyone but me." He set off down the road again, not caring if she followed.

Of course, she did.

"Where are you going?" she called.

"To make camp far enough away from your town so I can sleep."

"I know the best spots for travellers to camp between towns. I'll show you."

He could probably find them on his own, but he did not refuse her offer. Something told him he needed to hear more about the job she wished to offer him.

He let the silence swell between them, wondering if she would break it with chatter. Most people could not abide silence for long.

This lady was not most people.

He smiled in the dark.

"What's funny?" she asked.

A thought came to him, and he ran with it. "What would your husband say, if he could see you now, following some assassin you barely know down the road, away from your home?"

He expected her to stop and blush, or come to her senses and turn back.

Instead, her voice was cold as her steps never slowed. "It might surprise you to learn that the lands of Mirroten are quite extensive, so in truth, I have not yet left home. Besides, I imagine my husband is far too busy doing important things, instead of watching what's going on down here. But if he were watching over me, I imagine he'd approve of my willingness to do what I must for those I care about."

Now he was the one who hung his head in shame. "You are a widow. I'm sorry for your loss." He refused to focus on the spark of hope that leaped into life at the thought of her having no husband.

"As am I, but I still have my son. He'll be a man soon, old enough to claim his birthright."

There was a bitter note in her voice, but it seemed that the bitterness was directed at him, not the son.

"There's the camp I use when I trade with the other towns." She lifted her lantern and pointed.

The clearing held little more than a fire pit ringed around with stones, and a small pile of firewood left by some kindly traveller.

Or the lady herself?

No, surely one of her servants.

She made no effort to help him as he set up some kindling and set it alight. Soon, he had a small fire going.

Without rising from his knees, he held out his hand to the still standing woman. "My things, please?"

Wordlessly, she handed him his travelling sack, which felt heavier than he remembered it.

Perhaps because she'd packed his freshly laundered clothes, a flagon of wine and other provisions. Mirroten might not be the friendliest town, but at least they were generous with their hospitality.

The least he could do was share what little hospitality he had here. He spread the striped cloak on the ground for her, and set the wine flagon between them.

"Now, please sit, my lady, and tell me about this commission you have in mind."

She set the lantern down beside the cloak. "Sara."

Her name! His lady finally had a name! He couldn't remember the last time he'd felt this jubilant. "If it please my Lady Sara, will you sit and share a cup of wine with me while you tell me what you desire?"

He didn't mean it to come out so seductive. He just…she…

She laughed. She laughed so hard she fell to her knees and rolled onto her side on the striped cloak. "It's Sara. Just Sara. And Tola was right!"

No, he would not fall into this trap. There was a reason few assassins lived as long as he had.

"You live in the grandest house in Mirroten, and the town and all the land surrounding it belongs to your family, does it not?"

She nodded once.

"So much land would not be granted to anyone less than a knight. So, your husband…"

She laughed harder. "My husband was a goatherder, and a good man. He had a silver tongue and a sweet smile, but he never held a sword in his life, nor did he need to."

So the land was hers. "What of your father?"

She sobered. "My father was a good man. He took his place on the town council, and he was so busy running the estate he had no time for swordplay or horses that weren't for working. My brothers, had they lived…some of them hoped to be trained as knights. Much like my grandfather, and his father, whose swords are still mounted on a wall in the house somewhere. I think it was my great grandfather who was a crusader knight. The king gave him the estate to honour his service in the Holy Land."

That must have been the very first crusade – a more honourable affair than the one Zoticus had joined. Though he'd seen tavern brawls more honourable, if truth be told, so that wasn't saying much.

"Which would make him a baron, and you…Lady Sara, liege lord to everyone who lives here."

Slowly, she shook her head. "No. Their liege lord will be Tobias, my son." She lifted her gaze to meet his eyes. "Enough banter. From what I have seen and what I have heard, you are a man of honour and honesty. If I ask you a question, will you tell me the truth?"

"I will not lie."

She inclined her head. "That is fair. Now, tell me – did you come to Mirroten to kill my son?"

Why would she think that? Had someone threatened her in the past? Surely they'd have wanted both her and the son dead, for the lands were hers.

She mistook his silence for something else. "If you have come to kill him, I will pay you double to stay your hand."

He should have told her the truth instantly, instead of weighing her words. Now he'd sound like he was lying.

"Triple."

What could he say? Triple of nothing was still nothing. He didn't kill children.

She leaned forward, her eyes glittering in the firelight. "Name your price. If it is within my power to grant it to you, I will give you whatever you want, if you will swear to save my son."

All he wanted right now was her.

Perhaps it was the cider he'd been drinking all day, or some intoxicating scent she wore, or the spell she wove with words alone…he no longer cared why.

He kissed her.

Twenty-One

May God forgive her, but once his lips touched hers, Sara forgot she'd ever had a son. She was aware of nothing but that moment. The tart taste of cider on his tongue, his warm breath mingling with hers, his fingers tracing her jaw as one kiss became all the seduction she could ever need to succumb.

Until it stopped.

Zoticus froze, and it was like kissing a corpse. Farewelling a love she'd known but briefly, which would never be enough.

She moved away from him, putting a more decorous distance between them. For a moment, she'd been willing to give him all of herself, but he'd declined. Good. One of them should be sensible when business dealings and lives hung in the balance.

Finally, he moved. "The castle in the mountains," he said, or something like it, before shaking his head.

"It's not a castle. It's a monastery. The Cloister of the Holy Innocents, built by the king to house the relics my ancestor brought back from his crusade. The remains of the Holy Innocents," Sara said.

Zoticus drew in a sharp breath. "Have you been there?"

She let out a laugh. "In case you haven't noticed, I'm a woman. Women aren't welcome in monasteries. Apparently we distract the men from their work."

"Men who are easily distracted must not be very good at their jobs."

Unlike him.

She sighed. "Perhaps. I don't imagine I'd be much of a distraction now. Perhaps they might allow me to visit."

"But first you wish me to save your son."

She eyed him across the fire. "First, I wish

to hear you swear you will not kill my son. Then, I want you to save him. If someone sent you to kill him, what will stop them from sending another?" She reached for the pouch at her belt, untied it, and tossed the pouch into his lap.

He lifted it, shaking it so the coins inside tinkled sweetly. "What is this for?"

"That is for ridding us of rats. I have no desire to be indebted to you. Now, what will it cost me for you to save my son?"

He gazed at her through the flames. He looked so long, she feared he was reading her soul. Finally, he said, "Lady Sara, the only payment I ask is the honour of serving you."

She wanted to believe him. Truly, she did. But he was an assassin, sent to kill her son. Though he talked of honour, she still didn't know what that meant to an assassin. Perhaps he had honour.

Or maybe he had none.

She wrapped the striped cloak around her and leaned back against the tree behind her. "Then we should get some sleep, so that on the morrow we can head back to Mirroten for my son."

"You would sleep alone in the forest with an assassin you barely know? You're braver than most men I have known, Lady Sara."

Better than sharing his bed, she thought to herself as she felt her face heat. Now that would be foolish.

"No, Master Zoticus. I intend to spend the night keeping watch while you sleep, so that you do not sneak away. We have a bargain, you and I. You desire honour, and I want you to save my son. Come morning, I intend to see both our wishes granted."

"If you truly knew my wishes and desires, you would hurry back to your own bed in Mirroten tonight, my lady."

His words made her spine shiver, but she refused to let him see the effect he had on her. He was handsome enough to consider making him her lover, but she'd be the one to bury a blade in his breast if he so much as shed a drop of Tobias's blood.

"You're on my family's land, assassin. Whether we are in Mirroten or in the monastery on the mountain or here in my camp, my power is the same." Even she heard the cold, naked threat in her voice — a tone she'd never used before. She suspected even Ahab would quail if he'd heard it.

Zoticus, the wretch, merely grinned. "Lady Sara, I suspect your power is greater than you know. I am, of course, yours to command. Sleep, you say? Then I shall."

He stretched out, rolling himself up in his own cloak, before resting his head on his sack of belongings. Within moments, he began to snore.

Twenty-Two

Sunlight filtering through the trees woke Zoticus, who had to admit he'd slept quite well. So had Lady Sara, it seemed, who had fallen asleep to the sound of his fake snoring. She was fortunate that he had magical means of keeping watch, that didn't rely on her ability to stay awake. Not that he'd expected to be attacked — there were too few people left alive to do so, after the plague had passed through. And he'd hear an angry mob from Mirroten a mile away — more than enough time to awaken and hide.

He broke his bread in half and used his

knife to spread the remaining cheese across both pieces. "Would you like to break your fast, Lady Sara?"

Her eyes flew open and for a moment they stared at him in shock. Then she recovered, sat up, and said, "Yes, thank you, Master Zoticus." She accepted the offered bread and cheese.

Even brave Melisende had suspected poison the first time he'd handed her food. Yet Lady Sara bit into her breakfast without hesitation.

"Aren't you worried I'll poison you?" he asked.

She shrugged. "If you poison me, you won't be paid. You may speak of honour, but a man who kills for a living expects to be paid. An assassin with your reputation would not have lived this long if he were a fool, and nothing I have seen so far has made me think otherwise, even if you do own a motley cloak."

He felt his cheeks redden. "It was a gift from a friend."

She rose, dusted off the cloak she'd slept in, and held it out to him. "Then I should return it. My thanks for loaning me such a precious gift."

He wasn't sure if she was simply being

courteous, or trying to taunt him. "If ever you have need of my cloak again, you have only to ask, my lady."

Her fiery eyes said hell would freeze over before she'd ask any such thing. But she finished her breakfast, then washed her hands daintily with a flask of water.

"I'm ready to leave as soon as you are," she said.

It wasn't long before they were headed back along the road to Mirroten. Somehow he'd ended up carrying his things and her lantern, so she had both hands free to pick berries from the bushes beside the road as they walked.

The first person who spotted them was a girl with flour-dusted skirts.

Zoticus glanced at Sara, wondering if she'd want him to hide so that she might pretend that she hadn't seen him, but she was too busy greeting the girl.

"Mistress Sara, you must do something. Ahab has everyone locked in the church, and he won't let Father Fazzio release them until they agree to go on a crusade!"

"Ahab has the whole town locked in the

church?" Zoticus swore. If even one of them was afflicted with the plague, they might pass the pestilence on to everyone. Better to burn the church down than release them, if they were all going to die anyway. Not to mention suffocating from smoke inhalation was a far more merciful way to die than succumbing to the plague.

The girl shook her head. "No, not the whole town. Just the children, and anyone who isn't married yet."

"Tobias?" Sara asked.

"Yes, him too."

For a moment, Sara looked stricken. But only for a moment.

Her hand landed on his arm. "Master Zoticus, you will free the children from the church. Take them to the travelling camp, where I will meet you with supplies for the journey."

What? What had he missed that suddenly he had to steal an entire town's children? They weren't rats, responding to a magic whistle. And there was absolutely no way he was taking children on a crusade. He wouldn't have even taken Melisende if he hadn't seen that vision where she helped him get justice from those damned knights.

"I'm not taking kids on a crusade!" he burst out.

Her hand on his arm squeezed gently. "Bring them to the travelling camp, and I will explain everything," Sara said. Then she grew thoughtful. "Goats. We'll need to bring the goats." She hurried off, beckoning for the miller girl to follow her.

Too late, Zoticus realised he'd somehow gone from saving one boy to kidnapping half the town. If it had been anyone else asking, he would have chased after them to argue, but instinct told him he'd be wasting his time today.

Lady Sara was certainly a force to be reckoned with.

He wagered she'd be wondrous in bed. A pity his vision had cut short last night's kiss, or he might already know.

At least if they were to journey together, they might have another chance.

Then again, maybe not with a hundred children coming along.

He sighed. He'd find a way. Eventually.

Or she would…

Twenty-Three

The people of Mirroten liked putting bloody big bars across their doors, Zoticus decided, struggling to unbar the church door. He'd pull out his magic key to do the job if he had to, but he shouldn't have to. It was simply a matter of the right leverage and…finally. He leaned the bar against the wall and threw open the church doors.

The town's children, huddled at the other end of the church, before the altar, squinted in the sunlight streaming into the windowless building. Two of the bigger boys, old enough to consider young men, stood before the group, ready to defend them.

Zoticus had to admire their courage.

The smaller of the two stepped forward. "You may tell Elder Ahab that our vigil has not changed our resolve. We will not go with you on a crusade to the Holy Land."

Zoticus did not remember madness being one of the early symptoms of plague, but it did seem like absurd ideas were spreading faster than usual through the town.

"Good," Zoticus replied. "Because one crusade is more than enough for any man. I'll not be going on another. Anyone with any sense will not be heading for the Holy Land, but in the opposite direction. Up into the mountains, maybe, until the plague has passed."

The boy frowned. "You mean on a pilgrimage, to see some holy relics?"

Yes. Some remote place with holy relics, high in the mountains. Somewhere so hard to get to, the plague had not reached it yet.

"You mean like the Cloister of the Holy Innocents? To see the jewel encrusted skeletons?" the bigger boy blurted out.

The smaller boy turned to him. "You've

been there?"

He shrugged. "Master Gojko journeys there once a year to trade herbs. They have some rather unusual ones that only grow high in the mountains, and because the Rialto traders can't go any further up the river, he buys extra to take to the Cloister. I used to go with him when I was younger, but now he leaves me to tend the shop while he's gone."

The apothecary's apprentice, Zoticus presumed.

"Could you take us there?" Zoticus asked.

The boy shrugged. "Maybe. Once you're on the right road, it's hard to get lost. Why? Who's going to the monastery? It'll be autumn soon, and the high passes won't be open much longer. One decent snowfall and you're stuck there until spring."

That sounded perfect. "We all are, if we want to survive this plague."

The smaller boy was not as trusting as the apothecary's apprentice. "Why should we go anywhere with you? This is our town. We're not rats, to be driven out and drowned."

Zoticus winced. He hadn't expected this to go well, but this was worse than he'd expected.

"Because Lady Sara told me to take you."

The two boys exchanged glances. The bigger one shook his head. "You take it up with her. I wouldn't dare argue with Mistress Sara."

The smaller one nodded. "I'd better get the goats. I'll never hear the end of it if I leave them behind."

Before Zoticus could stop him, the boy darted out of the church, toward the town green.

Zoticus stared after him. Should he go after him, or just save the rest of the children? Lady Sara had said to save all of them, but perhaps she hadn't considered him coming up against the obstinate goat boy.

"Do you think he'll come back?" Zoticus asked the apothecary's apprentice.

"Of course. Tobias said he was going to get the goats. It might take a while to get them all moving, but even he knows better than to cross his mum."

Zoticus's heart sank. Of course the boy was Sara's son.

"Take everyone here down the road to the first traveller's camp to wait for me. We'll meet you there, with or without the goats," Zoticus said. Without, if he had his way. Animals would only slow their progress up the mountain.

The boy nodded and started issuing orders to the rest of the children.

Zoticus headed for the town green. Saving Sara's son was proving harder than he'd thought.

Twenty-Four

"I haven't even managed to get the cart unloaded," Sara admitted as she opened the barn. "Probably a good thing, as now we have less to load. Wherever we'll go, we'll need supplies. It could be months before it's safe to come back."

"Where will we go?" Silvana asked.

Sara sank onto a bench, burying her head in her hands. "I don't know." When she'd asked Zoticus to save Tobias, she'd meant for the two of them to travel someplace far away, where they'd be safe from the plague. Two people could easily disappear, with enough coin to pay for whatever they needed along the way. But half the town…

Even Sara did not have enough coin to pay to feed and house so many. They'd have to rely on the charity of strangers, a chancy thing in good times, but if the plague had truly wiped out the other towns along the river, who was left that they could turn to?

If Mercurio had not gone far, perhaps he could be persuaded to take everyone aboard his ship. If they were to travel aboard a ship, though, they'd need to take all their provisions with them. She'd need everything on the cart, and most of the contents of her cellar, too. Not to mention another cart, or creatures who could carry things. Mirroten did not have anywhere near enough ponies to take a tenth of what she had stored in the cellar…

"I'll get the goats," she said.

"No need, my lady. You have only to wish, and it shall appear."

"Master Zoticus?" Even Sara had to stare as the man appeared in the middle of a flock of what looked like the whole town's goats. She shook her head. Goats were difficult to handle at the best of times, or so Tobias and her husband had told her. How an assassin could get them to behave so well…it would take some powerful magic.

"Mother?" Tobias appeared, and the riddle was solved. "Master Zoticus here said we were to meet you at one of the travelling camps along the road, before heading up the mountain, but Raphael told me it takes some time to get there, and they are not accustomed to hosting guests. We'd do well to bring our own supplies. Now, the goats have only carried sacks of hay down from the high pasture in the past, but if we could keep their loads light, we might be able to take some of the sacks of chestnut flour…"

Between the four of them, they managed to load most of the cart's contents onto the goats, and fill the cart with casks from the cellar. Silvana brought a second cart, which was soon full, too. Sara set the pigs loose in the chestnut orchard, hoping she'd be able to return before they ate next year's harvest. Surely she wouldn't be gone that long.

"Did you see Mercurio's ship on your way to Mirroten, Master Zoticus? He could not have gone far. Perhaps if I rode ahead, I could catch him and ask him to return for the rest of us. With his new ship, he can surely take us anywhere we want. Far from the reach of this plague."

He stared at her for a moment, then muttered an oath. "Mercurio the river trader made it to your town? No wonder the plague came here, too – he was carrying it aboard his ship. Yes, I found the trader's ship, but his corpse was already cold. The plague took him, too. The ship was tainted, so I burned it."

Her heart sank. "Then where will we go?"

Tobias made an impatient sound. "Have you forgotten, Mother? Master Zoticus is taking us up to the monastery in the mountains."

She blinked. It made sense, now that she thought about it. What better place than a church dedicated to the Holy Innocents to shelter her town's children from this scourge? "Of course," she said. "Let me get a few things from the house, and we shall go."

By the time she returned with a sack of clothes for herself and Tobias, she found only Zoticus waiting for her.

"Where is my son?" she asked.

He jerked his head toward the road. "He

and the miller's girl went on ahead with the goats and one of the carts, leaving the other one for you. I said I'd wait for you."

For a moment, her heart softened toward him. It was a sweet gesture, waiting to make sure she wasn't left behind. Like something a friend would do.

But Zoticus was not her friend.

"So much for protecting my son. What if something happens to him while you were waiting for me?" Sara snapped.

Zoticus merely shrugged, as if her anger meant nothing to him. "He's got a hundred goats and the miller's girl, armed with a stout cudgel. If anyone had wanted to stop us from leaving, they've had ample chance, yet I've seen no one. The last time I saw a town this quiet, it was Altino, and it was because everyone was dead. I didn't want to say it in front of the children, who all seem to be in good health, but everyone who wasn't locked in that church might be infected, or already dead."

Sara sighed heavily. "Yes, I haven't seen anyone about, either. Can it…can this plague really strike people down so quickly? One day they seem in perfect health, and the next day, they are dead?"

"Once the infection takes hold, death comes quickly. Usually a few days, but sometimes less. It can hide in the body, not coming out to kill right away, waiting several days or even a week. It can spread through rats, fleas…and sometimes, between one person and another, through the very air we breathe."

"Creeping in the dark, where we cannot see, only to strike us down without warning…this disease sounds much like an assassin," she said.

Zoticus frowned. "There you are wrong, Lady Sara. An assassin only kills where there is profit to be made from the death. This plague kills without a care for fortune or honour or virtue. It cannot be stopped. Whereas an assassin is mortal – we sicken and die like anyone else. As will you, if you change your mind and stay here instead of coming with us to this monastery."

For a moment, she longed to stay. This was home, and perhaps she could help those who were sick. The plague couldn't kill everyone.

"Don't even think about it, Lady Sara. I'll throw you over my shoulder and carry you all the way up the mountain myself."

Before she could stop it, a giggle escaped from her lips. She'd heard tales of barbarians in far-off lands who carried women away like that, but she found it hard to believe that this assassin, whose courtly bow was a thing of beauty, could be anything like those savages.

She regained her composure, hoping he hadn't heard her silly giggle. "If you plan to carry me, how will you protect my son? Really, Master Zoticus, you are the strangest assassin I've ever met." She swept past him to take the pony's bridle, urging the creature to start pulling the cart toward the road.

She thought he heard him mutter something, half under his breath, but she couldn't make it out, so she dismissed it as not important.

Not when they had a camp to reach before nightfall, and a long journey ahead of them.

Twenty-Five

"Stubborn woman," Zoticus muttered under his breath as Sara set off with the cart. He said it again when he saw her making the rounds of all the children, speaking to every single one, before she allowed herself to rest for the night, though he could see how exhausted she was. She'd given her cloak to a child who had none, refusing to let the child return it. She was the last to eat every night, though she was the one preparing the meals. And more than once, he'd caught her milking the goats in the morning, to make sure everyone had some milk with breakfast before they started travelling for the day.

The journey was torturously slow. They barely covered a third of the distance Zoticus alone would have done in a day, and sometimes even less than that. Between the smaller children and the goats, it would likely be well into autumn when they arrived at the monastery, but Sara would not countenance the suggestion that any of them be left behind.

She was the sort of lady any barony would beg for. Without servants or a husband, she saw to the needs of everyone in her care. Yet to everyone except her son, she was Mistress Sara, without her proper title, because they saw her as one of their own.

When she was so much more.

They'd been travelling a week when the road grew steeper, headed into the mountains proper, and it took all his concentration to keep the pony headed up the road, instead of stopping or turning around and heading home, which is what the silly creature wanted. This was why Zoticus didn't own a horse. Not because he couldn't afford one, but because relying on a creature with a mind and will of its own was a recipe for disaster. That, and once he'd ridden Godfrey's divine mare, Pegasus, every other horse seemed as slow as this grumpy pony.

The next day, the road grew steeper still, and the miller's girl almost tripped over her own feet as she ran to him.

"Master Zoticus, it's Mistress Sara. She's fallen behind," the girl gasped out.

"You take the cart. I'll see to Lady Sara," he said, heading off.

He found her at the very back of their procession, leaning heavily on a goat that did not appreciate being anyone's crutch.

"Lady Sara, are you all right?" he asked carefully.

"I'm fine. Didn't sleep well last night, is all. I think there was a particularly sharp stone under my back that I couldn't seem to dislodge. I'm fine."

The goat took advantage of her distraction to bolt toward its fellows, higher up the hill, heedless of Lady Sara, who would have landed in the dust if not for Zoticus, who swooped in to catch her.

Then she began to cough.

"Lady Sara..." he began, not sure how to

say what he dreaded.

"I'm fine. I just breathed in some of the dust that stupid beast kicked up when it ran away, is all. I'll just take a drink and be fine."

He handed her his flask.

While she drank, he palmed his healing amulet. He'd surreptitiously used it to scan each of the children in turn, relieved when their blood had shown no signs of the plague, but somehow he'd never checked Lady Sara. Now, it might be too late.

He pressed his thumb to one of the sharp claws holding the green stone in place, hissing as he felt it break the skin. A drop of blood was the price of certainty, and with Lady Sara, he needed to be certain. She had to reach the monastery on the mountain to realise his vision. She couldn't possibly have the plague. She couldn't.

He touched the amulet to her side. To heal her, it was best to have skin contact, but to simply see what ailed her, her dress would not impede his diagnosis.

"Please don't let it be the plague," he prayed silently as he searched her blood for signs of the dreaded pestilence. No, and no and no – it wasn't there.

Only then did he allow himself to breathe again. As always, Lady Sara was right. She was fine.

But just to make sure…

He lifted her off her feet and carried her to the nearest cart. "You shall ride up here for the rest of the day."

"I can walk just fine," she protested.

"That may be, but you didn't see that goat's expression. I'm sure he's not far away, plotting vengeance with all the other goats. You'll be safe from him and his friends up here, where he can't reach you," Zoticus said.

"I'm not afraid of my own goats!"

"Stubborn woman," he muttered.

Thankfully, she didn't hear him that time, either.

Twenty-Six

Zoticus didn't need to say it, but she knew he suspected it, as surely as she did. Once she'd started coughing, it was only a matter of time before she died of the plague. She kept herself apart from the others, mindful that the disease could be spread from one person to another, and she did not want any of their deaths on her conscience. Not when she would likely die soon herself.

She rode in a cart now, instead of walking alongside it. No one said a word, but she could feel Zoticus watching her. Waiting for her to die?

She wished she had let him seduce her, that first night in camp. One last memory, to take with her into whatever came next. Instead, she'd die wondering whether Tola was right...or whether he'd prove to be a good lover after all.

"Lady Sara!"

She almost thought she could feel his arms around her, laying her down, loosening the lacing on her gown, preparing to make love to her.

If this was to be her last thought on this earth, then at least it was a most wondrous dream.

Twenty-Seven

They rounded a bend and Zoticus took his eyes off Sara for a moment to take in the sight of the mountain monastery, the castle from his vision.

It soared above them, clinging to the cliffside like some sort of magical creation, ruling over the world. Thank heaven the gates were open, because the place would be nigh impregnable if they were shut.

A slight cough drew his eyes back to Sara. She toppled sideways in her seat, ending up slumped against a barrel that was all that kept her from tumbling out of the cart altogether.

Zoticus called for a halt. He lifted her out of the cart, not caring about anything but her right now. The kids – goat and human alike – parted to let him through.

He marched into the castle bailey, shouting for a healer.

But no one came.

He shouldered his way through the doors to the great hall, still shouting for help, but there was not even a fire lit there, though someone had laid one in readiness. He tugged off his cloak and spread it out on the flagstone floor, before laying Sara gently on the fur.

He lit the fire, making sure it was well alight before he dared to take his eyes off it. Sara needed warmth and healing, and he wasn't sure he was powerful enough to help her.

The children had followed him inside the hall, and some approached the fire, holding their hands out to warm them.

They were alive because of her. They owed her.

"Search the castle. See if you can find someone, anyone. Lady Sara needs a healer," he said.

Tobias, Raphael, Silvana, and many of the other older children spread out to obey his orders. The younger ones just stood around and looked lost.

For the first time in he couldn't remember how long, Zoticus knew exactly what that felt like.

Sara coughed weakly, her breath rasping in her throat.

He untied the lacing on her gown, hoping that would help her breathe, but still she struggled.

"I need a healer!" he howled, hoping whoever was here in the monastery would hear him and come help.

"I haven't found a healer, but I have found the best bedchamber. Mistress Sara will be more comfortable in a bed than here on the floor."

Zoticus stared around, looking for the source of the voice. Silvana, the miller's girl. He'd learned her name and others on the journey, but now he could scarcely remember his own name.

"Is there a fire there?" he demanded.

"I lit it myself, before I came down here. The bed could probably do with an airing, but if we stoke the fire hot enough, that should at least drive away the damp air." Silvana beckoned. "Bring her."

Zoticus bundled Sara up in his cloak and followed the girl.

The feather bed was piled high with furs. The fire had done little more than take the chill out of the air, so he set Sara down and proceeded to wrap her warmly.

"What else can I do for her?" Silvana asked.

"Find her a healer," he said.

She nodded and left.

An eternity passed while Zoticus held Sara in his arms. Her breathing was loud, but as long as she still drew breath, he could help her. He hoped.

"There's no one here. The whole place is empty. I've brought Raphael." Silvana shoved the boy forward. "Now I'm going to see if I can get the kitchen fire started, so we can cook something hot for dinner."

Raphael, the apothecary's apprentice, stood awkwardly beside the bed. "I found the stillroom. There are many herbs hung up there, most of which I recognise, and shelves full of jars that could contain anything. It will take some time, but within a few days, I should be able to make something to help Mistress Sara. What would be best for her cough is oil of rue, but that will take weeks…"

Oil of rue. Hadn't the witch's girl sold him some?

Zoticus reached into his pouch, and the vial materialised in his hand.

"Only a few drops," he muttered to himself, holding the vial over her lips. Carefully, he counted out three drops before corking the vial again.

The boy was still there.

"Do what you can," Zoticus said. "I have enough oil of rue to do for some days yet."

Raphael left.

Zoticus pulled his healing amulet from beneath his tunic. He sliced his thumb open again, smearing blood across the stone, before touching the amulet to Sara's throat.

This time, he wasn't looking for plague. He wanted to know what ailed her, in the faint hope that he might be able to fix it.

Her throat was inflamed, but the infection went deeper, coating the passageways carrying air to her lungs. No wonder she had so much trouble breathing. If he could but lessen the inflammation…

"Master Zoticus, you're bleeding on my mother's gown."

Zoticus palmed the amulet as he rose from the bed to face Tobias. The boy's face was pale.

"Is Mother…is she…?"

"She lives, though she is very ill. Perhaps now we are no longer travelling, she will be able to rest and recover," Zoticus said.

The boy nodded feverishly. "Good. Very good. For a moment there, I thought…" He shook his head. "Is it the plague?"

"No! I think she took a chill, and the rigours of travel made it worse," Zoticus said.

"Some of the girls have found the kitchen, and they say they will prepare dinner for everyone. The younger children have found what we think is the monks' dormitory, and they are busy bringing in straw for the beds so that we might sleep there. There is a sort of village green where I have left the goats, but I will have to milk them before the sun sets. The carts…." Tobias continued, but Zoticus stopped listening.

He'd brought them here because he'd seen Sara in his vision, running across the bailey, and nothing else mattered but her. She had to recover, because she still had to appear in his vision…

Tobias had finished talking, and he appeared to expect a response.

"Good, good," Zoticus said. "See that everyone eats and gets some rest, and ask the kitchen to send up some broth for Lady Sara."

When the boy had gone, Zoticus set the healing amulet to work again. He wasn't certain, but he thought the swelling in her throat had lessened a little. Just a little more, and she might find it easier to breathe.

For the first time in his life, he wished his mother were here with him. With the powerful magic running through her veins, a single drop of her blood would heal Sara in a matter of moments.

But he was all Sara had, so he'd do his best. Hoping that she'd wake up, and thank him, so he could deliver that terrible line about being honoured to be of service, and see desire burn in her eyes. Or maybe it was just irritation.

Right now, he'd settle for seeing her eyes open.

But they didn't open at all again that day, or during the night.

Twenty-Eight

Slowly, Sara became aware of voices. There was Tobias, Silvana and occasionally Raphael, always talking in hushed tones so that she could not always make out the words. Regret smote her – had she passed the plague on to them, too, so they were all dead? Served her right for trusting an assassin with her son's life. For the first time, she wondered if he'd receive a bonus for killing her, too, or whether that was always part of his plan. Or the plan of whoever had sent him. The Bishop of Rialto, most likely, who had always coveted the rich lands around the monastery. If they were all dead, then the lands would fall to him.

There was someone else there, too. Someone who moved silently, never said a word, and smelled strongly of rue and other medicinal herbs. One of the monks, preparing her body for burial? She wished she could have told him she'd prefer for her body to lie beside her husband's, in the churchyard in Mirroten, but she knew as well as anyone that the dead could not talk, let alone make their wishes known.

At least the strong-smelling monk didn't leave her. It was comforting to know that she was not alone. Perhaps that was why it was customary to hold a vigil before a funeral – if the soul had not yet been taken to heaven or hell or wherever they went in between, the loneliness was enough to overwhelm them.

Well, it threatened to overwhelm her. Only the scent of the monk and the gentle touch of his hands kept her from screaming out into the void she'd found herself in. No bishop should be able to steal her boy's birthright.

And then one day, the voices were no longer quiet.

"It is unseemly that you are alone with her,

when she is so vulnerable. She is a virtuous widow. Were she well, I know she would not allow you to enter her bedchamber. I have been remiss in my duties to my mother to allow it to go on so long. But it must stop." That was Tobias, speaking with unaccustomed authority. She hoped whoever he was speaking to could not detect the nervousness in his tone.

"Would you rather I did not heal her? She has been very ill, nigh unto death. If I had not been here, nor would she."

It took her a long moment to place the second voice, because she wasn't as familiar with it as her son's, but those smooth tones could only belong to Zoticus the assassin.

"I am grateful for your assistance, Master Zoticus, and will happily pay you for your healing services. That someone like you has such skills came as a pleasant surprise, but your services are not required here any more. As you say, she is improving, and will wake soon. What will it do to her, if the first thing she sees when she wakes is an assassin? I will not have her frightened. You must go. Raphael can heal her now."

A pause. "Perhaps we should take this discussion outside her chamber. Lady Sara needs her rest. I would not wish her to wake to heated words when she has suffered enough."

Footsteps and the sound of a door closing. The scrape of a bar being laid across the door, too, if she was not mistaken. Tobias was taking no chances that anyone would enter her room. The door must have been well made, for she could not hear their conversation, if it continued at all, once the door was closed.

Then Zoticus's words hit her. Nigh unto death.

Near, but not quite. She was alive.

A flood of feelings overwhelmed her. Regret at not seeing her husband again soon. Joy that she might see and speak to her son again. Anticipation, that she might thank Zoticus for whatever it was he had done. And uneasiness, because he'd said there was no cure for the plague. So whatever he'd done for her, it would surely come at great cost...

The scent of rue assailed her nostrils again. The monk was still there.

He would know what Zoticus had done, surely, for the monk never left. He would have seen all.

"Tell me, by what miracle have I survived the plague?" she asked softly.

Gentle laughter was his first response. "There are no miracles here. You survived because you left Mirroten before you were infected, along with the young people you commanded me to save. You fell ill because you took a chill, I believe, likely the night you spent with me in the forest. Travelling took its toll, and infection set in. Stubborn woman that you are, you hid your weakness well, so that the infection was far advanced by the time we arrived here at the Cloister. Healing you…that took magic, I'm afraid. But I will show you if you wish."

She opened her eyes. Zoticus stood before her, clasping something in his hands that she could not see. She scanned the room, and was surprised to find that they were alone. "Where is the monk?" she asked.

"There are no monks. The Cloister was deserted when we arrived, and none have returned from their quest for plague survivors. I last saw them in Altino, burying the dead. It is possibly none of them will return, for corpses carry the plague, too."

She took a moment to digest this. No monks, and Tobias had said Zoticus was her healer. She reached for his hand, which he allowed her to bring to her nose. Sara inhaled deeply, once, twice, three times, just to make sure. "You smell of rue," she said.

"Oil of rue helps to ease a cough, like yours. It has also been known to bring on visions of the future, and I hoped…" He shook his head.

"What did you see of my future, Master Zoticus?" she asked, curious.

He pulled his hand from her grasp and looked away. "I saw nothing I did not already know."

Evasion. Interesting. She would ask him again later. Other questions burned more brightly on her tongue.

"And what of my son?" She'd heard his voice only a short time ago, so curiosity and not worry fuelled this question, too.

He smiled. "Your son is snoring, asleep outside your door. He is not a particularly effective guard, but he is a dutiful son. No one can unbar your door without waking him, so you may sleep soundly."

"Yet how are you here?"

He spread his hands wide. "An assassin has many secrets. Surely you do not expect me to share them all?"

She folded her arms across her chest. "Only this one."

He jerked his thumb at the wall hanging behind him. "There's a servants' stair behind that tapestry. It comes out near the kitchen, hidden behind another tapestry."

She nodded. "So if I asked you to bring me dinner, you would be faster than anyone else, who would have to convince my son to unbar the door first?"

He laughed. "If you're hungry, that is a very good sign. I admit I am not as good a healer as I am an assassin, so to know that I have successfully healed you is…most gratifying."

"You said you would show me how you'd healed me," she said slowly. "Tola said you might have magic. Is it true?"

"Now that is a secret I have never shared outside my family," he said.

She'd known Tola long enough to hear how magical bloodlines worked. "That's because they have magic, too." She fixed him with her gaze. "You said you would show me if I wish. Well, I do wish."

His courtly bow made her smile. She'd never thought to see it again. "As my lady desires."

He thrust out his hand, as if to seize her breast.

Suddenly she became aware that she was only wearing a thin shift, and not the one she'd been wearing on the road. This one was cut so low, if she leaned forward, her breasts would spill out.

"Did you undress me?" she demanded.

He stepped back, dropping his hands by his sides. "I did consider it, but the miller's girl, Silvana, took your clothes for laundering. When I returned, I found you wearing a fresh shift. Should you wish to change again, I'd be more than happy to assist you. I'm not unfamiliar with helping women out of their clothes."

A few of those courtly bows, a smile just like the cheeky one he wore now, a handful of courtly compliments delivered in that cultured voice so deep she felt its vibration in her belly…he wouldn't have to lift a finger before women removed their clothes for him.

There was a definite question in his eyes, now, too. After all, she was lying in an enormous bed in nothing but a thin shift. It would only take a word for him to join her. If only her breath hadn't caught in her throat...

She blinked and that look in his eyes was gone.

"You're still not quite well, Lady Sara. You did say you wished to see how I heal you."

She eyed his hand, once again headed for her breast. She still couldn't see what he held in it. "Perhaps you should tell me first."

He flipped his hand over, and showed her the amulet resting on his palm. A cloudy green stone, framed in an ornate silver setting. A thick leather thong dangled from it, as though he normally wore it around his neck.

"This is a healing amulet, given to me many years ago by a powerful enchantress. Its healing powers are activated by my blood, and my blood alone. While I wear it on my person, it helps my body to heal faster, saving me from many a wound that might have been mortal, and destroying diseases, including the plague, when they come into contact with my blood."

Sara nodded slowly. "So it has a price, this healing amulet of yours. The magic in your blood. The witch who gave it to you must have been very wise."

Zoticus smiled. "That she is. What she did not tell me is that I might use it to heal others, too, but as you have already guessed, it comes at a price. A blood price. The magic in my blood activates the amulet's healing powers, but the amulet must be close to the person I wish to heal. The magic is strongest when it rests against the skin, near the wound or sickness. So for your infection, I would place it over your heart, or at your throat."

Only a fool allowed an assassin anywhere near their throat. Then again, Sara suspected he posed even more danger to her heart.

"You're the healer, Master Zoticus. Where will it do the most good?"

Twenty-Nine

If he placed his hand at her throat, he knew he would cup her face and kiss her. If he put his hand on her chest, though, he'd have to remain rigidly in control, concentrating only on healing her and not the deliciously soft flesh beneath his fingers.

"I would prefer your heart," he said without a word of a lie.

But then he had to swallow manfully as she pulled the neckline of her shift down to expose half her breast. By all that was holy, he wanted…

"Please heal me," she whispered.

Zoticus shook himself. He'd never been this distracted by a woman, not since before he became an assassin.

He took a knife and sliced open his palm, then laid it atop the amulet. The stinging pain helped him concentrate on what he should be doing, and not anything else.

The swelling in her throat had gone down, but the infection still lingered in her blood and in her airways. He focussed on burning it out of her blood and the rest of her body, until none of it remained.

There. It was done.

Gasping, he pulled away from her, and the amulet tumbled to the floor.

He dropped to his knees, feeling for it in the darkness, for the fire had died down to embers. He'd been healing her for a long time.

Pain pierced his hand, and he drew the amulet out from under the bed. It was a thirsty thing, but worth the blood price he'd paid for healing her. He'd do it again, even if Sara had been infected with the plague instead of some simple infection.

"It's done. You're completely healed, Lady Sara," he said. "Your body will still be weak as you recover, but the illness is gone."

He headed for the fireplace, so that he might mend her fire before he left.

"How did a man like you become an assassin, Master Zoticus?" she asked.

He had yet to meet another man even remotely like himself, but he did not correct her. "It was so long ago, I scarcely remember," he lied.

"Please try," she said. "Because you've spent years shedding blood for a living, and tonight you've shed yours to save my life. I want to understand how you can."

He stayed silent for a long moment, determined to fix her fire. Far too soon, it was again blazing merrily, licking at a fresh log.

"I have a twin sister. Now, she's a powerful enchantress in her own right, while there isn't enough magic in my blood to cast a spell without an enchanted object to focus it. So she used her elemental magic as easily as breathing, while I spent most of my time in the woods around where we lived. Our mother was the village witch, much like your friend Tola, so I would hunt and trap in the forest, and bring back meat for our table.

"One day, my sister's friend went missing. We were not much older than your son Tobias, but everyone else our age was settling down and getting married, having children. All except us and her friend, Amice.

"Now, Amice was fond of stories, and there are plenty of them, telling how some brave, noble knight or lord or prince finds a girl in the woods, saves her from something fearful, and makes her his wife. It was no secret that Amice dreamed of marrying a knight, at the very least.

"And it so happened that a party of knights came to our town, on their way to a tourney of some sort, but they intended to break the monotony of their journey with some hunting.

"A few days after their arrival, Amice went missing. And my sister, who could level a castle, drain a lake or stir up a storm so strong it could blow a grown man down, could not find out where the girl had gone. So she asked me to track her, and I did.

"It took me hours, but I tracked her to a camp where the knights' had spent the night. But the camp was empty, and the only prints I found leaving the camp were all from horses' hooves. So when Amice left the camp, it had to be on horseback."

"Oh, the poor girl!" Sara said.

Zoticus shook his head. "Oh, she was willing enough, I wager. She wanted to marry a knight, and she'd found a whole company of them. She'd have her pick and live happily ever after, or so I thought. So I went home to tell my sister.

"My sister, who'd seen more of the world than me at that point, being an enchantress and all, feared even more for her friend. She knew not all knights and noblemen were honourable, and even if these ones were, she still wanted to make sure her friend was happy. So she sent me off after them."

He sucked in a breath. Should he tell her, or not? His instincts told him yes.

"That night, I had my first vision, though I thought it a dream at the time. I saw Amice in the forest, lying in a pool of blood. Even thinking it was a dream, it was enough to spur me on after her.

"Now, this was a mounted hunting party. They followed whatever prey took their fancy, which led them a merry chase. I was a boy on foot, following their tracks. But I knew they were going to a tourney, and when they got there, they would stay for some time, so I kept on following those tracks, hoping I would find them eventually.

"They stopped to camp and roast a deer they'd caught. When I found their camp, they could not have been gone a day. But the knights were all gone. Only Amice remained.

"I didn't see her at first. She was huddled in the bushes, weeping, and when she saw me, she tried to hide. Of course, I hadn't tracked her over so many miles to be fooled by a few leaves, so I pulled her out and begged her to tell me what was wrong.

"Her story started out like any of the tales she loved. The knights fought an impromptu battle for the honour of sitting beside her, and the winner…well, I don't know if it was that night or later, but he took her into his bed, telling her all manner of stories about how much he loved her and wanted her for his wife. For a few weeks, she was completely under his spell…until they approached the town where the tourney was to be held, not a day's ride from where I'd found her.

"On the last day, after he'd satisfied his lust, her seducer told her he no longer loved her, and they all rode off, leaving her there.

"I was horrified by her tale, but offered to take her home. That only made her cry harder, until she produced a knife and stabbed herself in the chest. Then she tore the knife out of her breast and flung it across the clearing. By some terrible mischance, she'd pierced her heart, and there was no saving her. Within minutes, my vision lay before me – her body in a pool of blood in a forest clearing."

"Did you love her terribly?" Sara whispered.

Zoticus laughed. "Amice? By all that's holy, no! She was Zoraida's best friend, and if I so much as thought about kissing her, my sister had promised she'd set fire to my bed. Oh, my life would have been so much simpler if I'd fallen in love with Amice. Then, I'd never been in love in my life, and the village girls knew me as the enchantress's twin brother, son to the village witch, with no magic of my own. As far as eligible bachelors go, I think I was just above the pig boy, and that was only because I was better looking."

Sara smiled faintly. "Were you more modest

then, too?"

"Heavens, no! If anything, I thought I was invincible. Like most boys that age do. So I swore on Amice's body that I would seek vengeance for her lost honour. A boy against trained tourney knights. I was a hunter, not a fighter. I must have lost my mind.

"Luckily, by the time I reached the tourney grounds, I'd regained my wits, and instead of challenging them or something else equally stupid, I filled a vacancy for a stable boy at the inn where they were staying. I listened to the gossip, watched the tourneys, and soon worked out that I was no match for any of the knights. Worse, the one who'd seduced Amice had a new bedwarmer, and the girl could not have been more than twelve years old!

"When the tourney was over, I attached myself to Sir Seducer's party as a groom. We hadn't been riding long before I discovered that not only did the man pick up a new maiden to deflower in every town, but he had a wife at home, waiting for him.

"Now, I'd grown up with enchantresses. I knew women ruled the world, and I thought my best chance would be to tell the knight's wife about his crimes. Until I met the girl."

Zoticus took a deep breath. "Lady Gemma was the most exquisite girl you'd ever seen. She looked like an angel, and she could not have been a day older than I was. Younger, perhaps, in years, but not when it came to the ways of the world. She had eyes as pale and hard as twin diamonds. Because unlike the peasant girls her husband had seduced, Lady Gemma's father was a knight, who'd insisted upon marriage between his daughter and his fellow knight. Whether money changed hands or they were just very drunk, I know not, but Lady Gemma only warmed her husband's bed for a few weeks, before he tired of her and returned to seducing innocents like Amice.

"Lady Gemma also wanted vengeance on her husband. And she began by taking her husband's newest groom into her bed."

Sara's jaw dropped.

She really was the virtuous widow her son thought she was, if that shocked her.

"Lady Gemma, young though she was, ruled her husband's estate. He was off chasing virgins or tourneys or deer for most of the year, so she grew accustomed to giving orders and having them obeyed. And she was no different in the bedchamber. It turned out I was not her first lover, and she was most particular about how she wished to be made love to.

"At first, I thought it was a fitting fate for Sir Seducer to learn his wife had lost her heart to me, as Amice had to him. But as I became more familiar with every bit of Lady Gemma's body, I soon learned that she had no heart…and that she was inexorably winning my own.

"How could I not think myself in love with her? She insisted we make love multiple times a night, pleasuring her in between, and if the other grooms found me asleep in the hayloft after another strenuous night, they just muttered that I was Lady Gemma's lover, and let me go back to sleep.

"This went on for some months, until one night Lady Gemma claimed to be ill, and banished me from her bed. The next morning, a servant brought a message from her that she wished me to deliver a letter to her husband, wherever he might be, and to attend her in her chambers that night.

"Any hopes I'd had of sharing her bed again before I left were dashed when she greeted me with the letter I was to carry, and a whispered promise that she would consider taking me into her bed again if I were to make sure her husband never came home, so she'd be free to marry again.

"And, like the fool I was, I believed her.

"When I caught up with Sir Seducer – I cannot remember his name, for all my names for him were epithets then – it was at the start of another hunting expedition. I joined the other servants, and waited for my opportunity. I had never killed a man before, but I was determined to do this for Amice and Lady Gemma.

"Sir Seducer shot a stag, then dismounted so that he might finish it off. The other knights had started chasing another target, so he was alone.

"Then, the only enchanted object I owned was my flute, the same one I used to summon the rats in Mirroten. That day, I used it to bring a boar. The beast gored Sir Seducer in the back, and then gored him again as he lay writhing on the ground. His friends heard his screams and came to help, but there was nothing anyone could do. He died in agony, several days later, and I was jubilant when I headed home to tell the good news to Lady Gemma."

Years had passed, but he never forgot that day. He'd been such a fool.

"She was at dinner when I arrived, and I had to deliver my news to her in the great hall, standing below her on the dais. She ordered that the house be placed in mourning, and dismissed me. Me!

"That night, I went to her bedchamber, just like I used to do, only to discover that it had been turned into a nursery. The bedchamber where I'd made love to Lady Gemma all those nights now belonged to twin boys, so tiny they could not have been long out of the womb. The boys' wet nurses stared at me until one of them had the presence of mind to direct me to Lady Gemma's new chamber.

"There, I learned that the boys were now Sir Seducer's heirs, though the knight had not shared her bed in years, and she would rule in their stead until the boys came of age. All the servants, of course, would swear to the boys' legitimacy, for they were hers, heart and soul.

"I delighted at the thought that my sons – for who else could be their father? – would have lands of their own and knightly titles. I promised her I would train them well, and spend every day teaching them to be better men than her now dead husband. And my nights would be hers, of course, as was her right.

"She merely laughed, tossed a pouch of coins on the floor at my feet, and said if I ever breathed a word about our arrangement or attempted to see the boys again, she would hire a real assassin to hunt me down and silence me forever. And so...I went home."

After a considerable amount of time begging Lady Gemma to change her mind, Zoticus thought but did not say. Lady Sara already thought he'd been foolish. She did not need to know the entire extent of his idiocy.

But her eyes were wide over the hand she'd used to cover her mouth. "How old were you?"

"When I went home, I was a few weeks shy of my eighteenth birthday. I spent more than a year in Lady Gemma's service."

"Have you seen your boys again?"

Zoticus grinned. "Several times. They both became knights, and while they do occasionally host tourneys, now they have come into their inheritance, they are far too busy managing the vast estate Lady Gemma amassed from her four former husbands to waste as much time on such things as Sir Seducer."

"Do they know you're their father?"

"No! Lady Gemma gave them plenty of father figures, before she chose widowhood again. She contracted some other assassin for the other husbands, as I would not take the contract."

"Did you regret killing the first knight?"

Zoticus hesitated. He suspected most people regretted their first kill, but he never did. "No. He preyed upon children, and felt no guilt for his actions. How many more girls like Amice and Gemma would he have harmed if I had let him live? Death was too good for him, but it was the only justice I could give them, so I did. If Lady Gemma came to me now and asked me to kill her first husband, I would still do it."

"Do you still love her?"

This time, there was no hesitation. "No. I don't think I ever truly did. I was in love with the idea of a woman who wanted me in her bed every night. A boy's brain is in the head of his cock at that age, as I'm sure you know."

Sara snorted with laughter, which sent her into a coughing fit. Zoticus leaped to grab the potion that soothed her throat, which he'd been keeping warm on the hearth.

He helped her sit up so that she could drink, and when she finally had the breath to speak again, she was so close…

"Have you ever loved a woman?"

"Yes." And he'd give everything he owned to lie her down and make love to her right now, but her son was right. She was vulnerable after being so sick, and he had no right to take advantage of this virtuous widow.

So he bade her good night, and took the servants' stairs up to the small chamber he'd claimed as his own.

Thirty

"Open the door, this is heavy!"

Sara woke in daylight to shouts in the passage outside her door. Though she'd been utterly exhausted from Zoticus's healing and whatever the sickness had done to her body, she'd lain awake for far too long last night, her mind churning through all the things he'd said.

He was an assassin, a rat catcher, a hero, a healer, a flirt…he'd been sixteen or seventeen, the same age as Tobias, when fate had turned him into….not so much an assassin as a vigilante. He'd gone after justice, killing a knight for crimes he'd committed, and only circumstances and the horrid Lady Gemma had turned him into an assassin, after the fact.

Such a horrible, heartbreaking story, that she wanted to be fiction, but he'd told it without leaving out his own foolishness, so she knew it had to be true.

He'd brought them here, to the Cloister of Holy Innocents, and healed her with his own blood.

Her thoughts darted back to that first day he'd appeared in the council hall, when he'd announced that he'd save the town from the plague.

He might not have saved everyone in town, but he'd saved enough of them. He'd said that night in the forest that he wouldn't lie to her. Had everything he said been the truth, even when she doubted him?

The door to her chamber burst open, and a parade of people came in.

First came Zoticus with an enormous wooden tub, like a larger version of the one they used to crush the chestnut shells. He set it down before the fire and waved the next person through. The rest were children, each carrying a bucket of water, which they sloshed into the tub. Then they headed out again.

"Four buckets each, and then you may go to the kitchens to get your apple from Sal!" he shouted after them.

"Master Zoticus, my mother is not well. You shouldn't shout like that in here," Tobias said.

Zoticus bowed in her direction. "My deepest apologies, Lady Sara. Now, how would you like me to shout at the children bringing water for your bath?"

Poor Tobias looked lost. He'd spent all his life herding goats and learning to lead the people of Mirroten, but Zoticus was outside of anything he'd ever had to deal with before. Even Sara wasn't sure how to handle him, especially after last night. But she knew she definitely wanted to.

"Your cheeks look flushed, Mother. Has your fever returned? Or is it too hot in here? Should I bank the fire? Or send Raphael down to the stillroom for some medicine? Or are you thirsty? I can send down to the kitchen for some goat's milk…"

"I'm fine. Truly, Tobias. Master Zoticus has taken good care of me. Who knew he had such healing skills? I am still tired today, but perhaps tomorrow I will be well enough to leave my bed. Don't worry about me." She managed a smile, hoping her cheeks had cooled. "I'll ask one of the children to bring me something from the kitchen to break my fast. I'm sure you have more important things to do."

He wrinkled his nose. "I've been trying to teach a few of them to take care of the goats. They're slowly grasping the idea that they must watch them all the time, but teaching them to milk the goats so far has been a disaster. Was I ever so fumble-fingered?"

"Well, you did learn young. As soon as you could walk, you wanted to help with the milking. It takes time and practice. Then again, perhaps your new goatherds simply don't have the right touch for milking. See if you can find some of the children who came from families that owned goats, and whose job it was to do the milking. Even if it's just to help teach the others, with extra skilled hands, the milking will go faster."

Tobias nodded. "Thank you, Mother. It's good to see you well again. I don't know how we've managed without you."

Zoticus stepped forward. "You'll have to manage for some time longer before Lady Sara is truly well again. She still needs rest."

Tobias opened his mouth to argue, but the bucket brigade had returned, and the noisy splashing and clattering as the children filled the bath up further prevented all conversation.

When they were gone, Sara got in first. "I still am terribly tired, Tobias. All I seem to want to do is sleep!"

"Your body needs sleep to heal. It's only natural. Once the children are done bringing up water for your bath, you should sleep again. The water can warm by the fire while you sleep, so it will be ready for you when you wake. In the meantime, I'll go down to the kitchen and fetch you some food." Zoticus bowed again, then departed.

Tobias waited a moment, then dropped his voice. "Mother, are you sure we can trust him? Father Fazzio said he's an assassin, and he has committed so many terrible crimes, the only way he can earn forgiveness for them is to go on a holy crusade. I fear for your life, leaving you alone with him."

Yet Sara had no such qualms. Not any more.

"He has healed me of his own volition, when he had plenty of opportunities to do me harm, yet he did not. He has already been on a crusade, which is more than Father Fazzio has, so I'm not sure the priest is any position to judge him. If Zoticus has a heavy conscience, then that is his burden to bear. He will be judged for his sins at the end of his life, as will we all. Rumours abound about his actions in the past, but who is to say any of it is more than common gossip? What I've seen of his actions since I've met him show him to be selfless, and somewhat of a hero. He saved my life, but he also saved all of us from the plague. We all should be grateful to him, you more than anyone."

"How can you be sure he didn't bring the plague to Mirroten?" Tobias persisted.

Sara considered for a long moment. She couldn't truly be certain but… "Anyone who comes into contact with the plague falls ill. Ysabel was ill before Zoticus arrived, yet Zoticus has showed no signs of illness. He's survived the plague before, but he was still very ill. No, the plague arrived before he did. Before Father Fazzio received word from his bishop about Altino. It must have been Mercurio. Zoticus said he'd seen Mercurio's ship on his way to Mirroten, and Mercurio was already dead of the plague. The hay he brought from Altino must have been tainted. I remember Ysabel and her father saying the first thing they would do with it was to restuff their mattresses..." She closed her eyes. "Poor Ysabel. Ahab wanted you to marry her, when she was old enough, you know."

Tobias edged away from her, as he always did when talk turned to marriage. "I have work to do, Mother. But it is good to see you recovering." When he reached the door, he hurried away.

When Sara could no longer hear his footsteps, the tapestry twitched aside and Zoticus stepped into the room.

"You're wrong, you know. I bear part of the blame for the plague coming to your town, even if it arrived before me. When I returned from that accursed crusade, we boarded three ships at Byzas that had been left behind after a battle gone wrong. The rats aboard carried the plague, and few of us survived the voyage to Rialto. I asked one of the Rialto merchants, a man I trusted, to see that the tainted ships and their cargo were burned. Perhaps he forgot, or perhaps he was too greedy to give up what he saw as his, but he did not burn those ships. And when he died, his sons inherited them. Not knowing their history, they sold the ships and the cargo…to your river trader, Mercurio. So while I may not have carried the plague on my person to your town, I am not blameless in the matter. I should have burned those ships the day they arrived in Rialto. By the time I did burn them, it was too late."

"I should have been more outspoken at the town council meeting, and insisted we take precautions to keep the plague out of Mirroten, and prevent its spread. Instead, I let Ahab overrule me, and allow trade to continue despite the risks. I knew the hay had come from Altino, and I could have commanded it to be burned, but it did not occur to me that it would be necessary until now. It was my duty to save Mirroten, and I failed. None of us are blameless in this, except maybe the children. Children you saved."

"I should have saved more."

"So should I. But we do what we can, try the best we can, and we'll never be able to save everyone." Sara sighed. "Perhaps you should have let me die instead of healing me. So many regrets…"

"No." Zoticus set his tray of food on the table beside her bed. "The moment I arrived in Mirroten, I knew I was not too late to save someone, at least. I knew you would survive the plague, but only if you left Mirroten."

"How…?"

He wet his lips. "I saw a vision of you. Here. Well, in the bailey here, not this bedchamber."

Sara paled. "You mean you saw me dead, like your friend Amice?"

"No. I saw you alive, very much alive. You run across the bailey. That's all I see."

Relief trickled into her chest, making it easier to breathe again. "Then your vision won't happen today, as I feel far too weak to walk across this room, let alone run anywhere."

Zoticus smiled. "Ah, that I can help with. You should have some of this broth, while it's still warm, and then see if you can sleep again. You'll regain your strength faster while you're asleep."

"Will you be here when I wake?" She wasn't sure why it was so important to her, but it was.

"Where else would I be?"

Thirty-One

By the time Lady Sara woke again, her son had already barred her door for the night. If Zoticus had had any sense, he'd have stayed on the other side of that door, and let her bathe in peace.

But as he evidently had no sense, he gave in to his selfish desire to watch over her while she slept. After all, he had said he'd be there when she woke, and he valued her good opinion. Perhaps more than he should.

He'd set out supper for the two of them on the table and checked a dozen times to make sure the water was warm. He'd left a pile of stones on the hearth, ready to drop into her bath to heat the water even more when she was ready. He'd even brought out his enchanted candle, which warmed a room better than any fire could. He was taking no chances that she'd catch another chill.

Lady Sara's eyes fluttered open. She took in the room with a single glance, then said, "Alone at last." There was a throaty purr to her voice, just like she'd had on the day he met her. She really was recovering.

Zoticus bowed his head. "I will leave you alone to bathe, if you wish it." Though he hoped she didn't.

"Some healer you are. What if I am too weak to walk to the bath? Please stay and stand watch while a stubborn old woman washes."

He snorted. "You're not old, Lady Sara. You cannot be a day older than me."

"But I am stubborn. I see. Ooh, is that supper? Am I allowed to eat something before I have my bath?"

"If your appetite has returned, it's a very good sign. Yes, if you're hungry, you should eat." He eyed her for a moment. "Do you feel up to sitting at the table, or would you prefer to eat in bed?"

"I haven't spent this long in bed since I was a new bride."

His mouth gaped. Had she really said that?

Sara winked. "It was so much softer than rolling around in the pasture or the hayloft, and when there's no one to interrupt, you can take more time to really enjoy yourself." She glanced at the door. "I take it the door's barred again?"

"Yes. Though your son found a padlock to fasten it with today, too, so he could sleep in his own bed, instead of outside your chamber tonight."

"Was that your doing?"

Already she knew him too well.

"Perhaps. It might have just been a happy accident."

He shouldn't have done it. Without the boy listening outside the door, he might do something reckless…

"I think we should have supper at the table," she said, thankfully interrupting his thoughts before they went too far.

"Yes."

He carried her over to the table, and, for a

time, they ate in silence. Zoticus finished his portion before she was halfway done with hers, so he headed for the hearth to heat up her bath. He used tongs to transfer the hot stones into the water, which hissed and steamed where the stones hit the surface. After a few minutes, he tested the temperature, then took out the stones. "The bath is ready when you are," he said.

A rustling sound behind him made him turn.

He could do nothing but stare.

She'd slipped out of her shift and stood naked beside her chair.

He'd never seen anything so beautiful in his life. He didn't have the words to describe her.

And then he did, just one: soft.

So soft he ached to touch her, kiss her, everywhere…

Which, of course, made him, her opposite, suddenly hard.

"I'll help you," he said, rushing to her side. He lifted her up and carried her to the bath, then let her down gently into the water. He dropped to his knees beside the tub, hoping she hadn't noticed. Then his traitorous hand picked up the washcloth and he found himself asking, "What would you like me to wash first?"

What happened next he could only describe as pure agony. Stroking the soap and the cloth over her skin, reminding himself every moment that he was her healer, yet aware of her every breath, each time she closed her eyes, and every time she moved to grant him better access to her magnificent body. At least when he was on his knees, his tunic hid his erection.

"I think I'm clean now." She sounded regretful.

Now he had to help her out of the bath, dry her, and get her back to bed. Without her seeing that his mind was full of very un-healer-ish thoughts.

He held up the towel like a shield. "Climb out, then."

When she was finally back in bed, mercifully covered by the sheets, he tried to form an excuse so that he could escape before she saw.

"The water's still warm. You should have a bath, too," she said.

"Yes." His tongue had turned traitor, too.

Now he had no choice but to turn his back and take his clothes off.

Thirty-Two

Sara knew she was wicked to watch Zoticus undress and climb into the bath, particularly when her body was most definitely showing her age and held no attraction for him, but she wasn't getting any younger, and this might be her last chance to see a good looking man naked.

The muscles that had only been hinted at when hidden by his tunic were all on display now. She could see how he'd lifted her so easily. Yet he'd been so gentle when he handled her in the bath.

If he'd shown the slightest spark of interest,

she'd happily invite him to share her bed. Actually, she wasn't above begging. She hadn't ached this badly for a man since…since…she could not remember.

"I can feel your eyes on me. What are you thinking?" he asked.

She wasn't sure whether she wanted to laugh or cry. "I was wishing I was a young maiden again, pretty and comely still, so that I might tempt you to come to my bed."

There. Let him think what he liked of her.

His shoulders hunched, then he turned to face her. "Lady Sara, I cannot believe that you have ever been more beautiful or irresistible than you are now." He slowly rose, and the water cascaded off him.

She couldn't stop staring.

"That looks painful," she managed to say.

"I've been thus…afflicted since you first took off your shift. I've never been so powerless to control myself since I was a boy."

Just the sight of him, jutting out so pointedly, made her braver. "Come to bed."

He began to dry himself. "I want to do that more than anything, but I keep reminding myself how deathly ill you have been, that you are still weak, that I should not take advantage of you while you are so vulnerable. I'm first and foremost your healer, and you should be resting."

Sara smiled. "I promise not to leave the bed."

Zoticus muttered an oath, half under his breath.

He hung the damp towel over a chair, revealing the full glory of his naked body.

No, she was not too proud to beg. Not when they both wanted this.

"On the road, when I fainted, I thought I was dying. My last thought, my only regret, was that I hadn't had my way with you, that night we were alone in the forest camp."

He stared at her for a long moment. "I'm a fool. I should have told you that night that no one had commissioned me to kill your son. I didn't know the boy existed until you mentioned him, and I would never accept a contract for a child."

She should have been surprised, but she wasn't. When she'd first heard he was an assassin, she'd put two and two together and arrived at a conclusion that simply wasn't possible. She would never have suspected such a thing of the man she knew now. The man who'd saved them all, including her. And that was only a part of why she wanted him so much.

She shrugged her shoulders and let the sheets fall away. She hadn't put a shift on after her bath, so now he could see everything, too. "We all have our moments of madness. Right now, I want to savour being alive, and celebrate how you saved me, and I want to do it all naked in bed with you."

She'd never imagined he could improve upon his courtly bow, but seeing him doing it naked was a memory she'd treasure. The way all those muscles bunched up just so…

"As my lady commands."

Thirty-Three

For a moment, she'd looked as nervous as a new bride. Then her expression had turned hungry as she'd talked of madness in that purring tone and Zoticus was lost.

He found himself kneeling between her thighs on the bed, a breath away from burying himself deep inside her.

"Yes," she whispered.

No. Once he was inside her, he wouldn't last more than a moment, and he might never have this chance again.

He leaned forward and captured her lips. This kiss was slow and deliberate, nothing like that first one he'd stolen with barely a thought, before a vision had mercifully stopped him from going any further. But now, the only vision he saw was her half-lidded eyes, begging him for more even as she returned his kiss.

Her breasts were soft as silk in his hands, until her hardening nipples made their presence known. Only then did he release her lips, leaving a light trail of kisses down her neck and collarbone.

"I want to feel you inside me, Zoticus," she said.

He wanted that, too, but not yet.

He ran his hand down her belly, through her downy curls and then slid his finger inside her. He hooked it…

She cried out, arching her back.

His fingers worked their magic, but it was her breasts that had his attention now, thrust up toward him as they were. He sucked hard on the nearest nipple, was rewarded by her moan, and took his time on one breast, then the other, until he felt her clenching around his finger.

"Yes, yes…" she whispered.

No.

First, he wanted to give her the pleasure of an unforgettable kiss.

He lifted her legs over his shoulders, so they spread beautifully wide.

With both hands now, he parted her lower lips, seeing them glisten in the candlelight. If he'd been in any doubt that she wanted him...

"What are you doing? I want you inside me, not...looking at my..." She blushed, like a bride seeing her first cock.

"You'll see, Lady Sara. I promise you'll like it. Just as I like looking at you." And then his tongue was too busy for talking, too busy tasting, for his fingers had brought her to the brink and it only took a few strokes to tip her over...

Thirty-Four

Sara had barely a moment to realise that Zoticus had slipped his tongue inside her before sensation overwhelmed her, and all she could do was scream his name.

When she opened her eyes, she saw he'd risen onto his knees, lifting her legs with him.

"Why…" she began.

His hot, hard head entered her then, and she no longer cared why. All she cared about was the tortuously slow thrust as he filled her. She could scarcely breathe, he felt so good.

"Lady Sara, are you all right? Did I hurt you?"

She opened her eyes to see his concern, but it took her a few swallows before she found her voice to respond.

"Heavens, no, but it's…so long…"

"Forgive me, did I go too deep? I shouldn't have…" He started to lower her legs, and it felt like he was starting to slip out of her.

"No! You're not too long. I mean it's so long since I've shared a bed, I'd forgotten it could be this good." Sara felt her face grow hot. "Please don't stop."

He laughed softly, then leaned forward to kiss her, pushing into her to the very hilt.

Oh, yes. She must have said it aloud, for he smiled and began to move, never taking his eyes off hers. He started off slow, but as passion kindled in his eyes, lit by the blaze between their joined bodies, each thrust became harder, faster, until she felt herself clenching around him, sucking in a breath to scream his name again.

"Oh God, Sara!"

They came at the same moment, the most exquisite pleasure marred only by its ending.

He covered her face and her breasts with kisses, still breathing hard. Then he threw himself down on the bed beside her.

"The second time will be slower, I promise," he said. "Slow and gentle, like I should've done the first time."

Her thighs still ached from the first time, and everything in between was tingling. Slow and gentle might be nice, too, but…

"Then the third time, I want hard and fast again," she said. As if anyone could make love three times in a single night.

Zoticus began to laugh. "And what does my lady command me to do on the fourth time we make love?"

"I don't know," she admitted, "but earlier, I had hoped you'd join me in the bath. Maybe…"

"Ah, speaking of baths, I should probably get us cleaned up." He produced a bowl and a wash cloth and proceeded to do just that. Until he started stroking the cloth between her thighs in just the right place, and she couldn't help but arch her back up…

The cloth splashed back into the bowl, to be replaced by his fingers and the rasp of his hot tongue.

"And the fifth, my lady?" he asked. "And

the sixth, and the seventh?"

His tongue rejoined his fingers and she could no longer think. All she wanted was him.

"Have me…however you like. As many times as possible. As long as…you don't…stop. Don't…stop…Zoticus! Oh my God!"

He was the very spirit of constancy, for he most certainly did not stop, though she screamed his name until she was hoarse. And she didn't want him to – not now, not ever.

One night would never be enough.

Thirty-Five

The next morning, Sara awoke to a light tap on her door. "Are you awake, Mother?" Tobias asked.

In panic, her eyes darted to the bed beside her, but Zoticus had already gone. Some hours ago, judging by how cold the sheets there were compared to last night. A pity. She wouldn't have minded one more round before breakfast…would it count as the eighth time in a night, if the sun had risen?

She really shouldn't be thinking such things with her son standing outside the door.

"Come in," she called.

Tobias shouldered his way through the door, carrying a tray with what she presumed was her breakfast on it. "I brought you something to eat, and a tisane from Raphael that he said will help you regain your strength."

It wouldn't be as potent as Zoticus's healing amulet, which he'd insisted on using on her again last night after the third time they'd made love, but she wouldn't refuse anything that might help her recover. She wanted many more nights like last night.

"Thank you," she said. "How did the milking go this morning?"

"A little better. With more people to show how it was done, instead of just me, we ended up with more milk in the buckets, less on the floor, and it was finished before breakfast, for the first time. Sal's been checking what provisions they have in the cellars here, and aside from a lot of cider, there isn't much to see them through the winter. There's an orchard of chestnut trees on the slopes below the monastery, and they're ready for harvest, so I set some of the boys the task of collecting nuts. Silvana said there's a smoke house beside the mill. It's not as big as ours, but it will give them something to do. She says she can operate the mill, too, if I find her a couple of hands to help. The apple trees will yield well in the autumn…" He stopped. "Forgive me. I want to show you everything, but of course I can't until you are well. Do you think you will be able to join us for dinner today in the great hall? Everyone meets there at midday, and so many people have asked about you. If they only saw that you are well, or on the way to it…"

If she could spend half the night making love with Zoticus, she could easily sit at a high table for an hour. She might need help getting there, but she could work that part out later. "Sure," she said.

"Wonderful!" Tobias kissed her cheek. "Thank you, Mother. Some of the children are so scared, they think you have the plague! Where they came up with such a silly idea, I can't imagine."

Given she'd suspected the same thing, the scared children weren't as silly as Tobias thought, but she didn't say so.

"We'll be safe here. I shall tell everyone so at dinner," she said instead.

Thirty-Six

Zoticus stayed away as long as he could, but eventually his feet found their way back to Sara's chamber. Perhaps he should have asked her permission to heal her again, but she'd looked so peaceful last night, sleeping in his arms, and he couldn't bear the thought that his selfish night with her might delay her recovery, so he'd fed more blood to the amulet than was really wise.

He'd been lightheaded when he made his way back up to his own cold bed, but it was for the best. Lady Sara was the virtuous widow everyone looked up to, and he would not take her reputation from her. She would have the strength to lead what remained of her people when it was time to return to her town, and he would be gone.

But instead of doing the sensible thing and creeping out the gate last night, he'd weakened himself so much from the blood loss that he'd decided to delay for another day.

The sight of her now was enough to make him both regret and rejoice in his decision.

She wore a fawn wool gown today, which looked golden in the sunlight streaming through the open window. Someone – heaven forbid she'd done it herself – had opened the shutters for her, and she sat in a chair before the window, where she might admire the view over the valley.

Then she saw him, and the smile that lit her face sent a bolt right through his heart. "Zoticus! I feared you were too busy to come see me today, and I need your help. I promised my son I would attend the midday meal in the great hall, but I suspect I will need your help getting there. Crossing the room and donning some clothes was not too taxing, but finding my way around an unfamiliar castle...I fear I might get lost and not have the strength to return to where someone might find me."

His heart sank. So his healing last night had not been enough to ward off any ill effects from their lovemaking. He'd have to heal her again today, before he departed.

"I'll take you down to the great hall, and bring you back when you are ready," he said.

He expected her to rise and walk with him, but she just sat in her seat, looking up at him expectantly.

She wanted him to take her in his arms again. Even after he'd exhausted her last night.

He swallowed. Then, selfish wretch that he was, he scooped her up and carried her out of the room.

She felt even softer clad in warm wool than she had last night. It took every bit of his willpower not to turn around and take her back to bed, where he would join her and…

No. If she didn't appear at dinner, someone would come looking, find them together, and that would not end well for her.

So he forced himself to march right down to the great hall, ascend the dais, and set her in the place of honour at the centre of the table.

Tobias's usual place, until today.

Her fingers wrapped around his arm, tugging him down to her level. He expected her to say something for only his ears, but first she kissed his cheek before she said, "Thank you," loud enough for anyone nearby to hear.

He glanced around. Some of the children had entered the hall, finding their seats. Then someone caught sight of Sara, sitting at the high table, and the excited chatter began.

Zoticus wanted to sit at her side, as close as possible, ready to help her in an instant, should she need him, but he forced himself to move down the table, to the furthest seat to her left, where he might watch her without being so conspicuous.

The Younger Council, as he called them, to distinguish them from their predecessors in Mirroten, entered the hall. Tobias and Silvana sat on Sara's right and left hands, and the others took their places along the bench until there was no space left, except for the careful distance the brewer's boy kept between himself and Zoticus.

When everyone was seated, Tobias rose to his feet. "I want to thank everyone for all their work over the last week, preparing the castle for the coming winter and helping with the harvest. We may be here until the spring, or longer, depending on how long before the plague is gone and we may go home, but when we depart, we must make sure that the monastery is better supplied than when we arrived. And to guide us in our preparations, joining us today is my mother, Mistress Sara!"

Applause and cheers rang out across the hall.

Zoticus frowned. Sara was still recovering. She could not be expected to shoulder the burden of setting an entire castle in order is such a short time.

Raphael raised his cup. "A toast to Mistress Sara's health!" he shouted.

The whole hall followed suit, then drank deeply.

Sara smiled graciously through it all, but when they sat down, she scanned the crowd, searching for someone. Once, twice, three times her gaze circled the room, before she saw something that turned her face deathly pale.

Zoticus was on his feet, striding to her side

before he could think. "Lady Sara is easily tired, and must return to her chamber to rest," he shouted. She did not resist as he lifted her from the chair and spirited her out of the room.

It wasn't until he laid her in her bed that he dared to breathe again. "What's wrong?" he demanded.

Her voice came out half strangled. "It's Tola, and her daughter, Swanhild. I didn't see them in the hall. Did they not make it to the monastery?" Tears spilled from her eyes.

Zoticus racked his brain, but he could not remember seeing them at all. "Swanhild wasn't among the children in the church. I don't think either of them joined our pilgrimage."

Sara started to sob. He hesitated only a moment before he pulled her into his arms to let her cry into his chest.

"Tola and Swanhild are witches. They have powers normal people do not. If anyone can survive a plague, it's a witch. They are likely in hiding somewhere, too, waiting for it to be safe to go home. If you wish, I will go and search for them, and wherever they are hiding, I will find them, and send them home to you," he said. It was the least he could do for her when he left – send her friend back to her.

She sat up, sniffling. "What would I do without you, Zoticus?"

She'd do everything she did before she met him, he suspected, and her life would go back to normal. It was for the best.

Thirty-Seven

Zoticus soon left, saying something about getting her some food. Sara expected him to return, but Sal brought up her tray instead, asking after her health and telling her how much more complicated it was running a castle kitchen compared to helping her mother in the inn back home.

Several hours later, Sal returned, swapping the empty dinner tray for Sara's supper, but Zoticus was still absent.

"Do you know where Zoticus is?" Sara asked her.

Sal shrugged. "Master Zoticus is most

mysterious, but in the mornings, he comes down a flight of stairs near the kitchen. I suspect his bedchamber is at the top of those stairs."

Sara thanked the girl, trying not to show her disappointment. She knew those stairs led to her own bedchamber, not Zoticus's.

But it couldn't hurt to take a look.

She closed the door, so no one would see, before pulling the tapestry aside. A spiral stair wound its way past the exposed archway, heading both up and down.

Down to the kitchens…up to where?

She craned her neck and thought she might see some light at the top, but she wasn't sure.

Was she well enough to ascend the stairs, to see what lay at the top? She could always stop and rest on the way, if she needed to.

One turn, then another, and partway around a third before she emerged into a round room, barely big enough for the pallet that took up most of the floor. Zoticus's sack of belongings sat beside it, and his cloak hung from a peg on the wall. The shuttered windows were all closed, but the light she'd seen came from a candle left burning beside his bed.

It looked like his room at the inn, or the cellar at the mill where he'd been held prisoner. Like he'd just left a moment ago, and he didn't intend to come back.

He'd talked of going to search for Tola and Swanhild. Surely he hadn't…

Sara fell to her knees on the pallet. "Please, no," she whimpered.

"What are you doing here?"

His footsteps were so silent, she hadn't known he was on the stairs until he spoke.

Something told her she should stand up, but Sara stubbornly stayed on her knees. "I came looking for you. You're leaving, aren't you?"

He inclined his head. "Of course. My work here is done. You and the children of your town are safe, the plague ships are burned, and the Bishop of Rialto wants a word with me. I thought I'd head down to Rialto, and tell him the only word I have for him is no, and maybe find your friend. Then, who knows? There are plenty of wicked knights in the world who are still breathing. I'd like to see how many I can stop."

"Did last night mean nothing to you? You said you loved me. Was that a lie?" she challenged him.

His shoulders slumped, and her heart sank along with them. She'd been a fool to believe him.

"Last night was wondrous, and I shall remember it all my days. Whether I love your or not, it does not matter, for an infamous assassin and a virtuous widow have no future together."

"Did you lie to me?" She had to know.

"Lady Sara, I have never lied to you. I love you as I have never loved any other woman, and I will treasure the one night fate allowed us to share together. Which is why I must leave you here where you will be safe, while I go and do…all the things an assassin does. Things of which you do not approve."

"If you leave, I would go with you."

"You cannot. They need you here."

She snorted. "They do not. Tobias has already taken leadership of the young people of Mirroten, and there are others who have already formed his council. You saw that as well as I did today. They will not be children much longer, and when they realise that, they will not need me."

He froze, his eyes fixed on the wall or on something far away. A vision, Sara realised.

"What did you see?" she demanded.

He dropped to his knees on the pallet, too. "The same as I always see. If I leave, you will run across the bailey in your black travelling cloak. Whether I will it or no, you will follow me." He closed his eyes. "Sara, I must keep you safe. You must stay here."

She grasped his hands in hers. "Only if you stay here with me."

He met her gaze. "I'm a selfish man, Sara. If I stay, it is only a matter of time before I am tempted to share your bed again. What will the children…what will your son say when he finds out?"

"Does it matter? I've spent my whole life caring for their town. You saved them. Don't you think we're owed a little happiness? And if we find it together, who has the right to judge us?"

Zoticus still didn't smile. "Well, the Bishop of Rialto, for one. If he is not happy with me, he might come after you."

"The Bishop of Rialto relies on my generosity to keep this monastery going. If he comes after me, he will soon find it very injurious to his purse. Not to mention, if he'd sent word earlier about Altino, he might have saved the people of our town. He will not like me laying those deaths at his door. He's always coveted my family's lands. Perhaps he delayed so that Tobias and I would die along with the rest of Mirroten, and he might have my lands for himself. Well, he shall not have them. All he will have is the sharp edge of my tongue."

He stared at her in wonder. "Is there anything you do not have an answer for? Anything you actually fear?"

"Losing those I love."

"Could you love an assassin?"

She cocked her head. "Only if you come back downstairs to my bed. This pallet is a bit small for the two of us…"

"If I share your bed again, I will never want to leave."

She smiled. "Then we have a deal."

Zoticus shook his head. "You drive a hard bargain, Lady Sara."

Sara laughed and reached under his tunic. "No, I believe the hardness is all yours."

Thirty-Eight

Just when Sara seemed to finally have recovered, she fell ill again. Instead of coughing, infection or the plague, however, this illness made her unable to eat without being terribly sick. She refused to drink anything but water, and no matter how much he used the healing amulet, it only seemed to make her worse.

"The sounds of me retching must have driven Tobias away from my door," Sara said one morning, when they emerged from her chamber to go down to breakfast.

Worry still ate at him, but that managed to

make him laugh. "Oh, it's not you who drove him away, but a girl his own age who has caught his eye. He's been sleeping with the others, hoping to get closer to her, since the night we first made love, or he'd likely have broken down the door at the sound of your screaming."

Sara blushed. She had the saltiest tongue when they were alone in their bedchamber, but she still blushed like a maiden. "You surprised me, that's all. I did not expect you to be such an accomplished lover."

Zoticus snorted. "The first time, maybe. But by the seventh time, and every night after the first, you were definitely not surprised."

The smell of cooking wafted up the stairs.

Sara froze, then bolted back to her chamber. Zoticus found her noisily throwing up in the chamber pot.

He dug out a rag for her to wipe her mouth and handed it to her when she was finished.

Sara stared at the rag for a moment. "How long since I've had my monthly courses?"

Zoticus shrugged. "You haven't had them since we arrived. I didn't realise you still had those. When women reach a certain age, they usually stop, leaving more nights for lovemaking." He wasn't going to complain. For three months he'd shared Sara's bed, and he knew he never wanted to leave it.

She swatted him lightly. "Yes, but I'm not that old. I still get them, or I did…you said once that the amulet let you sense the blood coursing through my veins, when I had that infection. Could you…could you use it to see if there is something else growing inside me?"

She climbed up on the bed, tugging the skirt of her gown up over her waist, baring her belly and everything beneath.

Zoticus's breath caught in his throat. He wanted to take his own clothes off and…

"The amulet," she reminded him.

Right. In a moment, then.

He pulled out the amulet, and she guided his hand down to her belly. For someone who ate so little, it made no sense for it to be rounded. Not as soft as he remembered, either. A chill went down his spine. There were other incurable diseases, worse than the plague, that he also could not heal. No, not Sara…

He could hear his heart racing, the opposite of her slow, steady beat. No, a heart rate that fast would have him breathing hard and feeling like it was bursting out of his chest.

He placed his spare hand at his throat, feeling for the rapid flutter he knew he should find there.

But his pulse kept pace with Sara's.

"I'm pregnant, aren't I?" Sara asked.

Pregnant? How?

Now he knew what to look for, he moved the amulet lower, and there she was. Heart beating like a frightened bird, tiny arms and legs reaching out for a hug she could not yet have, and all of her seemed to twinkle, like she was made up of a million tiny stars, sitting just beneath her skin…

Absolutely magical.

"She's beautiful," Zoticus breathed. His daughter. His and Sara's daughter. Which meant all those magic sparkles… "She's an enchantress. So much magic in her blood, she cancels out anything I can do with the amulet." Memory twinged, the shared magical memories from so many generations. "While you carry her, your blood mingles with hers. You should wear the amulet. It will heal you both, more than I ever could." He hung it around her neck, then helped her smooth down her skirts. "Let's go down to breakfast. If you're eating for two, you cannot miss a meal."

Sara shook her head, a look of wonder on her face. "I never thought I'd have another child. Not after Tobias. And a girl, too…she'll be born in the spring. If Tola were here, she'd be my midwife, or even Swanhild, but without them…I think I'm the only one here who has handled a birth before. And I'll be in too much pain to do everything myself. Where will we find a midwife?"

The first snowfall had closed the road the week before – not even the monks would be getting through until spring.

"I will do it. I've helped on a few deliveries before. My mother was the village healer, and she did most of them, but women would go into labour at the same time, and I knew enough to handle the easy ones…" Zoticus heard himself say the words, but they did not console him. This was Sara, not some peasant woman popping out her twentieth child from hips so wide she took up two places on a bench. "I'll find you a midwife, even if I have to dig through snow from here to Rialto. You and our daughter will be fine, I promise." The words felt right, though worry still niggled at him.

Sara's lips touched his, and all other thoughts flew away. "Thank you," she said. "You keep delivering miracles. Saving us, saving me, and now…you've given me the sweetest gift of all. A daughter I'd never dared hope for. If there were a priest in the castle, I'd make him marry us right now, for everything I have, everything I am…I would give you, and it would not be enough, to repay you for such a gift."

His heart soared. Yes, if he could marry any woman, he'd want Sara, but she'd never be safe. All it would take was one unscrupulous would-be client who threatened her life, and Zoticus would be forced to assassinate someone he did not want to kill. Worse, they might hurt Sara…

He would not let that happen.

But now was not the time or place, and there was no priest present, so he forced a smile upon his face as he said lightly, "Wait until the mite is born before you thank me. I'm told babies do nothing but cry and steal your sleep, not to mention the ordeal of her birth. You'll be cursing me, come spring, I'm certain of it."

Sara's smile only grew wider. "Come spring, she'll steal your heart as surely as you hold mine. You'll see."

He would, but he hoped he'd find a midwife well before then. He might have healed Sara once, but he knew he'd be tempting fate to take her health in his hands again.

Thirty-Nine

As Zoticus dug his way through the snow covering the road for what felt like the hundredth time that year, he cursed. He hated snow, he hated ice, and more than anything else, he hated the sulphur-coloured clouds heading their way that would likely dump another load of the stuff, undoing all his good work. Wasn't it supposed to be spring already?

If the snow didn't thaw soon, he knew he'd be delivering Sara's baby. He'd tried to confine her to her chamber, or even just the castle, but she was having none of it. Three times a day, she waddled out to the duckpond, determined to have eggs if the ducks had laid any. He lived in constant dread that she'd slip on the ice, or the stairs, or trip over one of the baby goats that no one seemed able to control. He'd even gone through his magic pouch, trying to find something that would keep her safe, or at least help her keep her balance. All he'd found was a cloak pin enchanted to keep the rain off whoever wore it, and Sara wasn't silly enough to go out in the rain.

She was, however, perfectly happy to waddle out for the second time today, wearing his warmest grey cloak, for it was the only one wide enough to fasten over her enormous round belly. Her words, not his, but no matter how much he agreed with her, he wasn't brave enough to say so where she might hear.

She disappeared around the corner of the woodshed, and Zoticus went back to work, shovelling snow.

A flash of light in the corner of his eye made him turn. If there'd been anything but clear skies there, he'd have thought he'd seen lightning, but he couldn't have. The storm clouds were still on the other side of the valley.

A shriek reached his ears – that sounded like

Sara. He dropped his shovel and ran toward the woodshed.

Another flash of light, on the far side of the woodshed, followed by silence.

He rounded the corner, to find no one there. Sara's footprints just ended, as though a giant eagle had swooped in and carried her off.

Oh God, she hadn't fallen into the duckpond...

No, it was still frozen over, and yards away.

"Sara!" he shouted. "Sara!"

Zoticus staggered through the snow, searching for some sign of where she'd gone. He found Raphael near the kitchen gardens, shovelling snow away from the plants. "Have you seen Sara?" he asked.

Raphael leaned on his shovel, thoughtful. "I don't think I've seen her today, but she did ask for some willow bark to be sent up, and water to make tea. But that was hours ago. I imagine if she has a headache, though, she'd have stayed in her chamber. Have you checked there?"

Zoticus wasn't sure whether to laugh or cry in frustration. The only times Sara stayed in her chamber were when she was asleep or making love with him. She wouldn't be there now. Not when he'd just seen her in the courtyard.

One of the younger girls – Zoticus guessed she might be six or seven – raced through the kitchen door, skidded across the ice patch outside, then broke into a run on the snow without breaking stride.

"Master Zoticus, Master Zoticus!" she shouted.

"I'm here, child. What is it? Is it Lady Sara?"

He hoped so, but she'd come from inside the castle. It couldn't be.

"Mistress Dalia demands your presence in the best bedchamber right now!"

Mother. No, it couldn't be.

"Who did you say wants me?" he asked carefully.

The panic in the girl's voice grew. "Mistress Dalia, the midwife, says you must attend her right now!"

He wasn't a praying man, but if there was one midwife he'd wanted here, it would be her. What she couldn't cure with her normal skills, she might with magic.

"Thank you," he said, breaking into a run.

He jumped the ice patch, skidding a little on the step, before taking the stairs two at a time to the upper levels. He could scarcely breathe by the time he reached the door to Sara's chamber, but…

"Heavens, it hurts!"

That was Sara's voice, raw with pain.

"Well, if that boy would hurry up and get here, he might be able to do something about that!"

He had to smile. His mother was the only person in the world who'd call him a boy.

"Finally!" Mother snapped when he walked in. "Get over here and help your wife up. She's about to have your baby, so the least you can do is hold her in the right position so it hurts less!"

He considered correcting her, but the pained groan that came out of Sara made him forget everything else. Whether she was his wife or not, he'd help her get through this however he had to. Thank the Heavens his mother was here to help.

He drew Sara off the bed, careful to support her weight as she stood up, before she doubled over in pain as another contraction gripped her. This was where most husbands panicked, needing to be sent out of the room in search of something that took a long time to find, sometimes quite forcefully. Zoticus understood some of their panic – he wished he didn't have to see Sara in so much pain – but he'd be damned before anyone sent him away. It might take all his strength to bear her weight when she wanted to collapse with each contraction, but he'd hold her, for as long as it took.

"After this, I don't want any more children," Sara said, before the next contraction caught her in its toils.

"Never fear, she'll be your last," Mother said, dropping to her knees at Sara's feet. She'd laid a pile of cloths on the cold stone, ready to catch the baby. There were more draped over a bench beside the fire, warming in readiness to swaddle the child when she was born. "Now, Sara, it's time to push."

The sounds that came from Sara's throat were more animal than human as she strained and pushed until finally, when his arms felt like they'd fall off after holding her up so long, a shrill child's scream rose from the floor.

With her red, scrunched-up face and bloody fluid coating her body, the girl looked more like a demon than a human, but Zoticus didn't care. He knew she'd be the most beautiful girl in his world before the day was done.

"Take care of the baby, Tick, while I deal with the afterbirth," Mother ordered.

He didn't hesitate. He scooped up the angry, bawling baby, and wrapped her in the softest, warmest cloth on the bench. When she seemed likely to wriggle free, he added a second cloth, but it just wouldn't wrap right. It had been so long since he'd helped with a birth, and he'd never been given the baby before. There must be some trick to it, something his mother hadn't taught him, but it was buried in his magical memories somewhere, if only he could find it.

"Give her to me." Sara's voice was soft and hoarse, but he did not dare disobey her order.

He turned, to find Sara sitting up in bed, her arms out in readiness.

Wordlessly, he handed the child to her mother.

It took scarcely a moment for Sara to wrap the baby properly, before putting the child to her breast.

Zoticus's breath caught in his throat. He'd never seen a more beautiful sight. The woman he loved holding their child.

"Stop staring at her breasts, Tick, and go get your wife some dinner. She's just fought the battle of her life, and she's eating for two. See that the meat is well-cooked, and that there is not too much wine with it."

He wanted to stay, but he knew it wasn't worth his life to disobey. Not with both women ordering him about.

When he reached the bottom of the stairs, he met Tobias and Silvana. "Is Sara all right?" Silvana asked. "Raphael said she'd gone into labour."

Zoticus broke into a smile. "Sara is well, and so is the baby. A girl. She's resting now, but they are both well." And in the best possible hands, he added to himself. He skipped the rest of the way to the kitchen, determined to bring Sara the best, heartiest meal he could provide.

Forty

Sara waited until Zoticus was out of earshot before she said, "You're mistaken. I'm not his wife."

Dalia waved a hand like she was shooing away a fly. "Pah, but you will be. My Tick has done some foolish things in his life – that cold bitch Gemma, for one – but finding you is not one of them. He's still an assassin, with all the dangers that come with that job, but he'll always come back to you. He loves you."

Sara's breath caught in her throat. "You mean I'll lose him, just like my first husband." She didn't think her heart could bear losing him, too.

Dalia chuckled. "Oh, no, you'll never lose him. True to his name, my Tick will stick to you until the end of your days. He'll outlive us all, you'll see. You, me, even his twin sister, Zoraida. This little one and Zoraida's daughters will be the only ones left when he's an old, old man, dying in his sleep."

Sara allowed herself to breathe again. "I'd ask how you know, but he has the gift of future sight. I take it he inherited it from you?"

Dalia nodded. "Tick always kept his gifts secret. No one outside the family knew he had magic at all. If he's told you, he already considers you family. He'll make you his wife, soon enough."

Sara wasn't so sure, but she didn't think it wise to argue with Zoticus's mother. Not only had she just delivered her baby, but she was a powerful enchantress who could probably turn her into a newt if she offended her. "Why do you call him Tick?" she asked instead.

"Twas Zoraida's doing. She complained that he always followed her and her friends around like a bothersome tick, when they were small children, and somehow the name stuck. Of course, it's no sort of name for a fearsome assassin, and it did not make him popular with the girls in the town where he grew up, but my Zoticus has made his name known and feared all about the world. I think more people fear him than his sister, though she has magic and he has little of it. Funny how things turn out." She fixed Sara with her steely eye. "Now, speaking of names, what do you intend to name my granddaughter?"

"I'd thought Rossa, after my mother, who had red hair, but I wanted to discuss it with Zoticus first…"

Dalia nodded. "Rossa. I like it. As will he, when he's done getting you the fanciest dinner the castle kitchens can provide. But I sent him away so that I might have a word."

Sara pressed her lips together and nodded. Her mother in law might say many words, but Sara's word was law here, and once her mother in law left, Sara would decide what might happen, not Dalia.

"Now, little Rossa here is a witch. A mighty powerful one, like her aunt and her cousin. Likely she'll be an enchantress, too, able to cast portals and any other spell she turns her hand to. She'll have a fairy godmother, most likely Zoraida's girl, Zuleika. I wish I could do it, but I won't live long enough to be there when she needs me. She'll have you and Zoticus, and that's good."

Sara found herself nodding. She'd have to ask Zoticus about enchantresses, and how to stop one from lighting the house on fire or shaking apart the mountain when she threw a tantrum. Cousins…she could deal with when she met them. She shifted so that she could switch the baby to her other breast, and hissed as pain erupted from her nether regions.

Dalia blinked. "By all that's holy, I forgot to heal you. Don't tell Tick!" She dipped her hand in the bucket that held the afterbirth, and it came up dripping with blood. She seized the healing amulet that hung around Sara's neck in her bloody hand, and held it tight for a long moment.

Sara felt a tingling sensation start in her chest, then spread like lightning through her body. Heat built uncomfortably in her nether regions, but it faded quickly, taking the pain with it, leaving Sara gasping.

"Little Rossa's blood is more powerful than

Tick's," Dalia said knowingly.

It was like comparing a candle to the sun. When she was ill, he'd healed her over an entire week, and she'd still felt tired. Now…she feared if she could listen to her heart, she'd hear her blood singing in her veins.

"When she's old enough, give her the amulet to wear always. It will heal her, like it healed Zoticus, even if she's on the cusp of death." Dalia laid a box on the bed. "I brought you some wedding gifts, too. Seeing as I won't be invited to your wedding."

Sara lifted the lid. Inside sat a black wool cloak, lined with silk, and fastened with a silver pin in the shape of a flower. "They're very fine. Thank you."

Dalia make an impatient sound in her throat. "Yes, they're fine, such as might be worn by a lady of your station, but it's the magic in them that makes them valuable. The brooch will heal you, much like the amulet does my son or your daughter, but there is no blood price to pay. I already paid it when I laid the enchantment on it. The cloak itself will be your armour. I placed a powerful protection spell on the cloth, so that as long as you are wearing it, nothing can harm you. The spell is not confined to the cloth, but the one who wears it. So if you were to simply drape it over your shoulders, and a rock fell from the mountain onto your head, the rock would bounce off and would not touch you.

"You'll never need the brooch, though you may find it useful. The cloak will keep you safe from Tick's enemies, and those who wish to control him through you."

Dread seized Sara's heart. "What about Rossa? Or my son?"

"Rossa will grow into her powers quickly enough. She's using them already. Look." Dalia pointed at the window.

All manner of birds sat on the sill, jostling for position, yet all staring at Rossa. Songbirds, scavenger birds, someone's hunting hawk and an eagle that normally lived high up on the mountain. Even an owl joined the strange flock.

Sara shivered. There was magic at work here – powers she did not understand.

Dalia rose. "Well, that's all, I think. If I think of anything else, I'll portal back here, but Tick is surprisingly capable for a man. He'll help you more than you know, though you still might have to tell him what to do from time to time. Take care of that little girl."

She waved, then drew a circle with her hand. A sparkling portal appeared, just as it had by the duckpond when Sara had felt her first contraction. Dalia stepped through it, and disappeared.

"Thank you," Sara said. Too late for Dalia to hear her, but no less heartfelt.

Forty-One

Three years ago, if anyone had told him he'd spend more than a day in a monastery, Zoticus would have laughed at them. Yet he'd spent two years living here with Sara, and as summer faded into autumn once more, he wondered how much longer it would be before it was safe to venture down from the mountains to see who else had survived the plague.

They'd had no contact with anyone outside the monastery since they'd arrived, and more than once, he'd caught the others discussing whether there was anyone else left.

Most of them had moved out of the

monastery, though, and last summer, a village had sprung up where a patch of forest had once stood. Some of the older children were children no more, forming their own households with their younger siblings…and a few had even taken a partner. With no priest to celebrate weddings, though, he wasn't sure how long the pairings would survive. Another summer? Or their entire lives?

He suspected Tobias and the miller's girl were one of the pairs likely to last. Likely because Silvana ruled the roost in their cottage.

Some, like himself and Sara, had stayed in the castle, but they'd moved from the monks' dormitories to more private accommodation when the weather was warmer.

Raphael had taken the solar atop the highest tower, and he was up there most days. Watching for what or whom, Zoticus did not know, but there was a yearning in the man's eyes that said he would not be settling into the new village any time soon.

He was up there now, hanging out the window, shouting and waving and pointing at the road.

Had someone finally come to the

monastery?

Zoticus clambered to the top of the bailey wall, so that he might see the travellers. Sure enough, he could see a party approaching, with wagons, horses and many men on foot. Too far away to see who, though.

Instinct took over. He might not have taken any commissions lately, but he'd been an assassin for too long to forget years of training, or to want to wear any colour other than his customary grey. Today, it allowed him to disappear into the shadows, leaning against the parapet that gave a guard the best view over the gate.

He could always close the gate, for news could be shouted from outside the wall, but something told him to leave it open.

"What's happening? What do you see?" Sara called up.

So much for being well hidden. She saw him, no matter what.

"There's someone coming up the road. A large party, like we were when we arrived."

Sara frowned. "I'll go get my cloak."

Which meant she was worried, and wanted the protective enchantment his mother had laid on the cloak. He wasn't going to argue – he'd do anything to keep her safe.

Slowly, the travellers ambled closer. They evidently weren't in any hurry to reach the monastery's walls. Perhaps they weren't fleeing the plague, and it was safe to leave. Maybe even return to Mirroten.

"Master Zoticus? Can you see them? I think there's someone important coming. All brightly coloured on a big white horse!" Raphael climbed the bailey wall, then pointed.

Zoticus was loath to admit the young man's eyesight was far better than his. "Do you recognise him?"

Raphael smiled sadly. "Who would I know important enough to own a horse like that? He's surely some nobleman. Maybe a prince, or even the king!"

If it was the king, it was a good thing Zoticus hadn't closed the gates. Kings weren't particularly fond of being shut out of parts of their own kingdom. But a royal party would be larger, with more horses, for knights did not walk when they could ride.

Whoever they were, he hoped they'd brought a priest. Tobias and Silvana, as well as some of the other young couples, were eager to wed.

Zoticus shaded his eyes. If he wasn't mistaken, the man on the white horse wore the Bishop of Rialto's colours. He could not yet see the man's face, but he wouldn't have been surprised if it was the bishop himself. Most of the men with him wore the drab tunics that marked them as monks. So some of them had survived the plague, then…or these were new ones, come to claim the monastery as their own.

"Rossa! Get back here! Rossa!"

The girl had taken more than a year to learn to walk, but it had only taken her a day to learn to run. Rossa came barrelling out of the door to the great hall, giggling madly, with Sara a few steps behind.

"Daddy!" the girl shrieked, heading straight for Zoticus, heedless of the riders already entering the bailey.

"Rossa!" Sara screamed, sprinting down the steps. The wind whipped her cloak behind her, so it looked like wings.

His vision. Zoticus dropped down to the bailey and scooped up his wayward daughter, turning his back on the new arrivals to take Rossa back to her mother.

"Out of the way, peasant! His Excellency, the Bishop of Rialto, is here to take possession of his new lands. Show some respect!"

That was a mistake. Zoticus turned to grin at the idiot who'd spoken.

The Bishop of Rialto's horse, however, distracted them all by rearing up and dumping His Excellency on his ample arse in the dust.

There was magic in the air, and he had not used any. Zoticus shot a sideways glance at Sara, wondering if her cloak had done it, but found his daughter staring fixedly at the horse, who was now back on all four hooves, bowing his head in her direction.

Interesting.

Zoticus stepped forward and held out his hand to help the bishop up. "What are you doing here, Ambrose?"

The bishop reached out to take his hand, then paled and shrank back. "Master Zoticus? I'd heard that you died with the rest of Mirroten!"

Sara's soft gasp at this bald statement of bad news hardened his heart against the bishop.

And what was this about the bishop's new lands? These lands belonged to Sara's family. Unless the bishop and the king believed she was dead…

Zoticus's grin grew wider. "Maybe the people who stayed in Mirroten died, but most of the town survived by coming up here to the stronghold. Including Lady Sara and her son, Tobias."

The bishop turned whiter than the snowcapped mountains behind the castle. "S-s-survived?"

"Oh yes." Zoticus held out his hand to Sara as he executed his best courtly bow. "Lady Sara, may I present Bishop Ambrose of Rialto? Ambrose, this is Lady Sara and her daughter, Lady Rossa."

He wasn't sure how well versed Sara was in political intrigue, but she understood well enough that when he'd introduced the bishop to her, instead of the other way around, he'd been telling her she outranked the man. She merely stood and stared, instead of curtseying, like the bishop evidently expected.

Muttering a curse under his breath, the bishop heaved himself to his feet, then managed a clumsy bow in her direction. "Lady Sara. It is a miracle indeed that the Lord chose to save you from the plague that killed so many."

She inclined her head just the slightest bit. The queen herself would have been proud. "Maybe a miracle, or maybe it is merely good planning. Master Zoticus brought word of the terrible tragedy that befell Altino, and helped by his good advice, we came here, where we've been safe. Sadly, not all the town chose to leave, and I am saddened to hear that those poor misguided souls have paid a terrible price for not listening to wise Master Zoticus."

Zoticus wanted to applaud, but he forced his hands to stay by his sides.

The bishop's face turned red. "My dear Lady Sara, you cannot possibly be serious! Zoticus is neither wise or good. The man is an assassin, and you are lucky he has not murdered you all in your beds! I insist on taking him back to Rialto with me, where he will face justice for his crimes. If you have placed your trust in such a vile criminal, it is only by a miracle indeed that you have survived!"

Zoticus opened his mouth to demand that

the bishop answer such an insult with his sword. He'd never murdered anyone in their beds. His hand clenched on the hilt of his own blade, ready to draw it.

Sara's hand squeezed his, keeping the sword firmly in its sheath.

She laughed. "Oh, you are most entertaining, Bishop Ambrose! To think someone has made up such malicious stories about dear, kind Master Zoticus. Why, every person here owes Zoticus their life, some of us twice over. Had he committed any crime here, I would have seen to it that justice was served, for I am, of course, the landowner here. But justice is a sword with two edges, one for punishment, and one for reward. Thus, for his services to me and my people, I have resolved to give him my hand in marriage. It would be most fitting if you would celebrate the marriage rites for us, here in the castle my family built, that has sheltered us in our time of need. This very afternoon. I insist."

Yesterday, Zoticus might have protested about the danger he'd place Sara in by marrying her. Today, he felt the peculiar urge to kneel before her and pledge his sword to her protection. Lady Sara had finally come into her own, and he'd be honoured to be her husband.

The bishop looked from Sara to Zoticus, as if he wasn't sure who frightened him most. "Yes, Lady Sara. Of course. I would be honoured. Ah, but about the castle. You see, I brought some monks, thinking this place was still a monastery…"

"After the wedding, my dear bishop. It is not fitting to speak to a bride about business. In fact, it might be more fitting that you ask my husband…"

The bishop was likely to die of apoplexy before he left the monastery, Zoticus suspected, judging by how red the man's face grew. He couldn't find it in his heart to feel sorry for the man, either. He could have sent word of Altino's demise all along the river, so that all the towns would have known to turn travellers away. Instead, he'd let them all die, only telling Mirroten when it was too late to save them. If Zoticus had not arrived, Sara and all the others might have died…all in keeping with the vile bishop's plan.

"Oh, you must wait until at least after the

honeymoon," Zoticus said, entering the game. "Such an honour, and such a noble bride, I will scarcely know what to do with myself, let alone my lady's lands. Perhaps we shall keep this castle for ourselves."

The bishop appeared to have difficulty drawing breath. Zoticus recognised the signs of impending death. He had only to continue in the same vein, and it would be assured.

By the time the bishop's attendants realised what was happening and Sara called for a healer, it was too late.

A good man might have felt guilt, but Zoticus had been an assassin for a long time, and he had no sympathy for men who played games with other people's lives.

"Is there a priest present? I think the poor bishop needs someone to administer his last rites," Zoticus said.

"And conduct the wedding, if the poor bishop cannot," Sara said.

A priest was produced, a young man who stammered his way through the Latin with all the quivering dread of a man who believed he'd be next if he didn't obey, and the bishop's soul was sent to his maker. Or the devil.

Zoticus left such matters up to those who understood them.

Before the sun had set, his own soul had been wedded to Sara's, and several other couples had come forward to take their vows, so a wedding feast was laid out in the great hall, to be shared between monks and the survivors of Mirroten.

As Zoticus surveyed the hall from the high table, in the seat of honour with his wife by his side, he wished he'd been able to save more. But in the battle between one man and a plague…he felt it was fair to call this a victory.

About the Author

Demelza Carlton has always loved the ocean, but on her first snorkelling trip she found she was afraid of fish.

She has since swum with sea lions, sharks and sea cucumbers and stood on spray drenched cliffs over a seething sea as a seven-metre cyclonic swell surged in, shattering a shipwreck below.

Demelza now lives in Perth, Western Australia, the shark attack capital of the world.

The *Ocean's Gift* series was her first foray into fiction, followed by her suspense thriller *Nightmares* trilogy. She swears the *Mel Goes to Hell* series ambushed her on a crowded train and wouldn't leave her alone.

Want to know more? You can follow Demelza on Facebook, Twitter, YouTube or her website, Demelza Carlton's Place at:

www.demelzacarlton.com